Girl in the Air

Girl in the Air

Book One in the Alice Brickstone Series

Tyler Pike

To Tamsin

CONTENTS

ABOUT THE BOOK

Girl in the Air is the first full-length novel in the Alice Brickstone thriller series.

Book two in the series—*The Feeling of Water*—is also available now. Although the events in *Girl in the Air* take place just before those recounted in *The Feeling of Water*, these first two Alice Brickstone books can be read in any order. Neither one contains any spoilers for the other.

ACKNOWLEDGMENTS

Many people helped to calm and guide me as I parented this book through an overexcited childhood. I owe a particular debt of gratitude to Emanuel Lieberfreund, Chris Cox, Gavin Angus-Leppan, Stephanie Cranford and Nicky Pullen. You guys are the world's best beta-readers.

Thanks also to my swimming pals, Jacinta Van Lint and Emma Van Lint, who refined Alice's stroke, and to all coconuts far and wide for doing laps of the bay with me and listening patiently as I shared my writing progress with you over bowls of flat whites at Café de France.

Thanks also to my yoga friends—you all know who you are. I hope Alice provides you with some laughs and some satisfaction.

A huge vote of thanks go to my irreplaceable editor, Tom Flood.

Now the hard part: thanking those who taught me to write, sweating over my PhD dissertation, arming me for an academic career as a sinologist. Thanks Dr. Derek Herforth and Dr. Tim Chan. It's not your fault I would eventually turn those sacred weapons onto a novel. I hope you enjoy the outcome.

My wife Tamsin has lived the writing of this book with me. Without your advice, your ideas, and your encouragement, Alice Brickstone would have never come into being and I would have wobbled and fallen down. It feels woefully insufficient to write you a thank you here, but to leave it off feels wrong also. So, thank you!

CHAPTER 1

It was five in the morning and completely dark outside. In late spring the sun wouldn't rise over the ski mountain for another two hours. For a few little creatures out there, the day had already begun. There was a rustle in the leaves below her window, probably a deer mouse making her way to a nest somewhere. She heard a tiny peep that could have been a downy woodpecker chick.

She rolled over, lingering in the space between her nightmares and her morning zombie routine, and remembered it was Saturday. Her swim team only trained once today but it was usually a strong session. She would eventually have to stumble out of bed, gather her bag, eat something and cycle to the pool.

Laying there a moment longer, she listened for any sounds in her parents' huge, empty house, but heard none. Her mom would also be hearing the morning noises from her meditation cushion in her yoga room.

What drove Mom to wake up so early, she wondered. Did she hear things when she meditated? Dad, for his part, would be dead to the world. It would take an act of God to wake him from the stupor of his hangover.

After finally motivating herself to roll out of bed, Alice

stumbled downstairs with her swimming bag, grabbed four ice cream sandwiches and an energy bar for breakfast on the ride. She took down her bike off its hooks in the garage, clipped on her helmet and cycled down the driveway.

Her bike tires hit the gravel road. There would be no other cars up here this early and no other man-made sound of any kind. Above the crunching of her fat tires, Alice heard a tentative whistle from a hawk. It could have come from the edge of the Knifespur Wilderness where the old growth forest began. Then she heard vast expanses of pine trees rustled by a tiny breeze as it meandered, pushed by the warming dawn.

Some different sound reached her ear, like the wind had twisted itself into words.

"Fat girl," she heard. "Regular routines. Easy target."

She knew it had been her imagination but still the road corridor through the trees looked suddenly ominous, dark and claustrophobic. She pedaled a bit harder.

After a few hundred yards, she let her attention drift again and she heard a very distant whisper say, "I'm going to get you today, fat girl."

She forced herself to focus on her breathing in order to shut her mind up. It was a survival technique she had learned through years of battles against her fears and memories. She had a bad habit of imagining worst-case scenarios. It's like that mad impulse to jump when you're standing on a ledge. She always imagined her brother dying by thousands of spiders, slow-moving steamrollers, or being dropped out of a plane, and she often thought that the same kinds of things would be waiting for her around the next corner.

She took both hands off her handlebars, finished her last ice cream and the energy bar, then sped up to ensure she got to the pool on time. The road passed only a few other houses before emerging onto the two-lane Colorado Highway 320. From there she had a straight shot downhill to town.

She was feeling more awake by the time she arrived at the

pool where her swim team trained every morning and every afternoon. It was an Olympic-length, fifty-meter pool in a new aquatic center on the university campus. She should feel grateful her dad's company had helped to pay for her swim team's pool time. Her coach had some idea this scrappy little squad may someday rival the quality of the elite Denver swim teams. Fat chance, Alice thought. Kids up here were too focused on drugs, mountain biking and skiing, leaving few girls who even bothered learning how to swim. Only Alice and one other girl on her team were starting to post some times that rivaled some of the better swimmers based in Denver.

She locked up her bike and walked purposefully toward the entrance. The automatic doors slid open and the welcome smell of chlorine billowed out, triggering her anticipation of the pain of her morning workout. Alice put up with the monotony of long hours in the pool because swimming enabled her to temporarily escape from herself, or at least from her endless droning anxieties. She felt like the exhaustion released her from those, as well as some from invisible burden. Sometimes, in certain rare moments, the feeling of the water was more than therapy and recalled the ecstasy of a flying dream.

Hesitant voices of other teenage girls in her junior squad were already echoing in the huge expanse of the domed building. The pool was like a solid slab of blue glass lit from within by circular lights. She heard a splash and saw the first person dive in to break the perfect stillness of the water. The water lights cast circular shapes that danced and changed on the roof.

Alice made her way to the change room, put on her swimsuit and grabbed her cap and goggles.

On the way to the toilet, she caught a glance of herself in the mirror and paused. She was, undeniably, getting stronger. People started gawking at her when she sprouted to six feet tall as a fifteen-year-old and she drew even more stares when she pushed up another three inches this year and ate her way to two hundred pounds. She saw some of the fat had transformed into long, bulging strands of functional muscle. She was taller, broader and stronger than most men. Still flat-chested but, for a swimmer, that was not bad news.

She tried out a pose like she had seen bodybuilders do and was pleased to see a very large muscular "V" shape form in the back of her arms, but one of her arms had a painful zit on it. She tried to flex the muscles of her huge thighs but there wasn't much definition and some fat pushed out from under the seam of her Speedos.

She went into one of the stalls, sat down to pee and recalled something her coach had said to her on the previous day. He had told her that if she posted a few good times in the swim meet in Denver next weekend, she could qualify for the western zone championships in California. There were four zones in the US and each one held championships attracting the best age-group and senior swimmers in its quadrant of the country. Since turning fifteen, a year ago, Alice became a senior swimmer and often had to compete against girls up to nineteen years old. She hadn't bothered racing any long course meets and hadn't yet posted a qualifying time for this year's western zone championships.

When he told her about next weekend's meet, one of the last opportunities for her to qualify, a couple of her teammates whispered to one another and giggled.

As she sat on the toilet, she stared at the closed door, taking shallow breaths and feeling stressed. She replayed that scene over and over: Coach talking, girls laughing at her. Why were they laughing?

The quiet in the change rooms shook her out of her trance and she realized she must be late. She jumped up and accidentally dropped her goggles in the yellow water in the toilet bowl.

Coach ignored her as she rushed out to the pool.

She swished her goggles around in the water at the edge to wash the toilet water off before putting them on and dove into her lane to start the warmup. The cold water gave her a jolt and she launched into a slow freestyle, her arms arcing lazily, one at a time, hands soft. Already a couple of laps behind the other girls, she pushed into a few faster laps and was surprised to feel her body sitting much higher in the water than usual. She felt strong. She also felt angry. The presence of such a huge wellspring of anger made her suspect it would be a good morning in the water.

After she finished her warmup laps she bobbed in the water and looked carefully at the whiteboard. In anticipation of next weekend's meet in Denver, Coach had designed the program today around some time trial sets at race pace. She loved that. She relished pushing her body way past the comfort zone. Her body was like a sledgehammer she could use to brutalize the water and deposit this anger she was feeling.

She noticed Madison had also been swimming very well today and had been on her heels the whole time.

When it was finally time to start the race-pace sets, Alice was feeling pumped. Coach had organized the starting platforms and touch pad timers to be in place today to simulate a race environment. He kept large databases with all their split times at practices and races.

Alice didn't really care about that stuff. She just liked effort, strength and the raw feeling of speed in the water, the rest of the world blocked out.

When Coach called the 200 meter freestyle—her favorite event—Alice climbed her block and Madison took the next lane over. A few other girls were also training for the 200 and they filled the next two lanes.

Alice thought for a moment as Coach set up the timing system. Four laps in the pool. Coach wants me to swim each lap faster than the last. That means I am only allowed to put in a hundred percent effort in the last lap, or maybe the last two laps. What a bunch of crap. I'm just going to go all out the whole time. I don't care what he thinks.

"Take your mark," Coach said into a megaphone.

Alice placed one foot back, reached down and took hold of the front edge of the block. She leaned back slightly and tensed her body for a fast start.

When she heard the electronic start tone, a fresh wave of anger passed over her, forcing her to pause for a millisecond, enough time to see Madison already launching herself off the platform ahead of her.

Bang. She launched into the air with a ferocious explosion of her core muscles and legs. Alice hit the water and one of her goggle eyes filled with water. It would be just an annoyance but she would not be able to see Madison very well underwater in the next lane. She held her arms above her head, hands together in a streamline position, biceps against her ears, and gave five very powerful dolphin kicks underwater.

She surfaced and began her stroke. Her body lifted to the top of the water again and she felt even more powerful than she had earlier. She felt like she was swimming downhill. She felt anger and strength in equal parts.

She made her first turn and decided to see if she really could swim the second lap faster than the first. She refused to grant her coach the satisfaction that he was right she was going to 'bonk' after going out too hard and she would have to swim the last lap with nothing left in the tank. Her body responded and she practically flew through the water toward her second turn.

She turned and hammered the wall again with her powerful legs. In the stillness of her underwater glide, something changed and she felt herself entering into another realm. It was as though she had broken some kind of mental barrier and found quiet. Time slowed; she was separate from her body and there was a kind of spotlight on her. She had split into swimmer and the swimmer's witness.

Okay, Alice, she said calmly to the swimmer, let's lift a little more. Two laps to go, each lap faster than the last. Keep your stroke long and your legs pumping.

The swimmer responded, moving even faster through the water. The swimmer's whole body was burning with the fire of lactic acid and her heart was pounding, but these details didn't matter to the witness. The witness told the swimmer to go faster and accelerate into the last lap.

She turned tightly and began swimming longer and harder. Suddenly the split between swimmer and witness was destroyed and the silence obliterated. Anger returned. She was hurting and her technique fell apart. Vaguely aware of all that, Alice refused to slow down and increased her stroke rate, throwing her arms over madly. Tasting lactic acid, she hammered her way to the wall and hit the timing pad hard enough to break a few fingernails.

She stood and gasped for air. She lifted her goggles and couldn't see anything but black dots. She gasped again furiously and felt sick. She retched but managed to avoid throwing up.

She was completely alone on the wall. It seemed a long time before she could breathe without making gasping noises like a dying person. She turned and saw Madison swimming hard into the wall, but she was so far behind. Wondering what was going on, she had a strange feeling she had swum too few laps.

She looked up at the pool deck expecting Coach to be laughing. She couldn't even count out four laps of the swimming pool. He wasn't laughing and didn't appear to be preparing to come over and yell at her. He was just standing there staring at the scoreboard.

Phew, she thought. He didn't notice.

Madison finally touched the wall, came up for air and looked straight to the scoreboard.

"Oh...my...God!" was all she could say, in between gasps.

A bunch of the other girls were starting to crowd around the scoreboard. Probably laughing at her, Alice expected. If she had any energy she would have slunk off into the deep water and disappeared, humiliated.

A couple of the other girls came over to Alice's lane. "Alice, you just broke two minutes. You just swam a 1:58!"

Eyes wide as eggs, Madison turned back to Alice. "Oh my God, Alice, what the hell was that?"

Alice didn't really know what to say. Her previous personal

best in training was a 2:06: fast enough for a top three finish at the western zone championships. A 1:58? That was only three seconds off the state record. It was only five seconds off the world record.

Coach ignored her and stopped above Madison.

"Mad Dog, that was 2:12, a personal best. Nice swim. That would have earned you a second place in the zones last year. Lap one, thirty-five seconds, then thirty-four seconds, thirty and thirty-five on your last lap. That third lap was a screamer. Your kick came in well but your stroke rate was a bit too high. That's why you bonked on the last lap. I'm confident that you could take three seconds off that time by lowering your stroke rate on lap three — long and strong. You're right on pace for qualifying for the zone champs."

Alice listened to Coach talking in this way to the other two girls but she knew nobody was paying much attention. They were all looking at her.

"You okay?" Madison asked over the lane rope. "I got a good start, way ahead of you, and then you caught me and were already about three body lengths ahead by the second wall. I've never seen you swim like that."

"I don't know..." That was all Alice could manage. Her body was starting to feel like it was made of cotton. She felt sick to her stomach again.

Coach moved all four girls into another lane to warm down and started another time trial with four more girls.

As she continued to warm down and loosen up, Alice tried to remember how she felt during the swim: the anger, the strange moment when she felt like she was two different people, the anger again. She was familiar with anger. It was like her best friend, but the other thing was new. The quietude she felt when she split into witness and swimmer did more than help her swim faster; it created a clean split between herself and her pain. All of her pain, not just her physical pain. She tried to recreate the split again but it didn't seem possible anymore. She didn't know how

8

to get there. There was only the rhythmic sound of the splashing and the rush of water against her swimming cap.

Although she couldn't split herself again, she noticed she felt different. Exactly how, she couldn't place, but definitely different. She decided maybe she just needed to puke or something.

Her next race pace set was the four hundred meter free, but she swam slower than she usually did in that discipline. She was hardly winded at the end and coach gave her a look of complete exasperation when he read her split times out. She had a few more trials but loafed through all of them.

Alice warmed down, got out and showered. She wanted to be alone now. Her stomach was feeling better and she had her mind on breakfast and coffee. As usual, she definitely wanted to avoid conversation with any of the other girls, but as soon as she emerged from the locker room, she knew that was going to be difficult. They were all standing there waiting for her.

Madison was there and her little fan, Bess, and several others were there with her.

"Alice, congrats on that swim." Madison was wearing her usual post-swimming gear: jeans and a sloppy t-shirt. She looked sincere and Alice could sense nothing to indicate she wasn't.

"Yeah." Bess pushed her hip to the side. "Your dad works at a pharmaceutical company, doesn't he? You must be getting some fantastic 'supplements.' Where can I get some?"

She walked by the girls in silence, looking at the ground. The swim had left Alice feeling blank and empty, as though she left part of herself in the pool. It was like the girls and the pool were part of a dream and she was not even the dreamer. It was like she and the girls were all together in someone else's dream.

CHAPTER 2

Alice cycled up to her favorite café on the hill and tried to recover a sense of normality by stuffing herself with a huge breakfast and two coffees. Most kids on the team couldn't stomach a coffee after the huge training effort. Alice was different. She didn't have breakfast waiting for her at home. She had a cast-iron stomach and she needed caffeine to give her the courage to face the rest of the day. Today, it didn't work; she didn't feel like facing the day. She had nowhere to go.

She cycled from the café to the university library to try to get some studying done. She couldn't think of anything else to do.

Locking up, she made her way to the rare books section, a place where she sometimes studied, and sat down at one end of a huge wooden table. The room was decorated like she imagined a library in the 18th century would have been. Light was angling in from stained glass windows located high up near the ceiling. It shone through them and sent shafts of color upon walls of hardwood bookshelves and onto the old manuscripts and dissertations shelved in them. There was a thick carpet and heavy, overstuffed leather chairs and couches with art deco floor lamps next to them. Alice's large wooden table stood in the middle of the room.

Students were not allowed to be here without a particular research aim and their request had to be made in writing and approved by library staff. As a result, hardly anyone was ever here.

She was only allowed in because of her dad. A few years ago he found out she liked to spend time at the university library and for her sixteenth birthday present, he bought her a lifetime membership with full borrowing privileges. He also made a large donation to the library, through which he permanently endeared Alice to the senior library administration. Alice ignored most of the library staff and only made an exception for one guy named Brian, who had his office near the rare books section. He was worth a laugh or two. He always wore a tight silk shirt buttoned to the top and tight pants. He spoke with rolling sing-song tones, always had something naughty to say, and was quick to help anyone who asked. He had a few interesting hobbies like hang-gliding and dressing up like a woman. They shared some common interests in films and Alice often borrowed from the library DVDs he recommended. He was the closest thing she had to a friend.

She stayed there for hours, occasionally lying down on the couch for a nap. When she was ready to leave to go get a late lunch, the big oak door to the room opened and Brian walked in, followed by a tall nun. He shot Alice a conspiratorial look and rolled his eyes. He was showing the woman to the dissertation section on the far side of the room.

She was dressed in orange robes and had cropped blonde hair and blue eyes. She noticed Alice right away.

Alice had seen her fair share of monks and nuns, as Hardrock was a magnet for religious types. Most of the nuns she had seen were Asian. She had never seen a blonde one before.

She was, Alice thought, beautiful in an unadorned kind of way, like a female version of Peter O'Toole in *Lawrence of Arabia*. The nun was about her parents' age. Alice could sense something of the desert in her. She even held herself in the upright, confident way Alice imagined a desert king or queen would. She had a long neck, relaxed shoulders and an obviously athletic body beneath the robes—like a dancer, Alice thought. She looked interesting, so why did Alice suddenly feel like throwing up for the second time today?

When their eyes finally met across the room, the nun smiled at her with eyes that seemed gentle, but Alice got a terrible feeling, deep in her stomach, like she had swallowed a bowling ball. A feeling like someone was standing right behind her, breathing on her neck, alerted Alice to the mental presence of the nun, surrounding and closing in on her. After a helpless moment when all Alice could do was stare, she eventually recognized that the nun was actively probing around in her head, observing her thoughts.

This was a trick Alice thought was hers alone to use on other people. She had been able to do it for as long as she could remember. It just took a deep breath and a shift into a different state of mind. There was a lot more to it than that, but by now it all came naturally to her. It was, however, a disturbing experience for Alice to be read by someone else. She did the only thing she expected might stymie the nun's effort; she forced her mind toward the most mundane crap she could think of. She started going through a stupid film she had seen the other day, calling up all the details she could.

The nun seemed satisfied Alice was just a dumb teenager, gave her a pert smile and turned away toward the books.

Alice breathed a sigh of relief and rubbed her belly a few times. She still felt sick but her stomach unclenched now they had broken their gaze. She tried to make sense of what had happened and stared down at her computer screen.

As Alice reflected, the nun sat down on one of the leather chairs to read.

She gathered her courage, looked up again and got another shock when she saw the nun's book had her father's name printed on the spine. Alice looked away again, thinking quickly. She realized it must be her dad's PhD dissertation; of course—he would have lodged a copy here when he graduated twelve years ago, before they went to India. Why had she never asked her dad for a copy? Why hadn't she thought to read the copy shelved in this room? Most of it wouldn't make any sense to her but maybe some of it would help her understand what he was like back then, before India. She had an intense desire to read it but an even stronger need to know why it was of interest to this woman.

Some tinny Indian music suddenly started playing in the nun's pocket. She pulled out a phone and answered,, "Hari Om"—instead of "hello."

After a pause, the nun said, "I think it was a pocket call." She spoke loudly, as though she was alone in an open field, rather than in a library. "I had just called her a quarter of an hour earlier, so my number was probably first on her list of received calls. It really was a miracle...Yes. That was another miracle. I had the call-recording app ready; all I had to do was to click start. It recorded the whole conversation about Helpharma's cruel and corrupt clinical trial practices in India. It is perfectly clear to me this was a gift from God and I know exactly how it should be used for His divine purposes...I'll tell you later."

Alice was now very afraid. She just couldn't believe she was in the same room as someone dressed in orange robes who was not only reading her mind and her dad's PhD dissertation, but also appeared to be plotting against her dad's pharmaceutical company.

After about twenty minutes, during which the nun devoured the dissertation and Alice pretended not to notice, the nun got up and left, carrying the dissertation with her. She would have asked Brian for permission to take it down the hall to the copy room, Alice guessed.

Alice quickly packed up her laptop in her backpack and made her way out.

Brian was sitting in the little office, waiting for the nun to return.

Alice didn't want to be stuck in close quarters in this office with the nun when she came back to return her dad's book, so she had to be quick. "Who is that woman?" she asked him.

He smiled. "Oh yes, it is a very nice day and I'm feeling fine, thank you sooo much for asking, dear. A little hungover, but nothing a brisk chat with you won't cure, I'm sure."

"Cut it out, man. I'll buy you a coffee if you tell me why she has my dad's dissertation."

"Ah, grumpy again today, are we?" Brian replied. "I'm not sure who she is or why she is interested in your dad's dissertation."

Alice turned to go.

"What about my coffee?" he called out behind her.

Alice made her way quickly to the library foyer, a big echo-filled room with a marble floor and a two-story high ceiling. The book checkout area was on one side and the security exit on the other. The walls were lined with old oil portraits.

Alice hung around waiting for the orange lady to come downstairs. She tried her dad's phone number but he didn't answer, as usual.

She soon saw the orange lady hurrying down the stairs, followed by six people who hadn't been there in the rare-books room. They all stopped right in the middle of the cavernous library entrance foyer.

Five of them were middle-aged men and women dressed in matching cream-colored cotton, thigh-length Indian shirts and trousers. It was a warm springtime day but several of them wore shawls over their shoulders, even the men. They all wore matching strings of brown beads around their necks. Alice thought they looked like monk-wannabees. They each had a mobile phone pressed to their heads and their combined chatter was out-echoing everyone else in the foyer.

The sixth person was different. He was taller and wore finer clothes. His shirt had an embroidered collar and he wore an Indian-style skirt, rather than trousers, with his bare calves sticking out. His calves were not ordinary. They were sinewy and long: very strong, like those of an athlete. He looked to be in his twenties, rather than pushing fifty like the others. Alice couldn't tell if he was Indian or perhaps Middle Eastern. He had strong cheekbones and clever, aware eyes which were searching the room casually. Alice instinctively took a step back so that when his gaze reached her part of the foyer, it would look like she was with a couple of other students.

The nun walked toward the exit doors, the others immediately following her. Alice followed a few other students out of the library and unlocked her bike, making ready to follow the followers.

A white four-wheel drive appeared and the driver rushed out to open the passenger side door for the orange lady. The Indian guy with strong legs moved into the driver's seat. Before getting in, the nun paused and one of the other people in white ran ahead and threw a colorful square cloth down on the seat for her to sit on.

The other five of her minions piled into the back of the car, the doors closed and the car rolled down the library road towards the nearest exit from campus. Alice followed on her bike, keeping up easily. They left campus and headed toward old Main Street and the center of town. Alice almost lost them at one point but a traffic light slowed them down and she managed to catch up in time to see them turn down a leafy street off Main. She noticed the street was packed with cars, as though there was a fraternity party. Most of the vehicles were old, salt-damaged mountain junk-heaps.

The nun's car pulled up in front of an old two-story timber house with decorative painted flowers on its timber work and an elaborate bay window in front. It must be one of those heritage-listed Queen Anne houses, Alice speculated. This house was the nicest one on the block. It had an elaborate alpine garden out front, flush with little ground-level wildflowers.

Everyone in the back of the white four-wheel drive jumped out and walked quickly up to the front door, kicked off their shoes and went inside without knocking. The orange lady and the Indian guy remained in the car and the car sped off. She knew she couldn't keep up with them this time, as they were driving uphill.

She swung her leg off the bike and stood there for a moment, wondering what to do. Another car pulled up and a group of people got out and walked up to the house. Alice quickly put her bike on the front porch and stood behind the others as they rang the doorbell. An Indian woman answered the door with a silent smile, turned and walked back toward the living room. She did a double-take when she saw Alice, who was a good head taller than the others. Alice's adopted group removed their shoes silently. She could hear one very loud male voice coming from inside and her interest was piqued.

They tiptoed into the room and sat down on the carpet in back. Sitting on the floor made Alice feel less conspicuous. The space was packed with people sitting cross-legged in front of an old, gray-bearded Indian man dressed in orange and sitting on a couch that had been covered in orange cloth. There was something familiar about him. Alice wondered if he was famous. Maybe he was that Bikram guy or one of the other big yoga gurus who have franchised yoga centers,. but he looked too fat to be a yoga guy. Maybe he was that big name guru from India who preaches about happiness. Alice had seen an ad in her café about it last year.

The fat guru was on the phone with someone. Next to him, another orange-robed man was sitting on the floor facing the crowd. Alice thought he looked European, not Indian. He wore very thick beads around his neck and appeared to think he was very important.

The lady who answered the door came by and served them small plastic cups of steaming dark stuff. It smelled like chai, her mom's favorite drink. It looked strong and Alice gladly took one as she listened to the gray-bearded man's phone call. He seemed indifferent to the huge crowd of people sitting at his feet and was speaking as though he was alone.

"Very good." The phone kept drooping down from his ear further and further, as though he was bored. "Then tell him Babaji sends his blessings... Yes, and tell him it would be great service to Holy Guruji if he could print seven thousand more for no charge." He finished the call with a mumbled *"asrivad,"* setting the phone down next to a gleaming silver cup of chai on a small table in front of him. He sat up straight and gazed out at the people on the carpet in front of him. The room became even more silent and electrically expectant. Even Alice sensed the excitement without knowing why. He looked slowly around the room, looking at each person individually.

When his eyes landed on Alice, she took the opportunity to take a deep breath and glimpse into his head but she could see nothing in the bearded man's mind. He was like an empty vase. She broke the connection and his eyes moved impassively around to other people in the room.

He closed his eyes and took a deep breath. When he opened them again, rather than uttering some words of deep wisdom, he looked at Alice again briefly and took the phone up again, found a number and held the phone up to his ear.

"Did you find what you were looking for in the library?" he asked loudly. After a pause, he said, "Yes. Try to have him meet us at the lecture tomorrow night."

He turned to look at a lady standing at a door that appeared to lead to a kitchen. She was dressed in a neat vest over a long white blouse.

"Where is this yoga ashram?"

"Number Fifteen Third Avenue, Red Tent Yoga Center, Babaji. 7:00 p.m. lecture."

He looked away. "Yoga Devi says it is in a tent on Third Avenue." Everyone in the room laughed on cue, apparently admiring his wit, and quieted back down immediately. He hung up the phone and looked back at Alice.

"Young lady," he said in a loud, patronizing voice, "how is your father?"

Everyone in the room was looking at her. Some were smiling at her warmly, others, squinting and pursing their lips, were noticing her workout clothes.

"He's okay, thanks," Alice responded weakly. That drew a few snickers from people around her. Alice didn't understand why.

"Send him our blessings." Babaji looked back at the neat vest lady. "Give her one flyer for the tent."

The vest lady climbed through the cross-legged people over to Alice, handing her a little flyer with the lecture details printed on it and a photo of the bearded man smiling gently at the camera.

"Take her to the kitchen and give her *prasad*," he ordered.

Alice reluctantly got up and followed the vest lady, tiptoeing around the cross-legged people on the ground and passing through the door she had been standing next to.

It was an old ladies' kitchen, common in Colorado better-homes-and-gardens magazines. There was an antique brass stove and oven, old fashioned brass fittings on the sink, little gilded framed pictures on the walls of things like bunnies and teapots with cozies on them. Instead of a portly Colorado grandmother at the stove, there were five or six large Indian ladies dressed in colorful saris. They were chopping and cleaning and cooking, crowding into the space. The antique stove was covered with huge steel pots and small saucepans. They also had set up an extra camping stove on a countertop onto which they had set up a big, black, flat skillet and were making flatbread, like tortillas. The smell was pungent, full of garlic, ginger, tons of Indian spices and bread smells. There was no laughter or joy, only concentration, and noise from a little stereo playing some kind of chants in Hindi.

One of the ladies looked familiar to Alice. As she tried to place where she had seen this woman before, suddenly a violent rush of unpleasant memories welled up and Alice knew who the fat guru was.

She used to sit at his feet when she was five and her family was in an ashram in India. She suddenly could even remember what the dusty carpet looked like. She had spent hours sitting on it, below the guru's chair, together with her twin, Thomas. Mom and Dad were usually sitting with them too, but not always. Sometimes it was just Alice and Thomas. Babaji would give them chocolates. Alice remembered wailing and chanting over loudspeakers in the distance.

Without saying a word to Yoga Devi or the Indian ladies, she rushed out the back door into the back yard. There were stone paths winding around beds of wildflowers. Alice took a few deep breaths and her head began to clear a little.

She suddenly noticed two young girls sitting on some decorative rocks under a tree and one of them had a pair of very dark eyebrows. Alice looked harder.

As she got closer, she saw it was Madison from swim team. She had to make a quick decision. Her first instinct was to run away, but she would have to go straight back into the house and pass by the ladies in the kitchen, through into the house, past the guru and all those weird people sitting on the carpet, before reaching the safety of her bike. Or she could hop a fence into the neighbor's yard, which would probably make her look like a criminal.

She looked again. Madison was sitting with another girl their age, or maybe a few years older. They were sitting on red flagstones, empty plates in front of them. They hadn't yet seen Alice. She walked over toward the girls.

"Hey, Madison," Alice managed.

"Alice!" Madison smiled hugely, eyebrows raised high over smiling eyes.

The warm welcome melted some of Alice's usual tension. She was confused, expecting derision, or at least a snide comment of some kind. Not that Madison had ever said anything mean; it's just what Alice assumed girls her age did to each other.

While everyone else inside was wearing beads and Indian clothes, these girls' attire looked comfortingly normal. Madison was dressed in a grungy, slightly torn flannel shirt and jeans which made her look much less like the elite athlete she really was. The other girl wore a t-shirt and jeans shorts. Her shirt had the words "out of order" written on it. They both sat there facing Alice with unapologetic warmth.

"Why aren't you guys in with the others, sitting with the holy guru?"

Madison's friend smiled. "Heard it all before."

Alice could hardly believe it. She kind of made a joke and the girls kind of smiled.

She sat down with them on the flagstones.

Madison's friend asked, "Why aren't you in there with Babaji?"

Alice didn't reply.

Out-of-order girl looked a bit nervous.

Madison looked at Alice on her left, the other girl on her right, and seemed to realize everyone was getting uncomfortable.

"Hey, you two," she said, "lighten up."

"You sound like my dad," out-of-order girl said.

Madison furled her huge eyebrows. "Where is your dad, by the way? I thought he was into this stuff too."

"No way. He was, of course, but he was one of the first ones to leave when all the stuff came out ten years ago."

"What stuff?" Alice asked.

Madison looked at her friend, as if asking for permission to answer Alice's question.

"Well," Madison started tentatively, "when Kirsty here told me this guru was coming to Hardrock, I did some reading on the internet. There are all these sites claiming he sexually abuses his followers."

"Really?" Alice said for the benefit of the girls. She had no sexual experience herself and had trouble imagining how some jerk like Babaji could force anyone to do something like that. She had read about sexual abuse in general but her knowledge came from dark fiction like *Girl with the Dragon Tattoo*, not from personal experience. She cast her mind back to the faces of the people sitting on the carpet in front of Babaji and wondered if any of them would follow him to a bedroom.

Kirsty seemed to get agitated and chimed in. "Mom says you can't really believe all that stuff on the internet. According to her, all those girls misunderstood Babaji. She says you're supposed to have a close personal relationship with him. He teaches thatenlightenment comes from getting close to the guru."

Madison said, "But getting close can't mean having sex with him. That would be as wrong as having sex with your math teacher, wouldn't it? Or worse, sex with Santa Claus. When I read those girls' stories, they really seem true. They're too scary and similar to each other to be made up. They trusted him and he repaid their trust by really hurting them."

Kirsty looked uncomfortable. "The question of abuse is very tricky..."

"So," Alice said, "why are you guys here? Hoping to get close to him?"

"My mother is one of his most devoted followers," Kirsty replied. "I grew up with Babaji's YouTube clips playing all the time."

"I'll bet your dad just loved that," Madison said.

"Yeah," Kirsty said quietly. "My house has always been like a battleground. Mom wants me to like Babaji and Dad wants me to hate him."

"Actually, Kirsty," Madison said, "that doesn't sound very fair to you. That's what I was saying to you before. You shouldn't let them do that to you."

Kirsty didn't say anything and there was silence for a moment.

"Well, I guess that's why you asked me to tag along with you today," Madison said cheerfully. "To make you feel totally awkward. By the way," Madison looked at Alice, "let me introduce you two formally. This is Kirsty. Kirsty, this is the famous Alice from swim squad."

Kirsty's eyes opened wide with surprise at the mention of Alice's name.

There was an awkward silence for a moment.

"You know, Kirsty lives out near you," Madison said, clearly in an effort to save the situation. "You live out near the Knifespur Wilderness, don't you, Alice?"

"Yep."

Kirsty finally looked up again at Alice. "I...I thought you couldn't talk?"

"What?" Alice asked.

"I mean, you're *the* Alice?"

"I guess."

"Now," Madison continued, trying to change the subject, "Alice, what brings you here, even though you have not even heard of this guy?"

Alice took a deep breath before she answered.

"I have heard of him," Alice said at last. "At first, I didn't actually know it was him. It's the...I mean...my parents used to be followers too," Alice said in her best attempt at a casual tone, "but I don't understand why."

Kirsty appeared to be recovering from her surprise that Alice could talk. "So if your parents aren't here, why are *you* here, Alice?"

Alice couldn't tell if it was an aggressive question or not. She looked at Kirsty. "It's weird. I ran into some lady in orange robes in the library today and she kind of freaked me out. I followed her here."

Kirsty pulled on her t-shirt. "You know, actually that is a really weird coincidence. Or maybe it's not a coincidence at all? I don't know if you believe in this stuff, but Mom would say 'it's the grace of the Guru' you ended up here."

"Yeah." Madison scrunched up her nose. "There are no coincidences to these kinds of people."

"So you know that orange lady, Kirsty?" Alice asked.

"Of course. She's Sadvhi Bhakti Devi." Kirsty shifted in her seat and pulled down the front of her t-shirt again. It was like a tic, Alice thought. "She's almost as famous as Babaji himself. When all those girls came out with their stories, she became his biggest defender. She meditates, like, ten hours a day. I once heard someone say she is more advanced than Babaji himself. Mom has made me watch some of her lectures on YouTube. They were pretty good, actually."

"What do you mean by advanced?" Madison asked.

"Spiritually advanced; I don't really know. Mom talks about Sadhvi Bhakti sometimes, saying she has these *siddhis*. *Siddhis* are like special yogic abilities. There is a list in one of my mom's yoga books. Things like flying, mind reading, predicting the exact time of your own death, knowing the future: stuff like that. I know it sounds stupid, but people in India really believe they are real. I don't know if this Bhakti lady has any special abilities though. They say if you have *siddhis*, you aren't allowed to demonstrate them or else the abilities just disappear."

Madison rolled her eyes. "So how do you get these *siddhi* things? Go to a lot of yoga classes?"

"Nope. They come to a spiritual person like blessings. They're a natural side effect of getting close to enlightenment."

The girls were quiet for a moment. Alice considered the idea Bhaki had demonstrated some kind of spiritual yogic power when she read Alice's mind in the library. That couldn't be true because Alice could do the same thing and she felt no more spiritual or enlightened than the rock she was sitting on.

"Actually," Kirsty said, breaking the silence, "this is Bhakti's mom's place. Her mom died last month and left her this house. They are making this the new ashram headquarters for Babaji in the USA."

"Seriously?" Madison asked Kirsty. "Her mom was Mrs. Schafer? She was a friend of my mom's. She was nice. They used to spend a lot of time chatting about gardening stuff. That's an old family. They've been here for generations—real locals."

Kirsty's forehead creased in worry. Alice wondered if Kirsty was going to ask her how she learned to talk, or something like that.

"Alice," Kirsty asked, "do you remember when we were in India together? When we were little?"

"What?" Alice tightened up.

Kirsty squared her shoulders to Alice. "Mom and Dad brought me to the ashram in India for a few weeks during Christmas. It was just me and you and...your brother. I actually remember you twins pretty well. You were inseparable."

"Yep," Alice said, looking at the ground. Her stomach was starting to hurt again. Alice noticed Madison elbowed Kirsty in the ribs, but Kirsty swiped her arm away and kept going.

"I was a bit older and I remember looking at you, wishing I had a brother. You guys kept staring at each other and smiling. You were so attached to each other. Everyone always thought you were the cutest things ever. I'm so sorry about what happened."

"Forget it," Alice said. Her face took on a cold Egyptian princess look.

"Yes, I'm so sorry, Alice," Madison said, putting her hand on Alice's. "We know about your brother. Everyone does."

Someone came out of the back door to the house. Alice saw she was a severe looking middle-aged woman dressed in more of those cream-colored fake Indian clothes.

"What on earth are you girls up to out here?" the woman asked in a reprimanding voice like an old-fashioned school teacher.

Offended to be reprimanded by a stranger, Alice reacted quickly by taking a deep belly breath, shifting into the right state of mind and locking eyes with this woman. Upon gaining access to her thoughts, Alice felt like she had entered a knife fight. The lady's head was full of unfiltered sharp voices cutting each other: cutting each other off, actually. Sentences were never allowed to be completed.

The only fragments she could hear clearly sounded like, She shouldn't be out here——

No, a rival voice cut in. One can't criticize.

I shouldn't be out here either, yet another voice in her head said. I should go back inside. That way, I teach her by example. Teach her to appreciate the blessings——

Shush! came another voice. Who are you to teach anyone? Some example you are, You're hopeless.

No! came one of the earlier voices, continuing the inner argument. Think positive about yourself.

That Alice Brickstone is abnormal. Wrong. Bad company.

No! You must not criticize. So long as Kirsty is on this sacred property, she is under Babaji's divine protection.

No! Not with that girl. She needs to be in there sitting at his feet. He is like her mother and father. You are just a custodian.

And so on. Alice could hardly make sense of the voices and didn't want to know how this lady knew Alice's name. She broke off the connection.

"Mom?" Kirsty was obviously concerned her mom seemed to have fallen asleep standing up. "Hello? Are you there?"

"What are you two doing out here?" the lady asked firmly after recovering from her Alice-trance.

Two, Alice wondered. Did she have trouble counting to three? Or was she intentionally ignoring one of us?

"We're just eating, Mom."

Kirsty's mom bent down, and with nervous hands, took the empty plates and cutlery. "Go on, hurry. Babaji was asking about you before."

Kirsty got up reluctantly and started to follow her mom inside. Madison and Alice remained sitting.

Alice was feeling sick again. That impossible heavy weight was pressing on her stomach. She could hardly think. She turned to Kirsty. "Listen, I gotta go. This whole thing is a bit much for me."

Madison noticed Alice's color had drained. "Hey, you look like you're going to faint. You okay?"

"Madison, give me your number...I'll call you. Sorry, I really

25

gotta go."

"No way," Madison said. "You look like you're going to collapse. I live a few streets down. Come on, I'll get you a cup of tea or something."

"Sorry. Gotta go." Alice hopped the neighbor's fence before she was totally overcome with the sick feeling and ran behind some decorative peony to throw up.

CHAPTER 3

Alice finally made it to the front of Bhakti's house, grabbed her bike and tried her Dad's mobile. It was the third time she had called him and the third time it had rung out. It was late on a Saturday afternoon; even if he was at work, he shouldn't be too busy to take a call from her. She kept trying his number as she cycled towards home with only one hand on the handlebars and the other hand punching redial.

She tried to relax by breathing deeply. She pedaled faster but her legs were feeling heavy and her neck and forehead were tight. She felt like she couldn't turn her head without pulling a muscle. Her hands were growing cold and clammy. Her vision was getting cloudy again, like it had been after her 200 free.

She looked up and saw the sun had already dropped low over the mountains west of town.

She passed her house and automatically continued toward the wilderness area, as she did most nights. She liked to cycle up the first hill just inside the boundary of the Knifespur to survey the last purple clouds of sunset. She wasn't thinking of purple sunsets tonight; she was just on auto-pilot.

When the road ended in a little gravel parking lot empty of

cars, she passed the posted trailhead and continued in her saddle, ignoring the prohibition against bikes in federally designated wilderness areas. She took a deep breath and wondered if tonight would be the night she ran into a forest ranger and got in trouble for cycling in here.

She wound her way up past landmarks that should have been familiar but today were not. The pine trees and the earth beneath them smelled musty, like they often do at the end of a warm day. The sounds of the distant highway were long gone and in its place was the familiar silence of the forest. She could hear things very far away. There was a whisper in the pine trees on the mountain, a chinook wind racing down toward her. It did not morph into a threatening human voice tonight.

The trail got steeper and her legs started to burn, but burning was better than the lifeless, fat slabs her legs had been only a short time ago. It was getting dark and she had to really concentrate.

She finally made it to the top of a rise and the forest opened up into a small meadow. If it were not so dark, she knew she would be able to see the little brook that snaked and rushed its way through the meadow.

She turned her bike around so it faced downhill, toward the east, and she noticed a few stars starting to appear between small gray clouds. The hulking shape of the ski area lay beneath the clouds. Below that were the lights of her town.

She thought she probably shouldn't hang out here long. She should just get home and wait until Dad arrived. She took a deep breath and started back down the trail.

She had a lot of experience in mountain biking down single tracks and she felt as though she hardly needed to touch her brakes. Within seconds she was already at her usual reckless speed. There was no room for thought, only the dark trail in front of her.

She recalled there were only two steep corners on the way down. She made the first one and started preparing for the second when suddenly the whisper returned.

"I have you this time."

Her body surged with fear. The voice was so clear. Definitely not just in her head. How could someone be up here in the forest with her, she wondered. Where was he? Distracted, she hit the bank completely wrong and launched into the air.

Her feet were still on pedals and she was airborne long enough to lift her arms instinctively in anticipation of impact. There was a moment of stillness and expectation as she and her bike flew, weightlessly, as though gravity had been unplugged. Then gravity returned and she smashed through a few pine seedlings, landed on her back and the bike launched away from her.

In the stillness following impact, she could hear the stream rushing nearby. Realizing she hadn't yet breathed, she took a big gasp of air. She continued breathing hard for a moment and tried to calm herself enough to move.

She had crashed her mountain bike before, but this time she hadn't had time to take it slowly. He might be upon her any second.

Painfully, she picked herself up off the ground and scanned her surroundings.

Before she could find her bike and escape, she saw an old Indian man with a huge, gray handlebar mustache. He was walking quickly up the path straight toward her.

She couldn't run and she couldn't find her bike, so she held her ground and tried to look big and scary, like what you're supposed to do when charged by a bear.

"Oh my goodness, thank God you are okay!" he said in a thick Indian accent.

It was the same accent as the whisper, more or less, but she thought this old man could not be the same person as her whisperer. The words, 'I have you this time,' and 'What a fat bloody Amazon,' could not come from the same person who could say something like, 'Oh my goodness.'

"Are you damaged?" he asked. "May I please help you with your bicycle?"

Alice wondered if it was the mustache speaking or if there was a mouth under there somewhere. The gray-haired comic-book mustache was as long as it was thick, stretching way beyond his face on both sides and ending in a tight upwards curl that appeared to be oiled with something. Everywhere else on his face was crossed with the deepest wrinkles she had ever seen.

He had a long body and his stride was graceful. He had obviously seen where her bike landed and he leaned down and plucked it up with one strong hand. It was a strange sight, such strength in such an old person. She noticed his dark fingers that took hold of the blue frame of her mountain bike were soft and relaxed even while applying so much effort.

He smiled at her.

She realized she knew his name. "Hello, Mr. Rao." Alice did not return his smile.

Mr. Rao's mustache moved as he managed to expand his smile even further. "Oh, I am so very pleased you remember me after all this time. I was so worried this day would come and you would not know me. Or that I would have made you nervous. This moment was just right. Come, come. It is dark and we should be having a cup of chai. Come. I have been searching for you. I will explain as we walk. Can you walk? That was one very impressive tumble. Come, *jau*."

He turned and quickly pushed Alice's bike alongside of him and headed down the trail.

Alice didn't follow him right away. She had a feeling she was on the verge of making a huge decision. She looked up at the darkening sky. The stars offered no advice.

"Lucky," the whisperer said from behind her.

She spun around and saw nothing.

"Don't worry, fat Amazon girl," the whisperer continued. "We'll meet tomorrow. You won't be so lucky."

Alice turned and forced her body into a run down the trail

and soon caught up with Mr. Rao.

"...and so you see, Alice," he concluded, apparently unaware she had not been walking with him the whole time, "it is not at all strange that I am here."

"Mr. Rao," Alice asked, breathing heavily after her jog down the trail, "what are you doing here?"

Mr. Rao stopped and looked at her. "Alice, have you not been hearing me the last few minutes? Heavens, you are a little bit nervous maybe. Nothing chai won't fix, *jau*. My cottage is not far."

She took her bike back from him and let him lead.

He started whistling after a while. When they reached the border of the wilderness area and the state forest, Mr. Rao managed to surprise her by turning immediately right, straight into the dark forest, away from the gravel road that led to her house.

She followed and soon realized they were following a nearly imperceptible game trail. She thought she knew all the trails up here but had never been down this one.

When the trail didn't switchback at all (as game trails rarely do), but rather plunged in a straight line to the west for what felt like ages, then began a long descent, she speculated they were heading for the next small drainage valley to the west of the one she lived in. The next valley had its own access road but it was basically just two lines of dirt tire tracks with weeds in the middle. She had cycled a little way up the road once, but never this high up.

Her parents had warned her that a crazy, old ex-con lived in a cabin over here somewhere. They said he sat inside with a shotgun and shot at anyone who got near the cabin. Mr. Rao did not look like he would own a shotgun.

She followed him in silence. The game trail eventually widened and spilled out into the two-track dirt road that had been cut into the forest and was now dimly lit by starlight. They followed the road uphill and after a while took a sharp turn up a little gravel driveway to the left. At the top it opened into a dramatic scene.

A large, cleared meadow, about an acre in size, harboring a cabin and a small barn, was utterly dwarfed by an enormous sheer cliff. The cliff made it feel like this was a hidden fortress. The trees shielded the property from the little road and one would definitely have to know it was here in order to find it.

As they approached the cabin and the barn, she saw it was all very carefully looked after. She could see up close that the windows were clean, the wood trim freshly painted and the chinking work between the logs was fresh. Each window had a window box full of chili plants. There was a herb garden out front surrounded with stones.

She turned her head to the barn and saw the back of a rusty old red VW bus sticking out. She thought this guy would make a really cute picture driving that thing into town with his big mustache practically sticking out of both the windows. How was it possible she hadn't ever seen him in it before? How long had he lived here in this hidden Shangri-La?

"Here we are," he said, opening the solid wood door to the cabin. "Come inside. I have a surprise for you. Oh my, you must feel there are very many surprises today. First, chai. Pardon the mess."

She leaned her bike against the cabin wall and followed Mr. Rao. As she ducked to clear the door frame, she watched him touch the feet of a Ganesh statue that was on a shelf right inside the front door.

"*Om gam Ganapataye namaha,*" he said and chanted a longer mantra under his breath.

Alice knew the long mantra he was whispering. She didn't know how she knew it. It was like a fragment of a bedtime story from a distant memory, but the memory began to crystallize when the smell of spices and incense flooded cabin. She remembered the ashram in India and that she used to stand and try to mouth the words of the chant together with her parents every morning. She would be standing with her brother. She and Thomas were exactly the same height and looked the same, except Thomas wore boy's clothes and she wore girl's clothes. They were both playing the game of trying to figure out these Indian words to these Indian songs that her parents somehow knew. When they finished the songs they would go as a family to have chai in the communal kitchen. Mr. Rao's place smelled exactly like the kitchen in the ashram in Rajasthan.

She looked around the one-room cabin as Mr. Rao chanted and moved around. It was very sparse. There was a single bed, tidily made, in one corner. Next to the bed was a small table with a candle. In another corner of the room there was a little round Persian rug with a cushion on it, set in front of a low window overlooking the back garden and the massive cliff. The other side of the cabin was completely full of kitchen paraphernalia surrounding a huge wood-burning stove in the middle. Next to the stove there was a small round table with three wooden chairs.

Mr. Rao finished his chant and went over to the kitchen side of his cabin. "Alice, please make yourself at home. I will make the chai. Your brother is here."

There was a moment of silence as Alice tried to register what Mr. Rao had just said. She looked around, saw no-one, and gingerly walked over to the little table. Not knowing what else to do or say, she sat down carefully in a chair that creaked loudly under her weight.

The minutes passed slowly as Mr. Rao pounded spices in a mortar, boiled them in a saucepan, added black tea, let it steep for a while, and then poured in milk.

She looked down to inspect the extent of the bruising on her hip, which was significant. She stared back at the chair across from her, thought she heard a voice, but then nothing. Nothing was there and there was no reaction from Mr. Rao. Alice could hear the sizzle of the saucepan that meant the chai was nearly ready to boil again. Mr. Rao removed the saucepan off the heat and added a liberal amount of white sugar. It smelled divine,

Alice thought. He poured it through a sieve into a metal pitcher, brought it over with two stainless steel cups and placed it all on the table.

Mr. Rao sat down, poured the chai, wrapped a piece of cloth around the bottom of each cup and handed one to Alice.

Alice took the cup, anticipating. The sharp metal edge of the steel on her lips reminded her of the ashram again. She took a sip and it was absolutely delicious. Sweet, sharp with ginger and cardamom, rounded by cloves and much better than the chai Mom drank at home. Much better than the chai at Bhakti's house.

She looked at Mr. Rao. "Thanks. Okay, please explain what you meant about Thomas being here. Go, I'm ready. This is going to be fun."

He said nothing. The minutes passed. Then as she watched him take another drink of his chai, something caught her eye. There were little streams of sparkling light flowing up within the steam above his cup. Suddenly the entire room seemed to be full of little flowing patterns of crystalline currents. She looked down at her hand and moved her fingers. The same pattern followed her movements, like she was moving her fingers through water. She looked at Mr. Rao and there was a long, elegant puff of swirling light coming down from his nostrils every five or six seconds. It was as though he was smoking some fluorescent tobacco.

She closed her eyes for a long moment and opened them again.

"Your brother has been through a lot, my dear," Mr. Rao said. "He is special, like you."

"What's all that stuff in the air?" Alice asked.

"Hmm?"

"Mr. Rao," Alice said, "Thomas is dead. How can he be so special if he's dead? Are you special? Are you dead or alive, by the way?"

"Oh, yes, very much alive. Thank you kindly for asking. Thomas is truly special, I don't know why. You are truly special too, Alice."

Then Mr. Rao paused and a look of intense discomfort shrouded his features. "As for myself," he said, mustache drooping, "I am not in any way special. I believe Thomas could make himself be heard by anyone with a clear mind. There is nothing at all special about myself."

After his disclosure was made, he brightened again. "Now, please look at me, young lady."

Alice looked at him, a little bit irreverently.

"Goodness gracious, you are very serious. Okay, now, I have one more little guess about you. I don't know if I am correct, but let us find out, shall we?"

"What, you think I'm a freak or something."

"Not a freak but maybe quite special, like Thomas. My dear, there are powers in this material world that have almost been lost—for many centuries. Some of us old yogis from the Himalaya still know something of these powers. No, not powers; just natural abilities people don't think they can have anymore. Most people are not living properly like some humans used to live a very, very long time ago. So many of us are so stressed and lost. Yes, it is nice we have so many interesting scientific advances, but really we all feel we are composed of a brain operating a sack of meat to go make money and get power over others. I am also stupid but I am not so stupid."

"*Siddhis*," Alice said, remembering the word Kirsty had used. She bent her elbow and put her chin in her hand and kept watching him and listening. There was a long pause and nothing was happening.

"Yes, *siddhis*," Mr. Rao said. "Very good. Now quit messing around, as they say." He became very serious and repeated, "You must really look at me."

Alice thought she knew what he meant. She took a deep breath and shifted her state of mind so that she could read him. She was surprised she hadn't thought to do this before now; the wipe-out must have jarred her more than she thought. When she connected, she almost gasped to behold his mind as a giant desert, an immense landscape of sand and space. There was no internal babble at all. No thoughts, no movement. Everything was the texture and color of sand. It was like no mind she had ever read before. She started to get the impression there was an ambient friendliness and...she could see he was very, very old—way more than a hundred. She didn't know what gave it away, but it was obvious. She blinked and withdrew herself. She stood up and took a step back.

"Alice," Mr. Rao said, smiling. "You were in my mind. See? You have *siddhis*."

"You call that a special power?" Alice exclaimed. "An Indian gardener who is over a hundred years old, or maybe two hundred, thinks that to be a little bit insightful is a special power?"

"Please," Mr. Rao said, with his hands open, "it is not so special to be a gardener." Mr. Rao smiled, looking embarrassed. He poured himself another chai. "I am a good gardener but many others can grow things. Perhaps not Indian chilies: at least not like my chilies. They are growing very well this year, I must admit."

"Mr. Rao," Alice replied, sitting back down, "I'm sorry. I didn't mean to embarrass you. This is all a little new to me. Can you just explain why you think my little mind trick is special?"

"Trick?" he said, looking offended. "That is no trick, my dear. It is just as I suspected. You are a truly remarkable young lady. You are doing what many, many yogis have tried to do for many centuries. You are not reading minds, Alice. You are seeing *prana*. You are sensing and influencing it's movement in my thoughts. We are all made up of *prana*. To know *prana* is to know who we really are, Alice."

"Mr. Rao, when you say yogi, are you talking about someone who wears yoga pants and goes to yoga classes?"

"Not necessarily, no."

"Then you mean the kind of yogi who goes to an ashram in India, like my idiot parents did?"

"Your parents are not idiots, Alice. No. There may be yogis who go to yoga classes and some who go see gurus in India, but they are not yogis because of the classes or the gurus."

"When you say guru, do you mean like that fat rapist guy my parents used to worship? Called Babaji? He's in town, you know."

"Yes, I'm aware he is in Hardrock. Tragic. Tragedy follows him everywhere and it has followed him here."

Mr. Rao looked through the window, as though trying to see something very far away and said, "Some yogis I met in the Himalayas had meditated in a cave for 60 years, 12 hours a day, and they had a little bit of what you have. They could read minds a little bit. But you, Alice, you do it like it is just...natural: like breathing."

Alice felt a wave of anger well up and she wanted to stand up and leave. Instead she looked Mr. Rao squarely in the eyes and said, with a challenge, "Okay. Why me?"

His smile disappeared and he responded in a similar, serious tone. "I don't know."

"Give me your best guess then."

He looked away, frowning. He appeared to think of something and he leveled his old eyes back on Alice.

"I am not one to make irresponsible guesses. There are many people in India who would say you were born this way and that you are a re-incarnation of a powerful yogi, but I would not presume to know what happens after we die."

Alice felt like he was just being diplomatic or philosophical. She narrowed her eyes at him in order to demonstrate her growing impatience.

"But it may be Thomas' death has something to do with the awakening of your abilities. Death is a mysterious thing and..."

"Excuse me, but quit messing around, Mr. Rao."

"You were shocked into silence when your brother died. Others thought it was a temporary silence and that you would get over it in time. They would be proven wrong. It would take you ten years before you uttered another word. But I felt like I perhaps saw something else in your silence that the others did not see."

"Sorry. Did you just say ten years?"

"Yes. Ten years: a long time not to speak. Everyone was quite concerned."

Alice's mind was whirling. Did people really think she had been mute until only a few years ago? She knew she liked being by herself when she was growing up, didn't have any friends and never condescended to answer any questions at school. She did, however, occasionally speak to her coach and sometimes even to her parents, though she never had much to say to them. But she knew she could speak. Had she really given everyone else the impression she was mute for all those years? Why had no-one mentioned to her their supposed concern?

"I was just quiet, like anyone would be if they had a twin and their twin died."

"Yes, but in that quietude you were awake and seeing things others could not see. Am I correct?"

Mr. Rao poured Alice another chai and continued. "Now, we don't have much time tonight because you should get home to your parents. This is my plan. It is probably very stupid. Maybe you have a better plan. But anyway, here it is. This guru, Babaji, he has a very interesting disciple called Bhakti. I knew her from the old days when she just arrived at the ashram. Back then she was just called Mary. She was just another smart girl who was lost. But now, something has happened and she may be the key to this funny business. She is what you may call a nut case."

"Babaji's staying in her house, you know," Alice said, her iciness and confusion defrosted somewhat by Mr. Rao's enthusiasm.

"Yes, and I think he may be here for some time. It is important you do not get too close to Babaji. He is a master of drawing people into his webs of tragedy. My plan is to keep our distance and slowly observe Bhakti and find out from this what is going on." Mr. Rao beamed at Alice and at the empty chair across from her. "Do you like my plan?"

Alice smiled and thought she had to be a little bit careful not to hurt Mr. Rao's feelings. "Mr. Rao, I actually have a little bit of a head start on that plan." She explained what happened at the library: Sadvhi Bhakti Devi reading her father's PhD dissertation, telling someone she had recorded an accidental pocket call that gave her some incriminating evidence about Alice's dad's company. Alice told him about the strange man with Bhakti in the lobby and how Alice chased the four-wheel drive on her bike. When she got to the part about going into the house where the guru was staying, Mr. Rao's eyes widened. She told him about her little conversation with Babaji, surrounded by his devotees, and the part where the guru said he knew who she was and had asked her to invite her parents to his public lecture that evening. Mr. Rao's eyes got bigger and bigger and by the time she finished her story, she grew slightly concerned that his eyes would fall out onto the table.

"But, oh dear..." he said and started chanting a long mantra that Alice didn't know.

CHAPTER 4

She started cycling home in the dark, pedaling mostly one-legged, as her left thigh was corked from the wipeout earlier. She knew she couldn't find the game trail back toward her house, so she had to just follow Mr. Rao's road all the way down to highway 320, then east toward her road.

She started to feel sorry for herself. She thought that was a good sign; maybe she wasn't crazy, she just needed some chocolate or something. She still couldn't reach her dad on his mobile. As she neared the turnoff for the road up the valley toward her house, she changed her mind and decided she would just head back into town to speak to her mother, who would be just finishing teaching her Saturday evening restorative yoga class. It was an easy ride, all downhill, and Mom could drive her back home. Maybe Mom would have some chocolate.

She cycled past the aquatic center and into the neighborhood called The Hill, where all the good cafés were, as well as a few boutique clothes shops and one other yoga studio besides her mom's. As she approached her mom's studio, she was struck by how peaceful and inviting it looked. It was on the second floor of an old brick building that used to be some kind of trackside warehouse when the railway used to come through Hardrock. The tall windows faced the ski mountain and Alice could see that Mom had dimmed the lights for the last part of class.

She locked her bike up and waited by the entrance. Eventually a slow gaggle of silent, fit, middle-aged women in Lycra were gently stepping down the stairs.

As soon as the last of them passed her, Alice climbed the stairs and shouted, "Hi, Mom," before ducking into the bathroom to wash some of the blood and dirt off. She did the best she could in the bathroom and emerged with just a little bit of road pizza on her knees and some bruising.

When she came out, her mom sucked her breath anyway.

"Alice, you have smashed yourself. Again." Alice's mom was a very fit thirty-five-year-old lady who held herself tall and proud, like a dancer.

"Lie down on that bolster right now and lean your head back. I'll be with you in a second when we're through here." She was standing with a student who was obviously putting her through the third degree about something.

Alice ignored her advice, walked to the far end of the room and stared out the window at the dark shapes of the mountains. She overheard her mom's student asking, "I was just telling a friend the other day that I am loving your classes and that I might be interested in committing more time to learning about yoga."

Alice had seen this many times before. She thought it was gross that Mom's yoga students were so grateful after classes. Alice never felt that way about her swimming coach and didn't understand why a yoga class would be different.

"Wonderful," Mom said.

"Do you run teacher training here?"

"No, but I can recommend a few different programs to you, if you like."

"Oh, that's too bad. Are those other programs in the same style you teach here?"

"I don't really teach in a particular style or tradition, but most teacher training programs will give you a solid appreciation of different approaches to teaching."

"Well, my friend is doing a teacher training program that is in a spiritual lineage of teachers in India. The first module involved a trip to the ashram in Rajasthan. She was just beaming about finding her true guru. Apparently having a guru has helped her take her spiritual practice to a whole new level."

Alice's ears pricked up, knowing that Mom's student could be talking about Babaji. She didn't know if there were other gurus preying on people here in Hardrock.

"So I asked her if I can apply and she said no. She got all mysterious and said it will happen when I'm ready." The girl shifted on her feet and continued. "So I wanted to ask you, what do you think of gurus? Do I need one? Am I ready?"

Alice heard her mom say, a little bit too quickly, "Look, Amy, in my experience most big-time gurus are more masterful at sounding enlightened than they are at being enlightened. There are so many agendas hidden under their halos. There are lots out there. Learn from them but just be careful."

"But what do you think of what my friend was saying about yoga? That the only authentic way to practice is under the personal guidance of a guru?"

"Sweetheart, commit to yoga, absolutely. It's a wonderful path. Sure, go see India. But total commitment to a guru can be dangerous. Believe me, I've been there. In my experience it's more powerful to commit to yourself. Commit to your practice."

Alice didn't know how the girl took all that but she heard her gathering her stuff and then she left.

Alice's mom came straight over and gave Alice a concerned look. Alice didn't feel like being mothered anymore and so she pretended to be all better. She helped Mom tidy up the yoga mats (students never put them away properly, Mom always muttered).

When Alice's mom sat down cross-legged on the carpet to calculate the takings and enter them into a spreadsheet on the laptop, she asked Alice, distractedly, "How was your day, sweetheart?"

Alice thought for a moment and decided to lay right into it.

"Well, after setting an unofficial national record in the 200 meter free, I went to see your ex-guru this afternoon."

When Alice's mom flashed a look of complete incomprehension, Alice continued. "You know the fat Indian guy who started an international cult, promising enlightenment if you gave him complete devotion, and has sex with you."

Alice's mom slowly closed her laptop and looked at Alice with eyes pleading she hadn't heard correctly.

Alice topped it off with, "He's in town and I went to see him at some house."

It felt odd to say so many words to her mom. Alice usually just said "Hello, what's for dinner," and that was about it. She hadn't bothered to talk to her like this for ages. But she knew Mom was shocked by what Alice was saying, not by her loquaciousness.

Mom tried to speak. "Okay, I can handle this. Okay. So you took yourself to see Babaji. Does your dad know?"

"I have no idea," Alice said, "but I do know that some lady in orange robes named Bhakti secretly recorded an incriminating conversation she had with Dad's assistant And now Bhakti's going to use the recording to blackmail him."

Alice was feeling sick again and the benefits of Mr. Rao's chai had completely worn off. She needed some food and sleep. Her mother noticed she was turning pale and ordered Alice to sit down. She ran and got Alice a glass of water, grabbed her things and helped Alice get back up. They locked up the studio and went downstairs. Alice's mom helped her throw her bike in the back of her four-wheel drive and they drove quickly home.

She focused hard on the passing scenery to try to clear her head. It was already dark and there was not much traffic around. The old-growth pines crowding the road near her house cast a deep silence across the landscape. Beneath the trees was a carpet of dry pine needles and sticks. Beneath that was moist, dark soil: hard to walk through. Beneath that, she guessed, was a network of underground streams gurgling forever along toward the Pacific Ocean. Beneath the ocean there were...more thoughts of her brother. How did he die? Why? Why had she survived?

Then the whisper came again. "She's coming."

"Mom, did you hear that?"

"Hear what, sweetheart? Are you okay?"

They rounded the final corner and Alice saw a few cars parked in front of their house. They pulled up into their driveway and Mom didn't drive all the way inside, so that it would be easier for Alice to put her bike away.

"I'm going upstairs, Alice," her mom said stiffly. The caring version of her mom had disappeared and Alice knew she had been chased away by the sight of those cars. They both knew who drove them—Dad's colleagues, who would be inside right now toasting each other and would be well into their third or fourth bottle.

"I'm okay, Mom. I'll see you inside."

The wind picked up and after her mom disappeared into the house, Alice turned to face the dark forest across the road.

"What a bloody Amazon she is," the voice whispered. "Well over a hundred kilos."

Before she could let herself hear any more, Alice snatched her bike from the boot of her mom's car, fled into the safety of the garage and pressed the button that closed the door. She stood there panting and watching the garage door slowly, too slowly, creak itself down until there was just a foot left, then inches, and it was finally closed.

Alice tried to sigh her fear away but was still haunted by the possibility that some evil whisper really was floating on the wind by her house, passing comment on her and threatening to kidnap her. She looked around, flipped on some more lights, grabbed a recovery drink from the garage fridge and tried to bring herself back to normal.

After hanging her bike up on ceiling hooks she had proudly installed herself last year, she was about to turn off the garage light and open the door that led in to the house when something made her look over her shoulder.

She nervously scanned the space, a large two-car garage that could really fit three cars. Shadows lurked and shifted everywhere. Her gaze was drawn to an area in the far corner where Mom and Dad stored their old bikes and camping gear—stuff that nobody had ever touched in years.

Something was different over there.

She walked slowly over, sipping her recovery drink for courage. Maybe there was a guy in here, she thought: hiding; whispering crazy stuff.

The wall shelves still contained unused sleeping bags, old ski boots and a couple of boxes of fishing things.

The floor beneath the shelves was cluttered with dusty frame packs and a few tents. Next to that were a couple of bikes with flat tires. None of that had changed.

She saw a tarp had been disturbed. It had been covering something leaning against the far wall. The whole pile was usually hidden by stuff leaning against it. All those things had been placed to the side.

She picked up a random power tool to use as a club. She walked over and forcefully pulled away the tarp, expecting to reveal a drunk crouching there, or a prowler or a rapist. Instead she only found a very unusual bike. Unusual because it looked like someone had stretched the front wheel out about five feet in front of the handlebars and stuck a big wooden box in that space.

Dad must have been in here today looking at it.

Curious about what he would have been interested in, she leaned down for a closer look.

The wooden box contained a little bench with seatbelts for two. Behind the seat was a huge rack holding a couple of massive saddle bags, a few camping things still packed inside.

She felt the smooth finish of the box and looked inside again. There were two colorful round objects on the floor. She plucked up her courage and reached inside, pulling out one of them: a tiny bike helmet with ladybugs painted on it. The other one had pink flowers.

She felt a pinch in her heart and closed her eyes tightly against the image of two little kids sitting in this box bike with those helmets on. Thomas and Alice, two little toddler twins in colorful bike helmets sitting side by side screaming with joy as Dad pedaled them confidently through the landscape of somewhere like Vermont or Yellowstone or Vail, Mom on her bike right behind, everybody packing tents and food and cameras and diapers and toys, smiling at each other in the wind and the warm air.

It had never happened. India happened first. Dad must have bought the bike, planning some great trip, and they went to India instead.

She covered the bike up and realized how stupid she had been to be afraid of a whisper in the air. It had probably been the wind. There were no such things as ghosts. Life was full of enough terrors: there was no need for her to invent more.

She walked resolutely back inside.

She heard voices. Before walking in to the living room, she paused in the snow room, chucked her bike shoes in a shelf with all her other shoes, and tried to remember and identify the cars she had seen out front. There had been two. One of them was a VW Golf she knew belonged to John. He was a regular at Dad's Friday evening cocktail gatherings. Alice knew he was older than Dad. His short brown hair was usually artfully gelled into a bed-head look. Every time she had seen him, he always had a perfectly manicured five-o'clock stubble goatee. His shirts always looked perfect, regardless of the time of day. She suspected he carried around spare shirts with him, pressed and ironed.

She couldn't remember the color or make of the other car. Some fancy four-wheel drive, like the cars that both her mom and dad, and most other people in Hardrock, drove. She guessed it was owned by Dad's executive assistant, a Chinese-American called Wei. She was older than John, and Dad had once said Wei was a real survivor at work. Not the smartest, not the most elegant, but she had always managed to get invited places and help him close the right deals. She had always worn black whenever Alice had seen her. She had a stylish strip of pink highlight in her bangs.

She felt a surge of anticipation as she pushed through into the main part of the house. She enjoyed trying to embarrass Dad in front of his stupid colleagues. She also liked trying to embarrass his colleagues in front of him. These were the only times when Dad showed some spirit. The alcohol probably had something to do with it.

Her dad and his two guests were sitting in the living room in front of the big glass windows facing east, magnificent views of the ski mountain in the distance. The gondola was a string of lights running up the mountain, taking people to an expensive steak restaurant at mountain top.

Conversation came to an icy halt as Alice walked in. Dad tried to smile but the other two seemed put off by her arrival. She looked down at her damp cycling gear, hugging and revealing her muscles and her fat, and smirked at the contrast she made with their smart-casual attire.

Alice reached down, poured herself some water from a pitcher on their table and looked up at Dad.

He avoided her look and lifted his wine glass to his lips. Alice's dad was a tall, bearded man with a balding head. He used to be strong but had become soft and slouchy. He was in his late thirties and was still handsome, but had an unhealthy air about him. She knew he could be funny when he was drinking with his employees because they seemed to laugh a lot, but she knew they didn't really care about him. She had read each of them enough times to know they all plotted against him and would do almost anything to unseat him and take his job.

Alice turned and smiled at them both to cement her power over them and plonked down in a chair.

They all shifted in their seats and took a drink.

Wei picked up on a story she must have been telling before Alice came in. "So this lady calls me last night. Seven fricking p.m. on a Friday night. 'Scuse my French, Alice."

"That was when we were meeting with the delegation, wasn't it?" asked Alice's dad.

"Yep. That was when I just stepped outside. She was saying I was listed as the main public relations contact for Helpharma and could she please speak to Nathan Brickstone, head of PR."

"I'm sorry, Wei," Alice's dad replied to her in an avuncular tone, "but you are our PR Officer. Fielding weird calls is in your job description. Who was it?"

Wei looked at him and shrugged her shoulders. "I don't know. I hung up on her, the bitch." She fumbled around in her handbag and fished out her phone.

"You hung up on her?"

"By accident. When I called her back later, she didn't answer and I could just hear the sound of some Indian guy in the background. It freaked me out. I thought I would let you know."

"What was the number?"

Wei was punching heavily with her skinny finger at the touchscreen in seemingly random places, cursing under her breath and clearly not finding the number she was looking for.

"That is strange," Dad said. "I wonder if it had anything to do with the delegation from the Indian pharmaceutical company we were hosting."

Alice was biding her time, waiting for a good opportunity to drop her bomb and tell Dad that it had indeed been a handbag call to Bhakti, that she had recorded it and there were going to be nasty consequences for Dad's company.

John slouched in his chair and flashed some artfully relaxed and clever looks at Dad and Wei as he spoke. He too appeared to be picking up on a story he had been telling earlier.

"Who cares. It was probably a handbag call. All these Indians are a bit amateurish anyway. That's part of the appeal. It's awesome. There is no bullshit red tape in India like there is here with the FDA. You just pay people off there and everything goes ahead. Imagine how many more people we could help with our products if we could halve our time to market?"

He took a drink and while swishing red wine in his mouth, he said, "I love India. We're good people, here at Helpharma," he continued, pointing at himself with a manicured finger. "Don't get me wrong," he concluded, smoothing down his goatee stubble with his fingers. Wei and Alice's dad nodded automatically, as though they felt that to fail to do so would break some unwritten law of nature.

"Yeah," Wei agreed in her normal voice. "I know the whole world thinks we pharmaceutical companies are all evil empires that need to be reined in, but we are just smart people trying to help save lives, so why all the stupid red tape?"

"I tell ya, not in India," John said. "We can do whatever we want there."

Alice was disgusted and no longer felt like telling her dad or these people about Wei's handbag call with Bhakti. Maybe a little blackmail will be good for their moral compasses.

Alice's dad looked hard at John. "You know why we can do whatever we want in India?" he asked rhetorically. "It's not because India is some lawless Wild West. It's because of the protection we enjoy through our new partners. Besides, if something does go wrong for us in India in spite of their connections, our company will wear it and they won't."

Alice wondered what it meant when a clinical trial goes wrong. It couldn't be good for the trial participants. She figured it was probably those poor people who would wear it before Dad's company did.

John's smug look had shifted.

Alice's dad lifted his glass. "Look, I hate dealing with ethics boards as much as anyone. I think it's fantastic things are easier in India. But just don't expose us to any bad press."

John flashed Dad a knowing look and they clinked glasses.

Alice was grossed out.

After her dad and his guests had a few more wines, they moved to the dining room and started hoeing into some takeaway Thai food.

Alice grabbed five of the plastic containers and went to the kitchen. She dumped the containers together into a huge salad bowl and ate it quickly.

She went upstairs, brushed her teeth and got into bed with her laptop.

The noise from Dad's party had escalated to ridiculous volumes. They had moved back into the living room and had put on some 70s music. They wouldn't notice if she chucked a couch down the stairs.

She put on her headphones and turned up the volume on a track with a heavy beat to drown out the noise from downstairs.

She woke up much later with music still playing in her headphones. She knew something was different. Taking off the headphones, she saw it was one in the morning. She was shocked to hear some strange sounds from downstairs. She snapped fully awake immediately and strained to listen.

"....she'll find out..."

Maybe Mom's voice, but strained?

"Shush, it's..."

That sounds like Dad, Alice thought. Were they actually talking to each other? That would be a first.

"Nathan, how long do you think you can... It's not right: it never was..."

That sounded like Mom again.

"...That's it, Victoria, you always...crazy..."

"Don't you dare call me crazy." This time Mom's voice was louder. "Women have been called crazy by men for centuries and it's going to stop now for..."

Alice was wide awake. She worked her painful body out of bed slowly and crept over to the stairwell where she could hear more. She sat down heavily on the top stair. She remembered she used to sit here when she was a little girl, and for the same reason. It had been a very long time since she had overheard her parents speak to each other.

"Sure, you go upstairs and hide in your cave," Alice's dad said. "Hide from the real world while the rest of us work."

"Is that what you have been doing?" Mom said. "Working? I'm sorry. I couldn't tell through the haze of your wine breath."

"Oh? How can you see my haze through your meditation aura?"

"At least I'm working on myself, trying to recover. You're killing yourself with work you hate. The man whom I thought I married was so interested in health. You were going to cure the world's worst diseases, as well as the common cold. You were meditating every day. And now…"

"Now I'm drinking myself numb every day after twelve hours at a painkiller marketing job. Ever notice the common denominator between those two occupations, Vic?"

"Yeah," Mom said louder now. "Do you? I see weakness."

"Since India, all I have done is make money for the family, for Alice. There's nothing amoral about that."

After a few moments of silence, Mom spoke again. She was now so quiet Alice had to creep to the top of the stairs to hear her.

"…Babaji, okay? I can't even stand thinking about him. I have spent the last ten years trying to get over him, and now that he has popped in to visit, all my meditation practice is out the window. I feel as betrayed and as bitter and as sorrowful as the day Thomas died."

"Aw, come on," Dad said in a gentler voice. "Surely all that meditation is in there somewhere. You've just had a shock."

"Just like all of the benefit of yours is there for you, but you've chosen to pour Shiraz on it for ten years."

Another pause.

"Look, Nathan, in some ways I am grateful for the money you make. We do have a nice house and I have the freedom to go run a yoga center that loses money and pretend like I'm doing something for the world. It's just I always thought family should come first. Our family is dead. It died with Thomas. The only light in the house is Alice. Actually, it's disgusting my yoga center is being propped up through the sale of your painkiller meds."

"Victoria, it is only Thomas who is dead."

"You're dead too, except when you are with Alice, which is hardly ever. I feel like I've wasted my life. I'm not even a very good mother."

"You are a wonderful mother."

"How would you even know? I'm a shit mother. I can't even bring myself to go to her swim meets. I meditate for another two hours to purge the guilt and feel strong for a while, and the guilt comes back like a big hairy monster strangling my heart. Meanwhile Alice is cycling all over this town doing who knows what."

"Victoria, you know she spends most of her time at the library and the pool. She has come so far, in spite of everything."

Another long silence.

"So why doesn't she have a single friend yet?"

Alice noticed her mom's voice was quieter now, as if they suddenly remembered Alice could be listening.

"I'm sure she has friends at school."

"You ever see her with anyone? Ask her coach, though he hates us so much you're not likely going to get any straight answers from him."

"Come on, she's a teenager. Teenagers are secretive."

"You're speaking like someone who has read a blog about parenting but who has never had kids. Ask yourself, Nathan, have you ever seen her play with another child? Ever? She's never asked to have anyone over here. Has she ever asked to go see someone else? Any sleepovers? Any birthday parties?"

"Maybe she's still getting over the traumas."

"She needs help, you callous, drunk bastard."

"Come on, calm down."

"I ask myself this question all the time and I have never found an answer that makes me feel sane. Why have I never given

Alice a single birthday party? Ever?"

"That's not fair. Every year one of us takes her out to a restaurant of her choice."

"That's great. Other girls get pink balloons, pizza, cupcakes and thirty friends for all-night pajama parties, and Alice gets to go out with only one of us, and no-one else, and eat caviar and prime rib. Again."

"You know as well as I do she hates anything pink and girly. She sleeps in her swimming suit, not pajamas. She's turning sixteen. She wouldn't know what to do at a girly birthday party."

"Nathan, is she okay? Just tell me you think she's okay."

"Victoria, she's fine, just a little independent."

Silence again.

"So that's it." Mom sounded tired. "You think everything is fine and we should go back to our hopeless lives and pretend like everything is okay."

"Everything is okay. We should be grateful for what we have. We live comfortably in a beautiful, natural place; we have a healthy, beautiful, talented daughter. We have our health."

"Usually that speech is supposed to end with 'and we have each other.' But we don't."

"Come on, don't be so dramatic."

"Our lives are a tragedy. If it wasn't for Alice, I would..."

"You would what?"

Silence again. Alice toyed with the idea of rolling something down the stairs, something big and heavy that would bounce all the way down noisily and break the old grandfather clock that had always lurked at the bottom of the stairs. It was a relic from one of her grandparents she had never met.

After a few more minutes of silence, and perhaps the glug-glug of a bottle pouring, Alice heard footsteps near the stairs. She jumped up, felt the pain in her legs and in her back, and made her way as quietly as possible back to bed before either of them reached the bottom of the stairs.

CHAPTER 5

She let herself sleep as much as she wanted on Sundays, which usually added up to sixteen hours or more. She smiled as she turned over and saw the clock read 3:00 p.m. The smell of chai floated up to her nose from downstairs, making her think of Mr. Rao. Suddenly all of the events of the previous day rushed back to her.

She ate some energy bars and prepared herself as quickly and quietly as she could. She had no wish to chat with her mom or dad today. She went downstairs silently, avoided the kitchen and her mom, took her bike down and cycled toward Mr. Rao's cabin.

When she arrived, she found him in the back, instead of the kitchen. His still form was just visible at the edge of the forest behind his house. He was below the dramatic one-hundred-foot cliff face. In the daylight she could see layered striations in the rock. The layers at the bottom of the cliff, near Mr. Rao, probably were deposited there hundreds of millions of years ago. Mr. Rao's back was straight as a rod, his legs crossed, hands crossed in his lap and eyes closed. A shawl was draped casually across his shoulders.

Alice gave up on him and went into his kitchen to see what

she could find to feed herself. To her immense relief, she saw a thermos of chai on his kitchen table, next to a plate of ten pieces of fresh Indian flat bread and a couple of bowls of spicy-looking curries. Never one to mind a bit of curry for breakfast, Alice demolished the food and poured herself a massive quantity of chai into a cereal bowl. She walked out and leaned against the house to watch Mr. Rao.

Drinking deeply from her bowl of chai, Alice gazed out above the trees into the sky. There were no clouds, only a light blue expanse framed below by the deep emerald green of pine tree tips. She thought of the blackness of space beyond the blue. If she could get high enough in the atmosphere, like in a rocket, she would see nothing but blackness and stars.

Closing her eyes slowly, Alice tried to remember what Thomas looked like before he died. She failed, but some long-lost feeling arose in her heart and caused it to beat faster. Something liquid brushed against her cheek and she opened her eyes quickly. As it had yesterday, the air around her again gained a liquid crystalline aspect. She looked out through the doorway and saw the treetops were even radiating the liquid ripples toward the blue sky, and in the distance, Mr. Rao was wrapped in the flowing vapor from the tree he was sitting against.

Alice looked down at her chai and saw it was the source of the liquid sensation flowing upward against her cheek. She waved her hand above it to interrupt the flow of the upwelling current and it felt cool, like water. The current also pushed against her hand. It was as strong as the flow of a kitchen faucet turned on full. She put the bowl down on the ground and looked around.

She noticed Mr. Rao's abundant chili garden was also emitting this same blue-green liquid. The garden was nestled against the base of the cliff, where it would probably attract a lot of sun. Chili plants stretched in rows for about the length of a small backyard swimming pool. Ignoring Mr. Rao, who was still meditating, Alice strode over and stood in front of the chili plants, holding both hands out. The flow pushed her hands upward until her arms were straight and she withdrew them. She looked up and saw that the flow continued up into the air for twenty or thirty feet. She stuck her face into the flow and again it felt like water on her skin.

The word prana came to mind. Mr. Rao had used it yesterday to lecture her about something. Something about how we are all made of prana and she had some special ability to read prana, blah, blah, blah.

It sounded like philosophical b.s. but what if he was right? Maybe this was prana? Whatever it was, could it hold her, she wondered. Could it support her body weight?

Alice leaned forward, as though she was about to dive into the pool, muscles coiled and ready.

With a burst of energy, she dove into the flow above the garden.

For a moment, she flowed along like a dolphin, feeling the gentle pressure of the chili energy underneath her and using a kind of underwater swimming motion to maintain her forward momentum.

She thought of Madison and imagined she would think Alice ridiculous for thinking she was swimming in the air.

Then she was not swimming in the air. She was landing hard into the chilies.

Alice moved her fingers and slowly slid her hands under her shoulders. She felt the dirt and pushed herself up, chest first, lifting her chin high to stretch out her neck. The chili plant under her chest tried valiantly to stand itself back up, but failed. She kneeled up and looked around.

Alice saw Mr. Rao fold his hands, press them to his head and bow forwards toward the forest. He unfolded his legs rather painfully, Alice thought, and stood up. He smiled at her before a look of horror flushed his features and he rushed the twenty steps to the garden.

"My garden! What have you done to my garden?"

"Sorry," Alice said, picking some chilies out of her pants

pockets. "There was a lot of prana above your garden and I wanted to try to fly. Sorry. Hey, thanks for the chai, Mr. Rao."

His face softened immediately. "You are very much welcome, my dear, and you are absolutely correct that prana concentrates itself around life. Prana loves places that have been nurtured with love."

"Why not places untouched by people?"

"Prana is also that life force that tries to keep balance in nature."

"So it gathers in places where natural disasters have taken place?"

Mr. Rao didn't answer. He was staring at the plants Alice had smashed.

"So," she asked, walking toward the house, trying to distract Mr. Rao's attention away from the garden, "what's up today?"

"This is a question I have been meditating on just now for many hours," he said, following her at last.

"Yes, I saw you sitting there under the trees, Mr. Rao."

"So you did, young lady, so you did. Lovely trees."

"And?"

"I still don't know what to do."

"Cool," Alice said. "An honest answer."

"But you know, I am running short on agarbhati, so let's go shopping?"

Alice faintly remembered that agarbhati was either the Hindi word for incense or for some kind of spice. It struck her as extremely odd she should be able to remember foreign words learned when she was five years old. She shrugged her shoulders, figuring she could tag along and get some more food. She followed Mr. Rao to his VW bus.

He didn't even need to go back inside his cabin to get anything. He opened the back sliding door for her, saying something about the view being better from back there, and she piled herself onto a bench that had no apparent seat belts. The bench was low and her knees were almost as high as her face. Mr.

Rao slammed the door violently, walked around and got into the front.

"Well," Mr. Rao said, "let's go shopping!" He turned the key but there was just a click. Mr. Rao paused as though in thought, then opened the door and ran out.

Alice watched him lope deeper into the barn and come out with some long, thin black hoses of some sort. He returned and went around to the back of the bus and opened the back hatch. Then he lifted off a rectangular lid, exposing what must have been the motor.

He was mumbling to himself. Alice heard him say something about bad fuel lines, and he might have said some other things about devils and bananas. Alice wondered if he was mad. His hands worked confidently and he soon closed the engine lid and the back hatch, ran around to the driver's side and jumped back in. He pumped the gas pedal a few times, turned the key, and after a few tries, the engine started weakly with a metallic, bleating sound.

Alice turned around again and realized the reason the bleating sound was so loud was because the motor was basically right behind her head.

Mr. Rao turned around to Alice and gave her a big smile, as if to say sorry and how fun, and stupid fuel lines, and my mistake, all at once.

As they bumped down his gravel driveway, Alice looked northwest and caught a glimpse of one of the higher Knifespur Mountains and saw huge swooping waves of blue air flowing above it.

Unfortunately, Mr. Rao's idea of shopping turned out to be a visit to a local Indian spice shop located in a dilapidated strip mall on the way toward the airport. The Hardrock airfield was a twenty minute drive further to the west and had some private traffic, as well as a few daily flights to Denver. Alice had seen the spice shop before, on the way to the airport with her dad, but had never been inside and never intended to. So after he parked, she said a brisk goodbye and walked away without waiting for a reply.

The secret to pulling off an exit like that, without having to deal with all the usual gentlemanly objections, was to be at least ten feet away before they could process what had happened. Just walk away and keep going.

She looked out over the ski mountain in the distance to the east. The huge bulk of it was her comfort, like a strong motherly presence. A strong mother, rather than the weak one she had now. It was only mid-morning but there were already some big white clouds gathering above the ski area. When the clouds darkened and the winds grew, as they did most afternoons here, Hardrock could expect angry bursts of rain, thunder and lightning. Morning storms were even louder and angrier. It was as though the mountain and the clouds schemed together to unleash some irrational vengeance on the town.

The long walk to Mr. Rao's place, where she had left her bike, would be most direct if she cut straight over private ranch land, rather than walk along the highway. She figured it was about ten miles through the ranch as the crow flies. If she jogged some of it, she could get her bike and cycle home in time for dinner.

The old split-rail fence was her first obstacle and she climbed it and set out across the alpine scrub. The knee-high brown grass and weeds ran along the fence for a couple of dozen feet. Then the ranch stretched all the way to the state forest surrounding both Mr. Rao's valley and the one where she lived.

This ranch didn't seem to be set up for any real grazing; it was just flat, dry, rocky land. There were random little skunk flowers and sage growing here and there out of the rocky earth. She had never walked in here before because it was so boring-looking. Maybe today she would find something interesting: some rattlesnake dens or something; maybe an abandoned plough or wagon wheel. There were probably lots of old arrowheads. All this land occupied by Hardrock used to belong to the Ute people and Alice had found arrowheads elsewhere over the years. She wondered if the land occupied by this ranch was stolen from the

Utes or purchased? Or both? What would they think of her walking around on their land? What would the rancher think, more to the point. She knew that some ranchers up here would shoot at trespassers.

She looked ahead and there were no people or vehicles for miles.

She looked up at the clouds that continued to build and billow above the ski mountain. It was definitely going to pour.,most likely before she made it home.

As she looked back over her shoulder to see if any clouds were gathering to the west, she saw something out of the corner of her eye. Toward the edge of the strip mall parking lot, something moved near the ground. She focused her attention there and saw it again. It was like a shadow; dark, like a coyote. It was a couple hundred yards away. Then she saw it move quickly, dashing between the heavier shrubs by the highway.

She stopped walking, turned and stared. The movement stopped and she saw nothing but scrub. Beyond that, there were no other cars on the highway. The traffic out here was light these days; how did that Indian guy stay in business? Crazy people on the way out to the airport, she supposed.

As she turned back toward her long walk through the ranch, she again perceived a moving shadow like a coyote. Then the coyote rose up on its hind legs.

A small man, not a coyote, was walking straight toward her. He was now about halfway between her and the parking lot and was no longer hiding behind anything. He still moved in a wary, coyote-like fashion.

Then she heard the whisper: "I have you."

It was immediately recognizable as the same voice that had whispered to her yesterday when she wiped out on her bike, and near her house the day before. It was a mystery to her how he was projecting his whisper to her, but she had seen stranger things over the past twenty-four hours.

Rather than freeze in terror, Alice put her hands on her hips and considered her options. Alice knew from his posture, and from the things he had been whispering to her, that this was someone hostile and dangerous. If she attempted to dash back to the strip mall, she risked being grabbed by him or worse. If she cut left and ran to the highway, a car might eventually come by, but there was no guarantee they would stop for her. In fact, around here, most people were petrified of hitchhikers and a six-foot-three-inch, two-hundred-pound girl would make any driver veer away and speed off. Her best chance was to stay in this dark field and run to the woods before he could. She could lose him in the forest which she knew like the back of her hand.

So she ran: sprinted, actually. She would have to ease off after five minutes, she realized, but hopefully, by then, her burst of speed would have dissuaded her pursuer. She was not the fastest runner at her school, but she was feeling fast: surely much faster than coyote man.

She focused on the dark ground about twenty feet ahead of her, rather than right at her feet. The ground was uneven; she needed advance warning of any obstacles.

She soon heard the sound of heavy breathing from behind her. The surprise to Alice was that it sounded like the rhythmic breath of an athlete. She guessed she was only ahead of him by less than a hundred yards.

After five minutes of flat-out sprinting, Alice had to reassess. Her pursuer's rhythmic breathing was sounding closer, so clearly she had failed to shock and awe him with her speed. Any second now, her legs would fill with lactic acid, her lungs would burn just a little bit too much, and her body would force her to slow way down. The pain was starting to take hold and she was tightening up in her hips and her stomach. She was already slowing down, even though she was maintaining the same effort.

Maybe that guy is tired too, she thought. Maybe he will slow down and give up soon. Maybe I dropped something in the parking lot and he's just trying to return it. Maybe I should just turn around, say hello, introduce myself, and find out.

She knew these were just doubts born of panic. She couldn't stop, or even slow down.

He was almost upon her: just ten yards or so behind her.

The world blurred slightly and she stumbled. She caught herself before falling, but the effort broke her rhythm and exhausted her. He must be just about ready to grab her shirt.

"I have you now," the whisper repeated as she attempted to speed up again.

She fought against her blurred vision and accidentally saw into his mind. She had never read someone before without eye contact and all the other little tricks she used, but there he was, open to her. There was no inner babble in his mind but she saw his name was Rajendra and that he was...cold. Calculating. Hungry. She sensed some kind of devastating threat hanging over him. This was a man desperately chasing her for his life.

Breaking off the connection, she realized her terror was close to shutting down her nervous system, which made her angry. Never before had she let a man, or any person, frighten her to her core like this.

Her anger cut into her like a hot knife and she felt herself split into a witness and a runner, like she had split in the pool yesterday. It was a huge relief to be free of her terror and anger. She was able to calmly observe her body and its pain. She could see the pain and the fear had been related, and now that the fear was gone, the pain was dissolving too. She sensed there were hidden reservoirs of energy available, both in her body and in the shimmering air around her. She tapped into it on behalf of the runner and gently encouraged her to pick up her speed.

The witness cajoled and encouraged the runner to improve technique. She straightened her torso, leaned forward and lengthened her stride.

Match that, scary coyote freak dude, she thought, and saw that she was pulling ahead of him.

She heard the rumble of thunder and remembered they were both running straight into an angry, dark Colorado thunderstorm.

This will be interesting, she thought.

She maintained the split between witness and runner and held her pace, concentrating on relaxing and breathing, running smoothly across the uneven dry terrain, weaving around prairie dog holes and sage.

A distant rumble of thunder collapsed the division between witness and runner, but this time she felt confident she could regain it when needed. The pain was there again, but it was manageable.

The uneven green line of the pine forest approached. She guessed it was only about five minutes away and she almost couldn't hear him behind her at all. She ventured a quick glance over her shoulder.

Nope, he was still there. About five hundred yards back, still running hard. She hoped to lose him in the forest but then she wondered if there was anything she could do to permanently dissuade him. She didn't know much about this guy, except the dark things she had briefly seen in his mind.

Perhaps she could lose him, double back and call the police? She could keep an eye on him until they got there. As she started to imagine what she could say to the police, she knew they wouldn't do anything for her. What could she say anyway? That he chased her for six miles across some ranch after whispering to her for the past few days. They would dismiss her as a crazy person. She was sick of being feared and dismissed as crazy by people in this town.

There was nothing to do but just run.

When she reached the edge of the ranch there was a sudden plunge straight into a dark, heavy pine forest. The terrain was now almost impossible to run through, but she kept moving as quickly as possible. There were huge, overturned blue spruces, thick with branches, old fallen lodgepoles covered in moss, young pines with branches at head level. Everything was an obstacle.

The secret to moving quickly in this kind of terrain was to relax, keep moving, just skim the edges of obstacles and maintain as straight a line as possible. It took a lot of experience and much more intense concentration than did the sprint across the prairie dog ground. She was pretty sure he would find it nearly impossible to keep up.

He was probably trashed by now. She was thirsty, so she guessed he was desperate for a drink of water too.

Although his breathing was not audible to her, his crashing steps were loud enough to tell her he was still chasing hard.

She heard another clap of thunder, much closer this time. Thunder up here was very different from thunder in a city and she knew coyote man would be rattled. To him, that thunder would have sounded like it was right on top of him.

She felt the wind pick up and caught the smell of approaching rain. Maybe hail.

She hoped he was on the verge of giving up on the chase.

When she struck Mr. Rao's two-track road, she decided against turning up to fetch her bike. He would catch up to her as she cycled back down this way. She dove back into the forest to continue on foot toward her own house.

Rat-face was about five minutes behind her. She kept weaving and dodging, heading vaguely uphill for another twenty minutes until she saw a metal sign nailed on a tree announcing 'National Forest Wilderness, Closed to Motor Vehicle and Motorized Equipment.'

She had misjudged the terrain and was too high up. She would have to continue along the wilderness border until she hit the road leading down to her house, then she'd have to sprint down the road.

She looked behind and squinted through the trees for any sign of him. She could hear him, but not see him. He had been lurking around these woods for the past few days and it was possible he would know to break toward her house right now and cut her off. She decided against going home directly.

Needing to lure him from going directly toward her house, she unleashed a blood-curdling scream, stopped and listened carefully, eyes peeled for any flash of movement in the trees below her.

He finally appeared and she turned and ran. She headed uphill toward a deep, dry riverbed lined with boulders, running further uphill through a depression for half a mile. The ravine was not visible until you were right on top of it, as there were dense trees on both sides. It was like a dark wound in the forest.

She knew a little game trail that led safely across the ravine. It was small, obscured by growth and hidden by boulders. If she could make it across and run some distance away before he caught up to that spot, there was a good chance he wouldn't ever find it and she would be able to just walk home as he struggled to find another way across the nearly impassable chasm.

Reaching the trail, she jumped through the boulders, moving quickly and fluidly, as though swimming. Careful to avoid twisting an ankle, she managed to reach the other side before she heard her pursuer.

She re-entered the forest and sprinted full bore uphill for a while to ensure she was well clear of the trail. When she reached a clearing in the trees adjacent to the ravine, she stopped and waited for him to reach a spot parallel to her on the other side.

She couldn't help but marvel at how pretty the little clearing was. The boulders of the ravine's edge formed a border on one side and the trees circled the clearing on the other. It felt secure, like the spot where Mr. Rao's cabin had been built. A single old bristlecone pine tree stood withered in the center of the circular meadow surrounded by soft grass.

Her heart quickened when she heard his crashing footfalls. She climbed up high on a boulder on the edge of the ravine and stood there facing across as he burst through some trees across from her.

Rather than plunging straight down the ravine in pursuit, he seemed to know Alice must have taken a trail and he started scanning the ravine in search of it. He was smarter than she thought.

She knew she should take advantage of the lead she had and dash home immediately, but facing him like this made her angry. She couldn't resist taunting him.

"Dude," Alice shouted, "thanks for the jog. I need a good training partner. Want to hook up again tomorrow?"

He ignored her and continued searching.

At thirty feet, he was close enough for her to see how weird-looking he was. Short and skinny, his head stuck awkwardly out of his 1970s tracksuit, making him look less like a coyote and more like a rodent. His eyes were flicking around, clear and black like a rat's eyes. His presence created a clarity around him that made Alice very nervous. He was probably Indian, at least ethnically. He was quite a bit older than she was, but still in his prime—late 20s maybe—could even still be an athlete, but not a very good one, she thought.

She didn't want this guy lurking around her house anymore. She needed to discover why he was chasing her.

"Hey, Rajendra," she said.

He looked up at her, surprised to hear his name. She took a deep breath, focused herself and shifted into the right state of mind. He looked away, searching the ground again. She couldn't get a lock on him, so she picked up the closest rock and threw it.

"I said hey! Rajendra!"

Her rock missed wide and he kept ignoring her as he searched the ground.

Time for drastic action, she thought. Alice lifted her shirt, unveiling her sweaty sports bra. "Hey, Rajendra," she said in her best attempt at a sexy voice. "I got something for you."

This time, he looked up and stared. "You can't run from me," he said in a calm, high-pitched voice. His English was good and sounded more British than Indian. "I'm going to give you a lesson in how real Indian men treat promiscuous whores. How do you know my name, whore?"

She took another deep breath and connected to his thoughts. Once again, she was met with a strong overtone of violence, fear and anger, but this time she could follow his thoughts clearly. It was easier than she had anticipated because of the orderliness of his mind. Rather than a barrage of voices arguing against each other, his thoughts contained only a single, confident line of narration. She was relieved the narration was in English, rather than Hindi or whatever language he spoke at home.

She must have found a trail through the boulders, his inner voice narrated. I haven't trained enough lately. I should have caught her before the tree line. Now I'll have to find the trail or I will lose her. If I lose her now it is possible she will contact the authorities, which will make it difficult to get to her later.

There was a pause in his thinking. Never mind, he continued. I'll catch her eventually. The fat whore will enjoy her permanent new home.

Alice caught an image of 'her new home' in his head. Rajendra was recalling a large clearing in some forest. Alice saw the image from a vantage point in the air, as though he had been flying when it was engraved on his memory. It was perfectly circular, just like the clearing she was standing in now, although the trees lining his clearing were much older and larger than these. Rather than a dry river bed, his clearing was situated right next to a small stream winding through a meadow on the clearing's edge. In the middle of the clearing there was a huge dead tree, and next to the tree was a little camping tent.

Rajendra did something no-one had ever done before. He forced his attention away from Alice, back to the moment, blinked, shook his head and returned to his search for Alice's game trail. The connection was broken. It was Alice's turn to feel shaken up. She felt violated. How could he have forced her out?

"Look," Alice said loudly, trying to distract him one more time before she left. "The way I see it, you have two options. One..."

BANG!

CHAPTER 6

At first Alice wasn't sure what had happened. She found herself on rocky ground and the hair all over her body was standing on end.

She remembered a terrible blinding light and a sound, loud and furious. Was she dead? What was that smell, like burning wires? Burning...wood. Her eyes were open but she couldn't see. Where was the world?

She rolled onto her side and her eyes were able to refocus enough to see the old bristlecone had become a geyser, pouring water into the sky. It wasn't really water. It was like blue liquid crystal—the same stuff she had seen above Mr. Rao's chili garden.

"Alice," a male voice said.

"Yeah?"

"Alice, try to get up."

"Thomas?"

Alice closed her eyes for a moment and opened them again. A tall boy was there in front of a burning tree. He was wearing a baseball cap on backwards, and jeans and t-shirt.

"Alice," he said, "you were almost struck by lightning but you're alright. You have to get up. He is coming."

"Who is coming?"

"That Indian guy you were speaking with. Alice, get up."

Alice closed her eyes, took a deep breath and opened them again. Of course there was no-one there. She listened and there were no voices either.

The Indian guy...was his name Rajendra? He was gone too. Lightning...had there been lightning? The old bristlecone was singed and burning. Her forehead hurt. She reached up and felt a splinter of wood protruding from her skin. She pulled it out. Something warm oozed down into her right eye. When she wiped it away, her hand came back maroon.

Then she caught a glimpse of Rajendra in the ravine. He had backtracked the fifty yards, found Alice's game trail, and was working his way across, making decent time. He'd be upon her soon.

Alice pushed herself off the ground with one hand, the other hand pressed to her forehead. Her legs felt heavy. She wondered if there were more splinters in her legs, or would a near brush with lightning affect her legs? Wiping the blood out of her eyes again, she looked back and saw Rajendra emerging from the ravine, walking up toward her.

He appeared to be smiling. He had cut her off and she could no longer head home.

She tried to walk uphill away from him, but couldn't make herself move very quickly. Glancing back, she saw he was only thirty meters away, walking steadily.

As she passed the burning tree, she realized she hadn't been hallucinating when she had seen it erupting blue liquid into the air. It was flowing outward over the edge of the ravine like a geyser. It looked similar to the stuff above Mr. Rao's chili garden that he called *prana*. She climbed the nearest boulder overlooking the ravine so that she could stand right in the flow. It felt like a powerful push on her back and it was also refreshing her battered body. She looked down. It was twenty feet to the bottom of the ravine. The boulders on the other edge of the ravine were thirty feet away.

She heard a footstep behind her.

Alice didn't look back. She took a deep breath, seeking inside for energy and confidence. She would really have to dig deep. She took another belly breath and dropped into the state of mind she used to read people.

"What is your plan, young lady?" Rajendra asked from behind her. "We're not thinking of jumping, are we?"

"Yep," she said, and she did.

She led with her hands together above her head in a streamline position, as she had been trained when jumping off the block into the pool. She tried to feel for the *prana* with the skin of her palms. It was definitely there. It felt glassy and cool. She stroked into it with one arm and the other, in a normal freestyle swimming style. She could feel it running along her chin and abdomen, but her legs were dragging and her kick was ineffectual. She sensed the heaviness in her legs would keep her from being able to make it to the other side but the act of concentrating on her legs instantly brought energy and levitation to them. It was as though the substance she was swimming through had an intelligence that heard her. She gave a powerful dolphin kick and her whole body launched upwards, enabling her to just clear the boulders on the other side of the ravine.

She realized she had no idea how to slow down. She responded in the best way she knew after years of mountain bike wipeouts. She curled up in a fetal position to absorb the impact. A pretty decent impact it was too, she thought.

After crashing through the brush and rolling to a stop, she picked herself up and looked back at Rajendra. He was standing on her start-block boulder, his little, pointy forehead creased in confusion or indecision.

It was as though he had seen a lot of weird things in his life and so he just shrugged it off. He ran down toward the game trail again in pursuit.

She started walking up the hill along the ravine, away from

Rajendra and deeper into the Knifespur Wilderness.

After ten paces or so, she was able to force herself back into a slow jog. It made her head hurt more, but her legs were at least working now. She looked back over her shoulder and saw Rajendra through the trees. He must have made it back across the ravine and was a couple hundred yards behind her, running faster than she was.

Come on, she urged, mopping blood out of her eyes.

What were the chances of getting struck by lightning, she wondered. The first huge raindrop landed on her head wound. The rusty smell of rain was suddenly everywhere. She could hear the wind pick up through the forest and knew a torrential deluge was nearly upon her.

She saw a little puff of *prana* up ahead, above some moss-covered tree branches, and she came up with a plan to get him off her back for a while, at least until she could get some help and figure out who had sent him after her, and why.

Drawn ahead by fear, and also by the possibility of another flight through *prana*, Alice pressed upwards and onwards. The rain started coming down so hard, it became difficult to see or breathe. She was moving well again, dodging trees and rocks up the gentle rise of the hill until the ravine shrank to a rough patch of boulders that could be more easily crossed by foot. No game trail was really necessary at this point.

She could no longer hear Rajendra and felt confident enough to pause for a second. She found a hollow rock and leaned down to drink. The rainwater was cold and tasted full of minerals. She saw stars and felt light-headed as she straightened back up, but felt well again as soon as she resumed her jogging.

Alice glanced back and caught another glimpse of Rajendra. Looking ahead, she began to see some light through the trees. She knew she was close to the cliffs above Mr. Rao's cabin.

The storm abated at the same time she emerged from the forest and she could see the cabin below. Beyond that, the rain receded toward the ski mountain, shrouded in streaked darkness.

The cliff seemed ten times higher than it had that morning. It towered above the entire landscape. It felt like the top of the world. She had only been up here once. When she had looked over the edge at the cute little cabin below, she had never imagined some Indian guy might one day live there, nor did she foresee she would ever be considering jumping off the edge.

Alice was soaked, injured, and about to do something stupid.

She heard the snap of a twig and knew Rajendra had arrived. His breathing was heavy from the pursuit.

She turned to look and was shocked to see him carrying some kind of weapon in his hand. That complicated her plan.

"Stop," he said, waving the stubby black gun at her. Alice didn't know what it was but she was pretty sure it wasn't a handgun. Maybe a taser?

"Enough of this," he said.

"I can't go anywhere anyway, Rajendra," she replied, indicating the massive drop with a sweep of her hand.

"Kneel down and put your hands behind your back."

"Naw," she said.

"Excuse me? Are you interested in learning what 50,000 volts feels like?"

"Not really, I guess," Alice said and looked around again. She was not feeling calm anymore. She glanced off the edge and was horrified by the height. It looked a hundred times higher than she ever imagined. Mr. Rao's cabin was like a tiny toy way below.

She scanned the air for *prana*. She could see some here and there, but it was nothing like the area around the lightning strike. She tried to imagine where Mr. Rao's chili garden would be. Was there enough *prana* above it to cushion her fall?

Then she saw a beautiful little black and yellow butterfly flitting in the air beyond the cliff edge. There was a trace of blue in the air curling gently around her wings.

"Kneel down with your hands behind your back."

"Okay okay," she said quickly to Rajendra, put her hands behind her back and maneuvered closer to the slick edge, nearer to where Rajendra was standing. She began to bend her knees and leaned forward slowly, as if she was having trouble kneeling and was planning on squatting instead. Rajendra pocketed his taser. Alice bent her knees deeper and looked out over the cliff. It looked like she was crouching at the end of the world.

She paused. Her hands were behind her, her knees bent, her chin lifted.

To Rajendra, she must have looked strange. Alice expected he would be wondering why she would pause in that position. She imagined him reaching back for his taser.

She burst forward off the edge.

CHAPTER 7

Alice was having trouble remembering what had happened. All she could figure out was she had been lying on a rock for hours. Her eyes functioned a little, but her sense of time and self had disappeared and were only just starting to return. Evening was upon her, she noticed, relieved she even knew what evening was.

She moved something and realized it was her arm. It was amazing, owning an arm. She held it up in front of her face and flexed her fingers.

Then the pain came to her like a ton of bricks. With its arrival, all her memories of the afternoon returned.

Although her entire body felt like one single throbbing bruise, she had the feeling there were no permanent injuries. She kept tentatively testing her arms and legs. As soon as she figured they worked well enough, she rolled over, pushed herself up onto her hands and knees, and stood, supporting herself by placing a hand on the base of the cliff. She looked up and couldn't see the top of the cliff. That was probably a good thing because it meant Rajendra couldn't have seen her either and would have assumed she was splattered all over the ground.

Alice stumbled toward Mr. Rao's house and looked around. It

was perfectly quiet. The storm clouds had gone, the sun was setting and the world seemed peaceful. She turned her head to look behind her and focused on the base of the cliff where she had landed after a hundred-foot plunge.

She lifted her eyes to the top of the cliff, searching for any movement, any sign of Rajendra, confident he would not be there. She could just see the clump of trees next to which they had stood before she leapt off. Just below that was a dripping shelf she had just missed on her way down. She followed the line of her exhilarating plunge down to the bottom where she had been saved by a cushion of that blue liquid air. The prana was still there floating like a heavy mattress in and above Mr. Rao's chili garden.

She knew Rajendra would have had a long walk. There was no other way down and the closest path around the cliff to Mr. Rao's was back across the rough landscape they had run together, down the hill to the lightning tree, down the ravine to Alice's house, bushwhacking back across to Mr. Rao's valley and up his road to his cabin. It would take at least half an hour in a flat-out run or a forty-five-minute fast hike.

Perhaps he had actually shown up in that time frame, seen her sprawled out at the base of the cliff and assumed she was dead. He would have patted himself on the back and gone back to pick up his car, or whatever he used to get around.

Alice found her bike and struck out toward home, vaguely thinking she would change clothes, get something to eat.

As she cycled, some of her clarity returned and she considered her situation. She already suspected Rajendra had some relationship with Babaji because, well, Babaji was an Indian jerk and so was Rajendra—or was that just a coincidence? Then again, Babaji didn't seem to be the type to work with gangsters and she couldn't imagine him exerting some terrible fear over someone like Rajendra.

She remembered Babaji was giving a lecture tonight. What else could she do but go and confront him?

She pedaled home as fast as her shattered body would take her. The garage door creaked open. Neither of her parents' cars were there. She was alone in this, as usual. She put her bike away and went inside. Her first stop was the fridge, where she ate half a block of cheddar cheese and chased it down with a couple of bowls of cereal. It was the best she could do under five minutes.

She didn't even take time to change her clothes, probably torn and bloody. She would deal with that later.

She left through the front door without taking a water bottle. Just as is: no phone, no wallet.

She cycled uphill to the wilderness area trailhead, left her bike, turned left into the woods and climbed back up to the ravine, soon arriving back at the scene of the lightning strike that had nearly killed her a few hours before. It was just as she remembered it. The boulders above the ravine marked one side of the clearing and the tall lodgepole pine trees curved around behind her in a big circle. Fine grass covered the forest floor, rather than the crunchy pine needles and mosses underneath the trees elsewhere. In the middle of the clearing, the lightning tree stood alone. She stood over what was left of it. The burned branches looked windblown, weaving their way toward the sky in a flame shape like the cypress trees in a few of the van Gogh paintings she had studied in school.

She touched her hand to her sore forehead, looked at the wet earth and saw two sets of footprints—hers, and others made by someone with small feet and brand-less running shoes. It confirmed for her that Rajendra wasn't just a hallucination. She walked over to where she had thought she had seen Thomas. There were no footprints, confirming that she had hallucinated him.

Above the tree she could see the heavy flow of crystalline air welling up like a geyser of blue liquid flame. The darkness of night made it brighter. The flowing stuff reminded her again of the van Gogh painting, Starry Night, with its curling shapes circling the stars in his night sky.

Before she could second-guess herself, she stepped up onto the boulder on the edge of the ravine and dove off into the night air. This time, the plan was to avoid landing at all. She had the vaguest feeling this was going to be possible, now that she had some experience.

She raised her arms above her head and lifted her chest, trying to feel the prana around her. She dolphin-kicked and picked up some speed. She was over the ravine and thirty feet up in the air.

She was concentrating too hard to feel any excitement about flying yet. She knew she had to get about ten feet higher to clear the treetops ahead. With a few stronger kicks and an experimental stroke with both arms together, like swimming butterfly in the pool, she easily cleared the trees. She was moving quite fast, much faster than she could swim in water.

She allowed herself to look around to get her bearings and saw she was well beyond the prana emitted from the lightning tree. Afraid she would plummet to the ground, she searched for additional pockets of the stuff and saw none. With the increase in speed, however, she could feel a light brushing of the substance everywhere. She felt like she was in constant contact with the liquid air.

Turning slightly so that she faced downhill, she saw her house about a mile down the ravine. At this speed she would be there in about a minute.

She sped up even more with a few stronger kicks.

Then it hit her. She was really flying through the sky.

"OH... MY.... GOD!!!" she screamed. She heard her shouts of joy echoing back to her. She hoped Rajendra heard her too, wherever he was.

It was like...swimming, but somehow there was no drag at all. She had learned most of the physics of swimming from her coach's screamed instructions. Every day for years she had been focusing on increasing buoyancy, decreasing drag, and increasing purchase on the water with her arms and feet.

Up here it was so different. The prana was thick, like water, but exerted no drag on her body. It was like intelligent water. It was so easy to feel.

The night was no longer silent. The wind was blowing loudly in her ears. Below her, the trees were moving steadily by. It was like watching trees go by on the side of a highway. Judging from the speed she was passing above the treetops, she was doing at least fifty miles an hour.

It occurred to her that when she reached her house, she would need to figure out how to stop. She wondered if she spread-eagled her arms and legs, kind of like the position a sky-diver takes, would it slow her down. She tried, but rather than slowing down, she lost contact with the feel of the prana and plummeted downwards toward the dark forest.

With only fifteen feet left before impact with the canopy of pine, she straightened her body into a purposeful dive. She felt the liquid air and just before she plunged into the trees, she lifted her chest and chin, skimmed across the treetops and upward again.

Okay, spread-eagle not a good idea, she thought. She had to keep swimming gracefully to maintain contact with the prana.

What would be a graceful way to slow down? She thought about airplanes. They always lift their noses before landing, providing a last minute bit of lift. She wished she knew more about how airplanes work. She vaguely remembered her friend, Brian the librarian, was a hang-glider enthusiast. She made a mental note to interrogate him about landing when she saw him next.

She was approaching her house. It looked small and strange from above. It was two hundred yards ahead and about the same distance below her. Alice imagined herself as a graceful super-jumbo jet and coasted, slowing herself while remaining in control. It was very difficult to stay in touch with the prana while decelerating. It felt like any second she would plunge toward the ground. She looked ahead and thought she might try to land on the road. Then she remembered all her aches and pains from the afternoon and realized the gravel would turn her into road pizza if she couldn't figure out how to slow down first.

Alice aborted the landing attempt and pushed off toward the sky. Forget it. Flying is more fun than landing anyway, she thought.

Swimming toward the stars, Alice was struck with a sudden fear that this was a dream. How would she know the difference? She looked down at the straight line of their dirt road, passing steadily below her, nearly hidden by tall trees spreading for miles to both sides, and thought the whole picture looked very different from her usual dreamscape. It was the level of visual detail that convinced her that this was real, not a dream. She could really feel the night landscape moving below her. She could smell it too. She could also feel the movement of her clothing against her skin. She definitely felt the pain of each of her bruises and cuts, the sensation of thirst, the temperature on her skin, the sound of the wind in her ears, the tears steadily running down her face from the wind in her eyes.

She was now acutely aware she really had to pee. This is not a dream, she concluded: gotta go the bathroom. Could she just wee in the air? How would she get her pants down without falling from the sky? No way, she told herself. She wished it was just as easy as peeing in the pool. Most elite swimmers just peed in the pool because the training sessions were so long, saving themselves the effort of climbing out. It was gross to see the long, yellow streams of vitamin-soaked urine, but they dissipated soon enough.

The pool...it occurred to her she might be able to land safely in the small outdoor pool at the aquatic center. Then she could really just pee in the water. She could already feel the relief to come as she thought about it. The pool would be covered already, but the cover might even further cushion her landing.

As she accelerated through the air and swam toward the

aquatic center, she remembered that people commit suicide by jumping off bridges, so she needed to figure out how to slow down to, at most, the speed of a platform diver. She remembered a physics problem in her homework in which she'd had to figure out how fast Olympic high platform divers hit the water. She didn't remember the math but faintly recalled the answer, that someone diving off the ten meter platform hits the water at thirty or forty miles an hour. Judging her current speed and how much control she was managing, Alice felt like she could slow down to well below forty before she hit the water, no problem. Probably could manage to get down to twenty-five, she thought. She just had to make sure she landed in such a way that she would avoid broken bones (or an exploded bladder). At least try not to belly flop, she commanded herself.

It was a fifteen-minute cycle from her house and she flew it in five. She slowed down her stroke rate as much as possible and descended toward the outdoor pool. Oddly, the lights were on in the indoor complex, shining out into the night. She thought that was very strange, as it must be at least eight o'clock, way past closing time.

She put it out of her mind and tried to plan her splashdown. Head first or feet first? Straight down or angled? She thought about the cover. It would not be fun to get all wrapped up in it and drown after all she has been through today. Best to enter feet first, at an angle, so her fall could push the whole cover over to the deep end. Then she would have a chance at crawling and swimming her way free of the cover, and pee like a racehorse.

She aimed at the very center of the pool. At the last minute she did a little lift-up, rolling her body so her feet aimed toward the pool cover. She tucked her arms into her sides, her chin into her chest and tightened her body.

It went fine, except rather than push the cover neatly along the surface of the pool, she pushed a hole right through it and shot into the deep end like an arrow. The water hurt. She felt the pressure on her ears from the depth of water. Then her feet hit the pool-bottom and her legs folded with the impact. She paused, ensuring she hadn't broken anything, and pushed off and upward toward the surface, which was completely black. She couldn't see the hole she had created so she had to settle for pushing the cover to create a little cavity of air so she could take a few big breaths. She held the cover up and breathed, treading water while pulling off her shoes with the other hand. Then she went back underwater and swam through the blackness toward where she imagined the side of the pool was. She had to swim with one hand in front of her in case she hit the wall. Just when she was about to give up and re-surface for air, she finally touched the painted surface of the wall, pushed aside the edge of the cover, and took some grateful breaths. She tossed her shoes over the edge and before leaving the pool, had a long, long pee.

Finally vaulting herself out of the pool, she started to wonder about the lights. Who would be using the indoor Olympic pool this time of night? She peeled off her socks, stuffed them in her shoes and walked barefoot toward the back entrance.

It was unlocked and Alice pushed right in to the sound of someone's rhythmic stroke in the water. As soon as she glanced at the swimmer, she knew it was Madison. Maddie has particularly relaxed hands, very flexible shoulders and a late breath.

Alice slowly padded toward the edge of the pool but Madison saw her on her next breath and let out a scream, fracturing the nearly silent air, and cut off as her mouth went back in the water.

At the same moment, a new scream came from behind Alice. She spun around and saw a baby in a high chair pointing at her in abject terror. Alice hadn't seen the baby before because she had been partially hidden behind the bleachers.

Madison spluttered to the surface, ripping off her goggles.

(Cough) "What the hell are you..." (cough)

Alice dropped her shoes and socks and held her hands out in a supplicating gesture. "Sorry, Madison! I saw the lights on and came in to see who was here."

There weren't any lane ropes for Madison to bob under and she paddled over to the side of the pool near Alice and vaulted herself out, pulling off her cap and shaking her hair loose as she jogged over to placate the baby.

"You scared the shit out of us!" Madison said, turning around. The baby was still screaming. "Why are you dripping?"

"I had a swim outside," Alice replied.

"No you didn't. The pool is covered at night."

"Yes I did. I went under the cover."

"There is a fence around the property. This is the only way in or out. You don't have a key. Seriously, Alice, what are you doing here?"

"Madison, what the hell are you doing here? The pool closes at seven. Who's the kid?"

Madison paused for a second, handing Billie a piece of meat she had overlooked.

Billie stopped crying.

"Alice, I come here a lot to get in some extra laps. They gave me keys this year."

"What? Swimming twice a day isn't enough for you?"

"If I don't put in extra sessions, I can't improve my times. The meet next weekend is my last chance to qualify for the zones."

She paused, looked up at Alice and said, as if in appeal, "I'm only cruising. It's just a little extra time in the water." After another pause, which Alice didn't fill, Madison finished, "It's relaxing. You wouldn't understand. You're always relaxed."

"What?" Alice was genuinely surprised. "Me? Relaxed? You think?"

Madison wiped the baby's face with a cloth and took her out of her high chair. "Billie's my baby sister. She's almost two."

"Pleased to meet you, Billie." Alice looked at her for the first time. She was covered in tears and was adorable. Rather than Madison's huge black eyebrows, she had cute little blonde ones, and blonde hair. While Madison had sharp, hawk-like features,

Billie was round and soft everywhere.

"You're not worried someone would walk in and take her?"

"Come on, Alice," she said. "I can see her the whole time and she likes the sound of the water. Besides, you're the only one who has ever come in here since I've been doing this."

"What about your mom and dad?"

Madison rolled her eyes. "No time. Billie's in day care all day. I drive over and pick her up from day care right after our afternoon training and I bring her back here. She eats a snack in her chair while I swim for half an hour."

"Wow," Alice was having trouble getting her head around the idea Madison had such a huge responsibility that she hid from everyone. "I had no idea."

"So what are you doing here?" Madison asked, chasing Billie as she ran toward the edge of the water. Madison just caught her before she ran right in.

Alice realized she would have to come up with something. "Okay, Madison, I, um, I'm here at the aquatic center because I had to pee. I was on my way to the yoga place where Babaji is giving his lecture. I'm hoping to find Dad there."

"The rest of the world doesn't have bathrooms so you jumped a six foot fence to pee in the outdoor pool."

"Well, kind of."

"You're gross—and weird."

"Probably." Alice looked down at her dripping clothes, which were not much cleaner for the dip in the pool. The blood hadn't completely washed out of her top and she smelled more like dirt than chlorinated water. Her cuts and bruises felt a lot better, though.

"Madison, do you have an extra change of clothes with you?"

Madison had followed Alice's gaze down to her shirt. "Is that blood? What happened?"

"I got struck by lightning. Actually I got hit by a splinter from a tree that got struck by lightning."

"Bullshit. Did you come off your bike?"

"Come on, Madison. Yes or no to the clothes?"

"Sure. But not underwear."

"That's great. Thanks so much."

"No problem. You ruined my sneaky swim tonight anyway."

Alice thought Madison's short hair was lovely, even though it was flat and bodiless after being pressed under a cap.

Madison walked over to her bag, reached in and found a set of neatly folded clothes for Alice. Madison was the only girl Alice knew who was remotely close to Alice's height, though Alice was heavier by at least forty pounds.

"Thanks," Alice said. "I think I'll go shower off first."

"Good idea." She reached into her bag again and pulled out a towel, handing it to Alice. "I think you do smell like barbecue. Were you at a barbecue?"

"Lightning," Alice said, walking away.

Alice went in and showered gingerly, feeling each cut in her torn body, pressing gently on a few nasty-looking bruises.

She started to wonder if the flying had been real. Otherwise how had she gotten all the way from Mr. Rao's house to the aquatic center?

She toweled off and put on Madison's t-shirt and shorts. They were jeans shorts, torn at the side of the legs, which just allowed her legs to force through. She couldn't get the button done up. Not even close. When she pulled on the t-shirt, she felt like one of those freak body-builder men at the gym. The t-shirt was much, much too tight and showed every muscle. It also showed each bump in her nipples. Her own sports bra was still wet, and although she thought she could get away with not wearing it, she felt too exposed. She pulled off Madison's t-shirt, wrung out her bra again and put it on damp, pulling the tight t-shirt over. She chucked her wet clothes into the garbage, looked in a mirror and cringed. She looked hideous.

"You look okay," Madison said.

"I look like a whale."

"You do not look like a whale."

"I look like a whale that just ate another whale."

"Oh, come on. Get over yourself. Let's go," Madison said, already chasing Billie out of the locker room into the pool area. "Alice," she said, turning her head back, "it may be hard to fit your bike in my trunk with all of Billie's stuff..."

Alice was having difficulty moving normally in Madison's tight shorts and t-shirt. She felt embarrassed, but at the same time, excited to have been shown so much warmth by Madison. She still hadn't managed to put on her wet socks or shoes and she padded along the tiles barefoot.

As she hurried to catch up, she replied, "I don't have my bike."

"What? Did you drive? You don't have a car, do you?"

"Didn't drive either."

Madison stopped and turned around. "Then how did——"

"Madison, can we just go?" Alice caught up to her and passed her, walking toward the door.

"Actually, Alice, I'm not going anywhere until you level with me. How did you get hurt? Was it your dad? Why are you here? How did you get here?"

Alice stopped. "Okay, Madison. Are you ready? If you call me crazy, I'm really out of here."

"I don't care if you leave. It's my car you want, right?"

"Oh, yeah."

"Spill it then,"

Alice walked back over to the pool area and sat down on the tiled floor. She started to wring out her socks and looked at her running shoes, which were also wet. Then she looked up at Madison, with a kind of desperation.

"I can fly."

Madison smiled. "Oh, so that's it. You got struck by lightning and can fly now. I should have guessed. That explains everything."

Alice smiled too, but she felt she had lost an opportunity. She tried again, even more desperately. "No, I'm serious, Madison.

I know it sounds strange, but I can show you. Do you want to see?"

"Sure, yeah, I want to see. Actually, I'll go stick my finger in the socket and then let's both fly around for a while."

Alice finished putting her wet shoes and socks on and stood up again. Her smile and openness was gone and she had become her usual self again.

"Forget it. Okay, my mom and I were eating barbecue and she dropped me off here because we saw your car parked outside and I snuck by you when you were swimming and jumped in the water outside to clean the barbecue sauce off my clothes. Now can we go?"

Madison was silent for a second and pointed at the cut on Alice's forehead. "So what happened to your head?"

Alice turned and walked outside. Madison followed her, carrying Billie and her bag and Billie's high chair. Alice headed for Madison's car, a crappy old Subaru wagon. She had never been in Madison's car. She had only been in cars with her mom or her dad. The whole experience of a couple of friends jumping in a car was completely foreign to her.

"You want to go to Red Tent Yoga?" Madison asked when she caught up. "That's where your dad is."

"Wait," Alice said, turning around, "how do you know my dad is there?"

"I dropped Kirsty off at the yoga place. It's right by Billie's day care."

"Oh. How is Kirsty?" Alice asked.

This time it was Madison's turn to ignore a question. They both got in the car. Billie fell asleep as soon as she was buckled in to her child seat.

Madison swung out of the parking lot and started driving toward the yoga studio.

"She said she talked to some Australian swami," Madison finally said. "Kirsty said he is really nice and wise and tried to talk her out of going to India. It had the reverse effect. She actually wants to go now. It seems she's not overly concerned about Babaji making sexual advances anymore."

"What do you think about that, about her going to India?" Alice knew this question was risky, as it was an inquiry into their friendship. She held her breath.

"Hate it," Madison said. Alice exhaled in relief. "She and I were going to take Billie and go on a road trip this summer. My parents agreed and everything."

"A road trip? To where?"

"I've always wanted to go to Yellowstone and Glacier. You been up there?"

"My dad doesn't have time to take us on trips."

"Yeah, my parents don't either. But they agreed to me going, as long as I planned to take Billie with us. It would give them a couple weeks to work without any kids around."

"Wow. Take Billie with you? That sounds...different." Alice couldn't imagine a sixteen-year-old being trusted with a two-year-old on a road trip to Wyoming.

Madison looked at Alice and back at the road.

Alice got the message. Don't criticize what you don't understand. "But it's hard enough for you to improve your times now," Alice said, ploughing ahead anyway. "Imagine what would happen if you took a month or two out of the pool."

Silence.

Alice looked over at Madison, whose face had turned white. Alice had definitely crossed a line and she knew it. "I just mean...you're better than that," Alice stammered. "You're really special, with your swimming. Kirsty is...different."

Madison didn't say anything.

Alice looked out the window toward the night sky, wondering what she could say to repair the damage. She tried to see any reassuring swirls of prana, but she could see only stars. She sank back into her seat, having insulted both Madison and Kirsty in the span of thirty seconds.

It didn't take more than a few minutes to drive to the yoga

place. The parking lot was completely full and cars spilled out onto the street, parking illegally. It didn't look anything like a tent and the old brick building wasn't red either. It was painted a creamy color.

"I'll drop you off, okay? I'm not that interested in Babaji and it's a school night."

"Sure. Thanks a lot, Madison."

Madison pulled up to the front door of the studio and applied the handbrake, leaving the engine running. "So," she said, "that wasn't barbecue sauce on your shirt, was it."

Alice looked at Madison. She seemed to have shaken off Alice's insult. "No. I'll tell you about it tomorrow. You got time for a coffee after swimming in the morning?"

"Um, I'm not sure. I'll try."

"Thanks for the lift, Madison, and for the clothes."

Alice watched Madison drive away, half tempted to chase after her and offer a tearful apology for being rude but instead, she turned away toward the door of the yoga studio.

CHAPTER 8

The night was cooling and the fall in temperature seemed to make the stars brighter. She looked up and almost decided to give up and walk home.

She caught the smell of incense from the studio and it called up some buried memories. She shoved them back into her subconscious mind, took a deep breath and opened the door to the studio.

She was in a small mud room full of shoes and jackets. There was also a wall of shelves containing yoga mats and a couple of benches. One of which was supporting the weight of the slouched form of...

"Mom."

Alice's mom spun her head around and lowered her phone, onto which she had been punching feverishly with her thin, bony fingers. She looked terrible. Her eyes were red from a very recent cry and she was still wearing her yoga clothes, with only a scarf wrapped loosely around her neck, not unlike Bhakti's stooges in the library.

"No...way...are you here. Alice; there is no way you are here. You can't be here. You are turning around right now and going home."

"Hi, Mom. Where have you been all day?"

"Sweetheart," she said in an exasperated tone, "I have been at my yoga center all day, like usual. I had four classes to teach back-to-back. I forgot my phone today and got home from yoga to find ten missed calls from you and a text message from your dad that he was here."

There was a loud sound of nervous laughter coming from the audience inside. Then Babaji's voice rang out as loud as if he were in the mud room with them.

"Darling." Mom squared her shoulders to Alice, "we are *not* having this conversation here. Please go home and wait for me."

"Mom, that's the problem. You never open up with me. You never say anything about the past. Now look what is happening."

Alice's mom sighed and looked to be in the early stages of a panic attack. "I'm sorry. But that's the way it is with Babaji. Everywhere he goes, he manages to spread confusion and misunderstanding."

"But, Mom, it's not like you can dictate terms to me. After all those years of silence I have every right to try to understand what is going on between Dad and Babaji."

"I cannot allow you to be dragged into this. You are nearly an adult, but not yet. When you are, *then* you can make your own mind up about this kind of thing but, for the time being, you are still just a sixteen-year-old. So I'm sorry but I forbid you from going anywhere near Babaji. No matter what you think your father has gotten himself mixed up with."

As she was looking at her mom, Alice realized she had left her mouth open. She shut it with a click of her teeth.

Mom cocked her head and looked carefully at Alice. "Is that clear?"

It had been a long time since her mom had spoken to her like this and she was a little shocked. "But, Mom, listen."

"No." There was a shakiness in her voice that told Alice she was about to cry again. "*You* listen..." Then she took a deep breath and calmed herself with a great effort. "Alice, honey, you have no idea. This man and his cult ruined our lives. I am so embarrassed to have been involved. Not just embarrassed. There is more. I...when you told me the other day that you went to see Babaji, I nearly threw up. I thought that was the end of it, but now this." She could not continue for a second.

Alice's heart was beating furiously.

"Now, you listen to me," she continued, tears rolling down her face. "I...will...not allow you to go through those doors, and that's final."

Alice kicked off her shoes and walked past her stunned, crying mother, through the door into the studio. A person dressed in yellow clothes was sitting in a chair right inside the door, like a guard. He immediately held up his arm to block Alice's entry, which wouldn't have gone very well for him, given Alice's size, but he seemed to recognize her and lowered his arm again. He smiled and indicated she could sit in one of the back rows.

Alice looked around and drew incense-tinged air into her lungs. The room was a medium-sized rectangular room that would hold about thirty yoga mats, she thought: a bit bigger than her mom's studio. The ceilings were just plain white tiles, like at Dad's office. None of the fluorescent ceiling lights were on. They had created some mood lighting by using up-lights around the edge of the room. Some were dressed in yoga Lycra but most people in the front rows were non-Indians dressed in something resembling Indian clothing, but not really like Mr. Rao's. His was more colorful, older, and fit him well. Like Bhakti's stooges at the library, these people wore long Indian shirts, cream or white, over loose pants of the same color. They wore them awkwardly, the wrong body parts highlighted, like fat bellies and elbows. Alice remembered, from Babaji's kitchen the other day, that real Indian women looked great in their *saris*, even if they were enormously fat. These fake Indians looked like they were wearing a uniform, rather than dressy clothing. Alice thought they looked silly, but she remembered she probably looked sillier, dressed in a t-shirt that was too small and a damp sports bra and jeans shorts that she couldn't even button closed.

There were some little kids present in the front rows. They were also dressed up like little Indians. Alice knew it was like a game to them. She knew because she had once been just like them.

There were a few musicians sitting up front, a little bit apart from the audience. They were readying their instruments—a set of tabla drums and a small box that looked like an accordion, except it was played on the ground like a piano.

Babaji was the focus of the room and Alice couldn't really delay it anymore; she had to look at him. He was sitting alone on a stage, propped up straight on a large sofa facing the audience. His legs were crossed beneath his orange robes.

Next to the sofa on stage, there was a very large altar, also facing the audience. The altar was a large coffee table, behind which they had built a kind of decorative wood backing. It had three large framed photos of other Indian gurus. Alice guessed they were in Babaji's lineage. An oil lamp burned gently away in front of each photo. There was an orange microphone in front of him. Alice wondered why it was orange. Then she saw the huge video camera aimed at Babaji and she realized the orange mic would probably blend in with Babaji's robes in the video they were making of the lecture. Or was it a webcast?

Alice sat down in a chair.

Babaji seemed to have paused his lecture and had closed his eyes for a very long time. The room was silent in anticipation. She looked around and saw that most of the people dressed in yellow also had their eyes closed. After a while, Babaji opened his eyes, looked around and down toward the musicians, who were poised ready to follow any order from Babaji.

He nodded at them and ordered, *"Bhajo re manva."*

They instantly started playing a song that sounded like a cross between Christian and Indian folk music. The lyrics were mostly in Hindi. Many people in the audience knew the song by heart. Many others sat with their eyes closed. Babaji himself appeared to be incredibly moved by the song. She noticed he wiped his eyes several times with a corner of his robes.

When the song finished, the room quieted again in anticipation.

After allowing silence to spread, Babaji closed his eyes and sat up tall in his seat on the sofa. His hands were clasped in front of him in a gesture of prayer.

Alice saw Dad. He had his eyes closed as well. He was sitting in a row of nicer chairs set up in the front, near the side of the stage. He was sitting next to a couple of other people in suits and ties, and also his stupid colleague, John, who was dressed in his usual smart casual getup. "*Ommmmm*," sang Babaji into the microphone. His voice was strong and some people in the audience joined him. He sang a long mantra she did not know, which ended with: "*Om...shanti...shanti...shantihi.*"

After another long pause, Babaji opened his eyes and looked around the room. The only sounds were from the occasional car passing by on the road outside.

"We are honored this evening to have the vice-consul of the Croatian consulate here with us." Babaji's voice was slow and reverent. "Welcome, your excellency, Mr. Barislava."

Alice looked over and realized Babaji was referring to a man in a suit who was sitting on the other side of Dad. The man held his hands up in prayer.

"Next to his excellency is Dr. Nathan Brickstone, the world famous scientist, a faithful friend of ours and a disciple for many, many years."

Alice watched Dad put his hand on his heart, as though he was indicating to the crowd that Babaji's words meant a lot to him.

Chills ran up and down Alice's spine. She knew Dad was probably there because he needed to find a way to get out of the predicament he was in, but in that moment he looked like he was playing the part of VIP disciple too well, with too much sincerity. How was Dad a faithful friend to Babaji, she wondered. Was he still a disciple? It was starting to look like it. Alice looked around at the response from the crowd. Nobody seemed to think there was much to it. Just a couple of VIP's: who cares? They were there to see Babaji.

She noticed a couple people craning their necks to stare. One of them was…Kirsty. She was up front, cross-legged, and dressed in a cream yellow t-shirt and jeans. Her choice of a cream shirt to match the cream uniforms worn by the others seemed to indicate she felt part of the group, but her jeans indicated she was reluctant to go the whole way. She was sitting next to her mom who was decked out in the full fake Indian getup.

Alice started getting really nervous. Seeing Kirsty's reaction to Dad's status at this circus brought it home to her. This sucks, Alice thought. Maybe I should have listened to Mom.

"They told me," Babaji continued, "the topic given for my lecture is 'yoga, off the mat.' I do not know who put it on the mat but we shall try to take it off the mat. Okay?"

Everyone laughed but Alice couldn't figure out what was funny. It was a lame joke.

"So, I will first introduce you to the word yoga, what is the yoga, and we shall see what comes next." Babaji closed his eyes dramatically and allowed another long pause.

"There was once nothing in the whole universe." He was speaking very slowly. "Only empty space, nothing. This is like the universal mother. Within this nothingness, within the mother, was the sound *Om*. Like we were chanting together and like the beautiful musicians were singing before. *Ommmmmm,*" Babaji sang again.

"This sound was like the embryo, the consciousness. Yoga is that which unifies the mother and the embryo. Within this sound was Lord Shiva. Shiva means consciousness; Shiva means bliss; Shiva means enlightenment. Shiva does not only mean destruction, like you say in English. Lord Shiva said, '*Ekoham*

94

bahusyami.' I am one and I shall multiply myself. He manifested the whole creation through his *yog maya*. Yoga here means that power that balances all of creation."

Who cares anyway, Alice wondered. Why would some fat Indian guy know anything about the origins of the universe? She looked around the room and saw the audience was looking bored. The mysterious power that held them a moment ago seemed to have dissipated somewhat. Dad closed his eyes and for the first time he looked like he wished he was somewhere else.

She saw Mom come in the door. She looked at Dad, then at Alice. She walked over and sat down in the chair next to her. The tears were gone and Mom had an absolutely livid look on her face.

Dad noticed her arrival and their eyes met. Mom raised her eyebrows at him and she lifted her palms as if to ask: What in God's name are you doing?"

Dad just held up his finger and he took out his phone. After a while he pressed send and Alice's mom's phone lit up and vibrated.

Alice looked over her Mom's shoulder and saw the message from Dad read: I'm sorry I didn't tell you I was coming here. It's not what it looks like.

Mom replied quickly.

Alice followed their texting conversation with curiosity.

It looks like you are sitting listening to the man who ruined our lives, Mom wrote.

Yes, Dad responded, but I didn't come here by choice. I'll explain later. Why are you here?

To bring you home. Please just stand up and walk out with me.

I can't leave yet. I still have to get Babaji to agree to something. We have a meeting after the lecture. Why on earth did you bring our daughter here?

Mom looked over, saw Alice watching and quickly turned her phone off and put it back in her pocket.

Alice noticed quite a few of the senior disciples she had seen in Bhakti's house before were absent tonight. They must all be in some room here somewhere, she thought.

Alice looked back at Babaji and resigned herself to sitting through the lecture, which went through many seemingly random twists and turns and finally descended into a series of Indian folk stories about a barber who cured a king of leprosy. Then Babaji said something that drew her attention.

"When a person has gone, only then do you realize what you have lost. Gone is gone."

He paused and looked around the room. Alice felt his gaze linger on her for a moment and her heart raced. What does he mean, she asked herself.

"In these modern times, it is very hard to keep friendships. We don't care. We think only about what we can get or about appearing good in others' eyes. Not about what we can give.

"In these modern times the relations between parents and children are also unhealthy. Also in India.

"The parents should always remember, your children don't need your toys. They don't need your money. They need your love.

"The children should always respect and love your parents. How many times did your mother and your father wake up and come to you when you were crying and sick? Love them. Do not forget them when they get old.

"It is like this also with the spiritual master. We come here to give. Even if there is only one person We will still come. This is because We are first a disciple. It is only others who may say We are master. The master never says he is master, he is always disciple. The disciple is always searching for ways to serve.

"Similarly, you should never think your candle—your love—is so bright it will never blow out. Do not think your love for the spiritual master is easy. Your love for your friends, for your parents, your children. You must protect your flame with your life. Any wind, any storm can blow out that flame if you are careless. We have a storm to go through and we must go through it together.

"What is that storm? What kind of storm can blow out the flame? That storm is *kusanga*: bad company. Now there is *kusanga* and *satasanga*..."

Alice saw Kirsty's mom turn to stare at her daughter, get her attention and point at Babaji, as if to emphasize his words. Kirsty looked down at her hands and back up at Babaji.

"...*satsang* is what we are doing. *Satsang* is when you are together with friends, discussing the inspiring things: truth, God, love, humanitarian work. *Kusanga* is different. It is when you are together with those people who talk about other things in this material world. Knowingly or unknowingly, they lead you away from *satsang,* from your truth. Your hard work is destroyed: gone in a second. Gone is gone.

"There may be here a few of you who are interested to do yoga, to go work in humanitarian projects around the world, to do something good, to give. Many young people have these thoughts. They see the world with more purity. But that love can be destroyed by *kusanga*. In one second, one advertisement on TV, one film, or one word from a classmate will destroy their good intentions. 'Why do you want to go help others in India?' they may ask. 'It is dirty and besides there are so many parties we can go to.' Then your love is gone and you are back in darkness.

"The negative people are negative because they have taken on the qualities of the people around them. The positive, spiritual people are rare. They have taken on spiritual qualities from others and have cultivated their own spiritual flame. Lucky are they who are born to spiritual parents. Blessed are they who meet their spiritual master in this lifetime. Fortunate are those who seek out the company of those spiritual disciples. It takes hard work. Every day, protecting the candle flame. Gone is gone. This is what I have to tell you. Gone is gone."

Babaji finally finished his lecture by reciting another long mantra. Then he sang *Om* into the microphone longer than Alice thought possible.

He had a good set of lungs; maybe could be a decent swimmer, she thought. She watched the audience collectively straighten up, close their eyes too, and sing with Babaji. They had plenty of time to catch up as his *Om* was so long.

As she watched Kirsty sit with her eyes closed, she again recognized a pang in her own heart. Even though she'd had a pretty wild day in which she discovered she had a Rajput recluse living in the forest near her house, had been chased through the night by a kidnapper and threatened with a taser, had jumped off a cliff and learned to fly, yet she still desperately wanted to be part of Madison and Kirsty's friendship.

Then again, maybe I really am kind of bad company for girls like Madison and Kirsty, Alice thought. I am, after all, pretty screwed up, at least according to Mom. I never had friends growing up. What does that make me: mental?

"*Prempuri.*"

Alice realized Babaji was calling her dad up to the stage.

"Come."

Dad jumped up and went to Babaji, who slowly stood up and held out his hand. Alice noticed Babaji had orange socks on. Dad supported Babaji's arm as he descended from the stage.

Babaji turned around and faced the altar. Dad let go of him and put his hands together in prayer, as did Babaji, and they both looked to be praying to the pictures on the altar.

When they finished their prayers, Dad and Babaji faced the audience again. Babaji beckoned to Mr. Bratislava and John, Dad's colleague. People in the audience stood up and circled Babaji as if he was God. Among them were Kirsty and her mom. Babaji stood with Dad and Bratislava, speaking quietly to them, and they formed a barrier between him and the audience.

He looked to be saying a long goodbye to Bratislava. Babaji pointed frequently toward Dad as though Dad was some kind of wise sage.

Is Dad really back into this, Alice wondered? He looks like it. Is that really bad? Some of the stuff Babaji says makes sense. Some of the people here look smart and Kirsty is here. Maybe I could go together with Dad in the back? Maybe I could ask Babaji about *siddhis* and about Thomas? Surely he could clarify a few things Mr. Rao said.

Alice's heart was beating fast. Her brain was flitting from thought to thought as though she had just had four double lattes. Maybe Mom is right; I am insane. What would Kirsty think of someone who has no friends and thinks she can fly? If she knew, she would totally call an ambulance and I would be sent straight to the Hardrock mental hospital, wherever that is.

Mom sat back down and seemed to be too stunned to do anything. Babaji shook hands with Mr. Bratislava and was standing with Dad.

Alice started to walk over.

The guru turned away from Bratislava toward the group of disciples who were waiting for him. He walked two steps over to Kirsty and said, loud enough for Alice to hear clearly, *"Kusang. Bad company. You should be very careful."*

As he spoke, he was looking directly at Alice.

Kirsty looked at her.

Alice was ready to say hi, but Kirsty quickly turned away without acknowledging her. She looked at Dad, who was also looking away.

Babaji turned and said something to Kirsty's mom, but Alice couldn't hear because of a roaring sound in her ears.

Why isn't Dad coming to my rescue, Alice worried. Or even acknowledging I'm here? Surely he has seen me? He must also know I'm *kusang.*

She was going to faint. She couldn't speak or move.

Babaji took Dad's arm and they walked together toward a back door behind the stage, leaving Alice standing alone.

She managed to turn her back on the door. She stood there trying to breathe. The audience members were milling around laughing and talking to each other. Some were looking at her with apparent disgust. Alice was in shock. A few approached the altar to say a prayer. She watched as a couple dressed in fake

Indian clothes pushed two little kids in front of the altar. They were maybe five and seven years old. The five-year-old had obviously been watching what everyone else had done and was excited to play the game too. Alice knew that feeling exactly. Memories of the ashram in India flooded back. She used to be the little star of the show, she remembered: she and Thomas.

Alice looked at her mom sitting in that same chair, alone, in obvious pain. For once, Alice felt a kinship with Mom. Everything was hopeless. She had ceased to worry about why Dad was here and what his dealings with Babaji were. None of that was important anymore.

Mom saw Alice, got up slowly and walked over. "Alice, you are hardly wearing any clothes. Where did you get those shorts and t-shirt? What happened to your head?"

Alice didn't respond. She didn't really understand the question. All she could do was look at her mom.

Her mom took her hand. "Let's go home, okay?"

"Okay," Alice said, finding a weak voice. She managed to move her legs and begin to walk.

CHAPTER 9

Alice woke up to her alarm after a restless night of sleep. She knew she had slept for eight hours, which was more than usual for a school night, but she felt like total crap. She was shaking. It was Monday and she had no interest in getting back to school or normality, whatever that was. Her body was tired and her head hurt. She touched her forehead and winced. It felt inflamed. Her lower back and leg muscles all hurt from the running. The entire back side of her body felt bruised. Her abs hurt from the effort of flying. She was freezing. She wondered if she had a fever.

The flying.

She bounced out of bed. Had the flying been a dream?

She fell back in bed, her head spinning.

As she tried to recover, she remembered last night: Babaji's lecture. She remembered the pain of being called *kusang*—bad company—by Babaji, and the passive agreement by Dad. Her memory reached no further than that moment. She didn't know how she'd got home or how she'd got into her bed. All she could remember was the feeling of being completely in darkness. Crushed. She fell back and could taste the darkness again.

Surely the flying had been real, she questioned. What was

real?

She looked at her alarm clock, saw that it read 5:00 a.m. and forced herself up again. She was going to be late for swimming.

She walked to the window, still shivering, hoping to see the air shimmering with flowing crystalline structures. Nothing.

She looked at the treetops beyond which the pink sunlight of the morning had started to color the dark sky. Nothing.

Everything looked normal. But what is normal now, she wondered. Her body hurt.

She turned away from the window and changed into her Speedos, stepped delicately into some sweats, and threw together her swim bag and a few things for school. She retrieved her phone from where she had tossed it on the floor. It was almost out of battery and there was a text message from some unknown number, which was weird. She only ever got texts from her parents. She tried to read it but she was having trouble focusing her eyes. She shoved the phone in her pocket.

On her way out, she thought of brushing her teeth. She went to the bathroom but couldn't remember why she had gone there. She splashed some cool water on the cut on her forehead. It looked terrible But she couldn't recall how it got there

She took three ibuprofens and swallowed five cups of water. She looked at her head again and threw the whole bottle of ibuprofen in her swim bag.

At least she was going to see Madison. The thought lifted her from her stupor slightly, like the first birdsong after a storm.

Stumbling into the garage to get her bike, she was surprised to find both her bike and her Dad's car missing.

She wondered if Dad had slept over at Bhakti's house after the lecture last night. Maybe they all just picked up and moved to India together and formed a big harem, she imagined balefully.

She knew these were delirious thoughts but there was no rational explanation for her dad's absence. He certainly wouldn't usually have gone to work this early.

She remembered her bike was up at the wilderness trailhead

and she shuffled slowly uphill for ten minutes and found it where she had left it yesterday before her big flight.

Pedaling back down her dirt road was easier, but her whole body hurt and it wasn't loosening up like it usually did after five or ten minutes. She lost her ability to concentrate again. All she could do was try to look at the ground approaching her front wheel. Nothing else would come into proper focus.

Her head was cold and damp. She realized she had forgotten to put on her bike helmet. She never forgot her helmet. She didn't even know where it was.

After a much, much slower cycle than usual, the familiar smell and sound of a normal morning at the pool lifted her spirits for a moment. Her energy lifted enough that she could act normal. She was going to see Madison and had even made arrangements to have coffee with her later. Madison was perhaps the only person in the world she looked forward to seeing. Alice felt she didn't deserve friends, but somehow Madison was understanding and sympathetic.

Chucking her bag on one of the bleachers, she started taking her sweatshirt off. Coach came up.

"What the hell." Coach looked her up and down.

"Sorry?" Alice pulled her sweatshirt the rest of the way off.

"Your head is cut and it looks infected."

"No it's not."

"Alice, you're shivering."

"So what; it's freezing today."

"It's warm. Alice, you need to see a doctor. You're not swimming."

"Someone telling me what I can and can't do. Just what I need. What am I supposed to do to prove to you people I care about something? I do care! Look at what I put up with to get to training!"

"I'll drive you." He turned to get his bag. "Put your sweatshirt back on. Now."

Alice looked at him and considered for a moment what to do.

She concentrated hard and managed to stop shaking. She looked down at the water and realized some of the girls had stopped swimming and were staring at her. They probably wouldn't want her in there with them if she had an infected cut and God knows she didn't want to make any more enemies today.

The world went dark for a second.

Coach grabbed her arm.

She looked around, startled, and recovered again. She grabbed her sweatshirt back off the bench and put it back on. She felt so cold. She tried to act normal.

"I'll ring Mom. Thanks anyway."

She strode out. No way was she going to let Coach drive her anywhere. No way she was going to call Mom.

She managed to get back on her bike and headed toward the local hospital. How nice it would be to just drift off the road and fall over into the grass, she thought, but she somehow kept pedaling.

Leaning her bike up against the hospital wall, she pulled herself together again.

One foot in front of the other, she thought.

There was no wait at the emergency room. Everyone looked bored at the sight of her minor injury. She filled out some paperwork. She had no idea what she wrote: something about her dad. She handed over her insurance card and her student i.d. Thankfully the intern saw her quickly. She was able to lift herself again, to act normal. It was just a cut on the head.

The intern was in a hurry and bought her act. He cleaned her cut, put some bandaid thing on it and wrote her a prescription for antibiotics. He let her check out without calling her parents. The whole thing only took about fifteen minutes. He also wrote her a note to get her out of school which she threw in the trash. She couldn't fill the prescription until nine in the morning: two more hours.

She went to the café to try to stomach a coffee. Hopefully Madison would still come to meet her after swimming. She passed an hour in a haze. Madison should have arrived. She knew she must not be coming.

Alice kept her eyes glued to the front door of the café and the window out to the street. She tried to wish Madison into coming, parking her Subaru somewhere nearby right now.

She imagined the conversation they would have.

"Hey," Alice would say.

"Alice, are you okay?" Madison would say, rushing in, face full of concern. "I saw you arrive at the pool and then you just turned around and left."

Ten more minutes passed and no Madison. It was 8:00 a.m., well past the time Madison would have needed to go to school. They both had first period off because of swimming, but second period started at ten after eight.

At eight-thirty Alice gave up. Now there was no-one. Mom hated her, Dad thought she was *kusang*, Kirsty thought she was *kusang*.

Alice made her way out of the café, unlocked her bike and walked it toward the pharmacy on the university campus. She felt like an old lady using her bike like a walker.

There was no activity on campus on a Monday morning before nine. Alice heard a lawn mower start up somewhere in the distance. She stood at the pharmacy doors for ten long minutes. Her shaking had begun again. All she could do was stare at the graffiti on the wall. After the place finally opened, she got her prescription filled. The pharmacist said the antibiotics wouldn't kick in for a day or two. She chased a few pills down with a bottle of electrolyte drink and a few more ibuprofen for good measure, and then she painfully mounted her bike. She pedaled past the library and began to head very slowly toward home.

It took her twice as long as usual, but when she finally got to her driveway, something compelled her past it. When she reached the trail leading up to the ravine, she dismounted, wobbled a second, closed her eyes and took a deep breath.

She was feeling cold again and realized she should go home

and go to bed. Instead she laid her bike down on the forest floor near the road, slung her bag over her shoulder and started staggering along the trail.

The higher she got up the ravine, the foggier her brain got. She vaguely felt there was a danger here or maybe that was yesterday.

She felt like she was a little girl again and wondered what Daddy would say. Nature is not your friend. Nor is she your enemy. You just have to treat her with respect.

She reached a meadow with a burned tree and remembered a dream of flying. Alice sat down by the burned tree, lay down and rolled over to look at the blue sky.

The next thing she knew, Alice was waking up from a long sleep. Now everything hurt: front of head, back of head, arms and legs, butt, whole torso—everything. She coughed twice. Some birds flew away urgently. Something else moved quickly away through the forest.

She had slept deeply and was feeling disoriented. It took ten or fifteen breaths before she recognized where she was. She sat up to look for her bag. It was there: by the lightning tree.

She crawled over on hands and knees, took her phone out. It was nearly noon. She had slept for three hours. There were a few missed calls from school. She turned it off again. She only faintly remembered coming here. She must have been totally delirious.

She got up and walked back down the hill to her bike, got on and coasted home.

When she got there, she could hear the landline ringing inside, so she just left her bike on the driveway and walked in to get the phone.   "Hello?"

"Hello. Is that Mrs. Brickstone?"

"Yes," Alice said emphatically, trying to sound grown up.

"This is Cathy at Hardrock High. Sorry to trouble you."

"No trouble."

"Well, Alice is absent again today. Given her...condition, I wouldn't usually call you. We have discussed it many times and the school is still supportive of her doing self-guided study at the library, under Brian's supervision. But today, one of her classmates is also absent. Kirsty Bell. A third classmate, Madison Percival, a girl on Alice's swim team, came to me to express her concern about Kirsty and Alice's absence. She also said Alice missed swim practice this morning, which apparently is a very rare occurrence. Likewise, Kirsty has never missed a day of school. Naturally I called Kirsty's parents before I called you. They know nothing about it and are understandably quite concerned."

"I see."

"So I don't suppose you have heard from Alice this morning?"

"No."

"Both girls also have their phones powered off. I will leave it to you if you think it wise to contact Brian to make sure that Alice is okay. I would just ask if you could please contact us if Alice knows anything about the whereabouts of Kirsty Bell."

"I'll call Brian right now."

"Thank you, Mrs. Brickstone."

Alice hung up and walked, stunned, into the kitchen. The clock on the oven read 12:00 a.m. Not too early for lunch.

So, Mom and Dad have Brian spying on me. Because I have a *condition*. What condition would that be? The condition of having traitorous, dishonest parents who do not love their daughter? Who care so little that they are content to let others do their parenting for them?

The refrigerator contained precious little of value today. Alice pulled out a family-sized frozen pizza from the freezer, removed the packaging and whacked it into the oven. The oven racks made a satisfactory slamming noise.

A condition.

Where is Kirsty, she wondered. Probably hanging out with Babaji, but it is odd her mother isn't there with her. Anyway it's none of my business.

When the pizza had been in the oven long enough to defrost,

but probably not cook through, she took it upstairs with her to her bedroom.

She tossed her stuff on the floor and kicked her shoes off. She lay down on the bed with the rest of the pizza. A condition. She wondered what her condition was meant to be. She mulled it over slowly. She sometimes skipped school and went cafés or the University library. Was that a condition? Other kids didn't do that, presumably. They skipped school and did drugs, which was apparently normal behavior.

Alice finished her pizza, leaned over the bed and put the plate on the floor. Staring up at the ceiling, she felt mildly sick. No fever anymore, but she was certainly not well. She was tired. The events of the past few days had worn her down. She took some deep breaths and slipped back into another deep sleep.

CHAPTER 10

Alice stood up on the starting block at the pool. Everyone in the audience was pointing at her. She shook the tension out of her strong arms and tried to focus on the race. Which race? Is it the 200 free or the 100? She started to feel cold.

Trying not to draw attention to herself, she reached down to check if she was wearing her Speedos. Her hand felt nothing but skin. She was completely naked on a starting block in front of hundreds of people and all of her swimming peers. Her goggles felt extremely tight on her eyes. She must have misadjusted them.

Then some bell rang. It didn't sound like the right bell for the race starter, but all the others were already swimming. I missed my start. Should I swim naked? The bell rang again.

Alice opened her eyes and the throbbing in her head resumed. She still felt sick. The doorbell rang again, reminding her of her nightmare.

She rolled over and pushed herself up into a sitting position on the edge of her bed. It took a moment for her to steady herself. The only things she could remember were she was sick, injured, and was at home.

The clock by her bed read 3:30 p.m. Should that be a.m., she questioned. She looked down and saw she still wore the same sweat pants and shirt she had thrown on that morning in an abortive attempt to have a normal day. There were some pine needles in her socks and in her hair?

She remembered a betrayal. By whom?

More memories returned. Her parents and her school had been spying on her because they thought she had some kind of condition. Her dad agreed with Babaji that she was spiritually evil, bad company for Kirsty. Apparently, Madison also felt that way, as she didn't show up for their first ever social arrangement.

She had a feeling they were all correct and she was bad company. Poison. Just yesterday she had actually convinced herself she could fly. She was both poisonous and delusional.

Alice managed to stand up and walk slowly to the window to see who had been ringing their doorbell.

She was startled back into full consciousness by the strange vision of a taxi parked in front of their driveway. The bright yellow contrasted sharply with the shades of green in the trees and grasses.

As she stared, a guy in orange robes appeared, walking away from her front door toward the taxi. They appeared to be the same style of orange robes that Bhakti wore. Before he got in, he looked up, straight toward her.

He saw her, put on a big smile and waved. His smile was so disarming, all she could do was wave back. He pointed at the front door and lifted his palms in question.

She nodded. Alice remembered Madison telling her Kirsty had been talking to an Australian swami. This must be the guy.

She acknowledged to herself that her parents would probably think a sixteen-year-old girl home alone shouldn't be opening the door to any man, but she didn't care. She climbed painfully down the stairs, overcame a head-rush at the bottom, and opened the front door.

"Hi, Alice."

She detected some kind of accent, British or Australian.

"I'm sorry to disturb you. My name is Shivapuri."

Probably Australian, she thought.

"I saw you and your mom at the lecture last night and I came out here today because I'm looking for your dad. I have some papers for him to urgently sign. I haven't been able to reach him on his phone."

"He's not here."

"May I leave them with you?"

"Sure."

He pulled out an orange folder from a briefcase and handed the folder to Alice.

She took a deep breath and tried to read him. His mind was a blank. Nothing. It was like he was a tree. She looked down and wondered why she was bothering. She should just go back to bed. She started to close the door on Shivapuri.

"Alice, you don't look well."

She looked up at him. She felt so sad she almost started to cry in front of this guy. Then she looked down again.

"Can I help you? Maybe make you a cup of tea?"

She looked up at Shivapuri again, feeling very sorry for herself. She recovered and made a decision. Alice definitely didn't want this guy making her a cup of tea and she knew her dad would not be planning to come home for at least three or four more hours, but she knew her dad would be furious if he knew she had let Shivapuri sit in their living room with her home alone. She liked the idea of angering her dad right now.

"Come on in. I'm a little sick today but you're welcome to sit in the living room and wait for dad to come home. He should be here any minute."

"That's very kind of you. I'll just pop out and speak to the taxi driver."

She pulled out her phone and texted her dad to tell him she was home sick and had let Shivapuri in to the house to wait for him to come home. She turned her phone off and took their landline off the hook. There, that should do it, she figured.

She watched Shivapuri come back up the walkway and looked him up and down as he kicked off his shoes and strode past her into the hall.

He was much shorter than she was and wore the same kind of orange monk robes that Babaji and Bhakti wore. He moved purposefully, as though he was heading somewhere undeniably important and nothing would stop him from getting there. His whole head was cleanly shaved and completely white, like he was used to wearing a hat, and his neck was sun burned and wrinkled. His age was hard to guess, like Bhakti's was. He could be anywhere between thirty and sixty.

She wondered how long it would take for her dad to get here after he failed to reach her by phone. Anywhere between ten and thirty minutes, she guessed. He probably wouldn't ring Mom to do the intercept. Shivapuri was more his problem and he wouldn't want her involved. Just enough time to grill Shivapuri for information about Babaji. She needed find out if Babaji had hired Rajendra.

She led him into the living room and offered Dad's favorite chair in front of the TV   "Shivapuri, Dad should be home any minute, but in the meantime, can I get you something to drink?"

"Just a glass of water, thanks," he said.

She smiled and left him sitting there. She strolled back to the kitchen and got him his water. Before she brought it out to him, she grabbed a large chunk of chocolate from her stash and stuffed it into her mouth for energy. She was still slightly woozy but was feeling much better now that she was inflicting stress on her dad.

She was still trying to swallow as she handed Shivapuri his water.

He seemed to notice and smiled.

"Ta. Alice, you look like you're feeling a bit better."

"Thanks." Alice sat down on the couch.

He slouched down and looked relaxed.

"So," she started, "Bhakti is blackmailing Dad into doing some deal with you and Babaji. Does that make you feel very spiritual?"

Anger flashed across Shivapuri's face but he controlled himself and looked relaxed again.

"I was not aware of any blackmail. It was your father who came to us, Alice."

"Sure. Yeah, I believe you. I'm sure you guys are all innocent, especially Babaji. You guys are all saints."

Alice saw something give in Shivapuri's posture. He slouched deeper and let go of part of his controlled mask.

"I can see that you're not going to be put off. It's just as well. You deserve the truth. She and your father used to work together at ashram. It's no secret that she wants and needs his expertise back."

"Back for what?"

"To re-invigorate her research. Ten years ago, Babaji helped your dad and Bhakti raise some local funding to research the health benefits of yoga and meditation."

"How original."

"You don't understand. They were onto something. It had to do with practicing under certain special conditions and with the guidance of an enlightened master. Everyone was inspired by their progress in such a short time but she hasn't had much luck since your dad left. When we heard that your dad was negotiating with a local company to form a pharmaceutical joint venture, she though it would be a good opportunity to bring him back to work with her. Babaji agreed and this contract details the terms of a cooperative research project."

"That's nice. I hope they have fun. How long have you been with Babaji?"

Shivapuri smiled at her as though he knew what the game was and was happy to play. "You wouldn't believe it but it has been nearly twenty-five years now."

"Wow. How many of those years at the ashram in India?"

"Twenty-four and a half. I have always been the kind of person that acted immediately once I knew what I wanted. As soon as I met Babaji, I knew I wanted to be with him in India."

Alice paused and looked at the clock. She had a few more minutes before Dad got home. She didn't really care about her Dad's little research projects anymore. All she wanted to know was how and why an Indian kidnapper was interested in her.

She took a deep breath and re-centered her awareness so she could read him, but again found an empty space where she expected thoughts and feelings. All she could do was back out and keep trying to learn what she needed in the old-fashioned way.

"Wow," she said, "that means you were there ten years ago when my family was there. What a coincidence. You must have had the opportunity to meet lots of hit-men and kidnappers in your day."

Shivapuri put down his water and squared his shoulders to Alice.

"Alice, yes, I was there when your family was there. I'm so very sorry about your brother. It was the biggest tragedy that has ever happened at the ashram."

He kept looking at her like he was expecting her to start crying.

She held herself tall and listened.

"I'm sure your mom and dad have told you all the details about what happened. It was such a terrible time for them and for you. Really, I'm so sorry for what happened. I can't imagine what it was like for you, growing up without your brother."

"No, they did not tell me all the details. All I know is there was a traffic accident and Thomas died in it."

Shivapuri looked at her with apparent concern and asked, "That's all they told you?"

"They barely told me that much."

"Alice, you must understand it isn't my place to tell you things your mom and dad have withheld. They must have their reasons."

Shivapuri slouched back in Dad's chair and clasped his hands together in a gesture to indicate that he was done with the topic. He had the manner of someone who was used to getting his way in a situation like this. He had not spent much time around people like Alice.

"Well, Shivapuri, before Dad gets home, can I offer you anything else? How about a medal for being yet another male authority figure who thinks he knows better than me? I think we have a gold medal in the kitchen. I'll be right back, okay?"

Shivapuri smiled. "Okay, okay. I get it."

"What do you get, exactly? You act as though the death of my twin brother was harder for you than it was for me."

"Alice, I'm so sorry. None of this is coming out right. No, you might not expect so, but it is hard for me. These are some of my most painful memories and I never dreamed I would be sitting here with you speaking about it like this."

He paused, drank some water, looked out the window, and then continued.

"I meditated and prayed for years in order to understand your tragedy. I think I have realized something about it that may be useful to you.

"Alice," he continued after another pregnant pause, "it was not a traffic accident that killed your brother. It was a complicated story, but in the end, it was a lot of mistakes and misunderstandings that resulted in your brother's death. Mistakes made by men who were confused."

Alice felt like punching him for being so vague, but at least he was sort of telling her something new, so she kept her fist to herself. She didn't know how to punch someone properly anyway.

"Does that make any sense?"

"Oh, sure," she said right away. "Some confused men killed Thomas."

"In fact," Shivapuri said, "most of them were scarred for life by the tragedy."

"Poor things," Alice said, putting on a fake frown. The only reason Alice had listened to all this crap was to try to get some real information at last—which didn't seem to be forthcoming.

"So who are we talking about?" she asked impatiently. "Babaji? Did Babaji kill Thomas?"

"I think almost every man involved in that sad story was culpable, Alice. There were Indians as well as non-Indians."

"You're not going to tell me who they were and what they did."

"I just can't, Alice. But I promise you, I know enough about the story to know that if your parents have withheld information, it was for very good reasons."

"So how do you recommend I find out those reasons?"

"Your parents may know more than they let on. At least your father should. But go easy on them. I can tell you from personal experience that it affected everyone in unpredictable ways. Your family was deeply affected forever. But so was ours.

"At ashram, something happened in the midst of all that tragedy. We all started to actually think for ourselves.

"Your tragedy helped us to recognize that heaven on earth was not going to be just handed to us. We weren't entitled to it just because we were disciples of a self-realized master. We had to work hard to create it for ourselves and for others. That is when my real spiritual practice began."

Alice rolled her eyes at him.

"It's like this, Alice. Sometimes a needle is needed to remove a thorn, a splinter. The thorn causes pain and the needle causes even more pain, but for a shorter time, and the thorn is out."

"Look," she said, leaning forwards, trying to look as imposing as she felt angry, "I'm not into all these vague Indian metaphors, Shivapuri, or whatever your real name is. You're in my house now and I want to know the truth."

Shivapuri paused.

They both heard a car on the gravel outside, driving quickly. Then the garage door opened.

"Alice, someday your dad will explain. Maybe soon, if you ask him in the right way."

He looked up at the entrance hallway from the garage.

"I am so grateful for spending these few moments talking with you. You are obviously an amazing young woman. It is easy to see that you, justifiably, are carrying quite a bit of anger about the events ten years ago and are not impressed with the amount of information about it that your parents have been able to share with you. Under the circumstances, I'm sure I would have been much angrier than you. I myself was just as angry as you are about some other terrible information that came out at that time. Before I go, I hope you'll let me share one last thing with you that I learned from my own anger."

Alice looked at him, challenging him to deliver more stupid, patronizing advice to her.

"It is this: anger, no matter how justified, hurts no-one but yourself. For a person on the spiritual path, it causes even more injury. That is because it kills your ability to see clearly."

"What?" she asked, not really caring.

"Just remember: anger is a thorn in your finger. It doesn't hurt anyone but you, even if you point your injured finger at the person who put it there."

"Not the stupid thorn metaphor again." Alice looked at him. She heard the car door slam.

"There is only one kind of needle that can remove that thorn. That needle is love."

Alice rolled her eyes at Shivapuri again.

Dad walked in pocketing his keys. Wei, looking angry, was walking behind Dad. Both of them were wearing black clothes as though they had just come from a funeral.

Maybe they need some love too, Alice thought.

As he passed the landline phone in the hallway, Dad placed the receiver back on the hook.

"Is everything okay here, Alice?"

"Great, Dad."

"But you said in your message that you were unwell."

"Yeah, this cut on my head got infected. I'm on antibiotics.

I'm going to go back to bed."

"Okay. Let me know if you need anything. I'll organize some dinner later."

Alice turned and started up the stairs. Halfway up, she turned and watched as Dad invited Shivapuri and Wei to sit in the atrium with views of the wilderness area. Shivapuri was taking out the paperwork for Dad to sign and Wei was reaching for it.

Alice sighed and went up to her room.

CHAPTER 11

Alice got her antibiotics and some more ibuprofen from the bathroom. Sitting on her bed, Alice chased the pills with water and touched her forehead gently, probing for inflammation.

It seems to be getting better, she thought. That scar must have come from the lightning strike. What about the chase and the flying?

She walked to her window took a few breaths of fresh air and returned to bed.

What had Shivapuri meant when he said Thomas had not died in a traffic accident, she wondered. Did the ashram cook accidentally poison Thomas? Was he accidentally left in the sun in a locked car? Did they even have kids' car seats at ashram?

All of these scenarios seemed as innocent as a car accident and no more or less worthy of being kept secret. It must be something else, she construed. Did Babaji sit on him?

She remembered Shivapuri had said, "I think almost every man involved in that sad story was culpable, Alice. There were Indians as well as non-Indians."

Alice suspected the perpetrators must be people she knew, otherwise Shivapuri wouldn't have given her the whole speech about pointing angry fingers at anyone. The two obvious choices were Dad and Babaji. Babaji fits perfectly, she thought; a man with no one to love him as a peer, the poor little guru. What about Dad?

She looked at the photo again and simply couldn't imagine any kind of scenario in which Dad could hurt a little kid like Thomas, even by accident.

She remembered Mom and Dad's argument the other night and realized their relationship may not have been that great back then either. Maybe it actually was Dad's fault?

She tried to think of other possibilities. Mr. Rao was there at the ashram back then, as was Shivapuri. What could their roles have been in Thomas' death? Shivapuri didn't seem to accept any of the blame, and when he spoke to her just now, he was depicting himself as an innocent bystander. But he could have been involved too. Mr. Rao doesn't appear to have a wife or even any family to speak of, but he doesn't give the impression of someone in any pain. Way too jolly. Besides, Shivapuri couldn't know that Mr. Rao and Alice had recently met again. He supposedly wouldn't even know Mr. Rao was in Hardrock.

The more she thought about it, the more likely it seemed to Alice that Shivapuri must have been talking about Dad and Babaji.

What had Shivapuri meant by love? Was it some yoga version of love? Masturbation? Or normal romantic love, like in the movies? What did that even mean? What was she supposed to actually do, and to whom?

She grabbed her phone to put some music on. She found some violent track, plugged in her headphones and closed her eyes.

How to even start? What do people do when they love each other? They say I love you, I guess. Got to start somewhere.

"I love you, Alice Brickstone," she declared as a kind of joke.

The joke didn't turn out like she expected. Her little declaration struck a chord somewhere in her chest and the chord was still sounding in her ears between the heavy beat of the music.

"I love you, Alice Brickstone," she tried again.

"I love you, Alice."

"I love you."

Something weird was happening. She felt sad and happy at the same time. Chills began to ripple the skin of her chest.

She tried to think about her day, about the solitary struggle to get to the hospital. It all felt distant, like the fever was returning. She felt separate from her actions today and from her body now.

She tried again. "I love you."

The distance between the observer and the rest of herself increased.

"I love you."

"I love you."

She was suddenly thrown into a huge, dark space. It was as though someone had pulled a plug in her mind.

"I love you."

With each subsequent declaration, the dark space increased in size and the darkness grew shades darker. The last traces of her ordinary consciousness were swirling down and away.

Yet she didn't feel alone. She had the feeling she was sharing the darkness with others. That realization suddenly shrank the space to a single point and it became light. Then she could think. Ideas came to her and passed by like passing leaves floating on a lazy wind.

She realized she didn't love herself. It was okay. The thought passed.

She realized she was still repeating the phrase, "I love you, Alice. I love you."

She felt herself drifting into sleep.

"I love you."

She woke up to the loud sound of a text message arriving. She recognized that the words "I love you, Alice" were still repeating and probably had not stopped as she slept. How long had she been asleep?

She touched her head and was pleased it was no longer angry or painful. When she opened her eyes she knew something was wrong.

It was dark but there were flashing red and blue lights coming through her window. She looked over at the clock and it read 6:00 a.m. She had slept for thirteen hours. Alice clicked open the text message that had woken her up:

Alice, the police were just here. Kirsty's parents can't find Kirsty. She didn't show up for school yesterday and never came home after. Her parents are freaking out. I heard you were home sick. I'm still going to training. Please call. - M

Kirsty missing? A rat face loomed in her memory. Rajendra must have given up on Alice and gone for Kirsty.

Alice had a flash of something she had seen in Rajendra's head: the clearing in the forest. The trees surrounding the clearing were old, at least forty feet high. There were a few big meadows near Hardrock that were that big, but there were not many places that had trees that high. It had to be somewhere deep in the Knifespur Wilderness.

She remembered there had also been a small brook running through the center of the clearing. Next to the brook was a tall dead tree with some kind of kite attached to the top of it. It was orange and shaped like a cone. She struggled for a moment and a word came to her. It was a windsock, like at an airport.

She thought she knew what had happened to Kirsty.

As she was about to call Madison, there was a knock on Alice's bedroom door. She pulled off her headphones, her ears smarting.

"Yes, I'm awake. Just a second."

Alice had slept in her clothes, so all she had to do was roll out of bed and answer the door. It was her dad.

"Honey, the police are here." Dad looked as though he hadn't slept yet. He was wearing the same black clothes he'd had on last night and looked tired and concerned. He looked as though he felt as strange as Alice felt. Alice couldn't remember the last time he'd called her honey.

"They are looking for a classmate of yours called Kirsty. I'm afraid she didn't come home yesterday."

"I haven't seen her. The last I saw her was at the end of Babaji's lecture, near you and the guru and his back door to some VIP room."

"Yes, that was the last I saw her too." He looked down at the floor, as though embarrassed.

"Perhaps you can come down and speak to the police?"

"Police. Okay, be down in a second."

Alice turned around and got her phone. It was a cool morning so she put on some running shoes and a hoodie.

After coming down the stairs, Alice ignored the police and went straight to the kitchen. After drinking a couple of large glasses of orange juice, she walked casually into the living room.

There were two uniformed police standing there in full gear. Both were women. One was short and stocky, the other was tall and thin, and looked like a model. Both appeared to be bored, like they expected nothing to come of this interview.

"Alice, sweetheart," her mom said from the couch.

Alice was almost shocked to see her there. She looked small and diminished. Alice was surprised she didn't look at all fresh. She was usually up at four every day to meditate for two hours.

"I'm so sorry to wake you up like this when you're not well."

Mom got up slowly, walked over to Alice and gave her a hug. For the first time, Alice thought her mom was fragile. She wasn't the strong person she used to be. Has she been eating, Alice worried.

She didn't have time to wonder about her mom. She didn't know how this kind of thing was done, so she just sat down and waited for the cops to speak first.

"Hi, Alice," the stocky one said. "I know this is probably a shock for you to wake up and have to speak to us straight away. We wouldn't usually be so rude, but we're on urgent business and your dad was kind enough to offer to wake you up."

"It's okay."

"It's about a classmate of yours, Kirsty Bell."

"Dad said she was missing?" Alice didn't have to pretend to be concerned. She was. She had more reason to be concerned, however, than she wanted to tell the police. She couldn't explain to them what she thought she knew, because the question would inevitably come: how could she know?

"Her parents reported her missing last night. She was last seen leaving for school yesterday morning on her bicycle. Her family lives up Leadville Road, not far from here, about five minutes down Highway 320 toward town. We're here to follow up with all of the people Kirsty has had contact with just before she disappeared. We need to know if Kirsty had been saying or doing anything unusual, or speaking to anyone new."

The tall policewoman took out a notebook, found what she was looking for. "Kirsty's mom told us you have had quite a lot of contact with Kirsty over the past forty-eight hours and she thought this was unusual because she had never seen you together before." She stared at Alice.

Alice didn't really hear a question in the sentence so she didn't say anything.

"Is that true?" the woman persisted, annoyed.

Alice felt strange about this encounter. The question seemed so unprofessional. "Is which part true?" she asked.

Alice's question appeared to fluster the tall one and the stocky one had to take over.

She smiled, trying to achieve a bit of rapport. "Alice, we're just trying to figure out what may have happened to Kirsty. Usually one of the starting points for us, in situations like this, is to look for anything out of the ordinary going on in the missing person's life. So, can you just tell us about any interactions or communication you've had with her in the past few days?"

"I just met her the other day. She was with my swimming teammate, Madison, at a house where this Indian guru is staying.

You guys know about Babaji, I assume?"

The policewomen both nodded.

"Kirsty was sitting with Madison when I met her. We chatted for a while and it turned out Kirsty lives around here. Also her family was in Babaji's ashram at the same time we were, ten years ago. Last night I saw her at the Babaji lecture. I wanted to speak with her again but I didn't manage to catch her."

The tall policewoman looked back at her notebook. "Her mother told us, and I quote, 'Ms. Brickstone walked toward Kirsty in a menacing manner. She was dressed inappropriately and bleeding from the forehead. I was frightened.'"

Alice looked at her and said nothing because the officer hadn't asked a question.

"Alice," the stocky one said, "can you think of any reason why Mrs. Bell would think you walked toward Kirsty in a menacing manner?"

"I don't know; maybe because she has the confidence of a deer mouse?"

The policewomen looked at each other.

"What is a deer mouse? How would you know anything about Mrs. Bell's confidence?"

"Deer mice, let's see." Alice was surprised by Dad's voice booming out over her shoulder. She had forgotten he was there. "Aren't they the kind of mice that have been discovered to be the main carrier of the dangerous Sin Nombre Hantavirus?"

By the tone of his voice Alice could tell he was smiling when he spoke.

The police women looked at Dad and were distracted for a moment, giving Alice the time to consider her response, which was probably Dad's intention.

"I don't know Kirsty's mom," she said, "but Kirsty told me she was concerned her mom had fallen back in with this guru, Babaji, and his cult. I went to the lecture because my mom and dad were there too, and I was kind of worried about the same thing Kirsty was. When I met her mom the day before, it was obvious she had no confidence. Anyway, I am guessing the only reason anyone would go to a lecture by this turkey is if they were suffering from very low self-esteem. That seems to be the case with my dad here. After the lecture, I was walking over to Kirsty to say hi, but her mom and Babaji took her into another room out back before I could reach her.

"And yes," Alice continued, "I was dressed inappropriately because this cut on my forehead had bled onto my other clothes and I had to borrow some from Madison at the last minute. Madison gave me a lift to the lecture. Madison is tall and skinny. I am tall and fat. I don't know about menacing but I'm sure I looked terrible."

The stocky one smiled at her. "That makes sense, Alice. Thanks." "By the way," she added kindly, "you are not fat."

"Alice." Dad placed his hand on her shoulder, which felt weird because he hardly ever touched her. "I was standing near Kirsty and her mom at the time and I didn't see you come over."

Alice's first reaction to Dad's comment was indignation, as what really happened was he had ignored her intentionally. She felt like ignoring him now, but she couldn't because some voice in her head said, I love you, Alice. It was like last night's declarations had continued through the night and they were still on auto-repeat now, softening her from the inside out. "If it seemed like I was ignoring you, I'm very sorry," her dad said.

She thought it would be impossibly hard to say something nice to him, but it wasn't. "It's okay, Dad." Alice turned to the policewomen. "I must not have been all that menacing if my own dad didn't even see me."

"It's not that important anyway," the stocky one said. "The main thing we need to ask you is if you can tell us anything that may help us find Kirsty. Anything at all."

Alice paused, pretending to consider her response. She took a few deep breaths, shifted her state of mind and prepared to read one of them. The stocky one was looking at her, so she was the obvious target. There was no jolt or shock as she connected; the woman's mind was orderly. Thoughts were forcefully laid out like in a spreadsheet. As Alice checked one column of her inner spreadsheet, it became clear the stocky policewoman didn't think much of Babaji or his organization and Babaji was unofficially her primary suspect. She was from a conservative Hardrock family raised on a healthy appreciation of the outdoors and suspicious of anything too liberal, foreign, or stupid. To her, Babaji was all three.

Alice broke the connection and said, "I have a bad feeling Babaji had something to do with this. He has a history of abusing girls Kirsty's age. It's all over the internet. You guys already know Kirsty was with Babaji in a private room behind the lecture hall."

The tall one hadn't noticed her partner's brief catatonic moment. "Yes, we know. We already spoke to your dad about that."

The stocky one regained her composure. "Alice, is it possible Kirsty may have gone to stay with a boyfriend? Or gone camping without speaking to her parents about it?"

"I don't know. I don't know her that well. I guess she could have gone somewhere. I just met her. It's just that it would have been a strange thing to skip school on a Tuesday?"

The policewomen looked at each other, then at Alice's mom.

"Hey," Alice pointed at the injury on her forehead, "I stayed home because I was feverish."

The tall one asked, "Alice, can you give me a detailed breakdown of your activities and whereabouts yesterday?"

Alice sighed at what she thought was a total waste of time. Time was ticking for Kirsty. She gave an abbreviated version of events, starting with her aborted attempt to join her swim team, the trip to the hospital, the café and the pharmacy. She left out all of the wandering in the forest near her house and said she just came home and went to bed. She didn't mention Shivapuri, in case her dad was trying to keep his liaison with the monk secret from Mom.

Her story seemed to satisfy the police. They reassured Alice and her parents that they would do everything they could to find Kirsty and could they please inform them if they had any other thoughts or information for them at all.

"So is Alice in any danger?" Mom asked tentatively. It was the first thing she had said the entire interview. "I mean could there be some kind of guy out there in the woods hunting teenage girls?"

"It's very unlikely, Mrs. Brickstone," the stocky one said, "but not impossible. In the meantime you should just take extra precautions. Alice, do you also cycle to school?"

"Yep. I'm sixteen but I don't know how to drive and I don't have a car."

"Could you get a lift for a few days, just to be on the safe side?"

"Sure," Dad told her, "we'll take care of it."

They gave Alice, and her parents, cards with their mobile numbers on them, and then departed.

Alice crumpled the tall one's card. The stocky lady was called Nancy Pelosi. Alice kept her card, moved to the kitchen and was making an omelet when Mom and Dad came in together. She used to be satisfied with half a dozen eggs but she was pretty hungry this morning and had already broken ten eggs into a bowl, whipping them with a fork. Her parents both wore faces of concern, mixed with guilt.

"Darling," Mom began tentatively, "we can't tell you how sorry we are that you had to go through that; it's all our fault. If we hadn't ever met Babaji, none of this..." She broke off, her voice cracking.

Alice was annoyed. No-one showed emotions around this house. Mom had no right to now. This was Kirsty's problem, and now Alice's problem, not Mom's. Why would Mom think these two cops were her own fault? More importantly, why wasn't Mom angry about last night? Alice had disobeyed her order—no, it was more like an impassioned plea—to not go into the Babaji lecture. Alice's annoyance grew to anger. Why was Mom so damn frail and pathetic?

"Oh, come on, Mom. You're being ridiculous. How could it even be your fault at all?"

Mom just looked at her.

A light went on somewhere in Alice's mind.

"Mom, it's not your fault."

Mom just stared. Dad looked at Mom with heightened concern. It was a look Alice now recognized, had seen a million times before over the past ten years and had always misread.

"It's not your fault, any of it." Alice walked over to her, aware Dad was watching. "Mom, it's not your fault. Come on."

She placed her arms around her mom's small torso and something broke. Alice quickly released her, afraid she had snapped her mom's spine, but when she saw Mom's face, contorted by tears, eyes closed tightly shut, she realized it had been something else that broke. She pulled her close again.

In her peripheral vision, she noticed Dad was looking away, but then his eyes snapped toward the stove. Alice saw the smoking frying pan a second after he did, Dad already dashing to the stove and grabbing the frying pan handle that he immediately released, cursing.

He shoved his hand under some running water.

Alice released her mom, who had opened her eyes and was standing with her mouth open, not breathing.

Alice sighed, found a hot pad, took the smoking frying pan off the burner and shut off the gas.

"I'm sorry, Dad. That was my fault."

"Alice, it's not your fault." He started to smile at his little attempt at a joke, but he darkened.

Alice suspected he was considering who was really at fault for last night and for the cops being here, and for many other things. She figured he was probably coming to the conclusion that of all the possible candidates, he was the guiltiest one.

He cursed again at his burned hand.

Mom had gone to look and was wincing. "This needs to get

looked at. I'll drive you to the clinic."

It must have been bad enough that Dad didn't argue. Besides, Alice realized, he really didn't appear to have slept last night. They could all use some time off.

Alice took the opportunity to speak. "Hey, guys, I'm not allowed to swim until this wound heals." She pointed at her head. "I think I'll take the morning classes off today as well, so that I can rest."

"That sounds smart, Alice," Mom said. "We'll be back in an hour or two and I'll take you in to school late, if you feel like it."

Alice took a box of cereal and a bottle of milk down, put the box under her arm, selected a large bowl and a spoon, and went up to her room. After pouring a half a bottle of milk over a bowlful of cereal, Alice rang Madison. She answered on the first ring. "Alice!"

"Hi. How was swimming?"

"Fine. How are you? Did you get my text?"

"Yeah, thanks. I just had a visit from the police too."

"What did they say?" Madison asked. "Do they have any leads yet?"

"No, but I think I know where she is. I'm going to go look for her right now."

"What? You know where she is and you didn't tell the police?"

"It's complicated but I need to go right now. I'm not sure if she's okay. I think I know who took her and he's a real dick."

"Alice, wait! Where are you?"

"At home."

"There is no way you are going after her alone. I'm calling the police."

"Okay, Madison: whatever. I won't be here when they get here. Seriously, I need to go help Kirsty and I just don't have time to wait for police or to explain all kinds of bullshit things they will want to know. I just need to go. I thought I would call you to let you know."

Alice paused. She heard a little voice in her head still chattering the phrase, I love you, Alice. At first she thought Madison had said it, but she realized it was just in her head.

"Madison," Alice continued slowly, "I also called because I wanted to say I'm really sorry if I was mean to you in the car yesterday. About how hard you work in the pool."

"Alice, as if that matters right now!" Madison paused. "If I bring you a takeout latte, will you at least wait for me before you do anything crazy?"

Alice thought she could use a coffee. "Okay. Thanks, Maddy. But just get a coffee from the pool kiosk. It's crap, but there's not enough time to go to the regular café. Ask them to make it a triple shot so that it doesn't taste so much like weak, dirty dishwater—and please hurry."

"Okay, see you in ten or fifteen."

Alice hung up and quickly plugged her phone in to power. It was low on battery after being on all night and she would need her phone this morning. She opened her laptop, called up some satellite maps of the Knifespur on the internet and started looking for any flat, football-field-sized clearings surrounded by tall trees, with streams running through them. Unfortunately there were quite a few meadowy-looking places but she couldn't tell if they were flat and it was really hard to see if there was a tiny little stream cutting through any of them. She also couldn't really see anything about tree heights.

This was going to be harder than she thought. The Knifespur occupied a huge, mountainous area.

It occurred to her to wonder about Mr. Rao. Where had he been throughout all her struggles yesterday? She put him out of her mind, closed her laptop and started getting ready to head out.

Alice had a water pouch she wore as a backpack for her longer hikes and runs. She filled it up. She remembered the feeling of flying the day before. It was cold up there. She found some tight-fitting cold weather cycling gear. She didn't want her clothing to flop around and slow her down. She put on ski socks because she knew she couldn't wear shoes.

She felt a bit itchy and tried to remember the last time she had changed her underwear. Not being able to remember was a bit disturbing, so she quickly took everything off and put on clean undies and bra and put everything else back on. Finally   she remembered how difficult it had been to land. What could be done about that? She sat down and thought hard. She was going to have to land in a meadow at twenty miles an hour. There was not likely to be a chili garden conveniently emitting a soft mattress of prana. All she could think of was a little kid's sled they still had in their garage, but there would be no way to carry it while she was flying.

She unplugged her phone, stuffed it into a pocket and rushed out of her room.

She ran into Mom's meditation room tofind a yoga mat, or something soft that she might be able to use as a landing aid.

She had almost never set foot in this room before. It was Mom's private space. There were lots of other so called private spaces in this house; why had Alice honored the sanctity of this one? The door was never locked but the room was forbidden as a vault. As she looked around, she realized how weird that was.

It was a large, carpeted room with no furniture, empty of everything except a meditation cushion, a few yoga props and a bookshelf. There were also quite a few photos on the walls. They were hung all the way around the room, precisely spaced like in an art gallery. They were small, framed shots of forest scenes. Some were close-ups of trees. She went over and looked closely at a particular tree shot and recognized it was her lightning tree— before the lightning. She puzzled how that was even possible that this particular tree appeared in a photo in Mom's room, unless Mom had taken those photos herself?

She took the lightning tree photo down and turned it around, looking for a signature or some evidence it was purchased from somewhere. The back just looked like old-fashioned photograph paper. Alice didn't even know Mom had a camera, let alone that she was a photographer. These pictures were stunning. Alice was no expert at photography, but she felt like each picture she looked at said something to her. It was as though her mom had captured something about herself in the pine trees and meadows. Something Alice had not considered before.

In the bookshelf she spied two large coffee-table books and pulled one out. It had a photo on the cover that looked similar in style to the pictures on the walls.

She flicked to the middle and opened her eyes wide on seeing a huge close up of her dad. He was captured in a moment of thought, looking down at something on the ground. His head was framed above by the outline of his car door. He must have been sitting in his car when the photo was taken, she realized. She turned the page and he was there again, this time looking forward. He looked determined and stronger in this photo. She found that almost the whole book was full of photos taken of her dad, apparently without his knowledge. Alice put the book down and went to the window. If Dad pulled out of the driveway, Mom could easily have taken those photos from this spot, she figured.

She went back to the book and found a few shots of her and her Dad taken a few years ago. One had them speaking together on the front lawn. Alice couldn't remember the incident but Dad seemed to be explaining something and Alice was looking at him as though she gave a crap.

In between the photos of Dad and her, and Dad by himself, there were lots more nature photos. Each was more interesting to Alice than the last.

Alice closed her eyes. She was struggling to reframe her view of her mom. Someone who hated Dad could not have taken these photos. A person who hid from life in this meditation room, and her yoga studio down the road, could not have taken the nature photos. These photos showed a side of Mom that was…impossible.

Alice tried to think if Mom had ever mentioned photography.

Well, maybe she had a few times. Maybe Alice had never listened properly. No-one had ever actually told Alice she wasn't allowed in Mom's meditation room. Maybe she just avoided it because her mom was usually meditating in it.

She thought of the photos of Dad and a tear sprung to her eye. The emotion caught her completely by surprise. What was that tear all about? Why would she feel so moved by a bunch of pictures?

She put the book back and was about to take out the other book, which looked older, when she heard a car pulling up on the gravel, brakes squeaking.

Madison.

No more time for sentimental photos right now.

She grabbed one of mom's yoga mats, an over-the-shoulder bag designed for carrying them, and rushed out of the room.

She ran downstairs and out front. Madison had placed two large coffees on her car roof.

"Hi, Madison!" Alice closed the front door.

"Hey. I got here as fast as I could." She held out a coffee to Alice. "What's with all that gear? You going to a yoga class?" Madison looked down and laughed. "In ski socks?"

Alice gratefully took the coffee and took a long drink. It was awful. As usual, the pool kiosk lady had made coffee without cleaning the cheap espresso machine and had burned the milk.

"Maddy, I really appreciate that you came out here and trusted me not to call the police."

"No problem. Now could you tell me what's going on?"

Alice felt as though she was past the point of trying to act normal.

"You know the other day when I dropped in on you when you were swimming at the pool at night?"

"Of course."

"I hadn't been to a barbecue. I was chased by someone who wanted to kidnap me. I don't know why he was after me. But I think this same guy must have got Kirsty."

"But Alice, why wouldn't you just come out and tell me that the other night? Why no police now?"

"It's complicated, Madison. You remember when I said I could fly?"

"Um, yes?" Madison nervously drank more of her coffee.

"I can fly."

"Right..."

"I really can fly. Like, without any help. That's how I got away from him."

"'Kay."

"I think I know where he took her. He can fly too. But he must have some kind of plane."

"You fly by...not having a plane?"

"That's right. It's not easy and you can save me some time by helping. Can I get on the roof of your Subaru and you drive about twenty or thirty miles an hour?"

Madison laughed so suddenly that she spat coffee out.

"Okay okay, so it's hard to believe," Alice said.

"You're going to fly away and find Kirsty. How would you know where he took her? Did he tell you the other day?"

Alice realized this was not going to work. There was just too much to explain. She smiled at Madison, took a final long drink of her coffee and looked around. The air was swirling with liquid crystal.

She left Madison standing there, put her coffee down on the lawn and opened the garage door. Not waiting until the door was fully open, Alice took down her bike off its hooks, hit the garage door button and cycled quickly out and down the driveway.

Madison was still standing where Alice had left her.

Alice cycled up the road a little way and stopped. She took a few breaths, tightened the yoga mat bag to her back, cinched up the shoulder straps to her water pouch, and got ready to do something that may result in her becoming road pizza.

She had a sudden flashback to a scene from Back to the Future when Christopher Lloyd and Michael J. Fox had to drive their time-traveling car a certain speed for it to work. She smiled and started cycling down the road as fast as she could. It hurt a little bit on her feet because she had no shoes on and her pedals were the clip-on type, but she managed to pick up speed.

She pedaled past Madison, who was leaning skeptically against her car like a mom watching a toddler do a trick. She kept going down the road past a little bend. She realized Madison probably couldn't see her anymore. She started coasting and centered her concentration on feeling the prana.

She pushed off with her hands and feet as hard as she could, lifting her arms toward the sky, searching with her hands for purchase in the liquid air.

She felt just enough pressure around her body and pulled back in a strong butterfly stroke movement, both arms arcing together, kicking powerfully with both feet.

She was airborne, but only a few feet from the gravel rushing below her. She needed to pick up more speed or it was going to be a short flight.

She heard the bike crash into the underbrush on the side of the road. Hopefully Madison would get it for her when she came searching. She blocked it out and concentrated on kicking with her legs, feeling the prana underneath her chest, hips and stomach. After a few more kicks, she pulled again strongly with her arms and felt her speed increase by at least double. She felt confident and buoyant enough to begin to crawl toward the sky and continue to increase her speed.

She was still below tree level. She wanted to lift herself above the trees and, with some luck, make a big arcing turn so she could swim toward the Knifespur.

It was much easier than it had been before. She was not wearing shoes, for one thing. Her feel for the prana was improving. She was able to begin to apply some of the refinements she used in the pool.

After managing her turn, she looked down and saw Madison.

"Thanks, Madison!!" she shouted.

Madison looked around but not up.

Alice didn't bother shouting again, remaining focused on her flying.

Looking ahead toward her destination, the Knifespur Wilderness, she considered the lay of the land. She knew the far western part of the Knifespur was occupied exclusively by craggy mountain peaks, probably inaccessible to Rajendra, and the far eastern side was well used by hikers and therefore probably unappealing to a kidnapper. She had explored most of the southern areas of the wilderness that were within a couple of hours' hike from the trailhead near her house and had never seen a clearing that big. That left the dead center of the park and the northward side near the Wyoming state border.

Unfortunately that was still a considerable area to search. All she had was the mental image of a large round clearing with a tree in the middle, but the tree had an orange windsock on it. That should be easy to spot from the air. That's what they were for.

Alice knew her search would be easier from a higher altitude, which meant moving faster, so she kept swimming hard and searching the sky for any further clues on how she might increase her speed.

From up here, she could just make out that the prana didn't circulate randomly but rather had certain patterns of flow. She searched, half by feel, half by visual cues, for any kind of current that may help her move faster, but she didn't have any luck.

She looked down and realized she had crossed into the wilderness area already and there was nothing but forest below her and ahead of her, and to either side. It was just beautiful, she thought, so exhilarating to be in the air, away from any people—all by herself—but if she fell from the sky now, it would hurt. A lot.

Her years of training in the pool were beginning to pay off as she made fine adjustments to her stroke and became more graceful in the air. With each adjustment she made, the prana repaid her by much larger increases in speed than she expected. It was as though the prana was an intelligent partner, She thought: more intelligent than water, that's for sure.

She ventured a wider look behind her. The sun was high enough in the sky over the ski mountain to indicate it was at least eight in the morning. She and Madison had already missed first period at school. She looked ahead and saw a clearing in the distance, but as she got closer, she realized it was much too small and there was no orange windsock.

Her phone rang in her pocket but she didn't dare take it out. She also didn't want to. It occurred to her that it was unlikely most of the Knifespur would be covered by a mobile phone signal, but there was not much she could do about that.

Her flight went on like this, with her searching, swimming and arcing through the air for about an hour. She had continued to increase her speed and elevation and could see quite a long way, but still no orange windsock and no clearing.

She began to entertain doubts. Perhaps it was all wrong. Maybe the clearing she had seen in Rajendra's mind was somewhere else in the world, like in Oregon or South Dakota, or Alaska, or maybe Kirsty hadn't even been taken by Rajendra.

Maybe she was wrong about a lot of things. Like about her Dad. Maybe he was totally innocent of everything and Shivapuri's words had created doubt in her mind about him. Why should she trust Shivapuri anyway?

These thoughts, combined with the effort of an hour of sustained flight, began to make Alice tired. Her head had started to hurt again and she realized she had forgotten to take her antibiotics that morning.

She lowered her chin so she could suck on the mouthpiece of her water pouch and soldiered on. Soon she realized she would need to turn around and head home or land somewhere to rest up before continuing. Crash land, more like.

Up ahead she saw another clearing. She squinted and scanned it carefully, hoping to see any glimpse of orange, but was disappointed. Nevertheless she descended for a closer look.

A huge gust of wind hit her suddenly from the side and she had to strain against it. As she lost altitude, she realized she was exhausted and struggling to keep aloft. The gracefulness of her movements had gone and she was almost flailing.

She reached behind her, while struggling to maintain a steady, slow dolphin kick, and pulled out Mom's yoga mat. She let it unroll, and owing to the speed she was flying, it immediately stuck to her chest and stomach and folded around her sides. It wasn't much but it would have to do.

The clearing was only a few hundred feet ahead. There was a long stretch of grass in the center of the clearing, slightly to the west, and she aimed for it. She just cleared the treetops and was perfectly lined up. Alice knew she needed to resume dolphin kicks to regain control of her flight so she could try to get a last minute lift before hitting the ground.

As she did, something caught her eye. It was either an animal or a person. Then she lost control altogether.

She could smell the grass already, as it was only ten feet below her. The wind was no longer deafening and she began to hear the sounds of the birds, and something else. Her sense of lift disappeared and her head suddenly plunged downward and her legs splayed upward toward the sky.

Maybe this wasn't such a good landing technique, she thought, in the split second it took before the back of her head hit the ground. She felt wet moss and everything went black.

CHAPTER 12

I love you, Alice.

Alice was underwater and was unable to breathe and the water was black and she couldn't see. Where was that annoying voice coming from?

I love you, Alice.

In the suffocating blackness, she held her breath and tried to orient herself, but there was no light.

Come on, get a hold of yourself, fat girl, she thought. When she thought it, those attempted words of self-comfort sounded like they were spoken by the same voice as the other voice. Whose voice was that? Who was there?

No-one was there. She could tell she was alone in this place. She was underwater. There was no way to take a deep breath, her only usual way of self-soothing. She could pretend to breathe. Maybe it would kick-start her real breath. She imagined she took a deep breath of air and something, not air but still something filled her lungs and her body and she was temporarily refreshed. That something also carried with it a kind of luminescence, though she wasn't seeing it with her eyes. It was light that was inwardly felt, rather than seen.

She followed the light and could feel it spread around her entire body. She could also tell something was darkening her throat and something was also dark at her right wrist. The light, instantly obeying her unarticulated wish, pushed itself into the darkness in those two spots and dissolved it.

The world rushed back into Alice's lungs and into her eyes. She gasped and stared at the person looking down at her.

"You're alive!! Alice, you're alive!"

Alice breathed and breathed and breathed. It was delicious and she was drawing it in and out furiously, feasting on it.

She looked at the person who had spoken.

"Kirsty?"

"Alice, how did you find me? I heard this sound and saw you lying there. You weren't breathing. Did you fall from an airplane?"

"Kirsty, is that you?"

Alice still felt disoriented but was starting to piece it together. She slowly sat up, being very careful with her right hand. It felt injured, but like an old injury. She flexed her fingers and they all worked okay. She placed her hand on her throat. Again, there had been some kind of injury there; she was unsure what kind. It was sore but it was not a big problem anymore.

She stood up with Kirsty's help, started wiping the mud and moss and grass from her face, and looked around.

As expected, there was a muddy yoga mat wadded up ten feet toward the tree line. She quickly looked away as she didn't want to draw Kirsty's attention to it.

"Never mind, Kirsty. I'm here now. Are you okay?"

"Well, yeah, but some Indian man left me stranded here. Where the hell are your shoes?"

"He's gone? Are you sure?"

"Yeah, he's totally gone. He flew away yesterday."

"Okay."

Alice took out her phone and was not surprised to see there

was no signal here.

"Kirsty, did he leave you any food? I'm starved."

"Yeah, he left me all this freeze-dried stuff, enough for about a week. He said Babaji or Bhakti would come and get me then."

Alice looked around at the little camp site. There was a very small tent and a stove. It was set up right next to the brook. She glanced at the tree in the middle of the clearing. The orange windsock was not there. He must have taken it with him. Alice began to relax.

"Okay, let's go have some lunch. Do you mind if I join you for lunch?"

"I just had breakfast! It's, like, nine in the morning, judging by the sun. But how did you find me here? Why are you on the ground? Did you fall out of a freaking airplane or something? Why are you not wearing any shoes?"

"Kirsty, I would be dead if I fell out of an airplane. I hiked in and I was so excited I found you that I tripped and face-planted on the ground. What else did the man who brought you here say?"

"He assured me that no-one but Babaji and Bhakti knew where I was and that this spot was a forty-five-mile hike through wilderness to anywhere. He said there wasn't even a trail and the only way in and out was his plane."

Alice checked her phone. Because she had already downloaded the area maps on her phone, the blue blip of her GPS showed her exactly where in the Knifespur they were.

"More like thirty miles," Alice said, "and there are some trails. But anyway, why did he leave you here?" Alice asked as they walked toward Kirsty's campsite.

"He said Babaji perceived that I was some kind of incarnation. Like I was a saint in some previous life. But that I didn't know it and I just needed a week of complete solitude and meditation and I would realize who I really am."

"Just a week, huh?"

"Seem's stupid now, doesn't it."

"How did he talk you into getting into his plane?"

"Alice, that is the weird part. I just don't remember."

"What is your last memory before the plane?"

"I just remember leaving home on my bike. That's it. The man said the foggy memory was part of the process. He said it was necessary so that I could begin to realize who I really am. He said I had to cut off all ties to my current life. He also told me my Mom and Dad are in full support of Babaji's plan for me."

Kirsty's camp had a gas stove with spare bottles, stacks of food and a pot full of water.

"Kirsty, you know you should string that food up somewhere so that a bear doesn't get it. Or raccoons."

"I don't have any rope. So how did you get here, Alice? How did you know where to find me?"

"Well, this guy that took you here, the guy with the plane...I didn't know he had a plane actually." Alice paused, tightening her face, aware that what she was going to say was not going to be well received. "Kirsty, I think this same guy tried to kidnap me the day before. I kind of interrogated him and found out that he was planning to bring me here. He failed and I guess he got you instead."

"Are you for real?" Kirsty accused, and looked down.

Only then did Alice realize Kirsty still wanted to believe this was all a benign plan for her to get enlightened.

"Let me get this straight," Kirsty said slowly, still looking down. "You were almost kidnapped and didn't tell anyone?"

Alice didn't really know what to say.

"How did you get here?" Kirsty continued, still not looking at Alice.

Alice was trapped. She liked Kirsty and needed her to believe what she was saying, but she didn't want to open up to her. She didn't trust her like she trusted Madison.

"Yes, for real. I'm telling you the truth, Kirsty. I have no reason to lie to you. That's what they do, not me." With a pang of regret, Alice paused and realized she would have to lie to Kirsty.

"I cycled some of the way," Alice said, "and hiked the rest."

"Oh. That was some trip," Kirsty said, still looking down, but now looking at the ground near Alice, rather than at her own feet. "Especially with no shoes."

"My shoes are still clipped to the pedals," Alice said, feeling a bit angry now. "I didn't want to ruin them by hiking on them. Hey, Kirsty, your parents are pretty worried about you."

Kirsty looked up. Alice couldn't read her expression.

"Are we really thirty miles in?" Kirsty asked.

"Yes, we are." Alice considered what she could tell Kirsty and decided she should be as open as possible about her situation. "Look, Kirsty. I want to get back right away and tell everyone where you are and that you're okay."

Kirsty stared at Alice with a look that slightly resembled the one Kirsty's mother wore the other day: a mixture of emptiness and righteous anger. It really frightened Alice. The young girl beneath the righteous mask reappeared and began to cry.

Then Alice really didn't know what to do. Raw instinct had shown Alice what to do when her Mom had fallen apart earlier, but this was very different. Alice knew a big hug was probably in order but she couldn't be sure. She thought she had waited too long and a hug would be awkward.

Kirsty just stood there, eyes closed, tears coming down.

Alice decided to just try to keep talking.

"Kirsty, um, I kind of understand how you feel."

Kirsty looked up and her eyebrows took on an angry shape.

"No, no, no," Alice countered, "I mean he didn't lie to me and say stuff about how I am going to get enlightened. He didn't manage to kidnap me at all. Okay, I know our situations probably feel different. But hey, look, Kirsty, everything is okay now. It really sucks what they did, but now you're going to be okay."

"Why should I believe you?" Kirsty said, wiping her eyes. "Why should I trust you?"

Alice didn't reply to that because she didn't really know the answer.

"My bike is stashed a short way from here and I can't carry you on it. But my phone has a GPS and I promise I'll send help to this spot. Everyone is completely freaked out right now and I'm sure they'll be here to get you this afternoon in twenty police helicopters with the whole National Guard. Okay? I promise."

Kirsty had lit the stove and was staring at Alice as though trying to decide whether to trust her or not.

Alice knew it wouldn't be right to manipulate Kirsty but she also knew she couldn't just say she flew here. She was going to have trouble taking off again, so she was going to have to wander through the woods and hunt for a source of prana welling up into the air, like out of the lightning tree and above Mr. Rao's chili garden. She didn't know how long it would take to find something.

"I'll need to give the police some information about this Indian guy," Alice said, stalling. "Can you help me with some more details? Like what time he left, what kind of plane he had: anything? It may be important."

"I have no idea." Kirsty matched Alice's angry tone. "I know nothing about planes. It was tiny though. Yellow, I think. It said 'gull', or something like it, on the paint. There were two seats in the front, side by side. I only vaguely remember arriving but I remember him leaving. I remember it felt like it was afternoon when he left."

Kirsty appeared to be warming up to her story. Alice realized this was her opportunity to get her talking.

"What else can you remember about the plane?"

"The plane had three wheels underneath. I remember the wings of the plane were over the passenger part. The doors opened upward and to the sides, like a sports car, and were mostly glass. The bottom of the door had the word 'Odyssey' on it, now that I think about it. The propeller was behind us, not in front like on a normal plane. After we arrived and I felt clearer in my head, I saw he had plugged these two huge batteries into a portable generator and seemed to be charging them. The generator, along with all the camping stuff, was already here. He must have brought it here before. While the plane batteries were charging, he just sat there meditating. For, like, four hours. It was so awkward. I didn't know what to do. I didn't want to knock him out with a rock because I didn't know how to fly the plane, or even where I would fly it if I could. I didn't know if he was friend or foe. So I just walked around for a while. He finally stood up and told me all that stuff about Babaji thinking me an incarnation of a saint."

Alice looked around.

"What direction did he fly?"

Kirsty pointed to a long stretch of meadow opposite to where Alice had landed. "He taxied his plane over there, took off and headed that way. I guess that's north."

Alice looked to where she was pointing and thought about Rajendra's plane.

"What time yesterday did he leave?"

"I don't have a phone or a watch but it was sometime in the afternoon. The sun was about there," she said, pointing at a spot above the tree line to the west.

Alice thought about flying and tried to put herself in his position. Judging from her brief experience, she imagined he couldn't fly at night. Recalling the huge gust of wind that almost took her out of the sky a short while ago, she certainly wouldn't want to fly at night. She could fly right into a tree or a power line. If he was the same, at best he had flown another leg of his journey and settled in for the night, then started flying again this morning. She might be able to catch up to him—if she could find him.

She thought about Kirsty's parents, scared to death their daughter was dead. She thought about her own parents, who would be worried about her too. Hopefully Madison would have told them something, but that would've put Madison in a difficult position too, she thought.

Should Alice go north or south, she wondered? North to

hunt a guy in a little electric plane who could be anywhere. Just a few moments ago she didn't even know electric planes existed. What would she do if she found him? Or should she fly south, back home, where she would have a lot of explaining to do. If she went home, at least she could get Kirsty some help and start the process of finding out who was responsible.

Then she had another thought. What if they all thought she was involved? She knew the tall cop lady was already suspicious of her. What would they think if she came back and said I happen to know exactly where Kirsty is, and gave them the exact GPS coordinates? Sure, Kirsty would tell them she had been taken here by an Indian man with a plane, but Alice would have to explain how she found Kirsty and how she reached this spot without her own plane.

Alice sighed. "Kirsty, I may have to take a rain check on that lunch. I'm worried about your parents. I think I better tell them you're okay and send someone back here to get you."

Kirsty looked at Alice and shrugged. She seemed confused. Alice really didn't want to look into her head. She never had much success reading her peers and now she was too afraid of what she would find in Kirsty's mind anyway.

She went to the brook and filled her water pouch. Kirsty followed her.

"Please, Kirsty, stay here and don't try to hike out. I promise to send help and they will be here this afternoon or tonight, or tomorrow at the latest. Okay, Kirsty?"

"I don't know. Why don't we just ride double on your bike?"

Alice thought about whether she may be able to fly with Kirsty on her back. If she found a huge prana source somewhere, or a cliff to jump off, would she be able to carry a person on her back and still fly? No way, she thought. She didn't know that much about the physics of what she was doing up in the air, but she knew by feel that she could not do it and carry anything heavy on her back. Besides, she had enough trouble landing as it is.

In any event, she really didn't know what would happen if

Kirsty knew she could fly. Not even Madison believed her.

"I know this area pretty well," Alice said, "and the trail I took on the bike is way too rough for two people. We would definitely end up both walking and it would take us at least two days to hike out. If I go by myself, I can get out this afternoon, before dark, and get you help straight away."

"What if that guy comes back in his plane?"

Alice shook her head. "He's not coming back. He took his windsock with him. I think he would need that windsock to land here. It's pretty windy."

Kirsty looked at Alice. "Alice, I'm putting a lot of trust in you, you know. I could die out here if you are lying."

"Why would I be lying to you?"

"It's just that...I haven't known you that long."

"Well, look at it this way. If I'm lying, the Indian pilot guy must have been the one telling the truth and Babaji will come out here and rescue you himself in six days. You'll have morphed into a saint, too, which will be cool."

"What if you are both lying?"

"Oh, give it a rest, Kirsty. What reason could I possibly have to lie to you?"

"What possible reason is there for me to have been kidnapped by an Indian guy?"

"That is a good question."

"How did you get him to tell you where this place is?"

"I told you, I interrogated him."

"How did you interrogate him?"

"Like this," Alice said, against her better judgement, and took a deep breath to lock in to Kirsty.

Kirsty's mind was, as expected, a shock for Alice. It was cacophonous, messy, full of fighting voices, fears and all the rest. Alice did not feel disgusted or terrified because she recognized something in Kirsty's mess. It was somehow familiar. In fact, it was more familiar than she wanted to admit. Like Alice, Kirsty felt anger about her mom's connection to Babaji, guilt about that anger and anger about that guilt. Deeper than that were memories of the ashram in India when she was a very young girl. Those memories had the same mix of exhilaration at being in such an exotic place and intense fears of the unknown. She still had a fear of losing her parents to an unfamiliar guru whom her mother worshipped like a God.

Where was Kirsty's father during all this, Alice wondered? She probed and found him, a normal-looking guy who was sick to death of her mom's interest in yoga, and in Babaji, but who stuck with her anyway.

Alice needed a detail, a fact that would convince Kirsty she had been prowling around in her head, and there it was.

She broke off the connection.

As Kirsty came back to normal, she appeared to still be waiting for an answer to her question, as if no time had elapsed.

"Kirsty," Alice started, "I get these feelings about what people are thinking. It's a kind of gift." Alice emphasized the word gift because she had seen that it was a word Kirsty's dad used when speaking about things he felt were Christian miracles he had personally experienced. "A gift, like the communication your dad had with your grandpa just before your grandpa died."

Kirsty's eyes widened. "How do you know anything about my grandpa?"

"I just explained how I know these kinds of things. That's also how I knew you were here."

Kirsty was struggling and she closed her eyes and appeared to accept what Alice had told her. Alice knew she was also remembering her grandpa as he lay dying and those miraculous moments that her dad had spent with him, speaking to him with no words, after he had lost the ability to speak.

"Okay. I believe you. But don't do that again, okay?"

"Sorry. I won't."

"It's freaky."

"Sorry."

"What other freaky things can you do?"

"You don't want to know."

"Probably not," Kirsty said. "Just hurry back, Alice, and tell Mom and Dad to come get me. When I thought they knew I was here meditating and it was all a plan for me to become special, I was only angry. All that reincarnation stuff is completely stupid. My friend Shivapuri would have even thought it was stupid. But at least I figured they would come get me as planned and I could scream and yell at them for being idiots. But now I'm scared."

"I don't blame you. I'm scared too. But I'm not scared of this Indian guy anymore. He has done his job and he's gone now. The scary people are the men who hired him, whoever they are. Anyway, all we can do now is get you out of here and help the police catch whoever was responsible."

"What, you don't think it was Babaji and Bhakti who hired him?"

"Probably. But I'm not sure."

Alice sat with Kirsty on the ground in silence for a minute. She had a feeling Kirsty needed just a little more company before Alice left. Finally, she felt like she couldn't wait any longer.

"Kirsty, I gotta go. I'm really sorry. But like I said, I totally promise, promise, promise to get you help straight away."

Kirsty looked at her with something like sympathy but Alice wasn't sure about that.

Alice took out her phone, dropped a pin on the map at their current location, took a screen shot, zoomed out, took another screen shot. Then she saw that her phone was down to ten percent battery. She risked one more shot, holding the phone up to photograph Kirsty standing there in front of her tent. It didn't exactly prove she was here in the Knifespur instead of in any other forest clearing, but it was something. She put her phone back in her pocket and tried to forget about how little battery was left.

"Okay. See you soon," Kirsty said.

"Yep. Try to hang up that food too. Just in case. Use that yoga bag I brought. I don't need it anymore."

"What yoga bag?"

"I left it in the dirt over there," Alice got up. She wanted to get out before having to bend any more truths. "I'll run get it for you."

"No, I'll walk over with you."

They walked over to the spot and Alice quickly picked up the mat and the bag and gave them to Kirsty.

"Okay, I'm off. See ya."

"Alice, why did you..."

Alice had already jogged off, entering the forest not looking back.

She moved as quickly as she could through the trees. It was impossible to run all out in this dense forest, especially wearing only socks that were, by now, completely drenched and muddy. Her feet were very sore and she kept landing on sharp things which had begun to create bruises and cuts on the soles of her feet. She could still jog if she focused on the spaces between trees, as she had done when she was trying to escape from Rajendra.

She tried to remember if she had seen any cliffs when she flew in earlier. It seemed like hours had passed, but really it was only about a half hour ago when she had crash-landed in Kirsty's clearing. She recalled seeing some kind of change in the topography just west of here, so she started veering to her right.

There was prana everywhere but nothing dense enough for her to dive into and get some lift to fly out of the trees. As she dodged around and over obstacles at her feet, she kept her eyes open for any change in the flow of prana at ground level. She had to jog like that for a half an hour and by then she was feeling exhausted again.

Finally she thought she had found what she was looking for. The terrain had changed and slowed her down. The pine needles and rocks had given way to moss. She felt slightly sad to be stomping all over it, aware that moss like this was probably old and was being damaged by her footfalls, but she could see it was emitting the same upwelling of prana as Mr. Rao's chili garden.

She kept moving forward, looking for the densest currents along the surface.

Up ahead, she saw a fallen tree, rotten, and draped densely with hanging vines. It was also glowing with prana. As usual, she threw caution to the wind and lifted her speed. If this didn't work, the worst that could happen was that she would face-plant onto mossy ground again, she speculated. She was nearly sprinting when she hit the end of the tree that was closest to the ground and managed a full sprint by the time she had run along the trunk to the highest part.

She dove upward, arms raised, chin tucked, abdomen pulled in and dolphin-kicked with as much strength as she could. She was airborne but capable only of horizontal movement. She desperately dodged as many trees and their branches as she could, scraping herself along many of them but avoiding any head-on collisions. In the back of her mind she knew this was fantastic fun and that she would try to remember it later in all of its adrenaline-filled detail, but the focus of her concentration was avoiding trees. If she hit one at speed, it was lights out: maybe worse. She needed to speed up and get above the forest.

She relaxed and found small ways to correct her stroke. Her mad dash between trees became more graceful and faster. She was unable to move her arms down from above her head and was only using the power of her legs and core muscles. It seemed to be working. A little at a time, she was working her way higher toward the canopy of pine. She scared some small wrens who were flitting around in the finer branches at the treetops and reveled in the idea that even if she hit a tree now, the branches were all small enough that a strike wouldn't kill her.

With one last effort she squeezed up above the highest trees and was skimming the forest.

She couldn't help but scream in joy and bliss, but immediately regretted it because she may have still been within earshot of Kirsty. She gained altitude and flew as quickly as she could, even faster than she had flown on the way out to Kirsty.

When she was within ten minutes of her house, she considered her landing problem again. She couldn't risk flying over town and landing in the pool at this time of day.

Her phone was ringing in her pocket and she knew she definitely couldn't look at it, but thought she could answer it and find the speaker phone button by memory.

Assuming it would be Madison, she shouted, "I found her! I'm on the way home!"

"What? Alice? I can't hear you very well. Did you say you found something?" a male voice sounded through the wind.

She placed the phone closer to her mouth and asked, "Who is calling, please?"

"Why, this is Srikrishna Rao, at your service."

"Mr. Rao! Where are you?"

"I'm very sorry, Alice, but I can't hear you very well at all."

"Where! Are! You!"

"Oh, I am at home. Where else should I be? Am I late?"

"Mr. Rao, can you get in your bus and start driving down your road?"

"What?"

"Drive! Bus!"

"Oh, yes indeed. Drive: but where? Do you need a lift?"

"Yes! Pick me up! Hurry!"

"Okay, okay. Yes, I will be there in ten minutes, just as soon as I can warm up the motor."

Alice shoved the phone back in her pocket as gracefully as she could and managed not to fall from the sky.

She veered to the right, aiming to fly down Mr. Rao's valley. She hoped her sense of direction wouldn't fail her. It hadn't so far but everything looked different from up here.

After ten minutes, she saw Mr. Rao's cliffs and his road snaking down the valley, but his VW bus was not on it.

She made a huge wide arc, circling like a jet waiting for landing clearance at an airport. Finally she heard his bus start up. She made one last arc in the sky and aimed for his road, hoping to time it just right.

She decreased her altitude, slowing herself as she had the previous two times, and finally saw his bus bump its way down his two-track driveway and turn onto the road. She was going too fast and was going to overshoot.

Mr. Rao's bus sped up abruptly, as though he had just found the accelerator. Alice thought she might just make it. She slowed herself more and was even able to kick a few times to speed up to match the bus speed. She saw smoke and smelled burning fuel.

Oh, Mr. Rao, she wondered, why now?

She had no choice but to land and she managed to bounce herself off his roof, landing again and sliding forward so her face was just over the windscreen. She looked down at Mr. Rao and his massive mustache. His face was a picture of bewilderment.

"Fire! Your bus is on fire!" she shouted.

Mr. Rao's eyes opened wider and he sniffed the air and slammed on the brakes. Alice plummeted forward off the bus and onto the dirt.

She closed her eyes, waiting to be run over by a VW bus. The impact didn't come. She had landed on her already bruised back, which knocked all the wind out of her, and she was struggling for air. She opened her eyes, trying to coax air into her lungs, which was easier than after the last landing in Kirsty's meadow, but still very difficult.

Mr. Rao looked at her in horror. Through her pain and distress, she smiled at him and waved. It was enough to jolt him back into action. He killed the engine, grabbed a heavy glove and a fire extinguisher from the floor of the cab and ran around back. Alice could hear him spraying the fire extinguisher foam into the engine bay.

While he was putting out his bus fire, Alice closed her eyes and attempted to breathe in the light that had helped her injuries earlier. It came instantly this time and she quickly used it to push some darkness away from some ribs in her back. This enabled her to inhale some actual air. She opened her eyes again.

When Mr. Rao returned, running, he looked sadder and more haggard. Alice had managed to roll over and sit up, breathing deeply.

"Oh, my goodness. How did you get on top of my bus? Are you okay, Alice?"

"Never better, Mr. Rao. Is the bus okay?"

"There was a fire. My old fuel line must have finally ruptured but I think the flames have not damaged everything so terribly. Nothing I can't fix. Just some new wiring, a regulator, the engine seal——"

"Mr. Rao, I don't really know what you're talking about."

"I'm just saying it couldn't be helped. Now that I have picked you up as requested," he continued, "walk with me back to the cabin and we should have some chai."

"Mr. Rao, I'm sorry but I don't have time for chai right now."

She took her phone out and saw a dozen missed calls from Madison from the last thirty minutes. The last one was at 10:30 a.m. She touched it and put the phone to her ear.

"Oh, you finally decided to call me back," Madison said with mock annoyance.

Alice smiled, hoping she had not lost her friendship by flying away.

"Sorry, I had to fly."

"Yes, you cycled off and left me standing there like an idiot."

"I found Kirsty. She's okay."

"Wow. I can't believe it. You just went and found her."

Alice could sense something strange in Madison's voice but she couldn't place it. It wasn't fear.

"Madison, I'm going to need to ask you a big favor."

"What?"

"I'm really sorry to ask, but it's the only solution I could think of."

"What?"

"Can I text you the info about how to find Kirsty and you get it to the policewoman who was at our house earlier?"

"Why?"

"Because I want to go find the guy who kidnapped Kirsty and left her in the middle of the Knifespur. I don't have time to sit down and explain everything to the police or I won't be able to catch up with him."

Alice paused, waiting for her to respond, but she didn't. Alice could smell burnt plastic and paint, and there was a ticking noise coming from somewhere.

"Madison?"

"Alice, it's a little bit complicated."

"What is?"

"Well, I'm here right now with the police and you've been on speakerphone."

So that was what was different about Madison's voice. Then she heard the voice of the stocky policewoman named Nancy who had been to her house.

"Alice, we don't think you had anything to do with this but actually, the situation has changed a little bit. We need you to tell us exactly where you are."

"Hi. Look, I will be happy to chat with you guys but first, please go get Kirsty. You'll need a helicopter. She's in the middle of the Knifespur Wilderness. I'll text Madison the maps. I was just there and she's okay. Please tell her parents."

"We wouldn't be able to send a helicopter without some way to verify your story. You haven't been honest with us. You told me only four hours ago you had no idea where Kirsty was or what had happened and now you know exactly where she is and who was involved. Your parents are worried sick about you. You need to tell me right now exactly where you are."

"I'm really sorry but you'll just have to trust me. Kirsty herself will explain everything. My phone is almost dead and I gotta text you the maps and make one more call. Please let my mom and dad know I'm okay. Bye."

Alice hung up, her heart pounding. She quickly texted Madison the screen shots she had taken of the maps where Kirsty was and also the photo she had taken of Kirsty standing there in front of her campsite. Her phone now showed one percent battery.

Madison was calling her back but she rejected the call immediately. She saw that the battery was gone and her phone was a brick.

Just as well, she thought. She didn't want to listen to anyone telling her what to do.

She had no desire to go home right now and get more advice from her dad about what to do and what not to do. The police would undoubtedly be at her house so she couldn't go home anyway—yet.

She looked at Mr. Rao standing there patiently.

"Mr. Rao, can I borrow your phone?"

CHAPTER 13

As Alice sat in the back of the taxi, she felt nervous and caught herself rhythmically bouncing her heels on the floor. She hated when her mom did that.

She thought about Mr. Rao and his burnt-out VW bus. He was yet another enigma in her surreal new life. She was grateful to him for a couple of things, most recently because he was prepared to leave his house at a moment's notice, no questions asked, and pick her up. She was sorry it resulted in his bus being destroyed. He seemed trustworthy but was he really trustworthy? She still hadn't managed to get a straight story out of him about why he was here in Hardrock and he hadn't divulged what he knew about Thomas' death. Perhaps there were cultural differences involved. Maybe he was embarrassed or it just wasn't appropriate for him to tell her this stuff. Overall, he seemed more trustworthy than a growing list of other adults, that was for sure.

Alice needed information about little planes. She could go online at the library but that might not be enough. She needed an advisor who knew something about planes. She needed Brian's help.

Her taxi arrived at the University gate nearest the library. She hardly noticed that people were staring strangely at her as she rushed through campus. For the second time that day, she lowered her coffee standards dramatically and bought a quick takeaway coffee from the student coffee kiosk before rushing up the stone steps and through the main library doors.

She stormed straight into Brian's office.

"Hi, Brian." Alice plopped down in a chair next to him. "Thanks for betraying me."

Brian looked her up and down with his mouth open. This was unusual because he always had some sly, witty comment.

"What, cat got your tongue, Brian? What does that expression even mean, by the way?"

"Girl, you're covered in mud."

Alice looked down at herself and saw she was not only covered in dried mud but also had torn her cycling jacket in the elbows and both cycling pant legs at the knees. Her face probably looked just as bad.

She had to remember to start looking in mirrors before she went places.

"Oh, I had a wipe-out on my bike. Sorry."

She grabbed a handful of Brian's tissues and dipped them in a glass of water on Brian's desk and tried to clean up her face a little.

"So," she continued, "what's your excuse? I thought you were cool. Why have you been spying on me?"

"Ah," he said, still gawking and fidgeting.

Alice thought Brian still looked more unnerved than she expected him to be. He was usually jolly and relaxed. He would have thrown a few decent insults into the conversation by now as well.

"I'm sorry," he finally said.

"For what?"

"For spying on you, of course. But you do realize it was the only way they would let you skip school and——"

"Yeah, yeah, yeah, I know all that."

"I'm an adult, you know, and you're a kid."

Alice took a deep breath and pulled herself together.
"Okay. Look, Brian," she said, tossing her coffee cup toward his trash can, but missing, "I'd like to make a request. From a wronged kid to the adult who wronged her. From now on, whenever you have the urge to call my dad or anyone to report about me, you come find me or call me and we have a chat beforehand. Okay?"

"Sure," he said, with a hint of smile. "If he calls me?"

"You say you'll call him back and you go find me or call me. Or that you're on fire. By the way, what kind of 'condition' am I supposed to have?"

"They don't know. But if you ask me, the word 'condition' isn't broad enough to cover how messed up you are." He held his hand out toward her and added, "Just look at you."

"Brian, I didn't come over here to chat with you about Dad. I know he's looking for me but I need to do something before I get in touch with him. It's really important to me. I need your help."

He looked skeptical, so she added, "Please."

"What?"

"Just one thing."

"Only one?"

"Only one. I need you to help me do some research about really small airplanes. And I need your phone charger."

"I knew there would be more than one."

"Okay, let's get started."

"I agree to your demands," he said as he handed Alice his phone charger. "But I have one myself," he continued. "A question, actually."

"Nope," Alice replied, plugging her phone in to Brian's charger.

"Nope, what?"

"No way. I don't know why everyone won't just leave me alone. You guys don't want to understand me, yet you want to control me and spy on me. I'm fed up. But for the moment, I'm asking for a little help, no questions asked. Unless that's too hard for you in your esteemed role as an adult."

"No, it's okay. I'm here for you." He cast his eyes down melodramatically.

Alice wasn't sure if he was being serious or not, but it was the best she could do for now.

They sat down together at Brian's computer and Alice explained she needed to know everything there was to know about a yellow, two-seater, battery-operated plane that may be badged Gull and/or Odyssey.

It was easy to find out that the E-gull was a leading make of electrically-powered ultralights and the Odyssey was their two-seater version.

"These are really interesting planes. You see," Brian said, apparently speaking from experience, "in the US, you don't need any kind of certification or license to fly a single-seater ultralight. Anyone is legally allowed to do it. The situation is different with a two-seater."

"How far can they be flown on a single charge?"

Brian looked but couldn't find anything at first.

"Here," Brian said, pointing at the screen. "Here's what you want." He was pointing at the title of an article on the E-gull in a trade magazine.

"How am I supposed to read that? It's restricted to subscribers only."

Brian looked at Alice with pity and said, "I am so disappointed. What do you do here in my library anyway? All these years? Do you just come for the library wifi?"

"You mean the library subscribes to that magazine?"

Brian flicked over to the library website, plugged in the info and wrote down a call number for Alice. He didn't say anything else, just handed it to her. Alice snatched it and strode off, feeling slightly violent toward Brian and frustrated that time was slipping away.

She ran straight to the correct section, pulled down the trade magazine and skimmed the article quickly. According to the article, everyone in the ultralight world was very excited about this new plane. The E-gull can fly for forty to fifty miles on a charge, depending on the conditions and the pilot. The two batteries require at least four hours of charge time. The fuel version of the same plane has a range of over 160 miles on five gallons.

Alice thought about it. Why would Rajendra use the electric rather than the fuel version?

She read on and saw the main reason electric ultralights were getting more popular was because they are so quiet. According to the E-gull designer, they are as close as you can get to the feeling of flying experienced in one's childhood dreams.

Well, that's something Alice had experience with.

It's not as quiet as you think, dude, she thought, remembering the wind blowing loudly through her ears during her maiden flight this morning.

That was obviously the answer. Rajendra needed a quiet plane so that he could kidnap a girl and fly off without anyone hearing him.

She ran back to Brian's office clutching the trade magazine.

"So you do know how to find a book in a library," he said smugly. "My happy feelings toward you have been restored."

"That's great for you, cowboy. I'm sure you feel very superior right now."

Alice noticed her phone had come back to life and there were a dozen missed calls from Madison and from her dad. She looked at Brian and wondered if he had already breached their agreement and called Dad while she was getting the magazine. She picked up her phone and began scrolling through the maps she had taken screen shots of.

"You better not have just rung my dad."

He shrugged his shoulders as if to say, I'm not allowed, right?

Alice looked back down at her maps. It was 11:45 a.m. now. She calculated that if Rajendra left Kirsty's clearing in the

Knifespur at two yesterday afternoon, he would have made it to just north of the wilderness area by nightfall, charged overnight and flown two more legs today.

"Brian, I need you to print out a map for me. It's got to cover about 200 miles north, east and west of the north edge of the Knifespur Wilderness."

"That's in Wyoming," he said, already calling up the maps on his computer. "Wait." He did a double take. "You mean, this little research project isn't for school."

"No, it isn't. Hurry, please."

Alice grabbed the map off the printer and put it on Brian's desk.

"Give me some of your dental floss and a thumbtack."

"How would you know I have dental floss in my office?"

"Just look at yourself," she said. "You're like a dentist ad."

"Okay, okay. Here."

She checked the map scale and measured out a piece of dental floss that represented ninety miles, thumbtacked it to a spot forty-five miles due north of Kirsty's clearing, and drew a big semicircle on the map with a red pen. Rajendra would probably be on the ground somewhere on this circle, charging his batteries.

She measured out another piece of floss representing 135 miles and drew another circle with the center in Kirsty's clearing, representing three flight legs. If he left at first light this morning, or something like 5:00 a.m., it would mean he would be landing on that 135 mile circle between 3:00 and 4:00 p.m. Or maybe if he got a tailwind, or didn't wait for a full charge, he could be there earlier, say 2:00 p.m. at the earliest.

Alice looked at Brian, who had been staring at her circles and obviously dying to ask questions but not daring to open his mouth. Enjoying her power over him, she looked back down at her map and tried to remember Rajendra's personality and imagine his plan. He was here for a job, which meant he was making money. He would be trying to minimize expenditure too.

"Brian, can someone rent these nice, new electric two-seater ultralights or do you have to buy them?"

"No, renting would be unlikely. The two-seaters would be used only by flight schools."

"So he bought it. He'll need to re-sell it. So where would you go to sell an ultralight?"

"I have no idea. eBay?"

"How about you try to get an idea. Just Google E-gull Odyssey for sale, or whatever."

Alice searched for Wyoming airports and saw there were three regional airports within the second circle on her map. A little bit more searching showed her that all three airports connected only to Denver. The latest flight to Denver was from Laramie at 3:45 p.m.

It was easy to find that the cheapest and fastest flight leaving Denver for India today was a 5:30 p.m. departure on United, with one stop in Frankfurt. It was actually the only remaining flight out of Denver that connected well to India in the afternoons.

"Here," Brian said, pointing at his screen. "I can't find any recent notices for an E-gull for sale. This is the only reference to an E-gull Odyssey on the internet that is not an advertisement. It may be useful for your weird little research."

He was pointing at a link on a website devoted to non-commercial freight. It was a conversation between someone who wanted an E-gull Odyssey shipped privately from the manufacturer in California to a barn in Laramie two weeks ago and picked up again and returned to another address back in California this afternoon.

Most of the online conversation between this private truck driver and his customer involved questions and answers about the plane dimensions, could it be shipped with the wings off, etc. The answers were from someone called John, and he seemed extremely knowledgeable about the plane, but Alice noticed that some of his sentences contained funny phrases sounding like stuff Mr. Rao would say. John must be Rajendra, she thought.

Perhaps Rajendra would never have dreamed he would be

discovered like this. He would be sitting next to his plane right now, chilling out, his generator humming, thinking about what movies United Airlines would have on his international flight, imagining that nobody would ever know he had been in this stupid country. Nobody knew his name, he left no clues and he would be in India before anyone even found that girl in the woods.

I'm coming for you, Rajendra, she thought.

Alice plugged in the address in Laramie and her phone showed her that it was 150 miles via roads. Probably more like 130 as the crow flies, she guessed. If she really was capable of sixty miles per hour, she could fly that distance in a couple of hours.

She looked back at her map and colored in a section of the 135 mile circle that was closest to the barn in Laramie. Then she looked at her watch. It was 11:50 a.m. She would have to get flying. If all her assumptions and deductions were correct, she needed to move fast to beat him to the barn before he arrived at two this afternoon.

"Thanks, Brian. Now one last question. What is the secret to landing a hang glider well?"

"Alice, I don't even want to know why you are asking that question, nor why you are researching ultralights. You cannot fly either one without serious training. Neither of them are like mountain bikes. Ultralights are not like hang gliders."

"You haven't really earned back the right to ask me any questions, but I will tell you it's not my ultralight and I'm not interested in flying it, or doing any hang gliding. I have another reason for asking. I just want you to tell me how you land a hang glider without wiping out?"

Brian looked at her for a long moment and finally acquiesced.

"Well, if you promise you are not going to do something crazy. The secret is to come in faster than trim, round into ground effect and stall the tips, not the nose."

"What the hell does that mean?"

"See? Why am I..." He froze at Alice's cold look. "Okay, okay.

Trim is the slowest speed you can fly without stalling and falling to the ground. Basically if you let go of all the controls and just let the glider coast along at its slowest speed, that's trim. Ground effect means that flying close to the ground gives you extra lift, like you're floating. Stalling means the wings are no longer providing lift. That is, you are falling toward the ground according to mother-gravity's wishes. If you stall the nose first, before the tips of your wings, you whack into the ground. If you stall the tips before the nose, you float down and can moonwalk run to a stop."

"So how do you stall the tips first?"

"You have to time the flare right."

"What's a flare? Something you wish you had?"

"It has nothing to do with my personality, thank you. Flaring an aircraft means to lift the nose at the last minute."

Alice thought about it and hoped some of that stuff might be applicable to her. There was only one way to find out.

"Brian, drive me home, okay?"

Brian finally appeared to have had enough of her demands.

"Alice, no, I can't just leave work, I'm not your personal driver and that's enough of this crap. I need you to tell me what is going on."

"Nope," she said, unplugging her phone. She grabbed the map print and yanked him out of his chair.

CHAPTER 14

Alice had Brian drive her to Mr. Rao's house in order to avoid her dad and any police. It was a good thing she had, because two police cars had passed them at high speed on the highway out of town and she suspected they would be headed either to her house or to Kirsty's.

Mr. Rao had organized a tow and been busy working on his VW when they arrived. He had come out of the barn to greet Brian and Alice with his usual overabundant warmth.

Before Brian left to head back to the library, he asked her permission to call her dad. She granted it, as it didn't matter anymore. She would be long gone before Dad would have time to drive over from her house to Mr. Rao's.

This gave her a good time frame to work from. It would take Dad ten minutes to drive over, so she had ten minutes to eat and have a chai before flying away—plenty of time.

"Mr. Rao, have you got any leftover food?" she asked as he closed the door behind Brian.

"Of course I do. But you will not be eating it. I will wash my hands and prepare some beautiful fresh…"

Before Mr. Rao had finished his sentence, Alice had already

popped the lid off some metal containers from his fridge and was shoveling it in her mouth.

"I see," he said, crestfallen. "Well, perhaps I could make you some chai and chapattis?"

"Yes, please," Alice replied. "But chai first. Please make the quick version."

This at least defrosted Mr. Rao's expression and he began to bustle around the kitchen making chai.

"Now I have something very wise to tell you which I have been thinking about ever since you left me standing there at the spice shop yesterday."

"I'm sorry, Mr. Rao," Alice said. "I just didn't really feel like shopping."

"No trouble. The wise thing I wanted to say has nothing to do with shopping. I have forgotten some of it because of the mental disturbance caused by the unfortunate blowing up of my VW. Before that I had a speech ready that was fit for the finest Hollywood movie. But now that it comes time to tell you, I realize it also may not be so wise. I'm not certain anymore. But you will be the judge. Somehow I believe it may be useful to you in these turbulent days."

"Yes, yes Mr. Rao, please hurry. I have to go."

"Yes, very well. What I can remember is this: I believe it is okay for you to trust people."

Alice rolled her eyes and kept eating. In reality, she was only half listening.

Mr. Rao placed a stainless steel cup of chai in front of Alice and began to beat some dough that had been under a cloth in the cupboard.

"It's like my old car. I know it has many problems. Some of them are quite serious. Design flaws even. Why put a carburetor on top of an engine? Why design it that way? All it takes is one broken fuel line and you have a fire. But you see, I know these things, which is why I feel I can trust the bus. It means my relationship with the bus is close. If I had some modern car that can be diagnosed only by some computer, I would not feel close to it.

"Likewise, when we trust a man, trust does not mean you must do whatever he says. It also does not mean you must fool yourself into thinking he can do nothing wrong. Furthermore, it definitely does not mean believing every word he says. That is only blind faith. If you fool yourself into giving a man blind faith, it will corrupt him. This is harmful to you, harmful to him. In fact, true trust requires you to get close to that person. You should remain fully aware of the weaknesses you know about him, and those you do not know about him, but which you know may be present. He should know that you know. You must protect yourself from his real and suspected weaknesses always. But trusting means that while you are protecting yourself, you may still offer him your respect and allow him to offer you what he can give and open yourself up to receiving from him as much as possible. Trusting him becomes a matter of trusting that he has something to offer, not that he is perfect. This is very important. Do you think this is important?"

"Who do you think I should trust? You?"

"Heavens, no. I am a doddering old man. Oh....well, young lady, yes. I see what you mean. You got me there. You mean why should you listen to my wise speech? Yes, perhaps I do wish you to trust me. To be perfectly frank with you, I don't know if I have very much to offer you except this chapatti," he said, placing a folded piece of flat bread on Alice's stainless steel container that still contained a few bites of cold curry inside. He sat down and poured himself a chai.

"But I hope perhaps you might also accept this piece of advice, given to you in the best spirit of friendship."

"Thanks. But Mr. Rao, why do you think I need advice?"

"We all need advice. It is how we grow. We grow by getting insight into another person's point of view. What they see and hear, how they interpret it. It never ceases to amaze me how every single person in this world sees it in a different way. India has more than a billion people and each one sees things differently, even though they may think they see them the same as others who share their social status and mother tongue. They do not. I learned this. I know you can read other people's thoughts but I suspect that you do not trust them enough to allow their perspective to enrich yours."

"People scare the shit out of me."

"That is exactly it! Because you see, they don't have to. It's completely up to you. It is in your hands. And I sincerely hope the police car coming up my driveway is not going to ruin your day."

Alice snapped out of her eating frenzy. Following Mr. Rao's gaze out the kitchen window, she could see a blue and white car snaking its way through the trees toward his house.

"Bye," she said, dashing out the door, changing her mind and running back for the rest of her chapatti and one more gulp of chai. "Thanks for the advice."

After bursting out the door, she immediately turned left, away from Mr. Rao's driveway, hoping the police wouldn't have seen her yet.

She dashed from tree to tree in the forest to the side of his cabin, getting as far away as possible while eating the rest of her chapatti.

The police parked in front of Mr. Rao's cabin and he came out to greet them.

So far, so good, Alice thought. At least no-one was shouting at her through a megaphone, telling her to put her hands up, or whatever they say these days. Yet.

She now had two options. Wait it out in the woods or try to fly away. The only other way out was to walk by Mr. Rao's cabin to get to the road.

Hiding and waiting was not Alice's style, especially since she had no idea how long the police were going to stay and question Mr. Rao. She had a feeling they were going to be there for a while. Time was passing in favor of Rajendra.

As soon as she felt she was deep enough in the trees to run

normally, she started moving in a circular trajectory toward the chili garden below the cliff. Once she reached his garden, she would be in full view of the police, but she couldn't help that now. She hoped they wouldn't be looking. They may even be in the cabin by then having chai.

She relaxed enough to feel and hear the bass drum of her heartbeat. That was very close back there. She wondered why she felt frightened of the police.

The answer came immediately—she must be a suspect now. They thought she had something to do with Kirsty's kidnapping. Otherwise they wouldn't have chased her out here.

Well, they would learn soon enough what really happened, she hoped. As soon as they could pull their thumbs out and get a helicopter out to Kirsty. Perhaps they were flying out there now. Maybe they had even found her already.

She realized why the police were here. It must be because Brian called her dad. Which meant it was her dad who had sent the cops after her, rather than coming here himself. He was probably too busy at work to bother with her.

She stopped jogging and placed a steadying hand on a pine tree trunk. She felt deflated. Eyes closed, Alice listened to her breathing. There was nothing in her mind because it was temporarily out of order.

In the silence, she could hear Mr. Rao speaking to a woman. It could have been the same policewoman who had interviewed Alice at their house. Or maybe not—it was too far to tell. She also couldn't hear what they were saying. Mr. Rao's tone of voice was steady and polite.

She imagined he was telling them Alice had not been here. He was probably attempting to explain the presence of two cups of chai.

She should trust Mr. Rao, she thought, but she just couldn't. As she punched Madison's number, she realized Mr. Rao was probably onto something back there with his garbage about trust. It was too big of a leap to trust herself to the mercy of the police, or to anyone else.

As usual, Alice was on her own, she thought, except maybe for Madison.

"Alice, you know the police are here," Madison said in a whisper, in lieu of saying hello.

"Yeah, it's okay."

"In one second they're going to see me on the phone."

"Tell them it's Coach."

"It's my swimming coach," Madison shouted away from the phone.

"Thanks."

"Yes, I'll try to make it this afternoon," Madison said awkwardly into the phone.

"Madison, I just needed to find out if the police are rescuing Kirsty."

"No, I won't be late to the pool."

"Why not? Do they want her to die out there?"

"It's too hard to organize the trip to the swim meet on such short notice."

"What, no helicopters?"

"Right."

"So when?"

"This afternoon."

"Okay. I guess that will have to do. Don't worry about me. Feel free to tell the police the truth; that I'm going after Kirsty's kidnapper."

"How?"

"I think he is using an electric ultralight. I'm guessing he uses it because it's quiet, which is why nobody heard him fly away with her the other day. But it also means he needs to land and recharge his batteries every forty miles. I found something on the internet that shows he is delivering the plane to a barn in Laramie, Wyoming, this afternoon and I'm pretty sure he's going to try to be on a 3:30 p.m. flight from Laramie to Denver, and a 5:30 p.m. flight on United to Frankfurt. You can tell the police that they can find the address too by googling E-gull Odyssey. It's on some private, non-commercial shipping website called uship.com. I'm going to try to get there before he does. The police can come too. It will be fun. But they should monitor those two flights and, in case I don't catch up with him, they should make sure he doesn't leave the country."

"How should I prepare, Coach?"

"You should quit swimming like a damn muppet," Alice said in a deep voice.

"Sorry, say that again?"

"I'm just kidding," she said in her normal voice. "You'll make zones because you're an awesome swimmer. I better go. I'll call you later. Like I said, feel free to tell the police all that. I don't want you to get in trouble on my account."

"Okay, Coach."

As Alice hung up, the smile left her face when she saw the policewoman looking out at the woods, right in her direction. She wondered if she had been speaking too loudly.

Alice thought fast. She needed a diversion. She thought of Mr. Rao, quickly rang his phone and prayed he had it nearby.

"Yes, yes?" he said in a whisper.

"Mr. Rao," Alice said, also whispering in the hope the police hadn't seen her yet, "can you do something weird? To distract the police?"

"Oh, my goodness. I am not sure I know how. Oh, well, yes. They think religion is weird. Okay. Please wait a moment..."

After a pause, Alice heard Mr. Rao say something loud in Hindi and she saw the policewoman turn quickly back toward Mr. Rao and re-enter the cabin.

She hung up, stuffed her phone back in her pocket and broke out of the woods, sprinting for the chili garden, determined not to look back, no matter what.

She reached the garden and dove into the beautiful, flowing air above the chili plants, relishing the feeling of prana against her stomach, driving her arms and thighs into it, accelerating forward and upward.

The difficulty was the cliff. She was flying straight toward it.

She dug in and gave a furious push with both arms, vaulting herself straight upwards along the cliff face. Now she was moving well and could feel the flow of prana all around her. With a surge of joy, she arched back, away from the cliff and straight into the deep blue sky.

Above the noise of the air in her ears, Alice could hear her phone ringing. She ignored it.

Excited to be underway and relieved to put some space between her and the police, she flew north, avoiding her own house and Kirsty's.

As soon as she was over the Knifespur, flying as high and as fast as she could manage, she pulled out her phone and promptly dropped it. She dove down and managed to catch it before it had dropped anywhere near the ground.

As she pushed back up to altitude, she clicked to her map application and saw the GPS was tracking her flight. It was satisfying to see the little blue dot moving northwards so quickly.

She clicked to another app she used to track her bike rides and it showed she was doing sixty miles an hour. She was about ten miles closer to Laramie than she had been at the library. If she had 120 miles to go, she would arrive in about an hour and forty-five minutes. Her phone clock showed 1:00 p.m., so she should be arriving at 3:00. She didn't know if that would be soon enough, as she had calculated Rajendra would arrive between 2:00 and 3:00 p.m.

Her phone battery showed fifteen percent and falling fast. She put it back in her pocket and settled into a relaxed rhythm for the long flight.

CHAPTER 15

She could hear virtually nothing because of the wind in her ears. Her eyes were sore and tears were constantly flowing and rolling back into her ears. It was not easy flying for such an extended period of time and her eyes and entire face were tired from scanning such a huge expanse of empty, cloudless blue sky, constantly searching for a little yellow dot. She had a pounding headache.

She jerked her head toward a flash in the sky below her that turned out to be the two-hundredth large bird, probably a hawk, arcing and circling its prey on the ground.

Alice realized she was again truly exhausted. How many times could she recover from this kind of exertion? She didn't want to take her phone out again yet and risk using up the rest of her batteries but she guessed she had slowed down by twenty percent or more. If this was a swimming race, she was not carrying much strength toward the final touch on the wall.

She had not seen any little yellow planes anywhere. Other than the strange sight of a commercial airliner passing above her about a half hour ago, she had seen no other air traffic. She smiled as she thought of herself as air traffic too.

As she pressed on and continued to scan the skies, her thoughts alternated regularly between Madison and Rajendra. They would drift to Madison and she would force them back to Rajendra.

What happened when Madison told the police all that stuff about Rajendra and his escape plan? Would Rajendra's plane be on the ground near the barn, or still in the air? Would she even find Rajendra out here in this huge expanse of empty land?

Everything below her was greenish-brown, interspersed with distant, dark blue ponds the size of pin-pricks and the occasional lake like a blue thumb-tack. She didn't know much about farming but she thought the square-shaped and circular fields below her must be irrigated hay fields. She was way too high to see animals but she knew from the experience of driving up here with her dad that there would be herds of pronghorn antelope milling around, dotting the cooler sides of hills, grazing in the less brown grasses.

Looking ahead, the horizon was bigger than anything she had ever seen before. She felt like she could literally see the whole state of Wyoming. She could see the slow curvature of the planet and she wondered what would happen to her if she just flew higher and higher into space.

Forty or fifty miles in the distance, just in front of the massive curving horizon, she watched yet another small mountain range rise up, inch by inch. She had already passed three small ranges so far. This time there appeared to be some dark shapes in front of it. Those must be buildings, houses. Laramie. The range must be the Laramie Mountains. She made out the shape of a much straighter road off to the east, running north and south with a great sense of purpose. That must be US Route 287, she hoped.

She was almost there.

To prevent her eyes from getting even more bloodshot, she had flown long stretches with her eyes closed. Now her eyes were again wide open and alert for any flash of yellow paint. Likewise, her hearing was straining beyond the wind-noise for the hum of any kind of engine.

She could feel Rajendra out here somewhere. Would he also be marveling at the beauty of these high country plains? Were his Himalaya this beautiful? Or would he just be bored with this job and wishing he was already on his international flight, sipping brandy?

For some reason, Alice had a feeling she was being followed. She couldn't turn her head far enough, so she began a giant arc across the sky, turning left and west away from Laramie.

At first she couldn't see anything, then she saw a flash of reflected sunlight in the distance. She could hear nothing but she suspected it could be Rajendra's little plane.

Now what? She felt exposed up here in the middle of the big, open sky.

During her flight she had been mostly looking ahead, left and right and downward, never up, so she immediately began swimming straight up toward the sky. She hoped to get so far above him that he couldn't possibly see her. She wanted to preserve the element of surprise. She wanted to sneak up on him and...what? She didn't know.

As she climbed upwards, she marveled again at how the prana didn't seem to mind what direction she swam; it supported her intelligently no matter which direction she flew. Gravity seemed not to be an issue. All Alice had to do was swim and her body always found purchase in the right places and met little resistance from either gravity or the air. Using the same level of effort she usually exerted in the water, she was swimming straight up toward the firmament at fifty or sixty miles an hour.

After five minutes of hard work, she was higher than she had ever been. She figured she must have just climbed over two miles. She could see the curvature of the earth in all four directions and the air felt a lot cooler and lighter. Laramie was about seven thousand feet above sea level, if it was similar to that of Hardrock, which made her more than seventeen thousand feet high right now. That was higher than any mountain in the Rocky Mountains.

She was elated.

Fortunately the prana also seemed to keep her warm, otherwise, she would be a floating ice cube up here.

She took a long drink of water from her Camelbak.

She kept an eye on the yellow speck in the sky. It was directly below her. It could have been a taxi on the highway if she didn't know better. She was surprised at how slowly it moved compared with that commercial airliner she had seen earlier. From up here, it looked like it was moving at walking speed.

She looked ahead at Laramie and roughly figured he would get there in something like ten minutes. If she was going to catch up with him, it was time for some race pace. She dove toward Laramie and began to swim as hard as she could.

Her hope was to land just after he did, right behind him, and somehow ruin his day. She had a plan to try out Brian's hang gliding advice: come in faster than trim, round out to ground effect, flare, moonwalk. Would it work? She definitely didn't want to face-plant in front of Rajendra and wake up with him standing over her, laughing like a rat. She tried to make sense of Brian's hang-glider jargon but it was hard to think as she strained her exhausted body in an effort to catch up to Rajendra.

After four minutes of effort she had managed to sneak up behind the little yellow plane. She could hear its high-pitched motor. The pitch of his electric motor was decreasing incrementally every ten seconds, like descending notes on a piano, as he got closer to the ground.

She thought about making one last mad push to catch him before he landed, to jump on his windscreen like a giant bug and try to make him crash, then jump back up into the air triumphantly just before he hit the ground, but she knew he had a propeller somewhere on that thing, which would be sharp. She didn't know if her formidable body weight would be enough to crash his plane. Probably not.

Much better to try to land first and confront him on the ground. Maybe she could sneak up behind him and pounce when he got out of the plane? Hit him with a rock? A stick? Tackle him like a raging bear? Hopefully some really great plan would take shape when it was time.

She watched him float down expertly toward a dirt road near a barn, land the little plane with no fanfare and hardly slow down as he taxied toward the barn.

It's business time, Alice Brickstone, she said to herself.

She slowed down to around the speed she figured was trim for her. Brian had said that was the lowest speed she could fly and still maintain buoyancy. She aimed straight toward the barn. She descended until she was just skimming along the road, hoping to feel the extra lift of Brian's ground effect. Thankfully there did seem to be a bit of extra lift.

She was doing twenty miles an hour toward Rajendra, who was standing in front of a big wooden barn. Time to flare. She lifted her chin and chest and arched her back while tucking her arms into her body to try to do her version of stalling the tips. She did seem to slow down to about ten miles an hour and was in a good position to land feet first, rather than face-planting as she had before in front of Kirsty. She was moving very fast toward the barn door and began to run madly in the air in anticipation of her feet landing on the ground.

She connected with the gravel surface, stumbled once, caught herself and ran, then slid along the ground.

She came to a halt right in front of the short, rat-faced man and smiled down at him, quite pleased with herself. Rather than offering applause or a compliment, Rajendra pointed his taser at her. This time he did not hesitate to fire.

Alice watched in slow motion as two little darts connected with her tattered, cloud-drenched bike jacket. The darts were attached to the gun with wires conducting electricity into her body.

The pain was unbelievable. Her body cramped from head to toe, left to right, inside and out. It was like she was lifting the heaviest weight possible in the gym, but with all muscles used all at once and maxed-out immediately, coursing lactic acid everywhere.

She went over like a felled tree.

Rat man walked casually over to her, still holding the trigger, sending current through her body.

He finally released the gun and casually pulled a little first-aid kit out of his coat pocket. As Alice watched, still immobilized, he dipped a syringe into a small bottle with no label and drew out some milky liquid.

He bent down and injected her roughly with the stuff, his beady little rat eyes never connecting with hers.

She was quickly fading into full sedation but had not yet recognized how far she had sunk. Something told her she had only seconds before she was totally unconscious and would wake up dead.

She shifted the last glimmer of her attention toward the prana around her and drew it into herself, providing immediate relief from the pain. The prana seemed also to know how to counteract the effects of the heavy sedative he had given her and naturally gathered itself into her brain and spinal column. She was not able to completely counteract the drugs but she felt she could just stay awake. She tried to move her fingers, but failed. She tried to move anything and had the same result. Her whole body was paralyzed.

The drugs made her feel completely relaxed, so it was easy to keep her face soft and eyes almost closed without twitching, so that she could play dead while she waited for an opportunity. An opportunity for what, she had no idea, particularly as she could not move.

She could see from where she was lying that he had scampered off to the barn, taken out several lengths of rope, and used the rope to help him wheel the plane in. She heard a very deep, loud, car motor start up. It idled roughly for a moment and she heard a door slam, then wheels spinning on the gravel.

Alice was not afraid. Her brain was just ticking along,

working through options for escape, analyzing his actions, working through more options. She was most curious how this little marathon runner was going to lift a two hundred plus pound girl into a car. Maybe that would be the first little hole in his plan.

As she watched his approach, she thought he was simply going to run her over and be done with it. Alice drew as much prana into her muscles as she could in the hope of inching away somehow, but she was still unable to move.

He drove straight toward her head.

This was it, she thought. She took a deep breath and closed her eyes all the way. An image of her mom came into her mind. She hadn't even thought of her all day. She had been obsessing over her dad, Madison, Kirsty and now rat face. With her death approaching, all she wanted was for her mom to be here.

Alice heard the wheel pass right next to her and skid to a stop.

She opened the slightest slit in her eyes again and saw Rajendra open the door over her head. It was an old car she could see, something from the sixties or seventies: dirty red. The interior leather was red, with plenty of tears and scuffs.

The engine was idling. Rajendra unraveled a long piece of thick rope, reached down to where Alice lay incapacitated and grabbed her hands roughly. He tied her wrists together tightly so that her arms were above her head, resting on the driver's seat.

Alice couldn't feel a thing.

He took the other end of the rope, scampered to the passenger seat, opened the door and ran off somewhere.

Alice couldn't see where he went. She listened hard but could only hear the distant call of a hawk. She wished the hawk could swoop down and carry away this rat in his talons.

After a second, Rajendra was back in the driver's seat, Alice's tied hands on his lap. He pressed the accelerator, the big engine growled and she felt the rope tighten against her hands, pulling her slowly up off the ground. Her head slammed onto the bottom of the door frame. She felt that one.

He lifted her head up by her hair and kept inching the car forward until her head was in his lap.

There was no way she could read his mind, so she would have to think it through and try to anticipate his moves.

Alice remembered something from Mr. Rao's rambling speech earlier today. He said something like, you can only learn by putting yourself in another person's shoes, not just by knowing what they are thinking.

She knew Rajendra was methodically and efficiently arranging her death. She had previously thought of him as impossibly different from her, more an animal than a person. That's not very fair, she realized. He probably has a mother too. What is your world like right now, little rat man?

She looked up through the slit in her eyes and saw his teeny chin buried into the bunched-up skin in his throat. She saw his thin lips pressed tightly together.

If she was Rajendra, this little, ugly man, what would she feel like? What would he want?

Home, she concluded. Maybe he would just want to go home, which was far away from here in a place full of people who were connected with each other through…old connections, blood, caste, religion and business. If she was him right now, she would want to get home. He probably had a lot of money waiting for him for doing this job. Maybe even a family to support. Maybe even children who loved him, in spite of his looks, in spite of his coldness. Children who didn't know what he did for a living and didn't ask. She remembered feeling that Rajendra was deeply afraid, not of her, but of someone. Perhaps if he did well here, the threat from his boss would dissipate somewhat. But there was something else, she thought. What? What made him so different from her?

She heard Rajendra grab something metallic, maybe a shovel. It must have been sitting on the passenger seat. He wriggled over and let her head fall to the seat. He sat on the passenger side and used the shovel to press down the accelerator, revving up the engine again and inching the car forward more until the rope had pulled Alice further along into the driver's seat of the car. Her big, musclebound bottom had slammed it's way over the door frame and up onto the driver's seat.

What makes you so different? She continued toturn it over in her mind. Are you at all like any of the people around here? Like my dad? No, nothing like Dad, but maybe like John? No. You are different even from John. You're smarter than him. What is it, she wondered. Why do I keep thinking of you as an animal?

Rajendra slid out from under the taut rope, out of the passenger side door, and Alice could hear him run and untie the rope from something, probably a tree. Her hands flopped down numbly onto the seat when the tension from the rope was released. She heard Rajendra rush back over to the passenger side, felt him cut her hands loose and saw the rope fly over her into the back seat of the car.

She heard him run around to her side of the car and felt her legs being pulled and shoved under the steering wheel as he pulled her hair to lever her upper body into a sitting position in the driver's seat. He had a lot of strength for a rat.

He slammed her door and her chin flopped down onto her chest.

Why are you like an animal to me, she wondered. Are you like an animal to everyone? You weren't this mean to Kirsty but you were probably instructed to be nice to her so she thought she had been taken out there to get enlightened. That's pretty weird.

"Hello?"

Alice heard a voice coming from a phone.

Rajendra was calling someone. He sat on the passenger side. "What is this girl doing here?"

"What girl?"

She didn't recognize the voice on the phone; the sound was too clipped. He sounded like he had an Indian accent but she wasn't sure.

"This big, fat Amazon girl. The one you asked me to get the first time."

"I thought you said she fell off a cliff and died. That's why you got the neighbor instead of her, remember?"

"Yes, very funny. So you put her here for me to take care of? To make sure she stays dead? Because you know that will cost you."

Rajendra wedged the phone between his right shoulder and his ear, shifting the automatic gear lever to drive and starting to push the shovel on the accelerator pedal to move the car forward.

"I don't even know where you are," said the voice. "No-one knows where you are. That's the way you wanted it."

Rajendra was steering them with his right hand, left hand on the shovel, and the car was moving toward the main road.

"I'm taking care of this girl for you but it is going to cost you double."

"You will not harm that girl," the voice said in a much higher pitch. "This is not a Hollywood movie. You do not take care of people in this country."

"You do not know what I can do. You don't know who you are involved with. You think you understand the world but you are like a frog in a well."

Alice saw Rajendra's hand grow tense on the steering wheel. "I will tell you something. You will pay me double. It is due in twenty-four hours. If there are any more surprises, or if there are any people waiting for me anywhere, or police trying to keep me from leaving this country, my friends back home will hold you personally responsible, and they are not as gentle as I am."

"I am telling you something, I do not even know where you are! How can I send someone to stop you from leaving the US? Why would I send you a girl?"

Before Rajendra could hang up, Alice heard the guy on the line say, "Hey, don't hurt her, okay? I'll pay you whatever you want."

Rajendra began to maneuver the car using the shovel to reach the pedals and using his other hand to steer.

Alice considered Rajendra's phone call. The guy at the other end of the call was a bit scared. He had panicked over her. That did not match with the boss who Alice knew was striking fear into Rajendra's heart, so Rajendra was working for more than one boss. His friends in India were not likely friends with the guy on the other end of the phone just now.

Rajendra managed to steer them one-handed onto the old, tree-lined road and they drove in silence for a few moments. Alice was still feeling very relaxed but she knew it was artificial and she was aware that there was not much time to think of some way to thwart Rajendra's plan to take care of her.

Rajendra appeared to be scanning left, right, and had moved the rear-view mirror so he could see behind. He was executing his plan but was nervous. He must still suspect Alice was not here alone.

The tree-lined road was quite beautiful. Through the slits of her eyes, Alice thought they looked like old cottonwood trees. There must be little drainage streams on both sides of the road for the trees to get that big out here, she thought.

They passed a few driveways leading away toward expensive-looking ranch homes. All of them looked closed up tight. Probably the same kinds of people as her dad, wanting to live somewhere nice but also near a local airport.

Over the drumming of the big car engine, she heard a different small plane track slowly overhead and after thirty seconds become silent. The airport must be close now, she thought.

She tried again to move her toes but to no avail. Her fingers were also still numb and useless.

There was a bend in the road up ahead and Rajendra had taken the shovel off the accelerator and used it to pump the brakes a few times. They slowed back down to a crawl.

Alice was helpless and felt hopeless. All she had the use of were her eyes and eyelids, and she couldn't think of any way to blink him to death. She still didn't want to alert him to the fact she was conscious either, because he might give her another dose of that stuff or just hit her in the head with the shovel.

He kept the car in drive so that they were creeping forward at a walking speed. He opened the passenger side door, the car still moving, and backed his legs out. He took one last look at Alice, who did not move: could not move. He took the shovel and wedged it deeply into the folds of her lower abdomen, which were soft as cream at the moment. He jammed the other end of the shovel onto the accelerator pedal, pushing it all the way to the floor. The rear wheels spun and the car shot forward. Rajendra appeared to panic for a second as the vehicle picked up speed. Alice panicked too; she had no idea there was so much power in this thing. It felt like a rocket ship compared with other cars she had been in.

He clumsily bailed out of the car. It clipped him hard on the way out. She heard him cry out in pain. The passenger door slammed shut. Alice was alone in a death machine.

She opened her eyes wide and willed her hands to work, but they would not. She still felt relaxed because of the drug and considered submitting to the car's trajectory into the trees. It would be easy, like falling asleep. She wondered if Rajendra had hurt himself badly enough to die. She wondered if Rajendra was still breathing.

She'd finally realized what made Rajendra different. He had no respect for life, not even his own. His survival was a game, a contest, like a marathon. That was not all. He had lost something. He played life like a game because his love for life had been torn from him.

Was she that different from Rajendra? She didn't care much for life either, at least before yesterday.

The trees were racing by the windows and the shovel dug into her stomach. She could feel it now. The curve in the road was only seconds ahead. The shovel was painful. The crash would force the shovel right through her, cutting her in half. That awareness made her alert. Rajendra had thought of one too many details to ensure her painful death.

She did not want her parents to find her here in this car, cut in half by a shovel. She would need to think twice as hard and twice as fast to undo his plans. She tried to split herself as she had before, in the pool. Nothing: only the beginning of pain.

She was beginning to feel prana around her again but she couldn't invite it in or use it to help her move. She knew prana was her last hope and she drew her entire being to focus on it. With that renewed focus, she sensed a spark within the prana. As soon as she did, it enveloped her. Time seemed to stop. There was no car, no road, no danger. No thinking. She was suddenly not Alice, a tall, strong girl. She was made of light, flowing like crystal. She was prana.

She had no inclination and no pathways for thought. She could only adjust her concentration like a laser target. She focused on the steering wheel and willed the wheel to turn. It inched to the left.

The car tires began to screech, groaning against the new trajectory. The motor continued to roar.

She shifted her focus to her right hand and arm, managed to reach down to the shovel, and drew it painfully out from her abdomen, relieving the crushing pain the shovel had been causing.

The motor stopped screaming and the car decelerated but she was still going to plunge into the cottonwoods at the curve of the road. She lifted her right hand to the steering wheel to turn it further, overcompensated, and the car careered toward the trees on the other side. She turned the wheel the other way and the car straightened out. She negotiated the turn and guided the car into the right lane.

Ahead of her she saw the blue and red flash of police car lights in the distance. This shook her totally back to herself. Time resumed. She could feel and move her limbs again.

She clumsily lifted her other meaty hand. She flexed her fingers and grasped the wheel. She managed to wiggle her toes in her ski socks and place her right foot on the accelerator, pressing down until the car sped up and leveled out to a steady fifty miles per hour.

Alice had never driven a car before but it seemed easy enough to keep the old car going in a straight line at fifty. She tested the boundaries a bit and noticed if she went too far over to the right, she started to hear gravel kicking up under the wheel wells. She drew it back a little and kept it there.

She tried the brake with her left foot and the car jerked to a slower speed, throwing her body into the steering wheel. Her right foot accidentally stood on the accelerator, shooting the car forward again. Her head whipped back. After a second of panic, she resumed her steady driving, staying clear of the brake. She vaguely remembered she never saw her dad use his left foot while driving. She wondered if maybe she needed to release her right foot and use it on the brake, but gently.

She tried it with faint pressure and she felt the car ease back. She tried to look casual for the benefit of the police, who were fast approaching. Fortunately they blew by her. She imagined that they were responding to Madison's call and were headed toward the barn.

Then, like a switch flipping on, the entire length of her body burst into pain, especially her head. Something was very wrong with the back of her head. She felt the spot and came away with a handful of red and black blood.

Through the near blindness caused by the overload of pain, she looked wildly around the front seats of the car and saw nothing she could use to tie around her head. All she had were her clothes. She very gingerly pulled the car over to the shoulder and jolted to a sliding stop in the gravel. She jerked the gear handle thing into park and pulled the handbrake up hard. The engine idled angrily. She painfully pulled off her pack and her cycling jersey, and wrapped one of the sleeves tightly around her head. She thought she may have felt or heard skull bones grinding against each other. She could hardly see for the pain, but it was the best she could do.

Or was it? She sensed the light was still within her mental reach and she closed her eyes, drawing a concentration of prana toward her wound. She could see a huge welling of darkness there and observed the light pushing it away until it was almost gone. The throbbing eased dramatically but she kept the cycling jacket tied on, just in case.

She put her water bottle in her lap and drank most of the rest of it through the straw, allowing her to think and see somewhat more clearly. Taking stock, she could see from the horse logo on the steering wheel and the general shape of the hood that Rajendra had gifted Alice an old Ford Mustang, probably from the Sixties. Her town hosted a Mustang convention every year, so she was vaguely familiar with them.

This one appeared to have never been restored. The red interior was a mess, but judging from her near-death experience a moment ago, the motor appeared to be more than prepared to push the car around, the steering worked and the brakes made the car stop. As it was Alice's first ever driving experience, she wouldn't know if this car was easier or harder to drive than her parents' modern four-wheel drives, but she felt as though she could handle it well enough after what she'd just been through. Perhaps all kids should learn to drive by being tossed straight into a crisis, she mused, rather than driving around empty parking lots at five miles an hour?

Remembering her promise to look in mirrors more often before going places, she adjusted the rear-view mirror. A dirty, bloody, battered, but strangely glowing face looked back at her. She drank some more water, spat some on her hands and did the best she could to clean herself up.

She recapped her situation. She had her phone, her credit card, a Mustang with a half a tank of gas, and it was late afternoon.

She felt for her phone and it wasn't there. She had a mental image of the cops finding it on the ground by the barn. She couldn't go back toward the barn and just ask for her phone back. They probably had her description and intended to bring her in. She couldn't go to the airport either because she looked like a war refugee, and also because the police would be there. Hopefully they were watching out for any Indians, as well as Amazons.

The experience with the prana had rejuvenated her somewhat but she still had no energy to fly.

Alice reached down with her right hand and shifted into drive. She pressed her right foot down on the accelerator and heard the engine roar. The car jerked forward. It was harder than she had thought to drive the car at slow speeds. The accelerator did not feel as though it could be pressed lightly enough to move the car slowly. It was all or nothing. She jabbed the brake to screech to a stop again and returned her foot to jab on the accelerator. Then she threw caution to the wind and pushed the accelerator halfway down, roaring forward.

She watched the speedometer climb to fifty, then she held the car steady, drove past the airport, managed to slow down for a few right-hand turns and cruised into town.

She felt more in control and drove along in the flow of traffic, pretending to be just one of the Laramie locals going about her business.   Her head felt much better, so she took a hand off the wheel, untied her cycling jacket and ran her fingers through her hair in a vague attempt to comb out the blood and dirt.

Alice wanted to live. She wanted freedom. She wanted to keep flying. She wanted nothing to do with Rajendra anymore. She wanted him to either find death, or to find his way home and never come back. It was likely he would continue hurting people but she hoped that his money would make someone happy who deserved to be happy. Somewhere in her head she respected that he wanted to go back home, which would be away from her. Let him be.

She wanted food.

She saw a McDonalds drive-through up ahead. She managed to slow down enough to pull into the McDonald's drive-through lane but she kept alternating between full brakes and a heavy accelerator. Alice ordered a large coffee, two bottles of water and two Big Macs. When the girl asked if she wanted anything else, she hesitated. She was starving, but something was different. She just couldn't imagine eating all that fat and meat right then.

"Can you take the meat and cheese off those Big Macs?"

"Excuse me?"

"Just Big Macs with no meat or cheese. Put more salad and pickles or whatever."

There was a moment of silence and then the girl responded.

"Okay, we can do it your way."

Before pulling forward, Alice checked herself in the rear-view mirror and saw she still looked like someone who had been hog-tied and dragged through the dirt, and smashed in the head.

She did the best she could with her appearance and jerked the Mustang to the pick-up window. She must have looked decent enough because the guy took her credit card, passed her order out and smiled at her.

She managed not to smash any obstacles on the way back to the road and found her way to a gas station. She didn't really need gas but she was starting to really get into playing grown-up. She jerked up to a gas pump, switched off the motor and got out.

As she stretched her legs, she realized she was feeling remarkably well considering what she had been through: three flights, a general anesthetic, a beating and a near-death experience. She knew she owed this feeling of vitality to the prana she had called upon to heal her wounds.

The air here was drier and the sky bigger and emptier than it was in Hardrock. Even on the ground, she felt like she would be able to hear a hawk call from miles away.

There was a Harley parked at the pump across from hers, loaded with travel pannier bags. There were no other cars at the gas station. A light trickle of local traffic passed her by. Alice suspected the road led to State Highway 230 and back to the Colorado state border.

She checked her appearance before going about her adult business of filling the gas tank and saw her torn bike pants and dirty ski socks with no shoes looked a bit odd. She   walked around the Mustang. It was a beautiful old muscle car, in spite of the scratches, dents and rust. There definitely was no place to fill the gas tank though. She walked around it again and had a feeling she was being watched.

"Missing something?"

She turned around and looked at the bald guy with tattoos who had spoken to her. He wasn't smiling but he didn't seem hostile.

"No," she said. "You?"

"No, but I'm not the one playing ring around the rosy." He pointed at the car. "That's a '67, isn't it?"

"Yep," she said, pretending confidence.

"All the first generation Mustangs fill up in the back."

"I know. I was just checking for scratches."

He cracked a smile for the first time.

Alice realised the car was so full of scratches, he must have thought she was joking.

"Nice bike," she said, trying to keep the friendly chat going. She was just another adult on a road trip, definitely not a teenager in a stolen car.

"You got quite a car there yourself," he said. "But those Sixties Mustangs don't exactly hug the road."

"Tell me about it," Alice said knowingly.

"You ever take it to the Hardrock Mustang Rally?"

Alice remembered all those loud car drivers red-necking around town every year. Normally her swim teammates and her parents either ignored the convention or expressed mild disdain. Today she felt a sense of community with those Mustang drivers.

"No," she said, smiling as knowingly as she could. "It's a bit too beat up. I'm saving up to get it restored."

"You do that, sweetheart."

Alice could see something twitch in his face when he said that.

She locked eyes, checked his thoughts and was surprised to see that he was feeling bad for calling her sweetheart and worrying he had given offense. Other than that pang of guilt, his head was full of confidence and warmth. He was on a road trip looking for something, or someone, but he was concealing exactly what it was. His mind was a comfortable place for her to linger but she realized she needed to get going before any police who may be out looking for her drove by. Standing up like this, like an Amazon, as Rajendra called her, she would be a dead giveaway for any passing police officer searching for a tall woman.

"Have a great ride," she said. "Hope you find what you're looking for."

He raised his eyebrows but appeared to decide Alice was just being friendly. "Hope you do too," he said, putting on his sunglasses and turning toward the bike. "Those scratches, I mean."

"See you around," she said, heading toward the pumps.

She grabbed a random gas nozzle, strode purposefully to the back, unscrewed the cap and wondered what kind of gas she was filling the car with. She hoped it was the right kind.

She went in to the gas station store, picked up a coffee, a pair of work boots her size and a baseball cap with the name of a motor oil brand on it. When she paid, the girl behind the counter looked bored, rather than suspicious.

Alice slipped on her boots, clomped back around to do a pee, and returned to the car.

She turned the ignition and with some hesitation, the engine roared to life. She wondered if she was supposed to have stomped on the gas pedal a few times or not. She took a long drink of her coffee, replaced it back in the cup holder and smiled, feeling like a real grown-up. She shifted into D and took the Mustang out to the road, heading south.

On the State Highway, she nudged the old car up to fifty-five, clicked on the old radio and found a local station playing something with a beat. Alice rolled down the window, rested her elbow out the window, wind blowing through her blood-caked hair, and smiled.

When she adjusted the rear-view mirror so she could watch for any police, she caught a glint of yellow in the sky.

She knew it was her imagination.

CHAPTER 16

Welcome to Colorful Colorado, the sign read. She had only been behind the wheel of the Mustang for forty-five minutes but Alice felt like years had passed since she flew above this spot the other way in pursuit of Rajendra. She had food in her stomach, caffeine in her blood and her own car—temporarily. She smiled again for the hundredth time since leaving the gas station.

She slammed on the brakes when she saw Madison's Subaru parked on the shoulder just beyond the sign.

After skidding for twenty feet wondering what the hell Madison was doing out here, she released the brake enough to unlock the wheels and managed to pull over without adding a new dent to Madison's car. Maybe it wasn't Madison's car.

"Madison? Anyone home?" she shouted too loudly. She opened the car door and got out.

Her heart was racing. Was it Madison's car? It looked like it. Beat up old Subaru. The glint on the windows made it impossible to see inside. If it was really Madison, how was she out here, an hour-and-a-half away from home?

It was only then that she heard the cries of a baby. Madison emerged from the other side of the car.

"Thanks. You woke the baby up."

"So I'm not a very good driver," Alice said, relieved. "Sue me."

"I didn't think you even had a driver's license and I'm sure you don't have a car."

"I don't. Isn't it cool?"

"Come here and help me with Billie."

Alice reached back into her new car and turned the engine off.

Billie's angry cries were growing rhythmically louder with each of her gasping inhalations.

She leaned in to Madison's car and saw Billie was strapped in to the car seat, tears flowing like broken glass all over her face, chin and throat, her mouth wide open with the effort of screaming. It was heartbreaking. Madison was next to her, frantically looking for something. The baby looked over at Alice and screamed louder.

"What makes you think I can help?" The screaming was undoing Alice's hard-earned calm. "She hates me."

"Help me find her binky," Madison said in a calm, but very loud voice. Alison wasn't sure if she heard correctly.

"What in the world is a bunky?"

"Pacifier. She chucked it somewhere."

Alice looked around the car seat and on the floor of the car but couldn't see it. She looked back at the baby and decided to try to reach her. She took a deep breath, got eye contact and dropped in.

The baby immediately stopped crying but kept her look of anger, helplessly staring back at Alice.

Her mind was a world of colors and complex emotions. Alice was completely taken aback at the complexity. Fueling much of the complexity was a desperate need for the safety of trustworthy adults. They were apparently in very short supply in this baby's world. Alice was impressed at the intricate strategies Billie had developed to secure adult attentions, and when that failed, strategies to fill the void. Many of these strategies involved eating lots of food. It all looked a bit too familiar to Alice.

She quickly discovered Billie was voraciously hungry.

"Madison, forget the bunky, she's starving."

The baby had begun to cry again as soon as Alice broke the connection and Madison resumed her desperate search for the pacifier.

"What? How do you know?"

"You got any food for her?"

"Yes, of course I do. It's in the baby bag. I didn't know how long we'd be out here looking for you, so I packed her dinner, but she doesn't usually eat until five-thirty. Go get that bag out of the boot for me, will you?"

Alice ran around to the boot and pulled out a large black and white bag stuffed full of random-looking fluffy things and a few other bags. She handed it to Madison.

"It's alright, sweetie, Maddie has yummy banana for you. You want banana?"

The baby glared at Madison and said, "Yeah" in a cute, clear voice with no trace of the nasty, formless screams she was producing three seconds earlier.

After being in her head and witnessing all the complexity, Alice was not at all surprised Billie could speak.

Madison peeled a banana and handed it to her.

Alice asked, "Did I just hear you say a second ago that you were looking for me?"

"Yeah."

"Why?"

"You said you were going out to Laramie, didn't you? To confront that dangerous kidnapper guy?"

"Yeah, but I asked you to tell the police, not to drive out here with your little sister. Don't get me wrong, it's really, really cool to see you out here, and you're the only person in the world who appears to give a rat's ass about me, but Madison, what were you going to do if you saw that guy? Have Billie cry at him?"

"Well, what were you planning on doing to him? I had no

idea what you were doing, but based on the past few days, I believed you. I believed you would be out here somewhere and I just thought maybe you could use a hand." Madison paused.

Alice didn't respond right away.

"And no," Madison continued, "I didn't tell the police about the barn, you idiot. If I did, I'd probably still be there right now trying to make up some story to explain how you were in the middle of the Knifespur and you were at a barn in Laramie a couple of hours later."

"What?"

"I didn't tell the police about the barn, Alice."

As Madison continued to help Billie eat her banana without getting it on the car seat, Alice thought for a moment.

"Don't your parents have other babysitters?" Alice asked more softly. "You shouldn't have to miss swim training."

Madison didn't respond. She just kept helping Billie.

Alice stood up and looked around at the brown landscape. Other than a straggle of greenish weeds on the side of the highway, everything was brown. Actually, gold would be a fairer description, she thought—but barren.

Now that Billie was quiet, the silence of this lonely stretch of two-lane highway was complete. Alice could hear nothing. No birds, no crickets, nothing. There probably were some ants and maybe a few mice. Actually there probably were lots of animals out here, but they were all silent, unlike the ruckus that nature made in the much greener areas around Hardrock.

Alice suddenly thought of something. "So did they find Kirsty okay?" she asked, embarrassed it took her so long to remember.

"I don't know. I guess it's not priority for police to call me when they find her."

"But they have reached her by now, surely. I promised her. It was hours and hours ago I sent you that stuff. You showed them my map photos and told them everything?"

"Yes, but like I told you on the phone, the helicopter thing is not as easy to organize as it sounds. By the way, they were pretty pissed off at you, Alice."

"So? Sucks to be them."

"I guess, but it would have maybe been better if you would have just come over and talked to them yourself, rather than driving this Mustang up to Laramie and back. Did you see that guy, by the way?"

"He tried to kill me. That's why I look all torn up like this. You remember the barbecue sauce thing? That was also him. It wasn't barbecue sauce. This guy is no joke. But now I'm actually pretty glad he got away. Hopefully we'll never see him again."

"More." Billie was clearly not satiated with one banana.

A girl after my own heart, Alice thought. To her, our discussions must be as meaningless as the twittering of birds, she thought. Alice smiled at Billie.

"Anyway," Alice said, "I'm just glad you didn't get anywhere near him, especially with this precious cargo."

"So what's the plan now?" Madison asked as she stuffed the banana peels into a plastic bag and unbuckled Billie, letting her get down and run around in the dirt next to the car.

"How long did it take you to get here from Hardrock?"

"Just over an hour. Why?"

"Let's get you to the pool. I'll look after Billie for you while you train. I'm not in any shape to go in the water with these cuts. It's no use both of us missing a workout."

Madison looked like she was considering Alice's suggestion. "Are you really okay to look after her?" Madison cocked her head and raised her huge eyebrows. "I mean, you're not too injured, are you?"

"I'm fine," Alice said. She watched Billie scamper off a few feet, squat down and look at something on the ground.

"You know...okay, let me be honest," Madison said, looking squarely at Alice. "It's not that easy to look after a toddler. You would also have to give her dinner and get her a bit cleaned up, because I'd have to put her straight to bed after swim training is over. I'd have to rush home because her bedtime is usually seven and we wouldn't be home till 7:45 and——"

"Hey, it will be okay. I promise. We'll be fine."

"You might have to do her diaper. You ever changed a diaper?" Madison looked at her watch again, and at Billie.

"No but I used to wear them, so I have some experience. Come on, let's go. I'll follow you."

"Alice...okay, let's see how you go. She needs a diaper right now. I'll watch."

"What? Is this a test?"

"Yes."

Alice walked over to where Billie was squatting down putting some rocks in her mouth.

"Billie, do you want a fresh diaper?"

"No," Billie said resolutely and ran a few steps away.

"Madison, she says she doesn't need a diaper, okay? Let's go."

"That's a failing mark, Alice."

Alice turned back and caught up to Billie, who was waddling away, and said, "Okay, come on. Your sister says you need a diaper, so let's do this." She plucked up the baby under her arms from behind.

"Noooooooo!"

When Alice held her up, arching and kicking, she saw she had wet herself all the way through her current diaper. It didn't smell like it was only pee either. She carried Billie at arms' length back to the car.

Madison had spread a diaper change mat out in the boot of the car and placed the fresh diaper and some baby wipes. Madison stood there smiling.

"Okay, Billie, just you and me." Alice tried to lay her down.

Billie kept struggling. She had closed her eyes and was crying loudly again.

Madison plonked a pacifier into her mouth and she instantly quieted.

"Wow, that's like an anesthetic," Alice said admiringly.

"It will give you about thirty seconds of peace. The clock's ticking."

Alice straightened Billie on the mat and pulled her shoes and wet pants off. Billie was still placid and Alice didn't want to show Madison that she felt squeamish, so she launched right in, pulling the tape off the front of the diaper and opening it up.

"Oh...my...God," Alice said, pulling her hands away.

"That's a serious one," Madison commented admiringly. "Good girl, Billie!"

"Okay, that's like a quart of diarrhea right there. You're going to have to talk me through it, Madison."

"It's not diarrhea; it's just normal baby poo."

"What do you feed this kid? Liquified cattle?"

"Step one. Wipe the old ketchup off your hands with a couple of baby wipes and gently take both of her feet in one hand. At least I hope that's ketchup."

Alice followed instructions quickly.

"Fine. Now start folding the diaper under her bottom. Try to use the diaper itself to wipe as much off her as you can. You can lift her up a little."

Alice gingerly put her right hand back down toward the scene of the crime and pulled the diaper slowly off Billie's skin with a squelching, sucking sound and wiped a huge gob of poop off, getting plenty onto her fingers as she did. She folded the diaper under Billie's butt.

"Gracefully done. Now clean her up. It will take about a million baby wipes."

Alice started wiping all the brown stuff off the poor girl's abdomen and private parts, legs, everywhere.

"Some poo usually gets up her vagina as well."

"Oh, ban, the poor liddle thig," Alice said without breathing through her nose. "She gets this dud to her everyday?"

"Only four or five times a day."

Alice followed instructions, and although only half a minute had gone by, she felt like she had been in a war.

"Here," Madison said, holding out a plastic bag.

Alice bravely grabbed the pile of baby wipes and the diaper and shoved it in the bag.

"Don't let go of her feet yet. Clean up your free hand as well as you can with baby wipes and put the new diaper on her."

Madison unfolded the new diaper, spread out the little tape wings and slid it the right way under Billie's bottom.

Alice lowered Billie down and let go of her feet.

Billie was starting to get restless and spat out the pacifier.

"One second longer, sweetheart," Madison said, putting her smiling face right in front of Billie's to block her view of Alice struggling to get the diaper done up.

Alice managed to wrap the tape things around and felt extremely proud.

"Done," she said to Madison. "Perfect."

"Well, it will do." Madison pulled out some clean pants from her baby bag and handed them to Alice.

"You want some nice clean pants now?" Alice asked Billie, raising her eyebrows.

Billie was already fed up and was trying to lift herself up.

Alice quickly put the pants on Billie's kicking legs and backed away, feeling as though she had just won an Olympic gold medal.

"Okay, let's hit the road!" she said to Madison, who was lifting Billie up and trying to calm her.

Billie kept struggling and crying as she was strapped in to the car seat.

"I shouldn't have let her walk around," Madison said, as if to herself. As soon as Billie was buckled in, she gave her the pacifier again and she quieted down.

"Okay, Alice, let's go. Are you sure you're okay driving? You're welcome to just come with me. You can leave that piece of crap here."

Alice thought about it but remembered the exhilarating feeling of driving on the highway, which was almost as good as flying through the sky.

"Hey, if I can change a diaper, I can drive a car. Let's hit the road."

"If you say so."

They both got into their respective cars. As soon as Alice started up the Mustang, she couldn't hear anything else. She watched as Madison did a u-turn and pulled onto the highway. Alice expertly put the gear into drive, gently nudged the accelerator and managed to get onto the highway behind Madison.

She swallowed the last little bit of cold McDonald's coffee, which would have tasted bearable if her hand didn't smell like baby poo. She put the cup back down on the passenger seat and rested her elbow out the window.

The sky was just starting to turn yellow with the approaching sunset. Alice smiled again for the millionth time. She looked ahead and saw that Madison was on the phone, which took the smile off her face. She hoped Madison was just checking in with her parents. Or maybe she was calling the cops and they would be waiting for Alice at the pool. Surely not, after all they had talked about just now—after the diaper!

Thankfully the drive was police-free and there were no police cars at the pool parking lot. Alice managed to park the Mustang next to Madison's Subaru without hitting it. They got out, stretched their legs, and smiled at each other.

Madison looked at her watch. She was just on time.

"You sure about this?" she asked Alice.

"Oh, yeah. No problem. We're gonna have fun, aren't we, Billie?"

Madison unbuckled Billie quickly and picked her up. Alice grabbed the baby bag out of the boot and ran back to lock up the Mustang. Then they rushed in to the pool together.

Before going in, Madison handed Billie to Alice. Alice hugged the toddler into her body and Billie squeezed her legs into Alice's side in return. Alice felt so proud she could burst. It was so different to be walking in to this place with a baby, she thought. She expected a comment from the guy at reception, or more.

Maybe he would call a bunch of people over to crowd around and say how cute Billie was and compliment Alice on how good she was with her.

As they swiped their cards to go through the turnstile, the guy at reception didn't blink, or even say hello.

Billie looked around, wildly curious about the splashing sounds of the pool echoing off the domed ceiling and the smell of chlorine and the humid air.

Madison was already rushing toward the locker room and didn't look back. Alice felt proud again that she was being trusted with Billie. She walked over to Coach.

At least he did a massive double take. "Mrs. Brickstone?" he said formally. "Is there something you need to tell me?"

"She's not mine, Coach. It's Madison's little sister. She needed a babysitter."

"You thought you would get a babysitting job instead of coming to training?"

Alice was glad he couldn't see her new cut on the back of her head, hidden by her new truck-stop hat.

"Coach, I'm still on antibiotics: should be good to swim by tomorrow morning."

"You look after yourself," he said quietly, nodding to Madison, who had just rushed out and was pulling her swim cap over her hair. She was holding her phone under her arm and her goggle strap in her mouth.

"Are you planning on making some calls while you swim?" Coach asked Madison. "What is it with you two? You think this is all a joke, don't you?"

Billie started pulling away from Alice and reaching toward Madison. Alice held her tight and took the phone and goggles from Madison.

"Sorry, Coach," Madison said when her mouth was free.

Coach walked away and Madison looked at Alice.

"Call your parents," Madison pleaded.

"'Kay."

"And feed Billie. Her dinner is in a tupperware container in the bag."

"Don't worry. We'll just be in the bleachers. I'll take her in for a shower after she eats."

Madison turned and dove into the pool to start her warm up.

Alice checked Madison's missed calls and saw five from her dad. She was tempted to check who Madison had been speaking to in the car a moment ago but she knew that would be a breach of trust, so she just hit her dad's number.

"Hello?"

"Hi, Dad."

"Where the hell are you?" he asked. "I've been calling you all day."

"Why did you call the cops on me?"

"You answer my question first. Where are you?"

"At the pool. I'm fine."

"Where have you been all day? You said you were going to stay home and rest. We came home after the hospital and you and your bike were gone. You haven't answered your phone. The police are calling me constantly. Can you imagine what we have been through today? With your mom's condition——"

"I lost my phone. I didn't get kidnapped; I'm fine. Wait, what condition does Mom have?"

"Never mind. So what were you doing all day?"

"Never mind. Why did you call the cops on me? I thought you were on my side. You're my dad after all."

"I am on your side, you ungrateful brat..." Alice heard Mom shouting something in background and Dad covered the phone for a second. When he returned, he said, "Alice, I'm sorry. I take that back. You're not a brat. I'm just upset. But, please, before we both have aneurisms, can you please, please tell us where you have been today?"

"After you guys left, Madison kindly brought me a coffee, which made me feel a bit better, so I went into the wilderness area for a while, then went to the library, then your spy Brian gave me a lift and I went up into the wilderness area again for a while, then Madison and I had a little drive with Billie and then came to the pool. Now, your turn. What condition does Mom have?"

"Your mom is fine."

"Oh. Thanks, that's so reassuring."

"I'm coming over there right now. Don't even move from where you are standing right now. Pretend like you are surrounded by land mines."

"Why do you think all us women in the family have conditions, Dad? What if we think you have a condition too?"

"What? Who? What are you talking about?"

"You think all women have conditions? What if we're all normal and it's just men who have the conditions?"

"Down!" Billie started to plead as she arched away from Alice.

"Who is that?"

"Madison's little sister. I gotta go, Dad. I'm helping look after her while Madison swims."

"See you in ten minutes. Don't move and——"

Alice hung up before her dad was through speaking.

She set Billie down and the babystarted to run toward the spot where she had seen Madison jump in.

"No, Billie!" Alice said, sweeping her up again. "You're too young to swim."

Billie started screaming and Coach looked over and gave her a nasty look. Alice walked over, set down the baby bag and Billie on the bleachers, and felt the panic rising as she searched for Billie's dinner. It turned out to be a very large container of cold spaghetti and meatballs. A girl after my own heart, Alice thought. There appeared to be no fork or anything in the bag, so Alice just opened it and waited for something to happen. Billie leaned over and put a hand in and started fisting it into her mouth, getting spaghetti sauce everywhere.

At least she is happy, Alice thought. What condition does Dad think Mom has? Something mental? Maybe something to do with her secret stash of photographs of Dad? But he wouldn't know about them. Come to think of it, Mom does look emaciated lately. Maybe she has cancer.

Alice had a surge of conflicted emotions at that moment, imagining her mom was dying of cancer. She felt strangely avenged, but for what, she had no idea. She already knew Dad was killing himself with work and alcohol, and that gave her no joy, so why should she be so twisted as to feel some kind of satisfaction to imagine her mom might be sick?

Anyway, she would ask Dad about it in a minute.

"More," Billie said, appealing to Alice, who was flummoxed because the tupperware was still full of pasta.

"More what?"

"More pesketti."

"But...there is more. Right there!" she said, pointing at the remaining spaghetti.

Satisfied with Alice's help, Billie resumed pawing the stuff into her mouth.

Alice sat up straight and looked around the pool area. It was one of the first times she had ever sat on these bleachers while her squad trained. She recalled she hadn't swum since Saturday, in the water, at least.

Coach continued to ignore her and was calling the swimmers together at the end of the pool to discuss the evening workout.

"More!" Billie said again, staring intently up at Alice.

She was super cute, Alice thought, but she had plenty of food left and surely she knew that. Why was she asking for more?

"There, Billie. There is more," she said, pointing again. "There."

Contented, Billie resumed eating.

She saw Dad rush through the pool doors, speak briefly to the guy behind the reception desk, and come walking through, followed by John. Fantastic, she thought. The first time Dad had been to the pool, her big moment, when she could walk him around her little kingdom, show him where she spent more of her waking hours than anywhere else. She also had wanted to grill him about Mom, and presumably be grilled about her day, and maybe for the first time try to have a real conversation with Dad and ... he brings along an employee. One who is a real jackass.

Alice looked down at Billie. "Let me handle this, okay? I don't want you to say something you'll regret later."

"Pesketti," she said, pointing at the last bit of pasta in the tupperware and smiling.

As he approached, Dad appeared to smile, but he may just have been clearing his throat. John appeared to be all business, or even like a soldier, loyal and in step with his squadron commander.

Both were dressed like they just came straight from work and they probably had been working at Alice's place, she realized. Nothing like a missing daughter to stop the important business of two pharmaceutical marketing executives. Dad looked tired and his shirt was wrinkled and had a bit of coffee on the front. John looked much better and his shirt looked fresh.

"How's the hand?" Alice asked, determined to stay on the front foot in what was probably meant to be a stern dressing down.

"Fine, thanks. So where have you been all day?"

"I already told you on the phone. Wilderness area, picked up by Madison, now here—with my new friend, Billie. Billie, this is my dad and this is John."

"You felt well enough to pop out for an all-day hike, by yourself, in an area where there may be a guy trying to kidnap girls, but not well enough to go to school?"

"I guess so. Dad, what is going on with Mom?"

"Alice, this is serious. I need you to understand this is not a game. They still haven't found Kirsty or the guy out there who may have taken her. The police this morning...didn't you hear them? You were even cautioned against cycling by yourself!"

"What is going on with Mom? Is she sick?"

"I promise we will discuss Mom later. She is waiting at home right now and has been in tears most of the day, worried about you."

"I can't leave right now; I've got Billie, as you can see."

Billie was climbing all over Alice and leaving spaghetti sauce hand prints all over Alice's torn cycling jersey.

"Yes, I thought so, which is why I brought John with me."

"Dad, I can't give Billie over to John. You can't be serious."

"Alice," John said, "I'm not here to babysit for you. I need to speak to you about Rajendra."

"You think you know more about him than about babysitting? Wait. How do you know his name is Rajendra?"

"As you may remember from the other night, we are hosting a delegation from a pharmaceutical firm based in Delhi. They are still in town. We were taking them around and one of them said he heard on the Hardrock Indian community grapevine there were some nasty Indians in town. Violent guys. Heroin traffickers. He told me because he was really surprised these kinds of people would have any interest in anything in Hardrock. I said resort towns in Colorado did, in fact, have a rising heroin problem and maybe that was it. He said these guys were different. You always knew they were around because people start disappearing and the emergency rooms get much busier."

Alice looked down and saw Billie had begun to rub spaghetti sauce into her eyes and appeared to be nodding off.

"You didn't answer my question about how you know his name."

"The police told me," John said, looking guilty.

Alice tried to remember if she said the name Rajendra to Madison, and if so, if she asked her to tell the police his name. After a moment, she decided John wasn't worth all this consideration and certainly wasn't worth having a conversation with.

"The scariest Indian in town that I know of is Babaji," she said distractedly, lifting Billie into her lap, "and he's not one hundredth as scary as you guys."

Billie responded by rubbing more sauce on Alice's shirt and starting to cry. Alice reached back into the baby bag and grabbed a pacifier and gave it to her. She immediately quieted and started to snuggle in to Alice's chest.

John appeared not to notice. "Yeah!" he said. "I didn't even know there was such a thing as an Indian community in Hardrock! Live and learn. Anyway, when your dad said an Indian might be responsible for Kirsty's disappearance, and he said you were off looking for this guy by yourself, I thought to warn you that these are not the kind of guys you want to be playing hide and seek with."

"I'll keep that in mind," Alice said to him, but she hadn't really been listening.

Her dad noticed she was not paying attention and tried to reinforce the point.

"Alice, I know you are not a little girl anymore, and I suspect you're too old for grounding and that kind of thing, but please listen to me this once. For your mother's sake, don't take any more big risks. Just let me and your mom drive you around for a few weeks. Stay away from the Wilderness area. Okay?"

That perked Alice up. "Are you really saying that you want to get up at 4:30 a.m. to drive me to swim team every morning? And drive me to the swim meet in Denver next weekend?"

"Well, yes. Your mom and I will organize all that. No problem."

"Okay, then," Alice said.

"It's settled," Dad said. Turning to John, he slapped him on the shoulder, "Thanks. I'll see you back at the office."

John appeared to dislike being slapped in the shoulder and was even less impressed with his quick dismissal, apparently hoping the conversation would have gone on a bit longer, no doubt so that he could turn it toward something that would serve to make him feel impressed with himself.

What a jerk, Alice thought. Not even worth reading. Alice looked down and saw Billie had fallen asleep on her stomach, so she took out a blanket from the bag and wrapped it around the kid. The shower would have to wait.

She looked around and realized her dad hadn't left yet, and appeared to be getting comfortable. Her teammates were continuing their laps and Coach was paying no attention to Alice's little domestic scene.

"Dad," Alice asked, "why didn't you ever teach me to drive?"

"What? You just turned sixteen."

"Madison turned sixteen and got a car. She drives herself to swim team."

"You want a car?"

Alice wanted to say she already had one but kept quiet about it. Then she realized her dad had quite expertly deflected the question. Wow, that's just what I do, she thought.

"Dad, why didn't you ever teach me to drive?"

"Alice, why are we talking about this? I will happily teach you to drive. Let's start this weekend. Okay?"

"What's wrong with Mom?"

"Nothing," he said, pulling out his phone, touching the screen and putting it up to his ear.

After it rang a few times, Alice could hear her mom say something.

"She's fine," he responded. I'm going to stay here with her until she's done babysitting for Madison, then we'll come straight home."

She heard her mom's voice raise but she still couldn't make out the words.

"Okay, see you in a sec," Dad said and pocketed his phone.

"If nothing is wrong with Mom, why did you say she had a condition?"

"She's just worried about you. Can you blame her? You have scared the shit out of us."

"Dad, don't curse in front of a sleeping baby."

"Sorry. So how did you get this babysitting job? Why aren't you swimming?"

"Just helping out; Madison's parents are out tonight. Why did you call the cops on me earlier?"

"Why don't they hire somebody else to babysit?"

"Dad, I wanted to help. Why did you call the cops?"

"I was worried. Are you kidding me? You disappeared! What were we supposed to do? And why is that a problem? Do you have something you are keeping from the police?"

"Not as much as you are keeping from me."

They sat in an apparent stalemate for a while, watching the swimmers go up and down the pool. As she hugged Billie into her chest underneath the blanket and sat next to her dad, Alice was starting to feel strangely comfortable. Something like the bliss she felt while flying.

"You want to get some pizza on the way home?" Dad's voice interrupted her mood and triggered her appetite.

The clock began to tick away quickly as Alice tried and failed to recapture the deep contentedness of Billie sleeping on her chest—and sometimes thought about pizza.

No words passed between her and her dad for ten minutes. He had gotten busy pecking away at his phone and Alice wrote him off.

A half hour later, two police officers walked in. The receptionist pointed over at Alice. His earlier nonchalance had probably been an act. She guessed he had been instructed to call an officer as soon as she set foot in the building.

They were far enough away that she could go to the bathroom and try to escape through a window, but she couldn't bear waking the sleeping baby. What would she do anyway? Hand Billie to Dad?

Besides, her dad was here. He had protected her before, when the police were interviewing her at home. She hoped he would protect her again.

Coach gave the two police a very dark look as they walked past him to reach the bleachers where Alice sat patiently waiting.

She didn't recognize either of them.

"Alice Brickstone?" one of them asked loudly. He was a fat white guy about forty-five years old. Alice disliked him immediately. His partner was cowering behind. She looked to be not much older than Alice and much less confident.

Alice put her finger to her lips and pointed at Billie.

"Are you Alice Brickstone?" he asked again, maybe ten percent quieter, but still louder than your average blow-horn. He was loud enough to make Coach look over again and give him an even more violent look.

"She is Alice," Dad said, looking up from his phone. He obviously hadn't seen them coming. He didn't appear to have expected them. "I'm her father. What can we do for you?"

"Mr. Brickstone," the policeman started, as you know, we have been trying to reach your daughter all day. You were to inform us when you made contact with her."

"She has apparently lost her phone and all is well. She called in from her friend's phone less than an hour ago and I rushed straight over here to pick her up."

"Ms. Brickstone," the policeman said, pulling out a notebook, "Mr. Brickstone, would either of you mind if we asked you a few questions?"

"Fire away," Dad said, putting his phone away.

"Ms. Brickstone, were you anywhere near a cabin occupied by an old Indian gentleman at about 12:45 p.m. today?"

"Yes," Alice whispered, trying to quiet the conversation down and make it feel less threatening. "My house is near there."

"You spoke to an officer at that time by phone," the policeman continued loudly, "and promised to come in to this Indian gentleman's residence to speak to a police officer who was there and answer some of his questions. Is that accurate?"

Alice kept her voice very low. "I thought that policeman on the phone meant you guys were at my house. I was just coming home from the library at the time. I went home and couldn't find you."

"Ms. Brickstone, did you provide information to police via a classmate of yours regarding the location of Kirsty Bell, the missing teenager?"

"You mean you haven't gone to get her yet?" Alice asked in a more urgent and louder voice. "What have you guys been doing all day?"

"We'll ask the questions, Ms. Brickstone. Did you provide information regarding the missing girl's location?"

"Yes. Why haven't you picked her up yet?"

"How did you come by this information, Ms. Brickstone?"

Thankfully, Billie hadn't budged this whole time. This was something like a miracle to Alice, not only because of the loud voices but also because Alice's heart was now racing and pounding right against Billie's head. Maybe that was soothing to her, she mused.

"Is she under arrest?" Dad asked, somewhat threateningly.

"No, sir, not at this point in time."

Alice caught the policeman's eye, dropped into the right frame of mind to read him and exploded into the violent world of his thoughts. It was terrible and she knew she would not be able to endure more than a few seconds in here. He was feeling extremely aggressive toward her and her rich daddy, didn't give a crap about the filthy sleeping baby, he hated he had been stuck with a new green recruit partner, who was a woman, no less, and he was ready to smash someone's face which, of course, he couldn't do right here. All he wanted was a few answers from Alice and he wanted to get out of here and go get a twelve pack of beer. He suspected Alice didn't know anything and had just heard something on the internet.

Alice gritted her teeth and searched a little deeper, looking for information about Kirsty and she saw that a helicopter had reached Kirsty's meadow about an hour ago but they only found the campsite and no Kirsty. The campsite appeared to have been ransacked by a bear. There was no blood though, so they didn't think the bear got Kirsty. One working theory was the bear knocked her unconscious and carried her off, as sometimes happens in this bear-prone area of the world. According to that theory, Kirsty would be buried somewhere for him to eat later. Volunteer Search and Rescue crews were organizing themselves and would enter the wilderness area on foot from trailheads near Kirsty's and Alice's house. Others were preparing all-terrain vehicles to join the search. They must allow vehicles in wilderness areas for emergencies, Alice guessed.

Alice dropped out and took a deep breath of relief to be free of the guy. Only twenty or so seconds had passed but the policeman's partner was looking at him strangely.

"I read it on the internet," Alice said.

"Exactly what did you read and where?"

"I went on the internet on my phone and read on some chat room that Kirsty had been kidnapped and dropped at a spot in the Wilderness area. I texted the stuff to Madison and then I lost my phone. I don't know where the website is anymore, and since I lost my phone, I have no way of checking."

As he was writing this down, Alice's dad glowered at him and added, "I'm sure you can find the chat room easily if a young girl can. Is there anything else we can do for you officers?"

"That will be all for now. You would do well to keep in closer contact with your parents, Ms. Brickstone. There are some undesirable persons in the area."

The two police walked away briskly, but not before receiving another look from Coach.

Alice's dad patted her on the shoulder, apparently completely satisfied that everything with Alice was now clear and okay, and his work and phone resumed their places higher in the priority rankings.

As Dad resumed his tapping on the phone, Alice continued to hug Billie until her heart rate fell again and her breathing came back to normal. She consciously relaxed her brow and loosened her jaw. She needed to be relaxed and clear in order to consider what, if anything, she could do about Kirsty.

Why had Kirsty left the meadow? Alice told her she would

send help. Didn't she believe Alice when she said she was a two-day hike from civilization? Idiot. Or maybe she had actually been taken away by a bear. Alice closed her eyes against such a thought.

It couldn't be. She must have tried to hike back to Hardrock. So assuming she had left straight after Alice, followed where Alice had entered the forest and aimed roughly south and east, Kirsty would have bushwhacked all afternoon through the woods and gotten five miles, or maybe about ten miles max. By the time she would have heard the sound of a helicopter, she would have no way to signal them. She would have been way too far away from the meadow to even consider heading back that way. She would have had to continue south and east and would have had to try to find somewhere to sleep tonight. She would be cold, scared and lonely.

Meanwhile, the search and rescue people would be just setting out looking for her and they only had an hour or two left of daylight. No way were they going to find her tonight, she realized.

There was also no way Alice could find her.

Or was there? Alice suddenly thought of the old megaphone Coach used to scream at them. Maybe if she could fly over the forest and scream into the megaphone loud enough and fly slow enough to hear Kirsty's response over the noise of the wind in her ears...

Alice looked over at her dad, who was still tapping away at his phone. She closed her eyes and tried to relax and rest. She would be grateful for it later.

An hour later, with Billie still asleep, Madison emerged from the pool looking very satiated, which helped her get over the shock of seeing Billie covered in red sauce, sound asleep and beyond hope of showering.

"I didn't want to wake her," Alice said. "Madison, this is my dad. Dad, Madison."

"Pleased to meet you," Madison said. "What did those police want? Did they find Kirsty?"

"Unfortunately," Alice said, "they haven't. She left the meadow and tried to hike out on her own. So the helicopter only found an empty campsite."

Dad looked very strangely at Alice.

"I'm guessing," she added, for her dad's benefit.

Billie was starting to fidget and so Alice shushed them and they all quieted down. Madison smiled and pointed at the showers and walked off. Billie settled again and Alice patted her rhythmically.

After reluctantly passing Billie back to a showered and smiling Madison, Alice quietly said she would use one of her parents' phones to call her later and they said goodbye.

Alice ran off to borrow the megaphone from Coach. She told him it was for a project at school and he said he didn't really care what it was for. He unlocked a door to the main supply closet by the pool and they looked into a dark, damp-smelling space full of the odds and ends used for pool maintenance. He gave it to her and she stuffed it into her bag and ran to catch up with Dad, who was still texting as he walked distractedly toward the door.

She followed him out.

She knew better than to try to speak to her dad about the Mustang, so she just left it where it was and went home with her dad.

Her wounds cleaned up reasonably well in the shower. She once again marveled at her newfound ability to call prana into herself to help her heal wounds.

She gave Mom the same short version of her day that she had fed to her dad and the police.

Mom looked very fragile so she added a few apologies and repeated the big hug she had given her that morning.

Somehow the hug didn't have the same effect. Mom still seemed weak and upset.

"Mom," Alice asked as they finally set out the pizza boxes on the coffee table in front of the TV, "Dad said you have some kind of condition. What's up?"

Mom looked over at her dad and back to Alice. "I know you said you just had a normal day, but I feel like I have aged a decade today. You can't do that to us, Alice."

"Mom, I said I'm sorry." She was. She really felt sorry looking at her mom slouching there in front of her, with bags under her red eyes and her twitchy hands.

She tried to read her mom again but failed. She never could read either of her parents.

The pizza was as good as she had imagined and she ate with Dad in front of the TV, Dad pouring his second or third glass of wine as he continued to text people. They were presumably work texts.

Mom ate like a bird, got up and slumped around cleaning and organizing things.

M.A.S.H. reruns started at 10:00 p.m. as usual.

The combination of a significant amount of food in her stomach and the memory of holding a sleeping baby on her chest made Alice feel remarkably calm, considering what she had been through today.

After dinner she excused herself and said she needed an early night. She suspected Mom and Dad did too. It was time she flew out to search for Kirsty.

CHAPTER 17

As soon as she closed the door to her room, Alice kicked off her shoes, stuck the megaphone in a backpack and took a big drink of water. She knew she was going to regret the water later when she wanted to pee in midair. She opened her window, letting in the dark air and bright sounds of the forest at night.

Without any further hesitation, she crawled out onto the roof, ran down the slope and dove off the edge straight toward the hard surface of the driveway.

She felt the prana buoying her body, and with a few strong strokes she was airborne, banking north through the night toward the darkness of the Knifespur Wilderness.

She was getting to know the topography of the Knifespur pretty well by now. She knew Kirsty was desperate but not completely stupid. She would have had a basic idea which way to walk, using the sun as a guide, and the moon, that shone brightly in the sky tonight.

She suspected Kirsty would be bushwhacking because the clearing in which she had been dumped was not serviced by any of the trails used by the local horse pack trip operators or by hikers. Alice hadn't seen any game trails out there when she was crashing through the woods, searching for a place to take off after leaving Kirsty. Kirsty would know the game trails wouldn't take her to civilization anyway. They would lead to and from watering holes, hiding places and food sources. So Kirsty would have just bushwhacked in a southerly direction, hoping to hit the town or at least the state highway.

Alice recalled there were two main draws out of the wilderness area to the south. One contained a stream that was flowing high and brown after the recent rains, surrounded by heavy undergrowth that would have made passage difficult, and the other was dry and more accessible.

It was in the latter where Alice eventually located Kirsty. She had been using the megaphone, shouting Kirsty's name every twenty seconds or so, and finally got a screaming response.

Alice shouted to Kirsty to stop and wait exactly where she was. She told her she was flying in a glider and couldn't land; the not being able to land thing was true, at least. Alice took note of the GPS coordinates using her mom's phone and promised to send help in the morning.

Kirsty shouted back that she was scared but okay. She was cold but she had water.

Alice flew around a little until she could find a bar of mobile phone signal, downloaded a map of the area, tagged the spot where Kirsty was and texted it to Madison to forward it on to Nancy, the policewoman. Then she returned to Kirsty, told her what she'd done and threw a backpack containing the phone down to her, so she could see exactly where she was. The backpack also contained a warm blanket and a jacket, some energy gels and the megaphone, which she should use to call out to rescuers in the morning.

After picking up the pack, Kirsty shouted through the megaphone that she felt a lot better, that there was an emergency signal on the phone, and she was going to dial 911.

The whole thing had taken two hours. It was midnight, the sky was clear and beautiful, and Alice was on her way home. The sordid affair seemed to be wrapped up. Rajendra was either dead or long gone, Kirsty was going to be okay, and all was well.

When she neared the boundary of the wilderness area, near Mr. Rao's house, she saw a little light bouncing through the trees along the main trail that lead up to the wilderness area.

Alice was impressed with the dedication of the search and rescue people to have someone running along a trail in the middle of the night.

She risked flying a little lower to try and catch a glimpse of who they were. She saw the trees thinning out on a rocky rise. The little light was bouncing along a ridge above that.

When she was close enough to see who it was, fear surged through her nervous system. It was the other Indian guy she had seen with Bhakti in the library. She remembered him as the odd man out. She hadn't seen him again since then, not at Bhakti's house that day, nor at the lecture. What the hell was he doing running up here, she wondered. He was obviously searching for Kirsty, but was he trying to help ensure she was safely rescued or was he trying to prevent her from ever being found?

She swam up to a higher altitude and made some quick guesstimates about his chances of reaching Kirsty before any of the official search and rescue teams.

He was running well. Not as fast as Alice and Rajendra had during the daytime chase, but steadily. Probably about six miles an hour, she estimated, impressive for someone running in the middle of the night along unfamiliar trails. He was on a trail leading due north into the wilderness area. She knew that after ten miles the trail banked to the east toward a series of high altitude lakes. In order for this Indian guy to reach Kirsty, he would have to break away from the trail at that point when it banked east and bushwhack three miles due west. He could potentially run the ten miles along the trail in two hours and the bushwhacking would take him at least another couple of hours. The best case scenario was he would reach Kirsty at four in the morning, but only if he knew exactly where Kirsty was, which was highly unlikely.

Alice didn't think she could do anything about him. She couldn't just drop a rock on his head. First because she didn't have a rock, and second because she was pretty sure she couldn't hurt him without knowing what his agenda was. She wasn't sure if she had it in her to injure someone anyway.

Alice didn't know what else she could do, so she flew toward home. On the way she saw where he had parked his white Lexus four-wheel-drive at the wilderness boundary near her house.

She continued flying above the road toward her house when she saw something else. There was another vehicle down there. She saw some taillights flash and could hear a low, growling engine. It sounded a little like her Mustang. Then the whisper came to her.

"What are you bumpkins doing out here?" Rajendra's ratty whisper said, reaching her like an anti-aircraft missile, killing her concentration and severing her connection with the prana around her.

She began to fall toward the earth, shocked at the knowledge that Rajendra was alive and nearby. She managed to recover just enough buoyancy to survive the impact with the soft earth as she rolled to a stop on the shoulder of the gravel road.

Alice lay on the ground going through a mental checklist. Legs okay. Feeling in all fingers and toes. Breathing okay. Head okay. Some cuts and bruises on my back. Should be okay. Hamstring hurts.

She had bigger problems. The headlights of a black Jeep rounded a corner, its engine thumping deeply, and they had definitely seen her.

"So that's where you are," Rajendra's whisper sneered. It sounded like it was coming from the opposite direction to the approaching Jeep.

"Lying on the roadside like a fifty rupee Delhi whore. If only these local idiots weren't here…"

Alice jumped up and waved her arms wildly at the

approaching Jeep. Wait a minute, she thought, what if the Jeep driver is Rajendra's partner? She turned and ran toward home. She heard the car skid to a stop and a door open.

"Wait, Alice?" It was a loud male voice, definitely not Indian. Young. She slowed to a jog. "Slow down, girl. We've been sent to give you a hand."

Alice turned around, bent over, and kept her hands on her knees, lifting her forehead toward the voice. It was the voice of someone big, trying to pretend they were small and not scary, like a mugger speaking to a toddler.

She heard the door close, and another one. He had killed the engine. Maybe another effort to soften their approach, but the lights were still on and she couldn't see anyone yet. Alice didn't respond.

"Are you okay?" the same voice said. "Why were you running?"

"Just out for a jog," she finally said. "You guys have engine trouble?"

"No, like I said, we have been sent to see if you needed a hand."

"You're not with Rajendra?"

"We're friends of Bhakti and your dad. Who's Rajendra?"

Alice stood up and walked as fast as she could toward the driver's side of the Jeep.

As soon as she got out of the glare of the headlights, she could see the two guys standing next to their doors. They were huge, about her size, or maybe bigger. They towered over the Jeep like it was a compact car. Both guys wore ashram yellows but they were way too small for them. She went straight for the back door, opened it up and jumped in. She hoped the car had decent suspension, because it was about to support six hundred pounds of people meat.

As soon as their doors were closed, Alice took some deep breaths to calm herself and said, "Thanks." She immediately noticed the car smelled disgusting, like dirty, wet dogs.

They both smiled at each other and the driver started the Jeep and gunned it down the road. The Jeep was quieter on the inside than she expected, but it was also a lot faster than she imagined, faster than her Mustang, that's for sure.

"Where to?"

"Home. Just ahead about a half mile."

The guys looked at each other. She could see the driver's eyes in the rear-view mirror but she didn't dare read him because he might wreck the car.

"How do you guys know my dad?"

"We don't. We're friends of your dad's friend, Bhakti."

"Names?"

"Prempuri and Sevapuri."

"Right. I can just picture those names on the back of your football uniforms." She decided to test them a bit. "So are you guys with that Indian guy with the huge calf muscles?"

They looked at each other. "Which guy?"

"The one who drives Bhakti around."

"Uh, yeah, we were looking for him too."

"Well, he's running in the woods just up there."

The guy in the passenger seat picked up his phone, punched a number and put it to his ear.

"We picked her up."

Alice heard a female voice on the other end of the phone, probably Bhakti.

"We'll go back after we drop her home. It's a good time." He hung up.

"Hey," the driver said suddenly, looking at her in the rear-view mirror. "Aren't you that famous retard girl, the one who used to go around fixing and cleaning things on other people's property without them knowing?"

"You shouldn't say that word," the other guy said. "Retard. It's not polite."

"Oh, excuse me. You are totally that retarded girl! You tried to fix my grandma's fence once. I remember. I was coming home from college to visit her and there you were, this little fat girl, with a screwdriver and a little bottle of Elmer's glue. When I asked grandma who you were, she just said you were that unusual do-gooder girl who can't talk."

He looked over at the other guy and said, "You know what I mean, don't you? You heard of her? She's like the village fool!"

"Sounds like she can talk now."

"Yeah. Hey! How did you learn how to talk? You get struck by lightning or something?"

"Come to think of it," Alice said, "yes."

"I knew it! Someone should write a book about you!"

"Thanks."

"They'd call it 'The Village Retard.'"

"That word is not very PC. Not cool," the other guy said again. He seemed a bit more serious this time, almost violent.

"So are you still retarded?" the driver asked her, peering in the rear-view mirror.

Alice suddenly flashed back to the call with her school counselor. Maybe she was actually developmentally disadvantaged. Maybe that's what her condition was.

"Probably," she said, looking down.

After a moment of silent driving, she saw they were approaching her house.

"Thanks for the ride, guys. I'm good."

CHAPTER 18

Upon waking, Alice was not aware of having dreamed, and felt disoriented. The room was full of unkind daylight. Suddenly concerned she had missed something, she snapped up into a sitting position and checked her bedside clock: 11:30 a.m. How could that be, she puzzled. How could she have simply slept through the five o'clock alarm and kept sleeping for another six-and-a-half hours? She checked the date on her phone, just to be sure she hadn't slept for a year. It was still a week before her birthday, so she had slept only for a night.

The first memory that came to her sleepy mind was the image of a cute little toddler eating pasta. Her feet found the floor carefully and she stood up: so far, so good. She used the bathroom, wracking her brain to remember Madison's mobile number. She had never had to know it, as it was programmed into her phone.

Somehow it came to her andshe rushed out to the landline and dialed Madison's number.

"Hey."

"Hi, Madison," Alice said quietly, hoping her voice wouldn't carry downstairs.   "They find Kirsty yet?"

"Good morning to you too."

"I don't think it's morning. I just woke up though."

"That's lucky. I had to wake up at 5:00 a.m. when Billie did."

"No swimming? No school?"

"Obviously, no. I just couldn't face any of it. I'm too freaked out. The police have been here, and the FBI. They were asking all these questions about how I got the map you sent me showing where Kirsty was. I didn't want to tell them it was from you because I seriously don't know how you know all that stuff and I didn't want to get you in trouble. I just said I found it on the internet."

"So you slept, like, three hours."

"You slept ten."

"I guess so. Don't your parents look after their own daughter?"

"Which one? To answer your first question, Alice, yes, they did find Kirsty. She had hypothermia but she's going to be okay: physically, at least. She's in the hospital. I just spoke to her. I can't go in to see her today because I have Billie. Are you going to go see her?"

Alice's mom turned the corner and glanced up from the bottom of the stairs. She looked gaunt, pale and tentative.

"Honey? You okay?"

"Mom, are you okay? You look sick."

"Did you just wake up?"

"Yeah, Mom. I'm on the phone."

"Oh, of course. Can you come straight down when you're off? There's food."

"Sure."

Alice put the phone back to her ear.

"Hey..."

"I heard," Madison said. "I gotta go too. I think my mom's emerging from her study."

Alice thought of cute little Billie and kind of missed her. "What are you two going to do today?"

"I may pop in to the pool later. I have to get in some extra laps and the pool is closed this afternoon for cleaning, which means some guy will come in for five minutes and dump some chemicals in the water and go drink beer somewhere. Billie will have her usual pasta by poolside while she watches me swim."

"Nice."

"So are you going to tell me?"

"What?"

"About how you got those maps? And how you reached Kirsty in the middle of the Knifespur? I assume you didn't drive that Mustang?"

"Not really."

"Alice, it's too far for you to have gone there and back on foot. So what really happened after you ditched me yesterday morning?"

"It's complicated."

"Well?"

"I flew."

"Which is a metaphor for?"

"Flying."

"Oh, come on, Alice."

Alice didn't say anything.

"Okay, whatever. That lady Nancy really likes you and keeps telling the others there must be an innocent explanation— innocent explanations. But you'll have to give it all to them this time, you know. This is getting very serious."

"Oh."

"I didn't tell them about meeting you on the highway to Wyoming Or about that Mustang. Most of what you told me was weird. Like that bit about some barn in Laramie. I didn't tell them any of that. They would have gone out of their minds."

"Okay."

"Okay, catch you later."

"Yep."

Alice chucked the phone down on its receiver as though it

was too hot to touch.

Life was too complicated. All she wanted was a few normal days. A good coffee from her usual café would be pretty welcome.

After showering last night she had put on clean underwear, so all she had to do was chuck on a sports bra, a t-shirt and jeans and head downstairs to face the world, or hopefully just to face her mom.

She made extra noise on the stairs and rounded into the kitchen, relieved to find it was only her mom there.

"Hi, Mom. What's wrong with you? You haven't looked good lately. And don't tell me it's just stress."

"Darling, what would you like to eat?"

"Coffee."

"I'll make you some. Sit down and start talking."

"About what?"

"Start from the moment you lied to us yesterday morning. About wanting to stay home from swimming and from school because you were sick. That would be a good place to start. Don't leave anything out."

Alice slumped into a chair.

"What about the police? Shouldn't we just record a statement for them? Or should I just wait until they get here in person so that I don't need to repeat the story?"

"Stop being clever and spill it, young lady."

Alice realized her mom was deadly serious and looked like she was too weak to be argued with, so she took her time and gave her mom a basic outline of yesterday's events.

Rather than say I flew, she always just said I went, and she left out the chase to Wyoming and the drive back in the Mustang. She suspected she would need to start providing an alternative explanation for the flying sooner or later, but not now.

Alice's mom put a large coffee in front of Alice. "Okay. Now—I already know the answer to this question but I'm just going to ask it anyway. You know, for clarification. You're telling me you snuck out of the house twice yesterday, after the police and your dad and I told you that you were to go nowhere without Dad or me driving you."

She tried to smile and offered Alice milk, which she accepted and poured into her coffee that she already knew was going to taste like dishwater and would do nothing to lift her spirits.

"Well, yes," Alice replied, "but both times it was for pretty good reasons, wouldn't you say?"

"The answer to that question depends on your point of view, doesn't it, Alice?"

"I thought I was the one who was good at answering questions with questions."

"Try answering a question with an answer right now. If you were me, Alice, would you think your daughter was right to sneak out of the house and try to rescue her friends from a kidnapper? By herself? Without telling anyone?"

Alice considered the question and thought her mom was pretty lucky she didn't know the rest of the story.

"Yeah, you're right, Mom. If we suddenly woke up one morning and changed places, like in one of those Hollywood movies, I would probably not be very relaxed about things right now."

"Okay, good. That's something. Now—the next major question I need answered with an answer is this. Do you intend to keep risking your own life to play hero? Do you intend to keep ignoring your father's and my wishes and keep ignoring the forceful requests from authorities like the police?"

"That's at least two questions and maybe three."

Alice saw her cheekiness had nearly knocked her mother down. She regretted it immediately and put down her coffee.

"Sorry, sorry. I'm sorry. No, I don't intend to keep doing that stuff. Okay?"

Alice took a drink from her coffee, which was still not doing anything for her, and saw that Mom was revived a little by Alice's apology.

"Mom, where's Dad? How's his hand?"

"He's at the hospital visiting a colleague."

"John got hurt?" Alice asked hopefully. How great would it be if John got hit by a bus?

"He didn't say exactly who he was visiting. Now, the easy question; where is my phone?"

"Mom, I'm really sorry about your phone. Really. I thought I told you last night. I lost it when I was running around. I know you use that to do all your bookings. I'm really, really sorry about it. Do you have any backup phone or something?"

"Never mind about my bookings; I'm so beyond worrying about my upcoming course."

"Okay."

"Now, I'm afraid we are required to pay a visit to the local police station soon. Officer Petrovic asked that I bring you in as soon as you were up and ready. She has called a few times already today."

"I haven't even eaten anything yet."

Alice's mom opened the oven door and pulled out a huge baking dish full of some kind of soufflé. Alice realized she had been smelling it the whole time but her brain had discounted the distant possibility that her mom had cooked something.

"Wow, mom. That smells incredible."

"So surprised?"

"Um, no. I mean yes. Thank you anyway."

Mom pulled out a plate and some silverware, got down some salsa and set the whole soufflé and a spatula onto a chopping board on the table in front of Alice.

"I'll go get ready. Enjoy. There are a dozen eggs in that soufflé, by the way, so don't feel compelled to eat the whole thing. If I come downstairs to find you gone, I——"

"Mom, I'll be here. Okay? See you in a sec. Thanks for breakfast."

After Alice finished the whole soufflé, she felt a little bit better and considered how she intended to explain the flying thing to the police. She didn't have a phone to check any maps or call times, but she thought she could remember pretty well. She grabbed a pen and an unopened electricity bill from a pile on the table, and started a schedule on the back of the envelope, listing only the approximate times the police could verify:

6:00 or 6:30 a.m. police were here

8:30 or 9:00 a.m. arrived at Kirsty's meadow

9:00 a.m. or 9:30 a.m. left Kirsty's meadow

10:30 or 11:00 a.m. texted Kirty's location to Madison

11:30 a.m. or 12:00 p.m. took a taxi to the library

12:30 or 1:00 p.m. had close encounter with police at Mr. Rao's cabin

She knew Kirsty's meadow was about twenty miles into the wilderness area over rough terrain with no direct trail. She had flown the distance in less than an hour. At best, she could have run or walked that distance in seven or eight hours, but if she was on a bike and could find decent game trails, she may have been able to do it in three or four hours. According to her schedule, she supposedly did it in two hours or less.

Well, it would have to do. It wasn't totally impossible anyway, twenty miles in two hours. They would have to believe her, as there really wasn't any other rational explanation.

So long as she didn't have to prove it by showing the police her exact route: so long as nobody had found her bike yet, discarded by the side of the road after she had used it yesterday morning to help her take off into flight: so long as nobody found her own phone, which she probably lost somewhere in the dirt near Rajendra's barn in Laramie: so long as the Harley Davidson guy at the gas station never says anything to anyone important about seeing a tall, fat girl filling up an old Mustang with gas at a Laramie gas station: so long as nobody looked carefully at the Mustang parked at the pool. She thought there would be quite a bit of her blood and hair in there.

"Are you ready?" Alice's mom asked, holding her bag. She looked slightly more relaxed. She had probably gone to her yoga room for a few minutes, Alice thought.

"Yeah, Mom. Let me get my swim bag in case we're still out later. I can't miss any more training."

"We'll see about that."

Alice ran upstairs again, packed a swim bag and remembered she had promised herself she would look at the mirror before going out.

Standing in the bathroom, she was surprised at the stranger glaring back at her. This person was not a fat little girl. Who was she?

She was distracted by how clean the mirror was compared with the one at her pool. Her mind grew curious about who had been cleaning this bathroom mirror all these years. Certainly not Alice.

She began to look around the bathroom with a kind of new appreciation. It was as though she flipped a light switch that had never been turned on before. She grew aware, for the first time, that the faucet wasn't surrounded with a ring of grime where the metal met the porcelain of the sink, like it did at the pool and most other bathrooms Alice used outside of the house. She turned toward the shower and saw the same was true of the bathroom hot and cold handles and the shower door. Spotless. Toilet. Spotless. Mom had even scrubbed the soap dish. Was that normal? The floor was spotless. Even the corners behind the toilet. She speculated Mom cleaned her toothbrush without telling her about it, as it looked clean too.

With a flood of guilt, she recalled walking past and totally ignoring her mom once just last week as she donned rubber gloves and stumbled around the house cleaning things. Another instance emerged in her memory...a couple weeks ago? She had seen her mom cleaning the downstairs bathroom and Alice was annoyed because she wanted to use it and couldn't. How often had she cleaned the house when Alice wasn't home? When Alice was home, how often had she ignored Mom while she cleaned? Alice had somehow never noticed who cleaned the house, like the cleaning lady version of her mom was an invisible slave.

Is there something wrong with my brain, she speculated. How could I have never noticed who did the housework all these years? How could I have not even offered to help? Perhaps another symptom of my condition? Surely a daughter should at least feel gratitude for a clean bathroom? She could say thanks every now and then for a free laundry service That has been provided to her for her whole life so far. Is that a debt? If so, how big? How can it ever be repaid? Alice was suddenly overwhelmed with the thought. When was Mother's Day?

Rushing down the stairs, Alice saw the back of her mom's head in the living room. She was sitting in a chair, which was unusual. Perhaps she had decided they didn't have to go.

"Ready," she called out. "Mom?"

"Mom!"

Alice walked over and saw her mom was dead.

She rushed over and grabbed her arm. "Mom?"

She wasn't dead. Her eyes fluttered open but her pupils were dilated and something seemed wrong. She looked at Alice in a strange way for a moment before her brain rebooted and she could focus.

"Oh, man, I think I dozed off there for a moment."

"Mom, you were not dozing," Alice replied. "You were out cold."

She tried to get up but Alice pushed her back down.

"No way, Mom: stay there. I'm getting you a glass of water.

"I'm fine."

"Stay."

After delivering the water, she saw Mom was prepared to stay seated for the time being. She dialed her Dad. He didn't answer, of course, so she quietly called 911, whispered the situation, acknowledged an ambulance had been sent, and hung up.

She considered whether or not she should tell her mom an ambulance was coming, but she thought she would just play it by ear.

"How's it going, Mom?" she asked loudly, as though she was an invalid.

"Not deaf, Alice. I'm sorry, sweetheart, I don't know what happened."

"I guess it's a good thing you didn't fall," Alice said. "Do you remember how you got to this chair?"

"I just felt faint and so I sat down. That's all."

"Mom, you have looked like crap for weeks. What is going on?"

As Mom paused, pretending like she hadn't heard the question, Alice wished again she could read either of her parents. She never had been able to and didn't bother trying again now.

"Well, I guess we should get going," Mom said, putting her glass down and leaning forward to hoist herself up.

"No way. You can't drive, Mom."

"You are in no position to dictate anything to me."

"Mom, you passed out. That's not normal. You look like a prisoner of war. You need to see a doctor."

"As soon as you can demonstrate a shred of good judgement, I'll start listening to your sage advice. For the time being, I think I'll rely on my own grasp of reality."

Alice looked around desperately for a diversion, but found nothing.

"Mom," she said with resignation, "I gotta tell you, I called for an ambulance. They'll be here any second."

"You did what?"

"Called 911."

They locked eyes and Alice felt like her mom was reading her, but suspected that wasn't possible. She wondered if her mom had the strength to get up and smack Alice, but she couldn't tell if the look on her face was one of anger or what.

Mom reached out, took her water and looked away from Alice.

Some kind of moment passed. Alice felt a sense of loss but didn't know what it was that had been lost.

"Mom," she appealed, "something is wrong and you're either not admitting it to yourself or you're not admitting it to me. I'm not buying any of that stuff that Dad said about you just being stressed. I'm sorry if you aren't happy with me for calling 911and I wish I could drive you to see someone, but I can't, and I can't reach Dad, so I did the next best thing."

Her mom looked at her again. This time Alice could tell it was a look of bewilderment, then a trace of a smile.

Alice repaid with a decent smile of her own. "I just want to say once and for all, thank you for cleaning my bathroom all these years."

Mom's smile turned into a snigger.

"No, seriously, Mom, I feel like I have been in a daze until now. I'm so ashamed I haven't offered to help with the cleaning and stuff."

"Aw, Blub," Mom said, tilting her head and raising her eyebrows. "Don't talk that way. That's just what parents do. They don't do it for the gratitude."

"Not all parents do. You should see what Madison has to do to keep her family going."

"What does she have to do?"

"Well, basically, she is like a nanny for her little sister. You know, the one I babysat last night."

Alice's mom darkened as the topic of last night was raised.

"Mom, I just mean I recognize that you do a lot. I'm going to try to help more."

"Alice, you do enough. All you ever do is help people. I can't tell you how many phone calls I have received over the years from people. 'Your daughter just tried to repair my car.' 'Your daughter just found my cat.' 'Your daughter carried my bags for me.' 'Your daughter splinted my son's arm.'"

"Yeah, and the whole time you were here working like a slave."

"It's my house. I want it clean and orderly. I can do it if I want."

"Just saying. I want to help."

As the ambulance pulled up, Mom tried again to sit up but was foiled by Alice's strong hand. It was the second time in two days the inside of their house was lit up by flashing blue lights. Alice let them in and pointed to her mom, who looked more embarrassed than unwell.

As Alice was getting her bag to take with her in the ambulance, she saw Mom whispering something to the paramedic. He nodded, saying something else. Mom got a panicked look and pointed at Alice. The guy shook his head. As Alice was walking over to find out what they were talking about, Mom started raising her voice.

"I'm telling you, I'm not going anywhere without her."

"Ma'am, we can't take you anywhere you don't want to go. It's your prerogative to refuse treatment. All I can do is recommend that we take you to the hospital for evaluation. There are any number of things that can contribute to your symptoms. We're not qualified to offer a diagnosis."

"Fine, then you have to take her in the ambulance."

"As I told you, under most circumstances it's against policy to take additional passengers in the ambulance. But I'm happy to call someone for you?"

Mom gave him Alice's dad's number, which rang out, as usual.

"There's no-one else."

"Your call, ma'am. An RMA is your decision."

"Mom," Alice said.

"Not now," her mom said while raising a frail-looking hand.

"Mom!"

"What?" Mom looked annoyed.

"Call Nancy."

"Who?"

"That policewoman who wants to interview me. She'll probably be here in, like, thirty seconds and would be happy to take me to the hospital if she doesn't take me straight to jail."

Mom paused, then agreed and gave Nancy's card to the paramedic. The paramedic spoke to Nancy on the phone.

Alice went in to the kitchen to get the envelope on which she had taken notes that would help explain her new version of events.

Mom was able to walk to the ambulance and, as expected, Nancy was there by the time the ambulance was ready to depart. She didn't look happy to see Alice, but she was alone, which was good news. Alice didn't want to deal with the other policewoman. It took too much energy to figure out what she was talking about.

"Get in," she said to Alice roughly after the ambulance had left.

Alice fought against an impulse to run away. The day was cool, the sky was clear and the lightning tree was a ten minute jog away. Easy. She would resist this time, she decided. For Mom.

Alice sat down in the front passenger seat of Nancy's truck, which was obviously her privately-owned vehicle. It was a huge Ram truck with four doors and some kind of air intake on the hood. It looked like it could be as old as Alice but probably was in better condition, at least at the moment.

Nancy walked slowly around to the driver's side, shut her door and paused before turning the keys in the ignition.

"Alice," she said, looking Alice in the eyes. "I am supposed to be arresting you right now."

"Where'd you get this truck?" Alice asked, marveling at all the mud on the floor, the various ranch tools piled in the back seats and the total lack of anything fun like a sticker or a little dashboard thing with a bobbing head.

"I am supposed to arrest you for obstruction," Nancy continued, ignoring Alice's impertinent question. "Do you know what obstruction of justice is?"

"Not really. But I could probably guess. Hey, what kind of gas mileage are you getting?"

"Ten."

"Is that good?"

"This is not meant to be a soccer mom car that gets good mileage and I'm no soccer mom."

"So why aren't you arresting me?"

"Because I like you. And I feel sorry for you. But I'm probably going to arrest you at the end of this car ride. Or maybe before. You'll be in the hands of the juvenile courts and out of mine."

"Oh." Alice was only half-listening. She was still taking in her environment and recognizing how different this side of Nancy was to the cop Nancy that came to her house yesterday.

"Hey, you're like a real local, aren't you," Alice said. In Hardrock, you weren't considered to be a local unless you were a third generation rancher or a Native American. Certain exceptions were made for non-ranchers if they at least hunted and fished, and wore a baseball cap with a motor oil brand on it. Everyone else was considered gentrified outsiders and treated accordingly, at least by the locals. Locals were culturally opposed to everyone else, like Alice's family and Madison's and Kirsty's, and everyone associated with the university and the ski area.

"So," Nancy said, "let's talk. Tell me everything."

"Okay. Hey, that lady Bhakti, I mean Mary Flowers, was a real local too. Must really bother you to see her all messed up like that."

Nancy didn't answer. Alice smelled the air and looked at Nancy, who was still gripping the steering wheel tightly.

"No offense but, um, there is some kind of nasty smell in this truck..."

Nancy dropped her hands to her lap and dropped her chin in defeat.

"No, seriously," Alice said. "I was in some guys' car last night and it had the same smell. Like dead, wet dog or roadkill skunk or something."

Nancy looked over at Alice.

"What guys? What car?"

"Yeah, totally the same smell," Alice said without answering Nancy. "But theirs was about a million times stronger."

"After all the warnings you have received that there are dangerous people around at the moment, you got in a car with strangers?"

"Yeah, they were strange."

"What car."

"It was a black Jeep. They were big guys. Dressed in ashram yellows, but they didn't fit, like they just borrowed them. I was out walking and they said they were friends of Bhakti. But these guys didn't act like Babaji people at all."

"What did they act like?"

"Like college football players, at least one of them. They called themselves Prempuri and Sevapuri. But I bet their names are Jeb and T.J. or whatever."

"What else."

"I...I think the football player guy may be a local, or at least he grew up around here."

"How do you know?"

Alice strained to remember what gave her that impression. There was a gap in her memory of the car ride. She thought there was something he said that was somehow important, but it was just beyond her grasp. All she could remember was he was kind of lopsided.

"I can't remember. But I think he had an old shoulder injury. In his right shoulder. The muscles were a little wasted and he favored that side."

Alice tried to remember something more.

"They were both big and tall. The football player guy was bigger and he moved like an athlete. Kind of like you. But not the other guy. He's just as big in his upper body but he wasn't really natural. He was all stiff, with skinny knees. I'm guessing he's a gym rat, not an athlete."

"What else. Why do you think one of them was a local?"

Alice started to feel agitated and almost couldn't speak.

"Juvenile court," Nancy added. "They will have total control over your life."

Alice pushed herself, but it was like trying to remember someone else's memory. It just wasn't coming.

"I...I can't remember..."

She simply couldn't remember the middle part. She knew it was a conversation of some sort, but it was like it was draped with black curtains and something told her something terrible was behind them.

"Something..." she pushed herself further. "I think they said something to me, something mean, like they...It was the shoulder guy, he said something mean to me, like he knew who I was, but... Nancy, I can't ..."

"You can't what?"

"I can't remember. Something mean."

Nancy sighed. "Did they say anything about bears, by chance?"

"What? Bears?"

"Never mind. Alice, how did you know where Kirsty was last night? She has reported that you delivered a survival kit, but she hasn't said how exactly you accomplished a feat that all the other search and rescue resources could not."

Alice started to recover and looked at Nancy. She didn't need to read her mind to understand Nancy was trying to help. She was trying to give her a way to get out of being in trouble, but she didn't think she could prevent that now.

"Um, I'm not sure, exactly."

Nancy paused, finally loosened her grip on the steering wheel. She started her truck, which made a throaty growl. Before putting it into gear, she turned to Alice.

"You are going to have to fill in a lot of gaps in your story, Alice. This is a very serious investigation now. Kidnapping is a federal offense and not only is the FBI involved, there are people here worried about terrorism and national security."

"Okay."

"I'm sorry your mom is sick," Nancy said as they pulled out of the driveway onto the gravel road. "What happened?"

Alice paused, and when she realized this was not part of the interrogation, she sighed and said, "She passed out. We were about to come to the police station to talk to you. She has been really gaunt and sickly looking lately."

After watching the trees go by for a moment longer, she added, "I keep asking Mom and Dad what's wrong with her, but they won't tell me. They seem to know something though."

"That sucks."

"Nancy, I know you want to interrogate me some more and arrest me, but can you do all that at the hospital? I'm kind of worried about her."

Nancy got on her phone via some kind of Bluetooth link and reported Alice's enhanced description of the two Jeep guys to some young guy and said to add that to the APB.

"The Jeep has some kind of crazy-huge motor that sounds like ten Harley Davidsons combined together into one ungodly machine," Alice said loudly for the benefit of the young guy on the phone.

"Did you catch that?" Nancy asked, got an affirmative answer, and added, "It sounds like it could be those guys who work for that suspected ice dealer. Ask Veronica or someone in the Task Force."

"What's ice?" Alice asked after Nancy hung up.

"It's a drug."

"So those guys are drug dealers?"

"Maybe they work for one. I think I know that car. It should be pretty easy to find them, now that you have condescended to provide enough information. You see now how that works?"

"I said I was sorry. So why did they stink? No, actually, let me make a hypothesis. This is fun." Alice thought about it for a moment then announced, "They faked a bear attack on someone."

"What? How did you know that?"

"You mean I'm right? Wow, that's really amazing. I just remember you asked me a weird question about bears a moment ago. It didn't make sense. You don't seem to have had any contact

242

with those guys and yet somehow you smell like them, or like something they had in their Jeep. Last night they didn't have a live bear in their car and they weren't injured, except for that old shoulder injury I mentioned. So they didn't have an encounter with a live bear. So they either had a dead bear in their car, or they had come in contact with one, carried it or something, or they had something with them in their car that smelled like a bear: like in a jar. I'm guessing it was that because how many dead bears can there be around Hardrock? At some point between then and now, they did something with that smelly bear jar that made someone have to call the police. I can't think of any reason some criminal guys would have something that smelled like a bear except for the possibility they wanted to hurt someone and make it look like a bear did it. You responded to that call and went there to investigate. That's how you got the smell on you. The only reasonable conclusion is those guys staged a bear attack on someone. Who was it? Some other drug dealer?"

Nancy looked over at Alice and smiled approvingly. It made Alice's spine tingle, maybe in a good way, or maybe it was horror. She wasn't sure which.

"A journalist."

Alice figured if Nancy could make all these phone calls while driving, she could afford to have her mind read and be out of action for five seconds. So she took a deep belly breath and locked in.

She didn't have time to admire Nancy's orderly mind this time or Nancy would crash the car. She quickly followed the thoughts concerning the journalist and found an unspoken sentence: The journalist is the cute Indian-looking guy with big, strong legs who has been posing as a disciple of Babaji.

Alice broke it off and thought for a moment. She finally put it all together. The journalist must be Bhakti's sixth man from the library. The same guy she had seen running around last night just before she saw the black Jeep.

Nancy thought he was cute? Well, Alice considered, he was

definitely cuter than all the other ashram people. She was again surprised at how many sides of Nancy there were. Weight-lifting cop by day, rancher on the weekend, and she had a thing for Indian men with big legs.

"Nancy, you know how I said I got in a car with those guys?"

"Yes?"

"It was near my house. I had just cycled up and found Kirsty in the woods. I gave her my mom's phone and those other things as a kind of survival kit. On my way home I think I saw that journalist guy. Those guys must have done the attack on him after they dropped me home."

Nancy's phone rang and when she pressed a button to answer, the young police guy spoke as if the earlier phone call hadn't ended yet.

"Veronica has ID'd your white males and we have local names and addresses."

"Organize a warrant and go pick them up," Nancy said. "Run it by Veronica first and make sure you're not stepping on any toes."

"Understood."

She looked at Alice and added, "It's time, I think, to try to try to get the judge to approve a warrant to bring in that guru and that nun, Mary Flowers, and to search the house."

"For soliciting a kidnapping? You sure we have probable cause? The boss says we have to make sure we have a lot of confidence before we take that step because of his senior religious status. So far, we can't find the small Indian man with the little plane and all we have is two teenagers who say he was acting on behalf of the yoga guru. We don't have any real evidence."

"Let's focus on the assault on the journalist. If we can confirm the link between Mrs. Flowers and the bear guys, we can get a warrant for conspiracy on the second degree assault. Then we'll see what happens with the rest."

"Understood."

After Nancy hung up again, Alice said, "I guess it's too much to ask for a takeaway coffee on the way to the hospital?"

"Yes, it is. Alice, this is not a coffee run and I am not a taxi driver. What you need to do now is to start filling in the details you left out about Kirsty's kidnapping. Like how you knew where she was—both times. And ..."

Alice didn't really hear the rest because she was already working on developing new hypotheses to chat with Nancy about. She was feeling proud of herself that she had guessed correctly about the bear and she wondered if maybe she could use the same kind of process to guess who rat-faced Rajendra worked for.

After a brief pause, she said, "I think you'll find something interesting about that photo of Babaji in Kirsty's tent."

"What are you talking about?"

"It will be something that looks incriminating."

"Why?"

"Well, you guys have seen the meadow, right?"

"I have seen the photos. There are forensics people there right now."

"Kirsty told you everything?"

"What is everything?"

"That her kidnapper told her Babaji had organized for her to be brought there to get enlightened?"

"Yes, she told us that."

"You saw the photo of Babaji in the tent?"

"What about it?"

"Well, like you said to your colleague on the phone, you can't find any evidence linking Babaji to the kidnappings other than what the kidnapper told his teenaged victim. That means that you have already checked the whole meadow and not found any evidence. Rajendra is smart. He would know that you guys would do more than check the meadow. You would try to figure who bought all that camping stuff. I'm guessing everything was cheap Indian camping gear, right? Stuff he probably brought with him from India? Stuff you can't trace?"

"Mmm," Nancy said, as though she wasn't really paying

attention, but Alice could tell she was listening.

"So that leaves the photo, which is also an obvious thing for you guys to analyze most carefully because it's a photo of Babaji himself. Rajendra would know that. Rajendra would also know you would figure out you can't get those photos anywhere except Babaji's ashrams. I heard someone at Bhakti's house say Babaji is really particular about that."

"Mmm?" Nancy said.

"So all you have to do to figure out who really kidnapped Kirsty is find out where that photograph came from."

"Mmmmm..."

"It's obvious. There was no ransom and no other motive for the kidnapping, so either the story Rajendra wasn't lying to Kirsty and it's true that Babaji wanted her in that meadow to get enlightened, or Rajendra was just trying to make it look like Babaji did."

"And the photo?"

"Come on, Nancy. If Rajendra works for Babaji and it's true he wanted Kirsty put there to get enlightened, then Babaji will have provided Rajendra with the photo."

"Mmm...."

"If, on the other hand, Rajendra did the kidnappings in order to frame Babaji, the photo will have a different history. Rajendra will have made it look like Babaji supplied it, but he won't really have..."

"Mmmm?"

"Oh, come on, I know this guy. He really is that smart. I kind of know how this guy's mind works."

Nancy pursed her lips, pulled over to the side of the road, put the car in park and turned to Alice.

"This is the big moment, Alice. This is the moment you level with me. I have three questions and your future depends on how you answer them. Number one, how do you know the kidnapper's name is Rajendra? Number two, how would you know how his mind works, Alice? Number three, how did you track Kirsty?"

Alice didn't answer and was quiet for a moment.

"Nancy," she finally said, "if I tell you everything, can you promise to keep it from my parents, if at all possible?"

"No."

Alice thought for a moment and decided to give Nancy a short version of the real story. "Okay, here you go. Two days ago, on Sunday afternoon, before the storm, I was running in the woods near my house and Rajendra tried to kidnap me too, and he kind of told me his name and what he intended to do with me, but I got away and I used the information to find Kirsty, and if my mom finds out, she might really die."

Alice saw Nancy's jaw drop, snap back up, and her cheek muscles tensed.

"If that is true," she said, "I find it difficult to understand why you were unable to tell me about it in your living room yesterday morning when Kirsty was reported missing."

Alice didn't hear a question, so she didn't bother to respond.

"Okay, back to the interesting stuff," Alice said, smiling. "So I think I can tell you how to find Rajendra. I think he's dead."

Nancy was shaking her head in disbelief, but Alice kept going.

"He mentioned something about a barn near Laramie airport where he was going to have someone pick up his plane which he was selling. It was an electric ultralight."

"You know that information... exactly... how and why?"

"He thought he had me and I overheard a phone call. I looked it up on the internet later and found details on a website called uship.com that people use to organize private deals for transporting things. You can find it too. Just google 'E-gull, Laramie,' and it comes up. E-gull is the kind of plane he has."

"Why do you think he is dead?"

"Well, something happened when he was trying to kill me. He got injured. I think if you look around that barn in Laramie, you'll find him. Or just ask around there if anyone saw any Indians that had been hurt really bad."

"He flew to Laramie after he was hurt really bad."

"Something like that. I don't know. I'm not a police investigator."

"That's all very cute, Alice. I'm sure the FBI will jump right on it and explore your theory."

"Whatever. I bet I'm right: seriously. Check all that Laramie stuff, Nancy"

Nancy pulled back onto the empty road and drove to the hospital.

"Alice, let's go in to see your mom and then we'll talk some more."

Nancy parked in the emergency drop-off area and they walked into the emergency department.

As they walked, Alice imagined what it would be like to be a police officer. She figured she would only last a week or two before getting fed up with people like Nancy's partner, and like those beer cops from the pool last night. She imagined what it would be like to be the one to knock on Bhakti's door, serve a warrant and bring in the nun and the guru. Now that would be cool.

She remembered Nancy was probably going to arrest her first, before they even managed to get a warrant to arrest Babaji. What would Mom think about her daughter getting arrested?

The Hardrock hospital was brand new and Alice faintly remembered being there recently, though she couldn't remember why. It looked more like a ski chalet than a hospital, Alice thought, with huge log and stone construction and grand, tall ceilings. The hospital seemed very peaceful, obscuring the struggles within.

"Hey, Nancy," Alice said before they spoke to the nurse at the reception desk, "is it okay if we don't mention anything about you arresting me? To my mom, I mean. Not right now."

"I haven't decided yet what to do with you."

"Well, thanks. I think."

The nurse at reception looked at Alice carefully, as though

she was appraising her, and asked, "How are you feeling, honey?" She appeared not to be put off by the policewoman standing there.

"I...good, thanks. Here to see my mom, Victoria Brickstone."

"Of course. She's right in the back. I'll buzz you through. Your head is healing nicely."

Alice put her hand to her head and tried to think about which head injury the nurse was referring to and why she would have known about it.

They got sent back through a set of security doors to a curtained-off area where Alice's mom was lying down on a bed hooked up to an IV and a blood pressure monitor. She looked worse than ever.

"I'm fine," she said as soon as she saw Alice.

"Yep. So why do you look like crap? Why did you pass out?" Alice asked, walking over to her.

"They said I was just dehydrated and had low blood sugar. I'll get some fluids and they'll let me go home."

"Is that before or after you do chemo?"

"Excuse me?"

"Mom, why do you look so awful? Like a cancer patient?"

"Is that Nancy?"

"Nancy Pelosi, Mrs. Brickstone. Pleased to meet you."

"Thank you for bringing Alice over. We just panicked back there and didn't know who to call. I...We just didn't want to leave her home alone after...."

"That was a good call, Mrs. Brickstone, and I'm glad you're feeling better."

"So where's Dad?"

"I just got here, Alice, about ten minutes before you did. They called Dad for me from the ambulance and he said he'd meet me down here. I'm sure he'll be here any second."

"Wow, he answered his phone. Wasn't he already here visiting a colleague?"

"Yes. I'm sure he'll be right over."

"Oh, yes, this hospital is huge. I'm sure he would need to get a shuttle bus to cross the two hundred yards to get to his sick wife's sick bed. What a caring husband."

Mom didn't respond and Nancy looked at Alice. Nancy appeared almost sympathetic.

"So, Mom, why were you so dehydrated?"

"Alice, don't worry about me. I'm fine. Really."

"Can I talk to your doctor? Who is in charge here?"

"She has already seen me and is confident I'll be fine after I get my fluids up."

Alice was getting more and more frustrated but didn't know how to break the impasse. The mention of fluids made her think maybe a cup of coffee might help her think clearly. Who knows, maybe she'd run into her dad at the hospital cafeteria?

"Nancy, can I buy you a cup of coffee?"

"Mrs. Brickstone," Nancy said to Mom, "would you mind if I borrowed Alice for an hour or two? I'd like to get some more details from her about the events of the past few days. I could get her back to you here, or if you have already been discharged, I'll bring her home. Does that suit you?"

"Of course."

"Let's give your mom some rest," Nancy said to Alice, guiding her back through the security doors and out into the emergency set-down area. Rather than jumping in Nancy's car to make a coffee run, as Alice had hoped, they continued around to the main hospital doors. There was another reception area there but Nancy seemed to know where she was going without asking for a room number.

"They have a café in here?"

"Yes, but we have somewhere else to go first."

They walked together through a deserted hallway until they reached some ward that appeared to be busier, though Alice didn't notice the name of the ward because she was looking for the cafeteria.

Nancy found her partner standing with Kirsty's mom next to a closed door. Kirsty's mom hadn't yet seen Alice. The door had a little window in it and Alice started to maneuver around so that she could see if Kirsty was in there.

"How is she doing, Mrs. Bell?" Nancy asked.

"She...what is this girl doing here?" Kirsty's mom looked like she had been through hell.

"I believe you have met Mrs. Bell?" Nancy asked Alice?

"Not really. Pleased to meet you, Mrs. Bell," Alice said, trying to act normal.

Mrs. Bell stuck a cold, fishy hand out for Alice to shake. Alice resisted the urge to crush it.

"Kirsty is responding well to the slow warming," Nancy's partner said. They are giving her heated fluids by IV and her core temperature is almost back up to normal. She's hungry and responsive. I haven't spoken to her again yet."

"What was her core temp again when they brought her in?"

"90."

"Mrs. Bell," Nancy asked Kirsty's mom, who had taken a step back from Alice, "how are you holding up?"

"Fine. Have you found the man yet?"

"No, ma'am, but we'll track him down sooner or later. There are a lot of people looking for him."

"Have you arrested this girl?" she said, flicking a thumb toward Alice.

Nancy ignored her question and instead asked politely, "Would you mind if we had a word with Kirsty? If she is up for it, that is."

Kirsty's mom looked conflicted and appeared to decide she couldn't really say no to a police officer, especially an imposingly strong one like Nancy. She didn't say anything and just held her fishy hand out toward the door.

They walked in, followed closely by Nancy's partner.

Alice saw Kirsty in a hospital bed covered with a heavy blanket. Kirsty's dad was in there too. Alice knew it was her dad from reading Kirsty in the meadow. He seemed much nicer than Kirsty's mom, but still quite surprised to see Alice there with

Nancy.

"Mr. Bell, this is Alice Brickstone. Alice, Mr. Bell."

Alice did another pleased to meet you and looked at Kirsty.

"Hi, Kirsty," she said tentatively.

"Hey."

"Kirsty," Nancy asked, "are you feeling up for another chat about what happened?"

"Sure."

"Are you okay if Alice is here too? I have heard both your sides of the story, and Madison's as well. Now it would be useful if we could work together to fill in a few gaps."

"Sure."

"Alice?"

"Yeah, course."

Alice saw Nancy's tall partner pull out her notebook and click on what appeared to be a voice recorder.

"Mr. Bell, can we do this in private?"

"Yes, of course," he said, walking briskly out of the room and shutting the door behind.

Alice concentrated on Kirsty. She seemed to be okay, more or less, with no obvious injuries or bruises, at least on her face or head. Her eyes moved between Nancy and Alice. They were tired eyes, but not angry or vindictive.

"Hey, Kirsty," Alice said, "I'm really sorry I couldn't carry you out yesterday, and that you got lost overnight."

Kirsty didn't say anything.

"Let's get straight to it. Alice tells me that your kidnapper, Kirsty, made an attempt on her as well. On Sunday afternoon. Is that correct, Alice?"

"Yep."

"It would seem logical," Nancy said, "that the kidnapper has been keeping an eye on both of you. Can we put our heads together and discuss all the times these past few weeks you have been together and who else was present? If possible, let's also try to come up with a detailed calendar of all the phone calls and photos or chats online."

Kirsty seemed hesitant, or suddenly tired, but slowly began to list the times she and Madison had called each other leading up to the other day, and when they went to Bhakti's house together, when they met Alice in the back garden. After that, there were a few more phone calls and text messages from Madison before Babaji's big evening lecture on Sunday night, when Kirsty saw Alice again, and then no contact between the girls until Alice showed up, out of the blue, at the meadow in the Knifespur.

"So you two met each other in Mary's garden on Saturday, then again at the lecture on Sunday night. Correct?"

They both agreed.

"No other contact by phone or by internet?"

They both said no.

"As far as you know, there's nothing recent on any social media that might link you two together?"

"Nothing ever," Alice said, "as far as I know, at least. I don't do any social media."

Alice expected strange looks from Nancy and Kirsty, but didn't get any. She speculated Nancy already knew all about her presence, or lack thereof, on the internet. Kirsty probably did too. Alice was probably a laughing stock at school because of it. She had never thought of that before.

"Nancy," Alice said, "we were also, you know, both kids at the ashram in India when we were little?"

"Yes, I know. So all we have are those two occasions when the two of you were in contact before Tuesday morning."

"Yes," they both said.

"Not even any phone calls or other discussions about Alice's upcoming sixteenth birthday?"

Kirsty looked at Alice and raised her eyebrows. Alice looked away.

"Is that a no?" Nancy asked.

Alice thought she heard an accusatory note in Nancy's question. She wondered how this could be relevant?

Alice looked at Nancy. "No birthday plans," she said in what she hoped was a confident tone of voice.

"Fine. Now we need to try to list all the people who you saw on those occasions you were together."

This discussion took them almost half an hour of pure boredom. Kirsty was exhausted and Alice was starting to feel tired herself. Police work, at least this kind, was boring, Alice thought.

Mercifully, before it could drag on any longer, Nancy's phone rang. Nancy nodded at her partner, who clicked off the recorder.

Alice's heart leaped as she thought the call would bring news about Babaji's arrest. She definitely wanted to hear about how it went. Alice dropped down into the right state of mind and stared at Nancy, hoping to get her attention and read her. Nancy turned away from Alice as she answered her phone, said "Excuse me for a moment," over her shoulder and walked out of the room.

Kirsty's parents immediately swooped in through the open door, concerned looks on their faces. Mrs. Bell glared at Alice.

Alice didn't pay Kirsty's mom much attention. She could still see Nancy through the little window in the door. Alice saw Nancy glance in through the window and was quickly able to lock in and enter Nancy's orderly mental world. Rather than dominating her, she tried to remain on the periphery so that Nancy could keep functioning and Alice could just listen to the phone call. The call sounded to be halfway through.

The same young male voice as before was on the line with Nancy again. "We found two sets of custom shoes in their vehicle that appear to be designed to leave animal prints, and a jar with remnants of some kind of foul-smelling animal fur. We're checking both against the evidence from the scene of the attack."

"Any progress on the warrant for the Indian gentleman and Mrs. Flowers?" Nancy asked, still looking at Alice through the glass, an increasingly curious expression on her face.

"No. Like I said, all we have is they told a sixteen-year-old girl something about an association with Mrs. Flowers. Ordinarily that would be enough probable cause for the judge, but not in this case, because of the suspects' high profile."

Nancy considered the problem and Alice observed her collecting information from her memory in an orderly way.

"Can Veronica tell you about any known associates of the two men you arrested with the bear shoes?"

"She says they work security for a dealer. The guy is one of her informants, so we're not getting his name unless we're sure it's relevant. She's sure her informant would have had no business interest in the attack victim."

"Have those bear attack guys been seen near Mrs. Flowers' house?"

"The officers who have been watching the house can confirm they have seen neither a black Jeep nor two large white males near Mrs. Flowers' house."

Nancy paused and said, "Okay, here's a way to get the ball rolling without exposing her informant at this stage. Write up a list of names of all the people we know are involved with the guru, including the guru himself, and ask Veronica to have a look. Ask if Veronica can advise of any possible connections between any of those people and the bear shoes guys and her drug dealer informant."

"Good idea."

Nancy clicked off and Alice closed her eyes to break the connection.

When she opened them again, Nancy had looked away and appeared to be speaking to someone else outside of the room.

"Alice," Kirsty said, apparently breaking the silence in the room, though Alice hadn't been aware of any. Everyone looked at her expectantly. "I just want to say thank you for——"

"You shouldn't speak to her," Kirsty's mom interrupted.

"Wendy," Mr. Bell said softly, "go easy on Kirsty. She's had a hard time."

"That's exactly why she shouldn't waste her breath speaking to someone like...her."

"You don't know what really happened."

"Well, it's obvious it had nothing to do with Babaji, so...I'm not stupid. Even Babaji said it. There is only one way this mentally-ill girl would have known where Kirsty was. That is if she was working with the kidnappers."

"Mom!"

"In any event, Kirsty, you need your rest," Mrs. Bell said. "I think we should all leave her alone."

"Mom——"

"You people..." Mrs. Bell addressed Nancy's partner, who was almost as shocked as Alice. "You people need to take this girl into custody. She should not be roaming the streets. She is mentally ill and dangerous. Ask anyone in this town."

"Mom! She's just different. There's nothing wrong with——"

"I am finished trying to censor myself about her! She is not healthy. Even Babaji said so."

Alice started feeling sick. Kirsty appeared to be trying to hide under the blankets. Fortunately, Nancy pushed open the door and came in. The room was totally silent, like someone was dying. Alice felt like she was the one dying.

"Everything okay?" Nancy asked to no-one in particular.

"Officers," Mr. Bell said. "I think we need to all leave Kirsty to her rest. She's had enough excitement for one day, don't you think?"

"Of course, Mr. Bell," Nancy said quickly, as though she had already thought about it and totally agreed.

Alice followed Nancy out of the room and was happy Nancy kept walking as her partner stayed for a moment to speak with the Bells outside of Kirsty's room.

After a few steps, Nancy looked back to make sure Alice was following.

"Come on..." She stopped and asked quietly, "You okay?"

"Yeah, fine."

"I think we need that coffee now."

"Whatever."

Alice followed her to the cafeteria, not noticing anything: not caring about coffee anymore, just following.

They got two filter coffees that looked like brown dishwater with cream. Nancy guided them to sit down.

"Alice," Nancy began. To Alice's relief, Nancy's phone rang again. "Yeah," she said into the phone.

Alice couldn't hear the other speaker this time and couldn't be bothered to do anything about it.

"Fantastic," Nancy said after a long pause. "Get it written up and issued as quickly as possible. Inform the chief and the Federal guy. I think I should be there to help with execution, so give me a call when it's ready."

After she hung up, she said, "Alice, I'm not sure what happened when I was out of the room but I'm guessing you were on the receiving end of some abuse from Mrs. Bell."

"Why?"

"I imagine some people in this town are...impolite to you."

"Why?"

"Why what?"

"Why do you imagine that?"

"You mean...never mind. So, here's my dilemma. Nobody at work believes you are just clever or insightful, or that you know so much about these kidnappings only because you just wanted to help your friends. Nobody but me. Even I had my doubts. I still do, in fact."

"Thanks," Alice said doubtfully.

"So let's say you're right and someone is trying to frame someone else for framing Babaji for two kidnappings. Now I'm going to violate all interview protocols and ignore all my training. I'm going to just ask you, who do you think really organized these kidnappings and faked a bear attack on a journalist, and why."

"One more."

"Excuse me?"

"Sorry. I just need another coffee to be able to function."

After another weak filter coffee with cream was organized for her, she thought for a moment, remembering the phone call Rajendra had made while he was trying to kill her with a Mustang. Then she considered what she could filter out and what she could say.

Before Alice could think of anything to say, they both heard a voice behind them.

"Excuse me, ladies! I am pleased to find you both here. I am just on my way to pay my visit to my new friend, Rama, the young journalist who was attacked by a bear. Would you care to join me?"

They both turned quickly to see a beaming Mr. Rao standing behind his bouncing mustache.

CHAPTER 19

As she paced behind some scrub near the parking lot, waiting for Mom to be discharged, Alice stubbed her toe on a large rock. Full of anger, she bent down and picked up the fist-sized stone. She threw it at the closest vehicle, which happened to be Nancy's truck. Fortunately, Alice had terrible aim and the rock landed far short of the truck and rolled to a stop on the blacktop. It reminded her of the rock she threw at Rajendra the other day. She felt impotent and pathetic.

The hospital was silent.

No-one besides my mom and Kirsty seem interested in getting sick or injured today, Alice thought. Oh, and that guy Rama is in there too. Why had Nancy been so intense when she forbade me to go speak to him? According to Nancy, he is none of my business and is too hurt to speak to anyone anyway, but it just seems it would be logical to ask him a few more questions. Nancy had posted a police officer at Rama's door to prevent visits from people like Alice.

Somehow Mr. Rao must have bypassed the guard because he hadn't returned through the hospital cafeteria. Alice looked around, impatient. She hated being reduced to a passive observer.

Finally the hospital doors opened. Rather than Nancy and Mom, Rama limped out wearing dirty farmer jeans and an old white t-shirt.

So much for being so injured he couldn't see anyone,

Alice thought.

She walked straight over to him. He seemed disoriented, but determined to find something or someone, probably not her, she figured.

"Hey," Alice said. "Apparently I'm not supposed to talk to you."

"What?" he asked distractedly. He looked squarely at Alice and his eyes gained focus. Alice noticed he looked a lot better without his hair all gelled-up like Tin Tin.

"You're Brickstone's daughter."

Okay, enough chit chat, Alice thought.

She took a deep breath and locked in on Rama. He was experiencing a tremendous amount of pain in spite of the drugs he had been put on. Alice recoiled. She caught two names in the swirl of pain: Nathan and Cristiana. It was all she could take, so she backed out of his head.

Nathan must be her dad.

"Dude, how do you know my dad?"

"It's a long story," he replied.

"Hey, look. We don't know each other but I have not had a very good day today and neither have you, so I would very much appreciate it if you cut the crap."

"Your dad...he..." Rama looked extremely disoriented for a moment and appeared to be falling over.

Alice grabbed his arm. "It's okay, Rama. Take a deep breath."

"Your dad is trying to help..."

"Who is Cristiana?" Alice asked.

That triggered something in Rama and he straightened up and looked at Alice with fiery, threatening eyes.

"How do you know anything about Cristiana?"

"I'll tell you if you tell me how you know my dad," she said, returning his fiery look. She was slightly taller than he was and the clash between them would have sent showers of sparks if their eyes were swords.

"I know your father because he gave me something that may prove my ex-girlfriend, Cristiana, was raped by Babaji ten years ago. It was a hard drive containing security footage from Babaji's bedroom in India. Now your turn. How do you know anything about Cristiana?"

"I can read minds."

Rama set his jaw and appeared to be holding in a scream.

"No, really. I'm not kidding. Think of something I couldn't possibly know anything about."

Rama paused and Alice locked in again.

He wasn't thinking of a number between one and a hundred or anything easy like that. He wasn't really thinking anything specific at all, because he didn't believe Alice could read his mind. He was just suffering, standing there in tremendous, searing, body-wide pain.

Then she saw something that she wished she hadn't.

"You are a freak," she finally said after backing out of his head.

"What?"

"I can't believe you did that."

"What?"

"I can't believe you removed your own catheter just now. Gross, but kind of impressive too. I suppose it is, like, a miracle you are actually standing up right now."

"I have no idea what you are talking about."

"Okay, so here's proof I can read minds. Just now you were remembering how you just removed your own catheter, which is some tube thing the nurse put in your bladder because they didn't expect you to be able to walk to the bathroom for another forty-eight hours. You had to Google it to figure out how to remove it without some kind of special syringe. Disgusting. Then you managed to get up out of bed. You showered and went to some injured rancher's room and stole his jeans and t-shirt and snuck out of the hospital without anyone seeing you. Gross, gross and gross—and impressive; you really should be in an induced coma or something."

Rama's anger subsided.

They looked at each other with mutual admiration, distaste and something like fear.

Alice saw in her peripheral vision that Nancy and Mom were emerging from the hospital, so she was nearly out of time with Rama. She held on to Rama's arm firmly.

"So can you tell me why you were so determined to get out of your death bed? Does it have something to do with Dad? With that thing he gave you to prove Babaji did something to Cristiana?"

"Sort of." He sighed and steadied himself on his feet. "Here's the short version of the story. After your dad gave me the hard drive, I moved out of Bhakti's house. I told them I had a family emergency but I actually just checked into a motel. But I think Bhakti somehow found out I had the hard drive. I left the drive in my hotel room and went out running in the Knifespur late last night, trying to see if I could find your friend Kirsty."

"That's by my house. I think I saw you."

"Yeah, I chose the airport hotel so that I could be near the Knifespur. I wanted to be able to do my bit to help find Kirsty. So…"

"Wait, wait; you were trying to find her? In the middle of the night?"

"Yeah. So? Some people knit. I like to run. Why not do something useful while I'm running? Anyway, Bhakti hired some guys to seriously hurt me and steal back the hard drive. They obviously have been following me and they caught up to me up there in the Knifespur. They made it look like a bear attack so that everyone in Babaji's group would think it was the spirit of his grandmaster who did it, because he is the patron saint of bear tamers back in Rajasthan. They would all think it was a miracle.

They probably still do."

"So you're not popular anymore with Babaji's cult."

"Nope."

"You just removed your catheter, stole some farmer's clothes and staggered out here so you can go find Bhakti and steal back the hard drive. You are a bad-ass."

"No I'm not, and that's not why I'm out here. It's difficult to destroy a hard drive, but it can be done, and if I can figure out how to do it on Google, I'm sure they can too. There's not much chance I can recover the hard drive now. The real reason I had to get out of this hospital is because I just received a message from someone."

"That's it? You just received a message? Like, a dinner invitation? Are you doing online dating?"

"I suppose you'll just pry it out of my brain anyway. There are some really nasty people who are setting Cristiana up to take the blame for Kirsty's kidnapping. They're threatening to hurt my parents and destroy my reputation if I do anything about it, or even mention anything to anyone."

He looked at Alice with fire in his eyes. "Including mentioning it to a teenage girl. You understand?"

"Hey, chill dude. Looks to me like you're ignoring the warning anyway and you're going to do something about it."

"Yes, I'm going to try to do something about it."

"You're a bad-ass, man."

"I can't believe they discharged you in your condition," Nancy said to Rama as she walked up, supporting Alice's mom, who was looking nervously from Alice to Rama and back to Alice.

Rama didn't respond.

From somewhere in the direction of the ski area, a hawk issued her raspy whistle and Alice was reminded of the big, open skies of Wyoming.

"Well," Nancy said, "since we are all here gathered together, I may as well give you some good news and some bad news."

She looked at Rama and said, "Rama, I have no idea how or

why you are out of bed, but the good news is for you. We have made three arrests in relation to your assault: two local men and Mary Flowers. We learned the two men are connected to Ms. Flowers through her brother, who is a known local drug dealer and a police informant. The men worked for her brother. We believe she hired them to attack you and make it look like a bear mauling, and to break into your hotel room and steal your bag."

"Did my tip help nab the guys?" Alice asked eagerly.

"Absolutely," Nancy said. "We found the jar of foul-smelling bear fur in their Jeep, as well as two sets of shoes that made bear prints."

"Any luck finding my bag?" Rama asked.

"Unfortunately, no," Nancy replied. "The entire group had decamped from Ms. Flower's house and had cleared it out. We made the arrest on the highway leading north toward Laramie."

"The highway?!" Rama asked, incredulous.

"What's the bad news?" Alice's mom asked nervously.

"The bad news is that someone in Mrs. Flowers' group filmed her arrest and posted it on the internet, and I'm afraid your husband is featuring in the background of the footage."

It was Alice's turn to feel incredulous. "Dad's with them?"

Mom was quick to defend him. "Your father most certainly has his reasons for being there, honey," she said quietly to Alice.

"In the footage," Nancy continued in a relaxed tone of voice, "he is standing next to someone we don't know. My colleagues who are investigating the kidnappings wanted me to ask you all if any of you can identify this man," she said, holding her phone out to them.

Alice suspected Nancy was wondering if the unidentified guy was rat-face, but when she looked, Alice didn't recognize the man. He looked Indian, but more like an Indian version of John. All prim and proper in stupid-looking clothes and with a fancy haircut.

Rama also shook his head, but when he looked at Nancy, Alice thought she saw a look pass between them. It was almost...romantic? How could he feel romantic about someone while being in all that pain, she wondered. She felt like telling them to get a room, but she was too pissed off at her dad for running off with a bunch of loonies to Wyoming.

"Hey," Alice said, impatient, "can we get going? I think Mom should get home to rest. And Rama needs..."

Nancy and Rama both turned to Alice. Rama looked very threatening indeed and he looked precariously close to another collapse.

"Do you mind giving me a lift to the nearest car rental agency?" he asked.

"Sure," Nancy said over her shoulder as she walked away to get her truck.

They all got in and Nancy set off toward Alice's house. As they passed the aquatic center on the way home, Alice looked vacantly at the parking lot and saw her Mustang. She was half-wishing none of the recent events had occurred, including all the flying, and that Mom was back to her normal self and Dad...well, she didn't know which Dad she liked least, the old one or the new one. Both were annoying, irresponsible and incomprehensible. She was sorely tempted to go home, ditch Nancy and all of her questions, kick off her shoes, jump off her roof and fly up to Wyoming to drop some kind of bomb on Babaji's shining new RVs.

"Hey, Rama," she said, leaning forward in her seat. Rama was sitting up front with Nancy.

"Yep."

"Can I borrow your mobile?"

He looked at Nancy, as though asking for permission to loan Alice his phone. Nancy just shrugged.

Alice watched him punch his security code and she memorized it. He held his phone out but was unable to turn around because of his pain and injuries. Alice had to unbuckle her seatbelt and lean up to get it.

She dialed Madison's number and held it up to her ear. After a few rings, the screen showed someone had answered but Alice couldn't hear anything.

"Madison? It's Alice."

"Predictable." It was a high-pitched male voice with an Indian accent. "I was relying on you calling about now."

"No way," Alice said.

"That is an odd way to greet an old friend," he responded. "One who was so kind as to loan you his car."

Alice looked up toward Rama to see if he or Nancy had heard Rajendra's voice, but they kept looking forward through the windscreen.

"Who would send a teenager to intercept a dangerous man in Wyoming?" Rajendra asked. "Who do you work for, young lady?"

Alice said nothing. Her index finger was shaking. She was listening hard for any sounds from Madison or Billie.

"Cat got your tongue?"

When she still didn't respond, he said, "Okay, Alice Brickstone. I actually don't care who you work for. I am now angry. Here's what you are going to do if you want your friend and this baby to live."

At that point, Alice had the presence of mind to switch the call to speaker phone and hold it forward towards Rama and Nancy. Rajendra's thin, high pitched voice rang out in the truck cab.

"You and your employers have caused me to lose quite a bit of money, so you will compensate me with as much cash as you think these two lives are worth. Your rich mommy and daddy will have plenty of cash in the house and I'm sure you are resourceful enough to get it without them knowing. Go home now, if you are not already home. Get the money. If you don't bring enough, I'll have to choose which of these two young lives to return to you and which to return to God. Since you love running so much, you will bring the money to me yourself, on foot. You will start running on the roads toward the ski area and you are to run up the mountain and wait for me at the top of the gondola. Is that understood?"

Alice looked at Nancy for help but she had her eyes closed, as though she was in as much pain as Rama.

"I asked you a question. Is that understood?"

Alice took the phone off speaker so that she wouldn't sound different, said, "Yep", and then put it back on speaker.

"Good. I will be watching you the whole time with an aerial drone. I will be calling you frequently. Stay on the open roads so that I can see you at all times. If you disappear from view, even to use the toilet, it will result in a death. Keep your phone on and answer my calls. If you fail to answer my calls, it will result in a death. Is that understood?"

Alice switched off speaker, said, "Yep", and put it back on speaker phone.

"Good. Now this is the important part. Listen closely. If you say anything to your parents or to anyone, I will kill the baby first, while the young lady watches, then I will kill the young lady. Is that understood? If you are not out there running with my money in ten minutes. or if you leave the highway, or if you tell your parents or leave anyone a note, text anyone, call anyone, or notify anyone of this phone call we are having, I will kill the baby first, then the young lady. Is that clear?"

Alice brought the phone back to her mouth. "Come on, Rajendra," she said. "What if my battery dies? Or I'm out of mobile phone range? Hardrock has lots of gaps in coverage."

"I have already investigated all of the coverage gaps and I know exactly where they are. As for your phone battery, two lives depend on it not dying. The clock is ticking, starting right now. Enjoy your run."

He hung up.

She was feeling such fear for Madison and Billie that she felt like screaming and crying and raging.

Nancy pulled the truck over and Rama was beckoning to Alice to hand him his phone. There was an eerie silence in the car as everyone considered what they had just heard.

Nancy was the first to speak. "Rama, I'll need your phone."

"Of course," he said, handing it to her.

Nancy used her own phone to call someone, probably her police station, Alice thought. She didn't put it on speaker phone. In a business-like voice, she greeted someone and read off Madison's number from Rama's phone and told her to locate Madison's phone and call her back. That was it.

"Can they find her phone without her permission," Alice asked, "and without a warrant?"

"Yes," Rama said. "They use cell tower data. It's called CSLI."

After a few more minutes of silence, Nancy's phone rang.

"Where exactly in Wyoming?....Does that correspond with the movements of the convoy of vehicles associated with the Indian guru?...Okay, time to involve the Feds. Some of them are still with you in the station, aren't they? Or have they all gone home?...Okay, tell them Alice Brickstone just tried to call her friend, Madison Percival, on that number and a foreign male picked up instead of Ms. Percival. Alice Brickstone ID'd the voice as belonging to a man who fits the description of the suspect for the Bell kidnapping. Give them the CSLI that you just got from AT&T. Tell them that the suspect is claiming to have taken Ms. Percival hostage and...just a sec..."

"Alice," Nancy asked, looking back, "what is Madison's sister's name and age?"

"Billie. She's a year and a half."

Nancy returned to her call. "He claims to also have taken Madison's sister, Billie Percival. Madison is sixteen, Billie is one and a half. The suspect calls himself Rajendra and has demanded a cash ransom from Alice Brickstone and has threatened to murder the hostages if the demand is not met. He instructed her to run alone from her parents' house to the top of the gondola. He claims to be following her with an aerial drone. Got all that?"

She paused again, listening, then said, "I've got Alice with me now...Yes, the first step will be to get a warrant to intercept the convoy, search every vehicle. But let the Feds do all that because they'll get it done faster."

The other guy said something that made Nancy smile. "Yep," she said. "Another relaxing day off."

She looked at Alice again and then returned to her call. "One more thing," she added, "after you do all the other stuff. It's a long shot, but check some website called uship.com and see if there is anything about an arranged pickup of an electric ultralight from somewhere near Laramie. It might have been the plane used for the kidnappings."

After she hung up, she tossed Rama's phone back to him, started the car and pulled back onto the road. She hit the accelerator hard and Alice realized Nancy's truck was every bit as fast as the Mustang, and probably faster. The speed was comforting. It felt like Nancy knew what she was doing.

"Sorry, Nancy," Alice asked tentatively, "but I'm just trying to figure out what I'm supposed to do now. Am I going to steal some money and run up to the ski area? Why do you think Rajendra would want me to run up to the top of the ski area if he is actually with Babaji in Wyoming?"

Nancy didn't answer Alice. Alice noticed her forearms; the muscles looked hard, like steel cables.

Nancy spoke to Alice's mom. "Mrs. Brickstone, given the circumstances, after we drop you at home, would you mind if I borrowed Alice again?"

"Of course, of——"

"Feel free to ring me anytime. The number is on my card. Did they return your phone to you at the hospital?"

"Yes, thank you. And you didn't let me finish," Mom said. "You may take her with you but you both must promise me to not leave each other's sight."

"Mrs. Brickstone, I think I have learned that making promises about Alice are difficult to keep. But I will do my best."

"Good enough. Now, as for you, young lady," Mom said, looking at Alice, "you are to do whatever Nancy says. Is that clear?"

"I will—if you tell me what's wrong with you."

"I...can't yet."

"Cool," Alice said, looking away and making it clear she wasn't promising to stay within Nancy's sight.

After a few moments of Nancy's very fast and precarious driving up Alice's road, Alice spoke up. "Nancy?" Alice said, feeling like stirring the pot a bit more. "You know, Rama may have something to contribute here."

Rama shivered and swiveled around so fast his face contorted with pain and he was unable to say what he obviously planned to say to shut Alice up.

"He, um," Alice said, looking away from Rama, while Nancy looked repeatedly between Rama and the road. "He received some kind of warning he is not supposed to tell anyone about. If he tells anyone, they'll hurt his family and ruin his reputation. I think it involves that dude next to Dad in the video."

Rama pounded Nancy's plastic dashboard so hard that Nancy slammed on the brakes.

"Is this true?" she asked him.

"I am not at liberty to say, obviously."

"I'm really, really sorry, Rama," Alice said, "but Madison and Billie need you. Don't be a jerk. Tell her."

"What, were you going to just jump in a rental car and chase the convoy?" Nancy asked him, speaking with anger for the first time during their short ride.

"Until I saw that video on your phone, I really didn't know where I was going to go. I believe you have met the elderly gentleman, Mr. Rao?"

"Yes," Nancy said. "He was at the hospital."

"The message came to me from him. But it's not his fault. He is under the same kind of threat that I am."

"So you are prepared to lie to a police officer also."

"No, I didn't lie. I don't recognize the guy in the video at all. It was the RVs behind them that made me curious."

"What about them?"

Rama used his phone and found the video showing Bhakti being arrested.

It took long enough that Alice started to get worried she had made a mistake giving Rama this opportunity to speak. Maybe Rama wasn't really in his right mind. She didn't know what his right mind was like. She was terrified Rajendra would call back any second.

He found the right video and Nancy leaned in to watch with him. He scrubbed to the end and paused it at a still shot of the RV. It was a pretty fancy vehicle, Alice observed. The make and model of the thing was printed on the side. Rama opened up a browser in his phone and looked up the RV. When he found what he was looking for, he held it up.

"Check it out." Rama showed his phone to Nancy. "The kind of RV they were standing in front of has a fully enclosed master bedroom in the back with an extra ensuite bathroom. It's huge."

Rama went back to the video and held up a still of the RV again to Nancy. "They've even hung orange curtains for Babaji. He can seal himself off for the long journey, while the drivers rotated up front and could keep going even when they had to use the toilet."

Rama went back to the arrest video and scrubbed forward a bit further.

Alice tapped her fingers on the back of Nancy's seat.

"Look, there's another one in front. So there are at least two top-of-the-line shiny new RVs." He put his phone down and looked at Nancy. "There is no way Babaji or Bhakti, or any of their Indian or local devotees on Babaji's tour of the US could have afforded to hire those things. I know enough about their finances to know that. I have never seen that guy next to Nathan before. I know most of Babaji's local and Indian disciples. Suddenly Babaji gets two brand new RVs. There was no hint of this in any of our planning meetings before I left to go stay in a hotel. Then I get a message from an unknown source that I am not to do anything that may harm Babaji's reputation or else somebody with enough information and resources to know where my parents live and where my ex-girlfriend live is going to hurt them."

Nancy raised her eyebrows. "You concluded that the origin of those threats against you is that guy in the video and that he is also responsible for hiring the RVs so that Babaji could get out of town."

"I bet he's also the one who hired Rajendra to get me and Kirsty," Alice said. "Now he's also got Madison and Billie."

"I'm not sure about that," Rama said. "I'm not sure about anything right now. That man in the video could have been anyone. Even if he is the one who told Mr. Rao to threaten me, it's hard to imagine the same guy would want to stage Kirsty's kidnapping. Such a stupid act would make Babaji look like a monster in front of the whole world. Why would the same guy turn around and try to muzzle me and stifle bad publicity about Babaji?"

"In any event, this is very different from the Bell kidnapping." Nancy put the car back in gear and pulled back onto the highway, spinning her wheels, accelerating hard. "It seems as though Rajendra is under pressure and is improvising. We need to find out why."

Rama's phone rang again. Alice saw that it was a FaceTime call. Nancy slammed on the brakes again, pulled all the money out of her wallet, shoved it and the phone into Alice's hand. Rama also grabbed all the cash he had in his pocket which was quite a sizable amount and added it to Nancy's stash.

"Get out," Nancy said briskly, "and pretend you just stole that cash and are running toward the highway with it."

Alice did as she was told and started running. Fortunately there was an evening breeze strong enough to blow some of the truck's dust away. Before she answered the phone, she looked at the wad of cash and saw that it was hundreds of dollars, maybe thousands.

"I got your stupid money," she said when she answered. Alice had recovered from the initial shock and was emboldened now that she was on foot near her house: at least temporarily. "Here, see?" she said, showing him the cash with the phone's camera and holding up her middle finger.

"That's not money," he said. "That's your father's change from last night's prostitute."

"You're a complete asshole," she said.

"That lovely comment just cost little Billie a finger," he said, "but don't worry. I'll chop it up and feed it to your close friend, Madison, so it all stays in the family."

Alice recalled how close she herself had come to being killed by Rajendra and she gasped out loud when she realized he probably was deadly serious about cutting off a baby's finger.

"Please, please don't hurt her. I'm so sorry, Rajendra. I'm just scared. I'm not thinking straight. Where do you want me to come bring you this money?"

She looked down and the connection was broken.

She turned around and sprinted up to Nancy's truck and jumped in.

"He's going to cut Billie's finger off," Alice said, panicked.

"Give me the phone, Alice," Nancy said.

"He's going to kill them, isn't he?" Alice said, handing Rama's phone to Nancy, who had already accelerated hard toward Alice's house.

"Alice," Nancy said, "this guy thinks he has scared you into cooperating, and that nobody knows about him but you, while in reality there is a whole team of highly trained people working on it. We have a lot going for us. We know Madison's phone is in one of the vehicles in Babaji's convoy in Wyoming. There are, no doubt, police vehicles heading to intercept them as we speak and the helicopters won't be far behind. We'll be able to intercept them within the hour. It is possible Madison and Billie will be there with them and will be recovered safe and sound."

Looking down at Rama's phone screen and back up at the

road, Nancy Bluetooth-dialed her colleague and said, "we just got a video call from the man who claims to have taken the Percival kids. But the call origin was different. Not from the Percival girl's phone. It's an email address that is just a long string of letters and numbers. Give it to the Feds too. I'll send you a screen shot."

After she did so, Rama took a deep breath and spoke up. "I need to say something here." He cleared his throat and sat up taller. "I wasn't exactly discharged from the hospital."

"Didn't think so," Nancy said.

"And I think I'm going to pass out."

"Great," Nancy said.

"Have you even had any water, dude?" Alice asked as they pulled up to her house and Nancy hit the brakes hard.

"Okay, people," Nancy said, "here's how this is going to work." She turned around and addressed Alice's mom. "Mrs. Brickstone, please give me your house keys and I'll run ahead and open the door. You," she said, pointing at Alice, "take your mom inside, carry her upstairs, if need be, and help her into bed. Get her whatever she needs. Then you are coming straight back outside and getting in this car. No detours."

"You," she said to Rama. "stay right where you are. I'm going inside to get you some water. What else do you need to keep you upright?"

"I've got some meds from the hospital. Just the water will be fine, thanks. Maybe some sugar."

"I'll get him some electrolytes and an energy gel from the garage," Alice said.

"Okay. Let's go. Alice, I need you back in this car in two minutes."

"What about Rama's phone?" Alice asked. "What if that freak calls back?"

"I'll keep his phone for now. You let me worry about that," Nancy said. "Just get moving."

As Alice helped her mom into the house, she thought hard about what Nancy said about Rajendra improvising.

Nancy had already gone inside and Alice heard the cupboards opening and closing as she frantically looked for a glass.

Alice picked her mom up easily and carried her up the stairs.

"You listen to me, Alice," Mom said. "I'm serious. Stay with Nancy."

Alice didn't answer and reached the top of the stairs, went into her parents' room and put her mom down in bed.

"Okay," Mom said. "I'm desperate. Your dad made me promise not to tell you until we were sure, but it seems you won't listen to reason. So here is what is going on with me. I'll only tell you if you promise to stay with Nancy."

Alice looked at her. "Do you need anything, Mom?"

"I'm pregnant, Alice. For some reason I'm having a lot of morning sickness and dizziness, but they checked everything out at the hospital and all is well with the baby. Just having a difficult first trimester."

Alice closed her eyes. She tried to take in what her mom was saying, but she could only think of Madison's baby sister, Billie. Am I going to have a little sister too, she wondered.

"You're pregnant?" Alice finally asked, opening her eyes.

"That's what I said."

"Why didn't you tell me?"

"Because your dad and I agreed it would be very hard on you if the pregnancy didn't work out. Normally people wait until they pass the three-month mark before they announce anything."

"Even to their own daughters?"

"Especially to their own daughters. I would very much like you to get me my yoga nidra relaxation cd from the yoga room and a glass of water. There's a glass in the bathroom."

Alice remembered the photos of Dad.

"Do you take secret photographs of Dad from the window?"

"Of course. But they're not secret. It's just a thing I do. I love him. Now please hurry so that Nancy doesn't get cross with you."

"So you don't really hate him?"

"Your father? Of course not."

Alice turned around, confused. She knew she would not be able to make any sense of her parents or their lives, so she forced her thoughts back to Rajendra.

She thought of Billie again, imagining her little stubby hands forcing bite after bite of pasta into a face covered with pasta sauce. The memory turned into an image of Billie crying in terror and pain as she held up her bloody hand with a finger missing. Thoughts of Billie blended with thoughts of an unborn baby in her mother's skinny, weakened body. Alice felt so angry that the world disappeared, like a TV turning off.

As soon as she could regain focus, she ran downstairs in a blind rage. As she ran, her thoughts whirled: stop Babaji's convoy, rescue Madison and Billie, kill Rajendra, get Dad, come back and look after Mom.

She dashed to the garage, grabbed a handful of energy gels and a big stainless steel camping water bottle, stuffed them into a backpack and thought about finding a weapon in case she had to face Rajendra again. She didn't think her dad had any guns anywhere and there weren't any knives, and even if there were, she couldn't imagine plunging one into a person. She needed something a bit more scary to frighten him off, like a power tool.

Her mind was racing. She wasn't a killer, but her anger was so real and there was nowhere else to put it.

She frantically scanned the garage and her eyes landed on her workbench. The last time she had done anything there was when she had used an angle grinder to shorten the heavy steel hooks she bought to hang her bike from the garage ceiling. An angle grinder, she thought: pretty decent weapon. A heavy hand-held thing with a spinning wheel on the end made out of something abrasive, and it spun fast enough to cut serious metal. Her dad had warned her repeatedly that it was the most dangerous tool in the garage, and had supervised her the whole time she used it. That was pretty much the only time he had spent some time with her this past year. The battery for it was still plugged in to its charger. Without thinking about what she would use it for, she attached the battery to the grinder and threw it into her backpack.

She dashed back out to Nancy's truck and jumped in the back.

Nancy was already sitting in the driver's seat and the truck tore out of the driveway and down the gravel road before anyone could say anything.

"This is the plan, Alice," Nancy finally said. "I just spoke to the task force that has been set up to deal with this new kidnapping and they have confirmed with the Percivals that their kids are not at home and are not accounted for. The team thinks it would be best if we could keep Rajendra thinking you're still following his instructions. It will give them time to reach the convoy and search the vehicles."

"What? I'm going to run up the mountain?"

"No. We think he's bluffing about the drone but he may have someone watching out for you at the top of the gondola. It is also remotely possible he is up there himself. There are not yet any good theories why the kidnapper has chosen to deal with you to ransom the girls. We're going to go along with his instructions, just in case. I'm going to get you up the mountain in the truck."

CHAPTER 20

They sat in the truck, which was still ticking and cooling after their furious drive up the cat trails to the top of the gondola. The ski mountain, like many in Colorado, had a front side facing south-west and it had several northeasterly-facing back bowls. The gondola takes skiers up to the top, from where they can access all the bowls or the gentler slopes of the front side. Alice had skied every inch of the mountain and always knew exactly where she wanted to go.

Behind them were the dim, romantic lights of the restaurant on top of the gondola that served hundred dollar steaks. The restaurant was also crawling with police who completely ruined everyone's dinner by swarming the place. They had arrived in a bunch of vehicles right after Nancy and had found no trace of Madison or Billie.

People inside had probably already forgotten about the police, had gone back to their oversized glasses of wine, and were gazing at the beginnings of the sunset over the Knifespur.

Rama's phone hadn't rung again and nobody had spoken during their winding drive through town and up the mountain.

Nancy's police colleague called again.

"Yeah," she answered, using Bluetooth to put the phone call into the truck's audio system. Alice figured that was more for Rama's benefit than for her's.

"We searched every vehicle," her colleague said. "No trace of the kids and no-one matched the suspect's description. Lots of them were pointing fingers at your journalist boyfriend who got attacked by the bear impersonators. There is a general sense among the people that he had something to do with the kidnappings. On top of that, the journalist seems to have disappeared from the hospital, so they've put an APB out for him."

"Cancel it."

"Cancel what?"

"Rama is with me. The journalist. I picked him up from the hospital an hour ago."

"Nice. Do I have your permission to carve your names into a heart on a cubicle in the men's bathroom?"

"No. So where was the phone?"

"They found the girl's phone, and get this."

"What?"

"Someone had it delivered to the convoy by courier."

"Bullshit."

"Scout's honor. It was in a cake that was delivered by motorcycle to an Australian man in the convoy. He's another monk like Mrs. Flowers. The guy signed for it at a gas station in Laramie and the courier left in a motorcycle. The monk said he didn't get the name of the courier service. The phone was hidden inside the cake. He didn't know it was there. We found it for him."

"A cake."

"Yep, a cake. The phone was on silent and was set to automatically forward all incoming calls to another number."

"Did you guys trace the other phone yet? The one he forwarded the call to?"

"We're working on it. It is not powered on right now. The

last time it was on was only for seconds but, Sergeant, I should tell you it's somewhere in the vicinity of the Brickstone house."

Nancy looked at Alice. "Send some people over there right now and call Mrs. Brickstone on the way."

"Already done; she was asleep, but she seems fine. The officers we sent will be with her in a few minutes."

"What about the Australian?" Nancy asked. "How did he get on first-name basis with the kidnapper?"

"He claims he is famous and that's why the kidnapper must have chosen his name as the recipient for the package. It checks out. His name is Swami Shivapuri and he's all over the internet."

"Did you find the guy in the video? The one with Indian looking features standing next to Nathan Brickstone?"

"Sure. He is carrying an Indian diplomatic passport. He hasn't heard of anyone called Rajendra and doesn't know the Percivals."

"Anyone else know anything?"

"They questioned them all, even the guru. There are dozens of people in this convoy, including Nathan Brickstone. The thing is, they showed evidence that they left Hardrock at noon. The Percival lady said she spoke to her daughter at half past twelve and she was fine."

"A diplomat," Nancy said. "That makes it complicated. So did they say why it took them six hours to drive the hundred miles between Hardrock and Laramie?"

"I don't know. Lollygagging; maybe they saw a moose."

"Where are they headed?"

"Chicago. The guru wants to see that big silver bean sculpture. Apparently it was made by an Indian artist."

"The feds let them go? Or what?"

"Under the circumstances, the feds said they had to let the convoy continue on their way. The famous Australian seems to be their spokesman. He pledged their group would check in with us every night until they reach Chicago. Right now, they're on I-80 Eastbound, probably traveling below the speed limit like good little tourists."

"Okay, so let's think this through. The suspect knew Alice would tip us off instead of following his instructions and that our first move would be to locate Ms. Percival's phone, so he already had couriered it to the Australian in the convoy. Which means that was a decoy."

"'Kay."

"If he knew Alice would tip us off, he also knew she wouldn't run to the top of the gondola with his money. So that was another decoy."

"Yep."

"What's the plan then?"

"The investigation is now focusing on locating the other phone and the Percival girl's vehicle. They're also combing all of the regional airports and DIA for any sign of a short, thin Indian man and the two kids. Meanwhile the feds want you to bring Alice's phone in so we can monitor it."

"It's actually Rama's phone," Nancy said.

"What did my dad say?" Alice shouted, unable to contain herself any longer.

"Who is that?" the guy on the phone asked.

"When you interviewed him, what the hell did my dad say, dude?" Alice shouted, louder this time. "Why is he driving to Chicago with a bunch of idiots who are probably criminals and kidnappers, instead of home looking after his pregnant wife?"

Nancy quickly said, in a calm voice, "Hey. I'll come in to the station now. I'll bring Rama and Alice."

"Yep," he said and the connection ended.

They all looked at each other.

Nancy called up some maps on her console's GPS and they all looked at the distances involved.

Laramie was a hundred miles north and the convoy was apparently heading east of Laramie on I-80. It was an hour's drive to the border between Wyoming and Nebraska and another 900 miles and fourteen hours across the huge expanses of cornfields in Nebraska and Iowa to Chicago.

Alice thought about it for a moment and looked at the map again: an hour to the border. The map showed a little town called Pine Bluffs right on the line between Wyoming and Nebraska.

They were quiet for a second and Alice looked through the windshield toward the rocky peaks covered with darkening purple light. Beyond those, Babaji and Dad were rolling along in comfy RVs. Maybe they were looking out the back window at the sunset. More likely, she thought, Babaji was in the back having a bath and Dad was in the middle having a business meeting with the Indian diplomat.

It occurred to her that it wasn't that far from here to Pine Bluffs. It would cut off the northward detour to Laramie. From right here, it was maybe a hundred miles as the crow flies.

"Guys," Alice said. "Rajendra is not in charge. He takes orders from some scary guys and one of them must be that Indian diplomat. He must have lied to those guys who searched the convoy. He knows where Rajendra and Madison and Billie are."

Nancy started up her truck and looked back to Alice. "That's a good guess, but it's just a guess at the moment. As Rama said, there is no motive. We can't do anything until there is evidence linking him to Rajendra. We can't beat it out of him. This isn't communist China. All we can do is head back to the station and wait for Rajendra to call."

"Madison and Billie are dead," Alice said. "It's my fault. I should have handled this myself."

"Alice, you have done the right thing. You just have to trust us now."

"I gotta go to pee," Alice said, grabbing her backpack and opening up her door.

"I do too," Rama said. "I'll go with her."

"Hey, wait a minute," Nancy said. "I'll drive you over."

"I'm going to just pee on the ground over there," she said.

Alice was already out of the car before Nancy could object and was walking toward the edge of a fenced-off cliff facing the forbidding peaks to the north-east.

Toward the convoy.

Next to the fence was a sign that had two black diamonds on it and the words: 'Toilet Bowl. Extreme Skiing. Experts only.'

She had skied this chute hundreds of times before. On skis, the strategy is to jump off the lip at the top, becoming airborne, and bring your skis sideways so that when the first thin section of skiable powder rises up to meet you, you can land briefly before careering off toward the left, airborne again, until landing in the larger section of skiable powder. This section funnels into a gentler glade through some stunted, high altitude trees. The last section is why it's called the Toilet Bowl: there is only one way out.

As she peered down over the ledge, it looked even more forbidding than when it was covered with soft snow. She saw only a cliff, a huge boulder, another cliff, and way below that was a steep scree field and then some trees.

She turned around when she heard Rama limping up behind her.

"Dude, you don't want to see this," she said.

"For a second there," he said slowly, "it looked like you wanted to jump off."

"Turn around already. I gotta pee."

"Okay, okay," he said.

She watched him turn around slowly, clearly still in tremendous pain.

"Wait a minute," she said. "Can you loan me your phone again?"

"Why?"

"I always check Facebook while I go to the bathroom."

"You have got to be kidding me."

"Hurry up, dude."

They faced off for a second. Rama standing awkwardly, Alice shifting her weight left and right, pretending she had to go to the bathroom.

"Alice, where are you going to go? What can you do?"

"Alright, forget the phone. Just turn around. Hurry."

He slowly held up his phone.

She took hold of it but he wouldn't let go.

He looked her in the eye. "Alice. Think about your mom. She needs you. Madison needs you. Don't run. You can't help anyone that way."

Alice thought about screaming at him, asking him what he thought he knew about what her mom needed, asking him what the hell he knew about Madison's needs, and about Alice's needs, and shouting at him to get the hell out of her family's business, to go get a room with his new girlfriend and butt the hell out.

She saw something in his eyes and held her tongue. Behind all the physical pain, she saw someone who really cared. It was not something she was used to seeing in anyone besides her mom.

"Turn around, Rama," she said slowly. "I gotta pee."

He pursed his lips, slowly turned around and began to walk back toward the truck.

Alice checked Nancy wasn't watching and she stuffed his phone in her pocket, kicked off her shoes, and as quietly as she could, she took a running leap off the cliff.

As her chest and stomach were about to hit the boulder where she usually made her first turn on skis, she wondered if she may have been a little bit rash. What if her heavy backpack prevented her from being able to fly well enough? As usual she managed to feel the tickle of prana just in time and gave a mighty pull with both arms, followed by a strong dolphin kick, and she just cleared the boulder. She was soaring down toward the scree field. Within a few more strokes she was curving up away from the slope and above the forest below. She swam hard toward the sky, hoping to get well clear of the ski area before Rama turned around to see if she had finished peeing.

Soon she had climbed well above the altitude of the top of the ski area where Rama was probably having to explain to Nancy that he lost Alice. Nancy would be jumping out of the car to look for her.

All they would find would be her shoes. Hopefully they would grab them for her. They were her good pair.

Rama's phone rang in Alice's pocket. Alice kept her momentum wth strong regular freestyle kicks and quickly pulled the phone out of her pocket, in case it was Rajendra again. She saw the call was from Nancy and she put it away.

For good measure she climbed another thousand feet or so and eased off, trying to glide longer, relaxing her body as her muscles continued to warm up.

As she always did in the pool, she picked up where she left off during her last flight and went through a checklist of all the little technique improvements that worked for her last time. She remembered that cocking her elbow in a certain way would let her get more purchase on the beginning part of her stroke and that a much slower kick rate worked better than a fast one.

She could already tell from the sound of the wind in her ears that she was not moving fast enough if she wanted to reach Pine Bluffs before Babaji's convoy. She had to try something new.

She had made two round-trip flights in the past few days. Aside from the takeoffs and landings, she mostly cruised by using a stroke that was similar to freestyle in the pool, without having to breathe to the side, of course. She had also occasionally tried a butterfly stroke which resulted in approximately the same speeds.

Because she didn't have to surface to breathe, she reasoned, maybe she could experiment with a hybrid stroke.

With that thought in mind she began moving her body through the prana like a dolphin, in long, slow undulations. She kept her arms moving in a cyclic freestyle motion. That wouldn't work in the pool because of the need to breathe to the side. Up here in the air, she could breathe normally and the combination freestyle stroke with a slow dolphin kick resulted in a much faster flight.

She fine-tuned her new flying style and felt like she was moving faster than she had ever flown before. The pitch of the wind blowing past her ears had lifted. It was almost deafening.

Above the scream of the wind, she heard Rama's phone again.

She stopped her arm motion, kept up the dolphin undulations with her body and pulled out Rama's phone. It was Nancy calling again. She pressed reject and tapped around one-handed, searching for any kind of runner's application that would tell her how fast she was moving.

Thankfully, Rama had three or four different running apps and the first one she opened was clocking her speed at a hundred miles an hour.

A hundred miles an hour—while not even using her arms.

She thought back to the maps she had seen on Nancy's GPS in her truck. She figured at this speed, she could catch up to the convoy when they hit the Nebraska border. It was just a guess, but if she was wrong, she could just back track along the I-80 corridor until she ran into them.

Then what? What was the plan?

She blocked that out and focussed on getting there.

Pocketing the phone, she resumed her new stroke and took in the incredible view below her.

For a skier standing at the top of the gondola, this huge mountain range between Colorado and Wyoming looks endless and forbidding. She often stood there on her skis, before plunging down the Toilet Bowl, looking over toward the next mountain, daydreaming that not much had changed over there for thousands of years.

Looking at it from above made it shrink. Alice could see that this mountain range only ran for about twenty miles. She considered the terrible geological forces that pushed these enormous things up ten thousand feet into the air. How many millions of years did these mountains take to rise to this height? Much less time, she figured, than the time it took for the ancient glaciers to push away huge expanses of rock and soil, creating paths between the terrible rocky peaks. The glaciers were all long gone but the valleys they left behind still grew deeper each passing year because of the endless flow of runoff from the snowmelt and the rain.

She relished the feeling of being so far from any other people; apparently, most people hated being so alone. She thought about Madison and Billie. If Rajendra had followed through with his threat and had killed Billie in front of Madison, how alone would she feel right now? How would she feel if someone did that to her?

She cringed and put it out of her mind and tried to let her heavy breathing, rhythmic movements and the white noise in her ears lull her into a kind of stupor. She wanted to achieve the kind of rhythmic numbness that she felt every day at the pool. One part of her knew she also needed a break from her mental chatter like she needed sleep.

Before she could get any relief, she began to get dizzy, perhaps because of the altitude. She grew weak. Within the fog into which her mind was descending, images began to well up from her memory, one after the other.

The first was Billie from last night, her face covered with pasta sauce. This immediately linked itself to a long-buried memory of another toddler. A young boy, broken and covered with blood, and not that much older than Billie, was lying on the dry earth. He was dying, or dead, she didn't know which. The little boy was her brother.

Alice tried to shake off this memory but knew she was losing the battle. This terrible image had always been there below the surface, just beyond her grasp. It haunted her dreams. It haunted the times between dreams and waking up. It lurked below the surface of every minute of every day since Thomas had died 11 years ago. Now that it had broken through to her conscious mind, it was there for good and she could think of nothing else.

As a result, she was also losing altitude. Some sharp rocks on a mountain loomed upwards toward her. Soon she felt she was tumbling downward randomly, head over heels through the darkness, wearing a heavy pack. Her enormous strength and miraculous abilities were useless. She was like a crumpled ball of paper, used toilet paper being flushed down the toilet. She didn't even know which way was up. There was nothing to grab—nothing.

After a few more seconds of free-fall, something in her broke free and she bore witness to her body's deadly, flailing plunge. As witness, she was free of the pain of the haunting image of her dead brother. As witness, she coaxed her body into a controlled downward dive. She coached both hands above her head, one over the other, palms down in the streamline position she used when gliding underwater. She witnessed her body accelerate through the wind.

She calmly saw the jutting rocks of a peak approaching and encouraged her body to take control and swim above it.

The inner split collapsed and she was back in her body, flying fast. The image of her dead brother was there, permanently stamped into the front of her mind. She was, however, able to think around it. She juxtaposed it with a different image of rat-faced Rajendra, and with this came a surge of anger.

Rajendra was not going to win this time, she thought. He can't win this time.

She climbed to her previous altitude, resumed her cruising speed, and even managed to squeeze a little more speed and effort out of her body than before—maybe up to a hundred and ten miles per hour or more.

She had to find the fancy Indian diplomat and persuade him to tell her where Rajendra and the girls were. She could feel the weight of the angle grinder in her backpack and wondered how she could use it to get the information out of the diplomat. It occurred to her she might need a backup plan.

After ten minutes of flight, it had grown much darker, but she could still see well enough to know she was passing over the last of the mountains before the land leveled out into the high altitude deserts of southern Wyoming.

She kept up her dolphin kicks and pulled out Rama's phone again. Up here in the deep purple sky, the light from the little square screen was painfully bright. She saw there were a few bars of coverage, so she typed a brief text message to Nancy. "I'm fine. Flying 100mph toward Wyoming Nebraska border. Making good time. Meet me there as soon as you can. - A"

She took a quick picture, smiling at the camera, the wind in her short blonde hair. The little light on the camera flashed because of the lack of natural light and she knew the picture would look strange and ghostly. Her eyes would look red, puffy and wet. Behind her head would be utter darkness. She didn't really care what she looked like right now; she just wanted them to know it wasn't Rajendra trying to trick them again. She texted the photo to them and pocketed the phone.

It started ringing immediately but she ignored it.

As she stared forward into the charcoal gray night through streams of tears caused by the wind, she saw the occasional light here and there, and a brighter glow in the distance. That must be Cheyenne, she thought. It was a medium sized city on I-25 just north of Colorado.

From left to right, all across the thin, dark horizon line, the land was now flat. That meant she was about halfway to Pine Bluffs already. Plan B was to wait for Nancy and Rama to arrive.

It was high time to develop Plan A, she exhorted herself, but no plan was forthcoming.

After crossing over the north-south-running I-25, she pressed on across the dry, dark earth to the east.

Keeping the thin lights of east-west freeway I-80 to her left, she focussed ahead of her, hoping she would arrive in Pine Bluffs well before the convoy.

She flew for a while longer. As she neared the spot where she figured Pine Bluffs would be, she banked to the left and let herself approach the I-80. The weak lights of local roads and little farm houses started appearing below her.

She pulled out Rama's phone, saw there was coverage and checked her location on a map. Sure enough, Pine Bluffs was only five miles ahead. She looked up and made out the glow in the distance.

She banked left and backtracked west along the I-80 corridor looking for a couple of flashy RVs followed by a line of cars. Even after tracking back a few miles and soaring up high enough to see five miles down the way, she could see nothing but a few individual cars and eighteen-wheel trucks. It felt as unpopulated and open out here as anywhere else in Wyoming.

She executed a big half-loop and half-roll and flew eastward a couple of hundred feet above the freeway, back toward the glow of town.

The lights of Pine Bluffs resolved and she soon came upon the freeway exit into town. It looped around and went down through an underpass beneath the freeway. She followed it to the left, flew above a frontage road and saw there were a few modern gas stations with fast food, beyond which were the little scatterings of buildings and houses of this town. She flew higher to broaden her view, not sure exactly what she was looking for. The town petered out almost before it began and ended in some kind of white statue. Alice descended slightly to see it more clearly and beheld a massive Virgin Mary overlooking the passing traffic on the freeway. Right past the statue was a sign that read: Nebraska. The good life.

She arced left over the Virgin Mary statue and saw there was another road just north of town that also ran east to west next to some railroad tracks and some grain elevators. The train tracks and the road crossed into Nebraska parallel to the freeway.

She pulled out Rama's phone and called up some maps, seeing the road below her was called the Lincoln Highway, probably the previous main artery out here before the I-80. She could see it ran nearly parallel to the I-80 all the way to Chicago.

Right where the old highway and the railroad crossed into Nebraska, there was a parking lot and some old, abandoned farm equipment and a few dark buildings. It was dark and completely out of the way. A perfect place to do whatever it is she was going to do.

All she had to do was find the convoy and figure out how to

divert them over to that other highway and to get them to stop at the spot she had chosen.

This would have been easier, she thought, if she had her Mustang. All she would have had to do was park the car sideways on the freeway somewhere just after the Pine Bluffs exit and light it on fire or something. They would take the exit and cross the border via the old highway.

She wondered if maybe she could find another car. She banked over the Virgin Mary statue and over the highway, following above a different little road into the hills.

A set of headlights wove slightly left and right, as though the driver was avoiding potholes, or was drunk. It was the opportunity she was looking for. She descended and took a big risk by going through her landing procedure. If this didn't work, she wasn't sure if she could find a way to take off again.

She managed a smooth landing on the gravel shoulder of the road just ahead of the oncoming car and slid in her socks until she came to a stop. She put on what she felt was a desperate expression and walked out into the middle of the road, waving her arms like a scared chicken flapping its wings.

The guy managed to slow down and stop without skidding or running himself off the road, and he opened the door of his beat-up car.

She strode purposefully over, still trying to look scared.

"Thank you so, so much for stopping, sir. I'm in big trouble."

A tired-looking man struggled from the driver's seat. He was tall and haggard in his rumpled farmer clothes. He didn't look sober.

"Can you give me a lift into town? My car broke down. Please?"

In spite of his apparent intoxication, he looked at her steadily and appeared to be sizing her up. Maybe he wasn't so drunk.

She tried to look cute but didn't really have much experience with that. She probably just looked fat.

"Young lady," he said slowly, "I'm not sure what kind of

trouble you're in, but I can tell you're putting on some kind of act. I wasn't born yesterday."

She didn't really expect this and didn't know what to say.

He squinted. "I don't appreciate the little flying trick you just did in front of my car."

"I...I'm really sorry about that, sir."

"I'm guessing there's no car, right?"

"I'm sorry. I just didn't think you would believe me if I said I was flying."

"Where are your shoes? Where did you ditch your hang-glider?"

She thought for a second. She was wary of this guy now. He was too observant.

"It wasn't a hang-glider," she said. "It was kind of something new."

"Anyway, that's none of my business. I reckon if you need a lift into town, I'm obliged to help, seein' as how you are alone here at night, with no shoes and all, and it's the gentlemanly thing to do. But I don't really want to hear any more wild stories."

"That would be great, sir. Thank you so much." Alice was already hustling toward the passenger door.

"That's no trouble," he said, more out of politeness than honesty, and eased himself back into the driver's seat.

As soon as they were underway, Alice took a deep breath and realized her heart was still beating fast from the adrenaline of her landing. She took another deep breath and smelled the familiar whiff of alcohol. It reminded her immediately of her dad.

"Are you a local?" she asked. She didn't have much time.

He didn't reply.

"Can I level with you, sir?"

Again, no response.

"It's not a story. I'm being completely honest now. I desperately, really need a favor and I'm happy to give you a lot of money for it."

He looked over at her, pursed his lips in scorn and turned back to watch the road.

"It's just that my dad is in a convoy of cars being driven toward here by a bunch of evil Indians who have kidnapped him and I need to borrow your car to cause a distraction on the freeway shoulder just past the Pine Bluffs exit. It's just to scare the evil guys into turning off the highway. I'll give you all the money I got. It's way more than a thousand dollars—and an angle grinder."

"An angle grinder? Young lady, why are you carrying so much money and power tools?"

"I just am. I don't want to make up a crazy story. I just am carrying that stuff. It's totally not stolen. So can you help?"

He was silent for a long while, long enough for Alice to get nervous. Then he appeared to think of something and he looked back at her.

"You're the girl on the TV, ain't you."

"What TV? What do you mean?"

"It was on the evening news. We get some of the Colorado TV news, you know. They had this human interest story tonight about you." He looked at her again. "I swear it was you. They put on a photo of you. It was your face. Then they interviewed your friend who was that girl who escaped a kidnapping. She was sayin' that you're different but everyone should support you. That sound familiar?"

"I'm not sure," Alice said, feeling confused.

"I didn't mean to offend you."

"I just don't know...what you mean," she said awkwardly.

"That story was touching. I didn't know you was someone famous. I don't know why all those people think you're so different. Aside from the socks and the hang-gliding at night, of course, and hitchhiking on a farm road, and the cowboys and indians story with your dad. Other than those things, you seem like a nice enough girl."

He paused again. "I reckon I could use a bit of money. But

the thing is, I can't lend you this car for the purpose you say, seein' as how my son is a policeman in this town, and also I have a meeting at a local watering hole I got to get to."

She was feeling hurt and confused, and somewhat desperate, but didn't know what to do about any of that.

"But tell you what I'll do for you," he continued. "If any of that stuff you said is true, I'm sure my son will be happy to help you. He works in the local police station. He ain't none too proud of his dad, you understand, but he'll do the right thing if you talk to him direct. I raised him right. Wasn't a good example, but got the job done somehow despite myself."

Alice looked out the window, trying to figure out what to do.

"The thing is, he's not in the station right now. He and his partner are on speed trap duty tonight. You okay with me dropping you off where he's hid?" the man continued.

She didn't know what to say, so she just said okay and opened her door. It made a loud creaking noise. Before he could do anything about it, she planted her right foot on something—probably the car seat—and managed to push off into the air with some strength. It was like jumping off a starting block into the pool.

She was, for the time being, airborne. She already could feel the prana taking her weight. She used her stomach as a sail to give her some lift as she scissored her legs to create enough drag to swing her around so that she was facing the direction the car had been heading. The guy in the car had slammed on his brakes. She swam hard and accelerated forward and upward, leaving him far behind.

He was a pretty nice guy. She didn't have time for a long chat with a local police officer, even one who was well raised by a drunken farmer. The drunk guy had, however, given her a different idea.

She flew up a couple hundred yards into the sky above and saw the glow of sirens. She couldn't see where they were coming from because there was a pine-tree-covered bluff in the way. She banked left and swam a couple hundred yards above the I-80, which curved slowly around the bluff, and behind the bluff she saw what appeared to be an innocent little speed trap on the highway exit. A police car was there issuing a ticket to someone. Alice flew back west along the freeway for a mile or so and saw another police car backed in behind some scraggy trees, probably pointing his speed gun toward the freeway.

She had a plan. It wasn't a perfect plan but it felt good.

She flew west along the highway past the police car hiding behind the sign with his radar gun and continued for another mile. She figured it was enough room for her to get a good head of steam.

She kept up a dolphin kick and pulled out Rama's phone, clumsily clicked around with one hand until she found the camera app, turned it on video and switched on the flash. Then she reached back and put it in a mesh pocket where she kept her gels for easy access. From there, the bright light of the flash would be easily visible to someone behind her.

She descended and looped back until she was accelerating eastward again, heading back toward town right above the surface of the highway. To the speed-trap cop, she hoped she would look like a speeding motorcycle.

She put herself in the right-hand lane and started swimming hard.

After half a mile she felt like she had probably hit something like a hundred or more. She imagined the guy in the police car would have his window down, speed gun pointed toward her. He would have been hearing nothing but crickets and distant car sounds. Until now.

She started screaming. It was a nice touch, she thought. The cop would be hearing some weird banshee shrieking sound increasing in pitch as she approached at very high speed. When she was almost upon him, she took a really deep breath and loosed an even louder scream. She held the scream as she passed him, imagining that the freaky loud sound would have immediately lowered in pitch because of the doppler effect. He would be staring at some huge number on his speed gun, while at the same time, hopefully, he would have peed his pants.

After she passed him, she kept screaming as long as she could stand it and continued to swim hard along the road as it banked slowly right toward town.

When her lungs had expended themselves, she allowed herself to take a deep breath and turned her head to look behind her.

Sure enough, the guy had put on his flashing lights and was about a half-mile back. Too far, she realized. She slowed herself way down so he could catch up a bit and see the glow from Rama's phone. When he was about a football field distance behind her, she sped up again and let him try to chase her.

She kept going right past the highway exit. When she saw that he was past the exit, Alice banked up sharply and swam hard toward the sky. She imagined he would have seen her tiny little light going up, up, up and disappearing above his field of view.

She switched off the light on the phone and banked lazily back around. She looked down and saw the police officer had pulled over onto the highway shoulder just beyond the exit. She watched him get slowly out of his car, looking up in her direction. Not seeing her, he walked forward five or ten steps, still searching the sky.

She pulled out her stainless steel water bottle from her backpack and flew over toward his car. Holding a bottle with one hand and swimming with the other, she centered herself right over the front of his car. She was about two hundred yards above him now. The bottle held a liter of water and was about half full. It occurred to her that she should try to wipe off any fingerprints, so she used her shirt to wipe down the bottle as well as possible.

She aimed and let the water bottle bomb go.

A feeling of utter panic gripped her. What if it landed on his head and killed him? She was tempted to try to sprint down and catch it. Before she could do anything about it, she saw it was on target and she heard a huge smashing noise. It sounded like a head-on collision between two heavy cars. The smash was followed by the sound of windshield glass crumbling into the car.

The policeman shouted out in fear, jerking his head toward his car upon hearing the impact. Alice panicked again, fearing some glass had ricocheted and killed him. She relaxed when she saw he was running over to inspect his car and appeared to be okay.

She didn't stick around to watch, as she knew she had done what she could. She expected the other police car to come over to help investigate and that they would set up some kind of perimeter, maybe even block off a lane of the highway with flares and stuff. They might even close the whole highway and divert traffic over to the old road.

Alice swam away from the chaos she hoped she had caused. She swam to a high enough altitude to scan the Wyoming horizon to the west, searching for signs of Babaji. There at the edge of the horizon was a long line of headlights. Her heart rate sped up again.

Preparing for confrontation, she popped her last energy gel, and of course, she suddenly had to pee. Well, what can you do? She stayed aloft treading prana and pulled aside her cycling pants. It didn't work very well and she ended up peeing all over her leg. Relieved, she resumed her flight toward the approaching headlights.

She had to be sure it was them, so she flew close enough to see that the first few vehicles were RVs. She ventured low enough to check the make of the motorhomes. The coloring and the branding matched exactly what she had seen in the arrest video. The back windows of the lead RV were enclosed with orange curtains, just like Rama said they would be.

It was nine o'clock at night. She imagined Babaji in the back, soaking in his evening bath. She wondered if that was a traffic violation.

She wondered what her dad was up to. Sitting around a little dining table in the back of the second RV, meeting with the dangerous guy? Sitting alone in a chair with a drink? Or maybe he had gotten off at the last gas station? Or maybe he was tied up? Or being tortured? Her imagination started working and she shook it off.

She followed above the convoy, thinking. The blue flashing lights came into view. It didn't appear the highway was closed but the convoy slowed down as they got closer to town and they all put on their turn signals, exiting into Pine Bluffs.

The RV drivers must have gotten scared, Alice thought. Maybe they thought the sirens indicated a roadblock waiting there for them.

She followed above as they passed right by the Exxon and the Sinclair stations and continued north the three blocks. They reached the grain elevator, turned right on the Lincoln Highway and started picking up speed toward the border.

Alice took out the angle grinder. She maneuvered herself so that she was above the lead RV. She watched as they passed a dark sports field on the right and another grain elevator on the left.

Five minutes had passed since they had abruptly slowed and exited the highway. The jostling would have sloshed Babaji out of the bath or out of bed or whatever, she figured. Someone would have gone back and knocked on his door to apologize and explain the detour. He would have thrown some clothes on, suddenly alert and wary. He would come forward into the main part of the RV to find out what was happening and to issue orders.

She swam with her free arm until she was just fifty feet above where she remembered Babaji's toilet should be. Rama had only shown her the RV layout briefly, but she had a good spatial memory. She figured a bullseye into the toilet bowl and down through the poo storage would stink up the cabin enough to make them stop pretty quickly. The angle grinder may even pop through something important in the RV's chassis and would put the RV out of commission, maybe burst a tire.

She chanced a look back and realized she had flown into full view of the RV behind her. All they would have to do was look up a little. She couldn't worry about that right now. The lower elevation was worth the risk so that she could be precise with her bomb.

She looked ahead and saw the weird collection of old fashioned street lights and buildings was approaching. She realized there was a point where the color of the highway changed abruptly: the state border.

She quickly wiped down the angle-grinder for fingerprints and focused her full attention on the roof of Babaji's RV. She switched on the power and the angle grinder began to scream as the wheel spun madly, ready to cut metal. She dropped her second bomb for the day.

This time the panic was far worse than before. This time she knew there was a decent chance she had just killed a man sitting on his toilet. Not an innocent man, but nevertheless a living, breathing guru, with a mother (probably?) and feelings (maybe?). As the power tool punched through the roof, she wondered if Dad was sitting on Babaji's toilet. She closed her eyes against all these thoughts because whatever had just happened, it was done. It was over.   For a moment, she thought they would just keep driving. She looked ahead and realized the only way she could get them to pull over would be to land on the RV and pound on the roof until they stopped.

She approached Babaji's RV and prepared herself to plonk onto the roof. Before she did, she saw the brakes come on.

She panicked again. What if she really had just killed Babaji? The brake lights had flashed a few times, as though the driver was unsure. Then the brake lights stayed on and the RV stopped so fast that the other RV almost ran into it.

She swam up toward the sky, trying to get away from a scene she knew would soon be on the national news: 'Popular Indian religious figure killed by an angle grinder dropped from the sky.'

She turned around and circled over the convoy from a great

height, squinting through the darkness, and watched them slowly pull into the old parking lot and line up in an orderly way. The two RVs parked side-by-side, then each car parked in the order they had been in the convoy. No-one was jumping out of their cars or running around in a panic.

Alice took a deep breath and considered her options logically.

Option one: fly away.

Option two: fly down and face the music. Try to find the diplomat and dig in his mind to find Rajendra and Madison and Billie.

Option three: hover here until Rama and Nancy arrived.

She couldn't think of any other options.

She had run away enough lately: time to be a real woman, she decided, and get down there to see what kind of damage she had caused.

As she descended, another option suddenly came to her. It was dark enough, she thought, that she could land somewhere unnoticed and walk casually into the chaos, pretending to have emerged from one of the cars in the back.

She looked carefully at the abandoned gas station, now full of Babaji's convoy vehicles. It was a big piece of land. She guessed it was about an acre, the size of a football field. There was a rickety old building in the middle, but it was too close to the convoy.

She saw that on the back side of the property there were a bunch of abandoned cars and semi-trailers, even an old boat and a tractor. Behind the tractor she saw another old building. Beyond all that was dark, empty grassland and the Virgin Mary statue rose up all white and bright about a half a mile further. Beyond the statue she could see the occasional car driving by on the freeway.

She picked a spot in the shrubbery behind some of the abandoned vehicles and managed a decent landing, sliding in some deep grass in her ski socks until she was standing behind a crappy old speedboat on a rusty trailer. She spun around and hid behind the boat, peering toward the convoy. She listened, hoping for her dad's voice.

She couldn't hear anything clearly and she couldn't tell what was going on. Nobody was screaming, at least. It was almost perfectly quiet except for the distant sound of cars on the freeway behind her.

Alice snuck around the old boat and began to creep out into the open. She needed to cross a hundred feet of open space before she could hide behind the old building in the center of the property. From there she would be able to see and hear them a little better.

One thing was certain; she felt much more vulnerable on the ground than she did in the air. At least in the air she could fly off somewhere. Down here, all she could do was scurry around like all the other ordinary people.

She decided to risk a run to the building. She made it, stopped and listened hard. She could hear the creaking of their cars as they cooled, but the voices were still only a distant mumble.

She heard the call of some nocturnal bird. It sounded like the high-pitched, nasal whisper of a hawk, probably a nighthawk. Nighthawks like to hang out around lights in order to eat moths and things. They make that whispery call when hunting. She speculated that the huge spotlights on the Virgin Mary would create a feast for nighthawks and every other kind of nocturnal bird. Maybe one of them wandered over here to have a look at all the commotion.

She peered around the corner of the building and looked carefully toward the cars. They all had their lights off but she could see the internal RV lights were all on, which lit the area up in a weak but warm glow. Perhaps enough to draw a few bugs for the nighthawk to eat, she thought.

She could see clumps of people standing together at a respectful distance away from the RVs. The people looked fairly relaxed, which was a relief for her. Some were stretching, some looking up at the sky, some just standing with hands clasped behind. Most of them appeared to have on fake Indian clothes like the ones she had seen at the lecture.

The closest clump of people was maybe a hundred feet away. She would need to walk through the line of old fuel pumps and across some more empty space to reach them. From there she could just slowly wander forward toward the RVs.

Suddenly Alice heard a liquid-spluttering sound and saw a woman squatting and peeing behind a pump near her. She withdrew and counted to ten before poking her head back around. The peeing lady was gone and Alice began to tiptoe her way toward the convoy.

She made it past the gas pumps and was creeping through the open space when she heard a familiar car approaching. Stopping in her tracks, she scanned the highway beyond the parked cars of Babaji's convoy and saw a cute little set of dim headlights and heard the sounds of a bleating VW engine, downshifting, slowing down, and then the squeak of dodgy brakes.

It couldn't be Mr. Rao, she thought. It just couldn't be him. How could Mr. Rao be here? Why?

The VW bus pulled past the RVs and drove around them. He bumped over some grass, turned, pulled up and parked just past Babaji's RV.

He hadn't killed his engine or his lights and it occurred to her that his headlights were shining right toward her like a spotlight in a theatre. Then she realized every single one of them had stopped chatting and stretching and was looking at her.

She froze in her tracks.

There was finally an angry shout from someone in the second RV. "Hey, you! Aren't you Prempuri's daughter?"

Alice couldn't run—her legs didn't work. She felt as though the exertion of her journey was just dumped on her like a bag of sand. She didn't feel like diving back behind a gas pump. She didn't feel like she could run forward toward the safety of a group of people. She just stood there, wondering why she should be so much more interesting to all those people than Mr. Rao in his classic VW—unless Mr. Rao had been expected.

Someone from the second RV ran over to Babaji's RV and jumped up through the side door. After only about ten seconds, Shivapuri emerged slowly. She watched Babaji descend the steps. He was helped to the ground by Shivapuri.

Alice hadn't killed him after all. He had no angle grinders sticking out of him. He wasn't wearing his usual orange and was dressed in a black t-shit and sweat pants. The contrast with Shivapuri's orange robes was stark.

Alice just stood there watching.

Babaji let go of Shivapuri's arm and made a good-natured, old man's groaning noise as he walked toward the center of the semicircle of vehicles. Shivapuri hustled up the steps, re-emerged two seconds later, carrying something, and ran to follow Babaji, but Babaji turned and gestured for him to stay.

Someone from one of the groups of people closest to Babaji ran over, bent down and touched his feet. He barely lifted his right hand in a gesture of blessing and did not look down.

Babaji ambled forward and stopped when he was about twenty paces from Alice. Everyone was watching. The place was whisper quiet again. The nighthawk called, chasing after another moth.

Alice looked around and realized it probably looked like an old western shootout. It was uncanny. She imagined it would be cool if Babaji had a six-shooter in a holster. If he drew it, her only move would be to pick up a rock and chuck it at him. She smiled at the image, in spite of her exhaustion.

Babaji appeared to have misread her smile because he nodded and smiled back at her. He turned and said, in a resonant voice, "Shivapuri, jau. Bring Prempuri and Amar Sing. Ask Yoga Devi to bring chai."

Babaji began to stride away from the cars toward the other abandoned buildings at the back of the property. When he saw Alice wasn't following, he called to her gently. "Come; let's have tea."

The invitation was strange enough that Alice almost turned to follow him, if only so that she could punch the fat bastard and finish their duel. She knew she didn't have that kind of violence in her, at least not at the moment. She just kept standing there.

Dad's bald head poked out of the door of the second RV. He looked desperately around, saw her and shouted, "Alice!"
She almost fell down to the ground right then. She wasn't sure if she felt relieved that he was actually here, or if she was touched he would shout her name in this kind of company, or what. She was overwhelmed with emotion.

He jumped to the ground more nimbly than she suspected he could and ran toward her. She still couldn't move, so she just waited. He slowed down and stopped in front of her.

"Sweetheart, are you okay?"

"Hi, Dad."

"But...how did you get here? How did you find us?"

"Can we just go somewhere? I need to talk to you."

"Of course," he said and looked back toward the RV. "It's just that I have...I just have to talk to this guy briefly first. You stay right there, okay? I'll be right back out. Then we can go in the RV and talk."

Dad turned away to walk back toward the RVs but he changed his mind. He paused and turned back.

Alice had already hardened up inside. After all she had been through to get here, he had just walked off.

"Hey Dad, that's great, you go have your meeting," she said. "No worries. I'll just be over having chai with Babaji."

She finally found the strength to pick up her feet and walked weakly toward Babaji. He had gone to the end of the gravel parking lot and was poking around one of the buildings.

She caught up with him. "Nice place, eh," she said.

He was peering inside through a broken window. "Take care," he said, "there may be snakes."

"Yep," Alice said.

He looked at her and then down at her feet. "Where are your shoes?"

She looked down at his feet. "I don't know. Can I borrow yours?"

Babaji raised his eyebrows with mock concern and turned back toward the RVs. Alice couldn't see Dad anymore but she saw Shivapuri hustling out of Babaji's RV and jogging toward them. Everyone was watching Alice and Babaji. It would have been quite a scene to them, Babaji walking off with some huge girl who had appeared out of thin air.

"Shivapuri-ji," Babaji called loudly. "First bring my house shoes and a torch."

Babaji turned back toward the window of the abandoned building. Alice walked around to the side of the little building to see if she could find another window. Babaji followed her. The painted metal siding gave way to painted wood panelling that had two gaping openings in it. Alice walked in, ignoring any potential danger to her feet from broken glass or snakes. Babaji followed right behind.

She could see the entire inside of the building and could just make out some stools in front of shiny surfaces. Some light landed on an old high chair. It had been chucked on its side. She felt sad about it, like it was a discarded child, rather than a child's chair.

"Whoa-ho," Babaji said knowingly from behind her. "It used to be a café."

Shivapuri reached them and shone a flashlight in.

So that's what Babaji meant by a torch. Must be British English, Alice thought.

"Wow," Shivapuri commented. "It looks like an old vintage milk bar from the fifties. I remember one of these things where I grew up in Australia."

Then he shone the light down near Alice's feet. "Hey, be careful, Alice. There may be old nails or glass on the ground here."

"Give her my house shoes," Babaji said.

Alice looked back and caught Shivapuri raising his eyebrows in surprise. He quickly turned his surprise into a gracious smile and handed her the orange slippers.

"Thanks." She slipped them on. They were cheap rubber sandals with open toes but Babaji must have big feet because they fit her okay.

"Come." Babaji walked back outside.

Alice and Shivapuri followed him. They all looked at the deep grass in front of the diner. The old diner shielded them from the spotlights on the Virgin Mary and created an eerie, nostalgic atmosphere.

Babaji seemed to be scoping the place out for something. "Shivapuri-ji, go get five strong boys. Tell them to bring sticks and torches."

"Ji," Shivapuri said and jogged back toward the people milling around. Alice watched them gather around. Most of the men dashed back to their cars, grabbed some stuff and ran over to where Babaji and Alice stood.

There were about seven of them, ranging in age from thirty or forty to sixty or seventy. They all wore yellow t-shirts and some kind of loose yellow pants.

"No sticks?"

"No, Babaji," one of them said, smiling obsequiously. "There aren't any trees around here."

"Find sticks," Babaji said quickly with a touch of annoyance. "Start in the grass over there," he pointed toward the pumps, "and march past this place here and all the way over there. Make as much noise as possible with your feet. Shine torches to make sure you are not standing on snakes. Look for the holes: snake homes. Keep marching up and back while we are here."

"Yes, Babaji," a few of them said. They were all looking at each other and smiling knowingly as if they had done something crazy like this for Babaji a million times before. Alice felt like they were not behaving like slaves, but rather like Babaji's accomplices in some kind of performance, a performance that had been staged many times before. Here we go again, their expressions said. Alice wondered why the hell they did it, but they did. They all somehow found tiny, useless sticks on the ground and began their night march against the snakes. Babaji walked forward to the place where the grass ended and the gravel parking lot began.

The lady with the neat vest Alice remembered from Bhakti's house emerged Babaji's RV, carrying a tray laden with covered, stainless steel cups. Alice wondered how she'd made chai so fast. She concluded she must have started brewing it when they realized they had been diverted from the main highway. Some strong chai would be good right now, Alice thought.

When neat-vest lady approached, a look passed between her and Shivapuri. He dashed over, took the tray from her and she sprinted back to the RV. She soon re-emerged with an armful of heavy linens and a folding camp chair and ran back to where Babaji and Alice stood with Shivapuri and his tray. She spread a thick, patterned cotton blanket on the ground.

"Here," Babaji said, pointing down in front of his feet.

Neat-vest lady unfolded his camp chair and placed it where he had indicated. She laid a small, finely-woven Persian runner over it so the chair was completely covered.

Babaji maneuvered himself around and sat down heavily. The chair creaked, Alice noted, but unfortunately didn't collapse.

"Table," Babaji said, and neat-vest lady ran back to the RV, returning in a moment with a small folding table she placed in front of Babaji. She covered it with a white cloth and Shivapuri set down the tray of chai.

Shivapuri sensed either Alice was about to collapse or Babaji intended to make a big deal out of her, so he gestured for her to sit down on the cloth blanket in front of Babaji.

She kept her backpack on, just in case she needed to make a dash for it, and sat down.

Shivapuri took a cloth napkin off the tray, wrapped it around one of the steel cups and gently handed her the chai.

She guessed there was some guru protocol that held she should wait for Babaji to have his chai first. She ignored it, chucked the lid off and downed about half the cup. It wasn't hot enough to burn but it was strong, sweet, and almost as good as Mr. Rao's.

She looked back toward Mr. Rao's VW bus. His lights were off but she could still hear his motor running. She could see him standing with two taller people she recognized as Dad and that Indian diplomat, Dad's new best friend. She saw the diplomat fold his hands and tuck his chin down to his chest, like he was praying to Mr. Rao or something. The diplomat and Dad shook hands and the diplomat pressed a phone to his ear.

Mr. Rao walked toward her until he was close enough to catch her eye. He stopped, looked around as though he smelled something, and looked at her again.

He was just close enough that she could see the wrinkles by his eyes, crow-footing into a smile. A sad smile, she thought, though she didn't know what it was about him that seemed sad.

He gave her a slight wave of his hand, turned around and walked back to his bus. He got in, backed out and left.

How could he just leave, Alice wondered, after all they had been through together? When she needed him most?

Alice looked back at Babaji and saw Shivapuri was organizing some little pills for him. They were from a plastic container that read 'equal,' whatever that was. He stirred them into a cup that seemed to be patterned silver, rather than stainless steel, and slid it closer to Babaji, who ignored it.

Looking back toward the RVs again, she tried to see where Mr. Rao had driven, but he was gone. She saw her dad and the Indian diplomat guy from the arrest video walking together toward Babaji's group.

The nighthawk called again and this time Alice caught a glimpse of something dark swooping down toward the RVs, then disappearing.

"Can Durga puri make the camera work?" Babaji asked

Shivapuri.

"Guru-ji, the cameras are both completely destroyed. Whatever came through your roof smashed them together with the hard drive from Sadhvi Bhakti devi-ji."

Alice considered this and realized she had probably destroyed Rama's treasured security footage. What terrible luck for him. She shook her head and took another deep drag from her chai.

After a second, Babaji responded, "Pity. This is a good time in India for a webcast. The background is very interesting, no?"

"This is a classic old diner. I'm sure someone has a camera, at least," Shivapuri said, moving away toward the row of cars.

"It can wait," Babaji said, gesturing for Shivapuri to return.

By this time, Dad and the Indian guy had sauntered up. Alice refused to meet his eyes and looked down at her chai. Dad and the other guy sat down next to Alice and neat-vest lady served them steel cups wrapped in cloth napkins. Alice kept ignoring Dad.

"A beautiful evening," the diplomat commented in a voice as sonorant and loud as Babaji's, but also thick with some kind of sing-song British accent. Alice looked at him and almost thought he looked like Rama for a moment, because of his carefully groomed hair and the chiseled jaw line. This man was softer and not at all athletic. There was a little fleshy overlap at his belt line and his forearms were much thinner than Rama's.

"Shivapuri," the diplomat asked, "what are your theories about what caused the damage to Babaji's motorhome?"

"It was something very heavy, about four centimeters in diameter," Shivapuri replied. "It came through the roof, went through the case containing all the electronic gear, through the floor, and seems to have lodged itself into the chassis of the vehicle."

"What could cause that kind of damage?"

Shivapuri didn't respond. Babaji didn't seem interested and was focusing on his chai. There was a long silence. Alice could hear conversation had started up again in low voices over by the cars. She took some deep breaths and tried to regain some of her energy.

"Prempuri-ji," Babaji said to Dad, breaking the silence with a voice louder than he had used before, "have you come to an agreement with Amar Sing-ji?"

Amar Sing must have been the diplomat's name, Alice figured. She looked up, curious what Dad would say next.

"I believe so, Babaji."

"Believe?" Babaji asked.

"The total investment figure is set, Babaji," the diplomat said. "The specifics of the technology transfer are, however, still not there. But I am confident all will proceed as planned. I have formally lifted the…sanctions."

Alice looked at Dad and saw his jaw was set and his teeth grinding. All this was some business deal after all, she thought. Dad was doing a business deal with that awful guy who may be responsible for organizing multiple kidnappings.

"Yeah, Mom's fine." Alice spoke loudly as though she was continuing some casual conversation with someone who was hard of hearing.

Everyone looked at her.

"She went straight to sleep as soon as we got home," Alice continued. "Wow, pregnancy must really tire you out, eh?"

Dad widened his eyes and looked at Alice. He started shaking his head, like he was trying to get her to stop talking.

"Tough day for her, though," Alice continued. "Dehydrated, low blood sugar: be even tougher for her if she wakes up thirsty or something, and no-one is around."

Alice let that sink in for a moment. She enjoyed the feeling that she had said something and everyone was thinking about it. She guessed that even Babaji was considering her words.

"Congratulations," Shivapuri said finally, placing a hand on Dad's shoulder. "We didn't know."

Dad recoiled slightly and did not look around at Shivapuri who withdrew his hand and walked away a few steps.

"Have some chai, Shivapuri-ji." Babaji indicated a place next to him.

Shivapuri took a cup for himself and sat down. Babaji closed his eyes for a moment and everyone was quiet. Alice felt the center of gravity shift from Dad's discomfort back to Babaji's presence. She didn't like it.

"So, Babaji," she said loudly. "Is it true you have sex with your followers?"

Babaji didn't move or open his eyes, but Alice saw his breathing change.

"That is an entirely inappropriate way to speak to a person of Babaji's stature, young lady," the diplomat said to her in a controlled voice tinged with violence.

Alice looked at Amar Sing. It was too dark to lock in on his eyes and he wouldn't look directly at her anyway. It was as though looking at her would be beneath him.

This made her feel even more determined. She felt like she was still in a kind of shootout, with Babaji and the diplomat lined up against her. She would win if she made both of them lose their cool or admit to some kind of wrongdoing. They would win, however, if they maintained their composure and superiority and everyone kept treating Babaji like a divine master and the diplomat like a respected VIP.

She had a sense she could get some results if she changed her manner. She tried to remember how Kirsty's mom spoke about Babaji.

"Babaji, I am sorry for being rude. I know you are a divine master. It's just that you're human too. I'm just curious; doesn't your body have normal human desires?"

This time the fancy Indian guy didn't reprimand her but he appeared ready to explode. Babaji still sat there in silence, eyes closed.

Shivapuri sat down next to Alice and smiled at her. "You see, Alice, the guru is not a person; he is a concept. He is that power that transforms the darkness into light. If we recognize that truth of the guru and allow ourselves to be open to his light, the darkness inside of us is removed."

Alice watched the guys stomping on the grass with flashlights and sticks. "Like those guys?"

Shivapuri looked over and said, "Yes. They are doing karma yoga. Seva. Service. It's part of the process. It's a great blessing to serve the guru."

"To serve the concept guru, or the guru guru?"

"Both."

"Which one are you?"

"Me? I'm neither. I'm also a disciple."

"Why aren't you out there with those guys then?"

"I was. I used to be those guys. Now I am serving in other ways."

"Like how?"

"Like talking to you."

"Is it hard?"

He smiled. "Probably harder than what those guys are doing, but much more rewarding."

Alice paused, recalculating, planning. "So how does a disciple get to be like those guys? Open to the light, I mean."

"Really, just trying. The wish to be open makes you open already."

"Open," Alice said slowly, thinking. "Open. Okay, I'm just thinking out loud, here. I'm just thinking that surely an open-minded person would say no to a stupid request, one that doesn't pass the common-sense rule? Or even goes against your better judgement?"

"Whose judgement?"

"Mine. Theirs. Yours."

"That's a lot of people. We all have lots of these kinds of voices in our heads: negative self-talk, imagined voices of others. It's only through years of meditation and hard work that we can filter through the chorus of voices in our heads and discover the truth."

"Meditation."

"Absolutely. Meditation supports any program of spiritual growth."

"What kind of meditation?"

"In our tradition, we focus on a mantra given by the guru."

"How about meditating on a photo of him, like in a tent?"

Shivapuri was clearly growing uncomfortable with this conversation. "A photograph is a perfect external cue to support the internal process," he said, "but in the end, mantra is all you need."

Babaji suddenly opened his eyes and interrupted Shivapuri. "Karma yoga is also a tricky path. We need constant guidance. We may think we are serving when we are not."

"Ji, gurudev," Shivapuri said immediately. There was silence for some time.

"For example," Babaji said, opening his eyes and looking down at Shivapuri, "sometimes a disciple believes he has come very far and has achieved more than his guru. Perhaps he thinks he is superior to his guru. He thinks he is beyond the advice of his guru."

Shivapuri immediately set down his chai and put his palms together. He cast his eyes downwards and narrowed them and smiled very slightly. It was like he was glad that he was being reprimanded. Alice thought his behavior was similar to that of those guys stomping in the grass. Shivapuri had fallen into a role in a performance.

"Ignorance may enter the disciple and yet he feels like wisdom has entered." Babaji paused, closed his eyes again and took a breath.

Alice saw his ring finger was slowly tracing the grain on the wood arm of his camping chair.

"He may make decisions. For example, he may imagine he is serving the guru by making arrangements that someone else is carried away to the wilderness to meditate."

Alice looked over at Babaji, surprised. He was clearly talking about Kirsty's kidnapping. She looked at Shivapuri and saw he had transformed from sacred servant to scared little boy. He slouched down as if to hide.

Babaji's eyes were still closed. "The young lady may be told it was gurudev's wish she was brought there."

"The disciple who thinks he knows gurudev's wish, but does not, is worse than the disciple that does not know anything. The disciple who thinks he understands, but does not understand, is in the deepest ignorance and in more need of guidance. To understand means to stand under. Not over. Water runs downhill, not uphill."

Babaji smiled at Alice. "Right?"

Alice didn't respond or smile. She was still trying to get her head around the idea Shivapuri was the one who did all that and tried to frame Babaji for it. Why would he do it? How could Shivapuri hire someone like Rajendra?

Babaji said something in Hindi to the diplomat and he looked at Shivapuri. For the first time, Babaji grew angry. "Those boys are following instructions and they are at least keeping the snakes away. Not employing them."

Alice's dad faced Shivapuri. "You?" he accused. "You organized the kidnap of Kirsty Bell?"

Shivapuri appeared to recover a little and sat up taller. "I did organize for her to be escorted to a peaceful place to meditate," he replied, looking Dad in the eye. "I truly believe that I have been serving gurudev and the lineage in doing so. I had nothing but good intentions. Babaji knows me better than anyone. Better than you do, that is certain. It is difficult for you to understand certain things, Prempuri, when you have been away from ashram so many years."

"Hey, dude." Alice patted Shivapuri firmly on the back. "Nice work, I'm sure you'll rot for it. Now where are Madison and Billie?!"

"I have no idea what you're talking about," he said.

"Rajendra kidnapped them. Where are they?"

He said nothing. Alice took a deep breath and locked eyes with him. Upon being tossed into the turmoil that was his mind at the moment, she saw he was telling the truth. He really had no idea who Madison and Billie were, nor did he know where Rajendra was. She broke the connection.

"That's insane," Dad said with the kind of conviction Alice did not expect. "It's simply insane to think kidnapping a teenager could be in anyone's best interest," he continued. He pointed his finger at Shivapuri's chest in a threatening manner. "Just because you've been in India for twenty-five years doesn't mean you have to lose your frickin' mind."

Babaji had closed his eyes again. Alice wondered how he stayed so relaxed.

It was Amar Sing's turn to become aggressive. "I take exception to the insinuation matā India can corrupt a man's mind," he said to Alice's dad. "You be careful, sir. You are treading on thin ice."

Alice needed to catch the diplomat's attention and read him to find out what he knew about Madison and Billie, but his eyes were darting all over.

The diplomat turned to Shivapuri. "You have overestimated the privilege of your status, as a sannyasin and as a disciple to a great spiritual personality. Did you think it would be so easy to get Babaji lynched so that you could inherit his throne? When my colleagues and I heard about your so-called well-intentioned plan, we took steps to ensure no harm would come to Babaji's reputation. That duplicitous journalist posing as a real Indian provided us the perfect opportunity. His harlot ex-girlfriend, who slandered Babaji in the past, will now have to face the music. Right now, as a result of the actions we took on his behalf, the American FBI is drawing up an airtight case against her."

After he finished his rant, he turned to give Alice a violent look, as if preparing to call her a harlot too.

She breathed deeply, locked in and started to tip-toe into his head. She was afraid she would be confronted with thoughts even more evil than those she had seen in Rajendra's mind. Before she could see anything, he shook his head and fought her out of it. She was not surprised he was, like Rajendra, able to evade her mind-reading. She didn't get any information from him, but had at least dissuaded him from saying to Alice whatever he had planned to say.

"As for you, sir," he said, turning back to Shivapuri, who had shrunk deeper into his spot on the blanket, "if Babaji had not insisted otherwise, we would not have gone to such lengths to preserve your reputation in addition to Babaji's. In fact, we would have devised quite a sticky lesson for you. Quite sticky indeed."

"Nobody will be doing anything sticky to anyone else," said a strong female voice, ringing out from within the abandoned café behind them. "Not today, anyway."

Alice spun around and a bright spotlight switched on. Two people walked out from inside the abandoned diner.

She had recognized the voice as Nancy's but didn't believe her ears at first. How could Nancy have gotten here so quickly, she wondered. Two hundred miles on mountain roads in an hour and a half?

Alice heard another car start up from the direction of the convoy of cars and the old Lincoln highway. She saw it was a police car, its blue and red lights switched on, siren sounding loudly, destroying the false quiet of the truck stop. The car blasted around the convoy and slid to a stop near their little group. The driver switched off the engine and turned another spotlight onto Babaji's little celestial gathering.

Alice saw two police officers emerge from the car. "Sergeant Pelosi," one of them said, "thanks for the heads up." He had a rural American accent not too different from the drunken old guy she'd hitched a ride with earlier.

"No problem, John," Nancy replied. "It's nice to see you again. As I mentioned on the phone, I was just here on a date with my friend and we went out for a little walk to explore the Virgin Mary statue and the monument area, and we got lost.

Then we happened upon this strange gathering of vehicles on this piece of private property. I believe this is private property, correct?"

"Yes, it is."

"We are very sorry for our accidental trespass."

"Happens all the time. I'm sure the property owners will overlook it," one of the officers said.

"Officers," Rama said, "I happened to have my phone out and we were recording some interesting nocturnal bird calls. By a complete stroke of luck, I believe the recording captured several of these gentlemen admitting to various felonies."

"Is that so?" the officer said.

Alice looked at Shivapuri and saw him drop his chin down toward his hands and slouch down even deeper. It looked like his vertebrae were slipping away from each other and there was nothing left to hold him together, or perhaps he had been an invertebrate all along.

She looked at Babaji, who had remained sitting exactly as before, his eyes closed.

If Babaji wasn't going to jump up and panic, neither was she, Alice thought. She decided to sit nice and tall and stay cool. Dad, however, jumped up, stood in front of Alice and took up what looked like a protective stance, as though he thought someone was going to open fire.

"Yes, sir. And..." Rama paused mid-sentence when he noticed Amar Sing had disappeared. Alice hadn't noticed the diplomat leaving. All eyes had been on the police when their car came tearing in and Amar Sing must have used the opportunity to slip away into the darkness somewhere.

"Where is the other guy?" asked the police officer.

"He's gone," Rama said.

There was silence as the police officers considered their options. One of them approached Shivapuri. "You are under arrest for solicitation to kidnap a minor."

Rama and Nancy had a word and Rama turned to jog back in

the direction from which they had come.

Alice was awestruck. She knew Rama had been in so much pain that he could hardly stand up. Now he was jogging into the dark.

Alice looked back at the police officers and wondered if they were the same ones she had bombed with a water bottle. She speculated Nancy must have called them earlier and asked for help. Maybe a cop from Hardrock, Colorado wasn't allowed to arrest somebody in Pine Bluffs, Wyoming, which would explain the charade about the bird-watching.

Remembering the diplomat had admitted to going great lengths to preserve Babaji's reputation, Alice knew he had been responsible for some of Rajendra's actions and was her last chance to find Madison and Billie.

She saw that Shivapuri looked like a garden slug as the two local police officers read him his rights, pulled him to his feet and cuffed him.

She finished off her chai and banged the cup down on Babaji's tray. Babaji was still sitting there with his eyes closed.

"Thanks for the tea," she said, and walked over to Shivapuri.

"Where is Amar Sing?" she asked him.

"It was for the good of the ashram community," he said quietly, still looking down. He had apparently not heard her question, or he was simply in shock.

"For the local school kids," he repeated, looking over at Alice, "in India. Their lives are better because of the things we do. Babaji's actions jeopardized all that."

"Whatever, dude." Alice said, still looking for Amar Sing but not seeing movement in the shadows.

She saw her dad make a dash across the parking lot toward the RVs. She ran after him in pursuit.

Nancy had reacted quicker and was right in front of her. "Mr. Brickstone, wait!"

Dad ran straight to one of the cars and was circling it when Nancy and Alice arrived. Alice saw the car was rigged up with a trailer, currently sitting empty.

Dad looked frantically around the trailer and turned to Nancy. "He's gotta be here."

"Who?" Nancy asked, taking hold of his shirt in a firm but friendly way.

"Amar Sing," Dad said, breathing heavily, making a faint wheezing sound with each inhalation and exhalation. "The diplomat...this car was towing something of his (wheeze wheeze). It was some kind of supercharged motorcycle (wheeze wheeze). It is fast. Not street legal (wheeze wheeze). He claimed it could go two hundred miles an hour (wheeze wheeze). He was bragging about it on the way (wheeze wheeze). He bought it in Denver and was going to ship it to India from Chicago (wheeze wheeze)."

Dad took a deep breath and appeared to calm down. "The trailer is here but the bike is gone. He must have taken it and driven away. I thought about it when he disappeared."

Alice heard two things in succession. One was the familiar deep growl of Nancy's truck pulling around the corner onto the Lincoln Highway. Rama must have gone to get it, she thought.

Immediately afterward, a ferocious high-pitched noise tore into the air. It came from a place behind the RVs, slightly ahead of Nancy's truck, and then disappeared to the east. All Alice could hear were fast gear changes and a screaming engine that was very quickly disappearing into the sound horizon. Nancy's truck lurched forward and accelerated hard after the motorcycle.
Nancy rushed back to one of the police officers, who got on the radio.

If that bike could really go 200 miles an hour, Alice figured, he would be a couple of miles into Nebraska by now. There's no way Nancy's truck could catch him. She could hear both powerful engines receding in the distance.

She ducked away and started looking around for some way to get airborne. How she was going to figure out how to fly faster than 200 miles an hour, she had no idea. That was almost double her fastest speed.

She heard a distant, popping sound and the engine noises went silent. Her stomach turned. She rushed back to where Nancy was standing. They stood together looking at the horizon to the east. Dad walked over to join them.

Nancy's phone rang. "Are you okay?" she asked breathlessly and listened for a second.

"Okay. I'll send one of the local cops over. Just stay put." She hung up and took a deep breath.

Alice started to notice a faint glow on the horizon. "What happened?" she asked.

"Rama's okay," Nancy said, obviously intensely relieved.

"And the other guy?"

Nancy looked at Dad, as though asking permission to speak.

"She's more mature than I am," Dad said. "Whatever you think I can handle, she can handle."

"Alice," Nancy said, "I am afraid Amar Sing was traveling at a very high speed when he hit a VW bus that was parked across the Lincoln Highway. Rama thinks Mr. Rao had taken it upon himself to form a roadblock."

Alice clenched up. "And?" was all she could say, fearing the worst.

"Rama doesn't think there could be any survivors."

Alice heard it but assumed they weren't talking about Mr. Rao. Surely Nancy meant Amar Sing couldn't have survived but that Mr. Rao was okay.

She looked at the glow in the east.

"He sacrificed himself to save you," Dad finally said.

"What?" Alice asked, still in shock.

"I think Mr. Rao knew the police were coming for Amar Sing," Dad said, "and he knew that if Amar Sing escaped, he would..." Dad looked at Nancy and back at Alice.

"He would what?" Alice asked, still staring eastward.

"Well, I guess it's all over now. We have been living under his threats for the last ten years..."

"If he escaped," Nancy asked, "he would what, Mr.

Brickstone?"

"Mr. Rao knows if Amar Sing escaped, he would re-issue the contract. The contract he had just cancelled. It took Mr. Rao and me all weekend and thirty million of my company's dollars, but we finally got Amar Sing to cancel the contract."

"What kind of contract?"

Dad looked at Alice and down at the ground. There was silence for a while. Alice was trying to form the question to ask Nancy about whether she meant Mr. Rao was okay or not.

Nancy said, "You mean, a contract on Alice's life, don't you?"

He didn't respond at first.

"Why would anyone want Alice dead?" Nancy persisted.

"Ten years ago, Sergeant, my family was at Babaji's ashram in India. We were just there to meditate and help out around the ashram. We really believed in what we were doing and believed that Babaji was an enlightened man, you know, like Buddha. Babaji found out I was a newly minted bio-science PhD and convinced me to help out with their ashram hospital. Then Mary Flowers showed up at ashram from Hardrock. She was a classmate in my PhD program and had always had a crush on me and did whatever I did. It drove Victoria crazy. Mary was like a stalker. Anyway, she showed up and Babaji thought it was some kind of divine opportunity and he asked us to work together to set up a research institute at ashram."

"Why would you say yes to that?" Nancy asked.

"You don't understand," Dad said. "When you are living with a bunch of people who think they are following a living saint, it rubs off on you. They convince you that every thought and action should be focused on him. He doesn't even speak to most of his disciples, so when he calls you to his room and gives personal advice, it is considered a real blessing."

"So how does the diplomat fit in?"

"Amar Sing is...was a local Maharaja. A Maharaja is what they call the hereditary kings. Maharajas don't have any rights anymore, after India gained independence from Britain, but they are still treated with respect and are at the top of the unofficial caste system. All these kings used to have royal gurus at their courts, in the old days, like in storybooks. Amar Sing considered himself a real storybook king and he thought of Babaji as his storybook kingdom's guru. His real kingdom turns out to be a bunch of local shady businesses which have since become international shady businesses. Now he apparently is...was some kind of diplomat."

Dad looked like his eyes were on fire. Alice was pretty sure he had never told this story to anyone before. At least not like this. Nobody dared interrupt him, not even Alice. He took a breath and continued.

"Then we heard from one of the girls there that Babaji might have been having sex with some of his young Western female disciples."

"Rama's ex-girlfriend, Cristiana."

"Yes, among others. She was leaving ashram to go back home to the US but couldn't get the money together right away, so she was stuck for a few days. She was so traumatized that she almost couldn't function. It was awful. Everyone said she had mental problems. She was ostracized like a disease. No-one talked to her, myself included. I was too busy."

"You were too busy working with Mary Flowers."

"Unfortunately, yes. Out of the dozens of people living at ashram then, Victoria was the only one who helped her, because that's the way she is. Of course, poor Victoria's loyalties were questioned by everyone at ashram. Cristiana naturally opened up to her. The story was terrifying, but the most terrifying thing was that suddenly others started coming to Victoria to tell her about questionable things that had happened to them too. Some very senior disciples started quietly coming to Victoria to say that they knew about some of the stories but that they were misunderstood, that Babaji was giving those girls special initiations that no-one else had any right to judge."

"Special initiations," Nancy said in disgust.

"We knew Cristiana was telling the truth. It was obvious to us. We realized Babaji wasn't who he claimed to be. We were devastated but I was more than that. I was furious. I was young and stupid, so I wanted some kind of revenge. In one of my earlier visits to Babaji's rooms, I found out from one of the senior disciples he had twenty-four-hour video surveillance in his bedroom for security. My anger at the time emboldened me to take some risks and I managed to sneak in and steal a couple of the storage drives."

"Which you held on to for all those years until you gave them to Rama. Why didn't you use them? What about Amar Sing?"

"We decided to take the kids and go home. We also gave Cristiana the money to get her flights. As we were preparing to leave ashram, somehow Amar Sing found out and he wasn't happy. In order to prevent our departure, he threatened to put a price on our children's lives."

Nancy covered her mouth with her hand. "How old were they?"

"Five. Twins; the cutest little innocent and happy kids you could ever dream of." His voice broke and Alice saw Dad was crying now.

"He threatened two five-year-old kids," Nancy said, tensing her jaw muscles. Nancy turned to Alice.

Alice closed her eyes in a useless effort to block out the memory that was welling up again.

"And...then what." Nancy turned back to Dad.

"Try to imagine you're just on a kind of peaceful yoga holiday with your family and suddenly you're caught up in the worst nightmare anyone could ever conceive."

"I...can't," Nancy replied slowly. "You couldn't just tell an embassy about it and try to get the hell out of there?"

Alice felt she was starting to fall apart. She didn't know what to do about it though. She couldn't speak. All she could do was to sit straight and act normal and listen to Dad tell the worst story she had ever heard. The worst part about it was she already knew the ending but there was nothing she could do to stop it. She couldn't undo her memories and she couldn't un-hear what Dad was saying.

"We couldn't tell anyone. That was one of Amar Sing's conditions. In any event, you can't just leave the ashram. There are armed guards at the gates and you have to wind your way through local villages and farm land for five hours before you even get to a regional airport, then you can wait for the one flight a day to get to Delhi. We knew that this guy had contacts everywhere and we didn't know how serious his threat was, so we had to take him seriously."

"So what did you do?"

"The first thing we did was to seek Babaji's protection. He had always seemed to have had our best interests at heart and he seemed to genuinely love the twins. They used to sit at his feet for hours."

Nancy turned around and looked across the parking lot at Babaji. He was still sitting in the same spot, eyes closed, as peaceful as ever. There was a policeman, speaking into a radio, standing next to him.

"We took our problem to Babaji," Dad continued. "He was quite upset about it. He acted very gracious and organized to help us negotiate with Amar Sing. He actually got Mr. Rao to help us. Mr. Rao was the ashram caretaker at the time. Mr. Rao took a gift and personal message from us to Amar Sing. He conveyed a promise that I would continue to help Mary with her work after we returned to the US."

"Why Mr. Rao?"

"Mr. Rao is...was not what he seemed to be. There are a lot of stories about him. He apparently lived in a cave in the Himalayas for fifty years. Before that, he was from a family every bit as wealthy and high-ranking as Amar Sing's. He was well over a hundred years old. Age matters in India. Babaji said Amar Sing respected Mr. Rao more than anyone on earth and he was right. I saw it with my own eyes. So we thought it was all okay, but it wasn't and…we made preparations to leave and…"

Alice stared at Dad.

"Amar Sing claimed it was a communication breakdown. The night before we left, someone snuck in the window of our room and killed Thomas in his bed, and only just missed Alice."

Alice saw Dad was speaking quickly now. It seemed he needed to move quickly through the worst part. She was grateful he did.

"We were in shock," he said, wiping his eyes and trying to pull himself together. "We didn't know what to do."

He turned to face Alice. "It was hard enough just to take care of you, Alice. We didn't know if you would ever recover. After all that you saw…"

Alice looked at Dad, then at Nancy. She wanted to ask what, exactly, happened to Thomas, but she still couldn't speak.

"Mr. Rao pulled some strings of his own, at great sacrifice to himself. He helped negotiate that the threat over Alice would be temporarily removed as long as I sent them a certain amount of funding each year and kept quiet forever about the real cause of Thomas' death. Mr. Rao also was persuaded by Amar Sing to agree to come with us to the US so that he could stay nearby and send me regular instructions from Amar Sing."

"You never told any authorities about this?" Nancy asked, obviously skeptical.

"Absolutely not. It would be so easy for him to re-issue the contract on Alice's life. He had already followed through on his threat once. You don't know what it's like in India. The poor people that work for him will do almost anything for money. For a couple of thousand dollars, you can buy yourself an incredibly good killer with international experience."

"Alice," Dad said, putting a hand on her cheek, "these last ten years have been hell for you and for us. Now I think it might be all over, thanks to Mr. Rao."

He turned to Nancy. "I have been slowly trying to find a way to get him to permanently let go of me and my family. I helped him establish his own pharmaceutical company in India and convinced my own company to work with him. In recent months, I finally set up a joint venture that I believe will actually bring profit to both sides. That's one reason he was here at this time, as part of a delegation to sign the deal. I just didn't know that Babaji also chose this moment to come back here and re-launch his spiritual empire in the US."

Then Dad looked suddenly afraid. "I need to be sure he didn't make another phone call after you all arrived. Can you let us know if they find a phone in the crash site?"

"Judging from Rama's description," Nancy said, "the only thing they'll recover from the crash site is a burned-out VW bus. It was cut in half by the impact. We don't expect to find a phone."

They stood in silence for a while. Then they heard the rumble of Nancy's truck and Nancy went over to help Rama down.

Rama looked extremely unwell. Alice suspected the jog and the chase would have taken an inhuman effort and that he probably needed to be airlifted somewhere. He surprised Alice again by walking slowly over to Dad and Alice, followed closely by Nancy.

"So, Mr. Brickstone and Rama," Nancy said in her official voice, "let me get this straight. We just recorded Shivapuri admitting to organizing the Kirsty Bell kidnapping to frame Babaji, so that he would inherit Babaji's religious empire. He presumably hired the Indian man named Rajendra to do the kidnapping for him. We also recorded Amar Sing admitting he found out about Shivapuri's plan and somehow organized that Rama's ex-girlfriend, not Babaji, would take the blame."

"That sounds right," Rama said. "Probably what happened is Rajendra got the job from Shivapuri and secretly contacted Amar Sing. It would be an easy way to double his money."

"Yes," Nancy said, "the photo of Babaji that Rajendra hung in Kirsty Bell's tent was purchased from Babaji's ashram in the name of Cristiana, and when they arrested her, they found on her computer a chain of emails between her and Rajendra discussing the kidnapping plans."

"You'll find that it was all fabricated," Rama said quickly. "She would never do something like that."

Nancy looked from Dad to Rama to Alice. "But who wanted the Percival girls kidnapped?" she asked. "And why? Where are they?"

Dad's phone buzzed with a text message, breaking the silence. As he read, he broke into a smile.

"I just got fired," he said. "John is taking my job."

Then his phone rang.

"Coach?" Dad asked, surprised, listening.

"Alice," he lowered the phone, "did you leave your bike unlocked at the pool?"

"What?" she replied, coming back to life. The world rushed back and she suddenly knew Madison and Billie could be alive. She grabbed the phone from Dad.

"Coach?"

"Hi, Alice," he said. "Sorry to be calling you all at home so late." Alice noticed a touch of slurring to his words.

"We're not exactly at home, Coach."

"Anyway, I was just driving by the pool on my way home and I saw that strange old Mustang that has been parked out here for a day or so. When I went to have a closer look, I saw your bike propped up against it. Your bike's not locked, so I thought I'd call you to ask if you wanted me to put it in the supply closet inside, so that it doesn't go missing."

Suddenly, Alice knew where Madison and Billie were. She was terrified that it was too late.

"Coach, forget my bike and go inside the pool right now—fast."

"What?"

"NOW!" she screamed, making Nancy jump up.

"Okay, okay, I'm getting my keys out. Keep your girdle on."

Alice put the phone to speaker and they all heard the jangle of keys and the sound of a glass door sliding open. Nancy was staring at Alice with a look of deep concern, but Alice didn't have time to explain anything to her.

"Okay, I'm inside. Now what? Hey..." he said, obviously lowering the phone a bit.

Alice's heart was beating in her mouth.

"There's a bunch of stuff floating in my pool. What kind of jerks would throw things..."

"Coach! What is in the water?" Alice screamed.

"What?" he asked, putting the phone back up to his mouth. "It's just some kind of doll floating in the water, and a chair of some kind."

"It's not a doll...Get Billie out!" Alice screeched.

"Billie? You mean Billie Percival?" he said, lowering the phone again.

They heard him set the phone down on some hard surface, then some water noises, followed by his footsteps again.

"No, it's not a baby," he said into the phone. "It's a doll. But there's some kind of noise...Just a sec."

They began to hear pounding noises and screaming, Madison's screaming.

"Jesus Christ," Coach said.

They heard his key noises again, and the sound of a door opening.

"Coach!" Madison's voice rang out through the phone. "Thank God!!"

"What are you two doing in here?" they heard him ask. "Is she okay?"

"Billie is fine." Madison's voice sounded calm. "She's just sleeping. Some skinny little jerk stole my phone and keys and locked us in here."

It really was Madison's voice. Alice finally lost it and burst into tears. She fell into Dad's arms and sobbed.

CHAPTER 21

The sun was out, not a cloud in the sky, the birds were singing in the forest near Mr. Rao's garden, Alice's wounds had mostly healed, much faster than anyone thought possible, and there was more food than she could possibly ever eat.

Alice stood by herself, looking around. She saw nothing but easygoing Colorado merrymaking. Madison and Kirsty were playing horseshoes, Billie was asleep in her pram in the shade, Coach was drinking long-necked beers with Dad, Nancy and Rama were cuddled up on a lawn chair and Brian and Mom were putting the last tray of tamales on the twenty-foot-long improvised log table. It looked like a feast for an army.

Alice wondered how all these people had moved on from the tension and horror of Pine Bluffs in just a week. How could they all be having a party where Mr Rao used to live?

As she continued to observe them, she noticed each person taking occasional long glances at the ground. She didn't need to read their minds to know they were recalling heavy memories. The sunshine drew their eyes back up, they would look over at Alice, and smiles would always return.

She knew they were doing their best to make her happy on her sixteenth birthday. In some ways she really was happier than she had ever remembered being since Thomas died. Rather than a nightmare that was never discussed, his death was now all out in the open.

Amar Sing was dead too. Rajendra had disappeared and was presumably back in India. Babaji had returned to India too. Shivapuri and Bhakti were in jail awaiting trial.

That just left Alice. Was she going to be okay? Ever?

"Can I get everyone's attention?" Mom shouted. "Gather round, please."

Everyone grabbed their drinks and shuffled over to the table where Alice was already sitting, eating the mountains of food with her eyes.

"Grab a seat and fill your glasses," Mom continued. Rama and Nancy came last, with Nancy supporting him with a solid left arm.

Alice sighed. Mom was going to embarrass her.

"First, to Mr. Rao, who died a hero."

They all raised glasses somberly and drank.

"I'd like to formally welcome you all here," Mom continued. "Things are different now. Our lives are different. We're selling the house and most of our stupid junk and moving into Mr. Rao's cozy old cabin. We are going to have a baby. Our little girl is different. She's growing up. She's sixteen now. But none of those things is what is most special about today."

Everyone went silent. None of them knew what Mom was going to say next.

"All of that stuff is important, but not special. Lots of people get pregnant and have babies. The babies have birthdays and grow up. If they're lucky, they may grow up to be as incredible as our Alice."

Alice looked at Mom and knew that what was unstated was that some babies don't get to grow all the way up, because they are dead.

"But that is still not that special. There are a lot of incredible people in the world too. What I think is most special today is that we're together. Here. Nathan and I are here with Alice, and all of you are Alice's friends, here with us to celebrate Alice's sixteenth birthday. You may know that it's her first birthday party in a long, long time. It's the first time she has wanted a party and the first time we have been able to throw a party."

Dad chose that moment to burst into tears and Mom had to stop her speech and go over to give him a hug. Coach got him a fresh beer and he recovered quickly.

"So anyway," Mom continued, "I don't have much experience with birthday party speeches, but I'm guessing what a mom usually says at her kid's birthday party is how proud she is. How her baby is growing up so nicely and achieving this and that.

"Well, she already knows all that. After what she has done these last few weeks...I actually don't even know all that she has done because I was kept in the dark, but what I want to say is this. I hope Alice is proud of us. We have been completely useless parents and we want to change all that now.

"Nathan was fired and I am closing the yoga center and folding up my mat. We're going to both be stay at home parents from now on. It's not just because of the new baby. It's because of our first baby too."

Mom turned to Alice. "Hon, a lot of kids get presents on their sixteenth birthday. Some rich kids even get stuff like cars. What we wanted to give you today is actually a formal request. Alice Brickstone, we want to invite ourselves into your life. We want to be here when you get home from school. We want to go to your swim meets. We want to take you on holidays. We want to invite ourselves to go hiking and camping with you. We won't take no for an answer. From now on, we're going to be the most annoying stalker helicopter parents Hardrock has ever seen."

"Hey, Mom," Alice said, "I appreciate all the b.s. but can we eat? I'm starving."

"We love you, Alice," Dad said, wiping his eyes. "Dig in, everyone. If there's anything left after Alice gets through with it, that is."

For the first time she could remember, Alice didn't eat so much that she felt like there was a car in her stomach. She even managed to chat a bit with people during the feast, and even to laugh once.

Dad was going to pour her a glass of beer from his bottle but Coach gave him a nasty look and Dad restrained himself. There was a big swim meet coming up, after all. Alice and Madison both planned to compete.

When everyone else had eaten themselves sick, they all migrated to the shade beneath some pine trees as Brian did all the washing up in Mr. Rao's tiny kitchen.

Alice was looking around for Dad because she wanted to ask him something, when behind her came the unmistakable, heavy sound of Nancy's boots.

"Can I talk to you, birthday girl?" Nancy asked.

"Sure," Alice said, still looking around for Dad, but there was still no sign of him and she noticed his car was gone.

"I thought he had changed," Alice said. "I thought maybe— just this once—he would be able to stick around. But he seems to have escaped yet again."

"Give him a chance," Nancy said.

Alice didn't say anything.

"Come on. Walk with me for a second?"

Alice looked at Nancy and realized she was serious.

"What is it?" Alice asked, alarmed, her adrenaline kicking in again, as it had so often since Pine Bluffs. She kept jumping at the slightest sound.

"Nothing like that, Alice: relax. I just want to talk."

As they walked slowly over toward the chili garden at the base of the cliff, Alice tried to figure out what Nancy was going to say. Alice hadn't flown anywhere since Pine Bluffs, so it wouldn't be that. Nobody could have taken a picture of her in the sky and sent it to the cops.

"What?" Alice asked at last.

"We found two stolen cars today. Just in the last few hours actually."

"Good work. A job well done," Alice said sarcastically.

"No, I think you'll be interested in these cars, and a plane. I'll tell you about the plane first. Somebody was cutting hay near Ft. Collins yesterday and they found a little yellow plane in their field," Nancy said.

"A crashed little yellow plane?" Alice asked.

"No. It was hidden there. The field was right near a roadhouse. That's like a bar near a highway."

"I know what a roadhouse is."

"Apparently a car was stolen from that roadhouse. Last week, on the same night Madison and Billie were kidnapped. No-one reported the car missing from the roadhouse until the FBI guys went over there today and started asking questions. It turned out some guy thought he just misplaced his car."

Alice rolled her eyes, well aware what alcohol could do to some people.

"They just found that same car in a long-term parking lot at DIA. I got the call a few minutes ago."

"Okay."

"The other car they found recently was a Subaru wagon. It was hidden really well. It was in a shallow ravine under some trees, covered with a tarp and some sticks and dirt."

"Where?"

"Not far from here."

They walked in silence for a moment, and then Nancy laid a hand on Alice's shoulder. "How did you know where Madison and Billie were?"

Alice was offended to be confronted with a question like that on her birthday, but she finally said, "Rajendra must have found my bike near my house. I left it out the night before, by accident. He must have been there watching our house, waiting for me to come out to look for my bike, and if I did, he was going to kill me."

"He was going to kill you? But he didn't kill Kirsty. Why would he suddenly want to kill you? Why was he after Madison and Billie?"

"I don't know. Mom got sick and we called the ambulance and you came, so Rajendra couldn't do anything to me. All he could do was get on my bike and follow us to the hospital. I bet that looked funny, because my bike frame is way too big for him. On the way he saw Madison's Subaru parked outside the pool. He had been watching me long enough these past few weeks to know the Subaru was Madison's car and that Madison and I had become friends. He must have been in a hurry to do something to me. He was very mad at me for escaping and hurting him, but he also is smart and he knew that he was running out of time to act. So he decided to hurt me through Madison. He went in and grabbed her."

Alice turned to Nancy. "But if that's true," Alice exclaimed, "I'm with you. I don't understand why he didn't kill her."

Nancy returned Alice's look and her eyes were getting bigger. She obviously hadn't put all this together yet.

"Maybe," Alice answered herself, "he didn't kill her because he saw she had a little baby with her. Maybe he's human after all. So he stuffed them in the closet and locked the door and stole Madison's phone and car keys. He drove her Subaru to that spot where he had his plane and flew over the mountains to Ft. Collins. He stole the drunk guy's car and went to DIA and caught a late flight to somewhere and went home to India."

"So," Nancy said slowly, "Shivapuri paid him to kidnap you, he missed and had to settle for Kirsty, and Amar Sing paid him to kill you but he missed and went for Madison?"

"I don't know. He's methodical, so he would have had some kind of reason."

"Methodical," Nancy said, stuffing her hand in her pocket. "So maybe when he failed to kidnap you the first time, it got personal for him. You represented unfinished business, which was bad for his reputation. He felt he had to stick around to finish the job. But when Amar Sing showed up and whisked Babaji out of town, and Bhakti was arrested, he would have known he was running out of time. There was too much pressure from all of us dimwitted police. He needed to leave the country. So when he failed again to get you, he had to settle for Madison and just run as fast as he could."

"Hey, you're pretty smart, Nancy. I forgot how smart you are."

"Smart enough to know you still haven't shared your secret with me."

"What secret?"

Nancy stopped, took Alice's hand firmly and looked her in the eye. Alice saw she was unnerved.

"Alice," Nancy said in a pleading tone, "I just need to know how you do it. How you get around so quickly. How did you reach Kirsty in the Knifespur before everyone else? How did you get from the top of the ski area to Pine Bluffs in an hour?"

Alice yanked her hand away, turned and walked away from Nancy toward the cabin. Nobody was going to grab her like that and demand answers. Some things had changed about her, but not that.

A big Ford truck was pulling up Mr. Rao's dirt road. Someone she didn't recognize was driving. She saw Dad waving to her from the passenger seat of the truck. It was towing a trailer that was carrying something under a cover. Dad jumped out and met her halfway.

"I know your mom said we weren't like all those rich parents who give their kids cars for their sixteenth birthdays. But..."

He turned around and indicated the driver of the truck.

"This here is Mike Meers. Mike, this is my daughter, Alice."

"Hi," Alice said.

"Pleased to meet you at last."

"At last?" she asked.

All the other people at the party were wandering over, including Nancy, who was smiling at her. Alice was glad she hadn't made Nancy too angry.

"Madison, can you come here a sec, please?" Dad asked, holding his hand out to Madison, who was carrying Billie.

"That Alice noisy car," Billie said.

"Shhh, Billie!" Madison said to her.

Dad squinted at Billie curiously, and then turned to address Alice.

"Your friend, Madison, told me you kind of fell in love with some car that was abandoned in front of the pool. At first, I didn't believe her, because you have never shown an interest in any cars. A rear-wheel drive muscle-car from the 1960s makes absolutely no sense in a mountain town like Hardrock, at least six months of the year when there is snow on the ground. Then again, I think I am learning something. I am learning to trust that you have your own ideas about things and they're likely to be different from my ideas, thank God. Anyway, you always have loved speed, so it kind of made sense. Madison promised me you really loved that car. So I looked into it and found it was a rental from Denver that someone had simply abandoned here in Hardrock. I arranged to buy it from the rental company and got it directly to Mike in Denver who, according to my contacts, is the best Mustang restorer in the world."

"Well," Mike said, "that's not exactly what we do."

"What do you mean?" Dad asked.

Mike was quiet for a second. "I don't restore them. I don't make high-gloss show ponies. That's not my thing."

Dad smiled and said, "Course not. Sorry."

Then he looked at Alice and said, "Madison here said you liked speed. Mike here does speed. He and his family have been modifying and racing Mustangs for the last forty-five years. They do everything in-house. I watched a TV documentary on them. That's what convinced me. They were saying on that show there is no other garage in the country that has all the skills under one roof like Mike has."

Mike appeared to be uncomfortable with the praise and he spoke up. "Young lady," he said, "your Dad didn't want me to build a quarter-mile dragster. He wanted a car for a sixteen-year-old girl: something safe and reliable. I told him to get lost."
He kicked the ground and continued. "Then he said some other things and I agreed. Then he said he wanted it back within a week and I said something a little bit stronger than get lost."

Dad smiled. "I gave him a blank check. Probably the last rich guy's gesture I could make on this planet, now that I'm jobless."

"Alice," Mike said, "let me try to explain what you have here, before we take the cover off and you can take it for a drive."

"Um," Dad said, "she doesn't have her driver's license yet."

"Alice," Mike said, looking at Dad with disdain, "this is not your usual crappy teenager gift car. Your dad wanted me to make it like my '67 coupe which he saw on the television. I had to explain to him my car took me twenty years to build. Your dad is a pretty stubborn guy, though. I guess you already know that. He cares a lot about you. Or he must. Anyway, we stopped all our other work and pulled together a team of the best in the business. Most of them said it couldn't be done in the time given, but we did it. It's one for the record books."

Alice started to look at the covered shape on the trailer. She was excited, but not sure what to expect. Was she going to be embarrassed driving around a crazy muscle car? Were people going to think she was an idiot, like those football players in their souped-up Jeep? Was it going to be some nasty thing with racing bling all over it and giant exhaust pipes? She would fit right in with all the criminal gangs in Denver. Nancy would love it.

She remembered the feeling of driving the Mustang from Laramie: the rumble of the engine, the power.

"What your dad brought to me was this rusty '67 Mustang coupe, all original, with sloppy steering, lackluster handling, hideous drum brakes and blood stains all over the upholstery. Every car has a past and every owner a story. This one has blood stains. The car had been driven into the ground. Given the time constraints, we just pretty much pulled everything and threw it away. We went with a light-weight small block stroker motor based on a 302 that just dropped right in the car with room to spare. The weight savings over a bigger block added horsepower while cornering and handle better without all that extra front-end weight too. In order for the vehicle to handle all that power, we had to put in a lot of the dragster modifications, like our custom-ground cam and a Ford nine-inch diff. We mounted the coil-overs in the trunk and we've got the geometry of it all pegged so well that you won't spill your coffee going over bumps. The brakes are disk all around."

Alice didn't really know what he was talking about, but it all sounded interesting. She liked the way Mike spoke, very down to earth and apparently knowledgeable. He did all that stuff with his own two hands, which was impressive. She looked forward to researching all of those words in the library later.

"So, like I said, we don't do show cars, but we didn't want it to look like a piece of crap either. We pulled all the panels, did the body work, replaced the dash and put in the bits and pieces Mustang enthusiasts like these days, and did all the creature comforts like power windows and better lights. Your dad said you were a big girl, so we gave you adjustable TMI sport seats, upholstered to match the original back bench, and redid the carpeting. Anyway, you can see for yourself."

He walked around, detached the cover and Alice couldn't believe what she was seeing. It wasn't a low rider. It wasn't nasty.

She didn't really have the right words for it. It looked new and old. She didn't think she liked old things, like Mr. Rao's bus, but this was different. This was a work of art. It was the same rusty orange color that it was before, but now was all clean-looking. It had a new thing on the hood that would scoop air in. It wasn't gaudy. Most of the shiny things with logos on them were underneath the car, which she could see clearly because it was up on the trailer. The tires were even beautiful.

Mike got up, sat in the driver's seat and started the car. It took a while for him to start it, she thought. She was worried he'd screwed something up, but it fired, and it sounded much throatier than it did before.

She looked around and saw Nancy and Rama both gazing at it with either intense interest or desperate envy. She couldn't tell which. Her mom wasn't looking at the car, but was looking at Dad with something like fear or pride in her face. Alice couldn't tell which. Brian was fussing with his clothes and Madison and Kirsty were just looking at Alice, holding their breath, as though they were worried she wouldn't like it and would walk off and leave the party in a huff or something.

"I love it!" Alice said quickly, for their benefit.

Mike slowly backed it off the trailer and beckoned Alice over.

"It can do ten seconds on the track but it doesn't have a roll bar, so don't ever try it. It's a beautiful car. You'll find it handles pretty nicely. You have to trust it. You'll learn. Enjoy."

"Come on, Dad," she said, smiling. "I think it's time for my first driving lesson."

ABOUT THE AUTHOR

Tyler Pike is an up-and-coming voice in the thriller genre. Before turning to novels, he was a sinologist, earning a PhD in Chinese poetry and lecturing at the University of Sydney in Chinese. He and his wife also spent many years studying Hindu philosophy, traveling in India and running a yoga studio.

When he is not writing, you'll either find him down at the beach with his young family or out on the open road.

Tyler Pike lives with his family in Australia and the US.

Tyler is different from most popular writers in that he endeavors to respond personally to every email and loves sharing his journey with his readers.

For updates on work in progress and free book offers, join Tyler's "reading group" on his website:
www.tylerpikebooks.com

Made in the USA
Charleston, SC
07 August 2016